POLAND

CZECHOSLOVAKIA

AUSTRIA

VIENNA

*R. Danube*

Kleinmutschen
Frankenau
Tömörd
Sarvar
Szombathely
Celdömölk
Györ

BUDAPEST

HUNGARY

*R. Danube*

Rozsäly
Püspökladány
Biharkeresztes
Orad

Timisoara

Banat

BELGRADE

JUGOSLAVIA

*Adriatic Sea*

Journey into Roumania 1950
  "    out of   "    1957

20  0  20  40  60  80  100
MILES

CHARLES GREEN

RUSSIA

CARPATHIAN MTS.

Burdujeni
Suceava

Jassy

Roman

Bacau

R. Siret

almeu
u Mare
Baia-Mare

Cluj
Apahida

ROUMANIA

u-Severin

Tecuci
Vladimiresti
Galatz

Muntenia

Constanza

BUCHAREST

Oltenita
Silistra

Mangalia

Caracal

R. Danube

BULGARIA

SOFIA

Black Sea

*THE LOST FOOTSTEPS*

# The
# Lost Footsteps

SILVIU CRACIUNAS

MK
9 martie 2010

Whilst every event described in this book is true, and none of the people in it are invented, I have deliberately altered the names, physical appearance, location and professions of those who are still living in Roumania, in the interest of their safety.

This book was begun after I escaped from Roumania, and each chapter was translated into English as it was drafted. The necessary editorial revision was then carried out with my close co-operation. I am grateful to Mabel Nandris, who did the work of translation.                           s. c.

ISBN   0-88264-176-x

© SILVIU CRACIUNAS, 1974

DIANE BOOKS PUBLISHING CO.,
TORRANCE, CA, USA, 1982

*This book is dedicated to*
THE RT. HON. R. A. BUTLER, M.P.
*in great gratitude*
*for the opportunity he gave me to acquaint myself*
*with the spirit of liberty*
*and humanitarianism in England*

# BIOGRAPHICAL NOTE

Silviu Craciunas, the son of an Orthodox priest, was born in February 1914 in Miluan, Roumania. After leaving school he studied medicine and then law at Cluj University. In 1938 he received his degree in Law and in 1940 his Doctor's degree in Law and Economics and Political Science. From 1934 to 1937 while he continued extramural studies at Cluj University he worked in the glass industry, and in 1941 became a member of the Board of the First Glass Factory "Gas Metan" in Medias-Roumania. Later in Bucharest he became a member of the Board of Directors of several sugar factories belonging to the Banca de Credit Romîn. In 1948 all privately owned factories were nationalised by the Communist Government, and Craciunas lost his posts.

## Foreword by SALVADOR DE MADARIAGA

On a first plane of experience, this book is a thriller. Once you have opened it, you must read it through, page after page, egged on by a tension of interest no novel can give. The waves of danger and escape succeed each other so relentlessly that you are hardly relieved from one when you are caught by the maelstrom of the next.

Then, you reflect that this is no work of fiction, but the account of the experiences of a European who has lived them in the XXth century, by your side. In fact, that it might have happened to you. The subhuman fiends who in these pages torture and torment their countryman or slave are men of our European stock, of our continent, of our Christian-Socratic civilisation—if heretical in that they follow the tenets of Communism. Bitter food for sad thought. Is the Christian-Socratic civilisation so thin a veneer over the skin of our Europe that it can be rubbed off by a mere forty years in Russia, fifteen years in Roumania, to the appalling degree revealed in these pages?

Think on. Then you find that the victim of these subhuman fiends was able to take the measure of their stupid cruelty and " escaped " to the free West by dint of courage and force of spirit, before he underwent it all over again and even worse. The author was in free Paris, at the dawn of what promised to be for him a life of public freedom and private happiness, when he decided to obey a call to return and renew the struggle in his native land. And you read in the baffling opening pages the peripatetics and dangers the protagonist lived through not to escape away from the asphyxiating atmosphere of a police state, but to smuggle himself into it, to assume the life of an outcast,

7

an enemy, an underground conspirator for freedom. Then you cogitate that there is something unbribable in the human spirit.

Of course, there is. For, as the story shows, this man was the object of the concentrated attack of a community determined to destroy him by means of the sadistic techniques which the Soviet police have developed by drawing on every branch of the sciences that control the workings of the body-mind of man. And it lasted for years. And he won. What does that mean but that, beyond and above the system of cells and of faculties which, so far as we can see, is the body-mind of man there is at work a force, a power, a spirit which can triumph over the worst attempts on its seizable and controllable tool among men?

One guesses that the man who has gone through so much should have something more to say on what happens to our spirit when we sail such uncharted oceans of experience. And the hope arises in us that some day, when his mind has lived down that nightmare, he may re-write his experience, stressing this time even more than he already does here how such outward things as prisons and escapes project themselves on the stream of thought and feeling that flows under our inner skies.

# CONTENTS

# *Introductory Scene*

March 1950

## INTRODUCTORY SCENE

MARCH 1950: this was my last chance to decide whether to remain in the free Western world to which I had escaped so recently, through so much danger, or to go back to my country, there to do the work which I had voluntarily undertaken, and to risk my life at every step.

We were still only seven miles from the Austrian village we had left two hours before. There, life had been predictable and safe. It was very easy to turn back, very difficult to go forward.

Not a blade of grass stirred in the deep silence of the night. Suddenly a searchlight flashed out on our left; its beam swung and searched the ground, yard by yard. We threw ourselves down, hoping that our carefully chosen grey clothes would blend with the withered grass.

The beam passed over us.

With every nerve taut, we waited for its probing to begin again. Great flights of migratory birds passed over our heads. The sky held the serenity of spring, but the starlight was too faint for us to see the Iron Curtain, which loomed ahead of us. It was only in my imagination that I saw the two barbed wire fences, six feet high, and the bottle-shaped mines buried in the strip between them.

During the week I had spent waiting in the border village I had calculated on a large-scale map every step we were to take tonight. I had looked for a terrain which could, I thought, if we were taken unawares, give us the protection we would need to scatter quickly and without a sound. For this reason I had chosen a bare hillside rather than the forest, where we might have stumbled over roots and crackled noisily through dry branches.

My two guides, Stefan the butcher and Paul the blacksmith,

had spent days and nights concealed in the bushes, spying on the frontier, studying the defences and the movement of patrols. During the day-time sentries were on guard on high watch-towers set almost a quarter of a mile apart; from these crows' nests, they searched the countryside through their field-glasses. At night, mounted patrols with bloodhounds, and guards hidden up to their necks in trenches, watched for even the suspicion of a movement. At all times, radio-sets, flares and telephones were ready to give the alarm at any sign of an attempt at a clandestine crossing of the border. What looked to the unwary as no more than a double barbed wire fence was, in fact, the unique and formidable Chinese Wall designed to keep two worlds apart.

Because I knew all this, for I had been here only a year before, I now sensed the presence in the darkness of a thousand ears and eyes alert and ready to surprise and to destroy us. And yet how careful they all were: not a rustle nor the softest whisper, never the flicker of a cigarette end or a match. We had only one thing in our favour: we knew that the monotony of their organised inaction, the silence which surrounded them, their state of permanent emergency, strained the sentries' nerves beyond endurance, so that the moment must come when their powers of concentration would flag.

Our time was limited. We had to cross before the moon rose.

"I'll go on alone to cut the wires," whispered Stefan. "Paul has a family. You'll look after my father if anything should happen to me?"

He had asked us this before we started, and he knew in fact that he could count on us as long as circumstances made it possible for us to keep our promise.

I shook his hand before he disappeared into the darkness. Paul followed him a little way, then stretched himself on the grass.

I had great confidence in Stefan's skill and courage but, as this was his first attempt at mine-disposal, the outcome was uncertain. The most dangerous moment of the operation depended on the least reliable of the human senses, for it involved groping with the finger-tips among hard tufts of grass, in an infuriating darkness, for the fine wires camouflaged by skilled military engineers.

For a long time, or so it seemed to me, I lay motionless on the damp grass. Although I had my overcoat on I was beginning to feel stiff and chilled. I suddenly felt the impulse to kiss the earth which had so generously protected me; to say farewell to it and to the tranquillity it had offered me. Quietly, I turned over and lay on my back, looking at the sky. The cold starlight caught me up into its magic world. I felt a wave of peace and utter reassurance flooding over me. God would sustain me on my road. I no longer wondered whether to turn back.

A rustling broke in on my thoughts and, looking down, I saw something dark and seemingly deformed moving towards me. It was Paul, crawling on hands and knees to tell me that Stefan had cut the wires; he had then had to wait for a patrol to pass. Now every second was precious.

I followed Paul. In a flash, it seemed, we had reached the fence; I could see it clearly now.

Until recently the two fences had been considered a sufficient barrier, but then it was discovered that experienced Austrian guides had found a way of crawling underneath by lifting up the lowest strand of barbed wire (stretched about six inches off the ground), and keeping it raised while their party, one after the other, got through. On the way back from Hungary to Austria, they had merely had to cut the wires; true, it left a hole and, once this was discovered, bloodhounds were rushed out in pursuit, followed by mounted patrols, but paraffin or pepper scattered on the tracks destroyed all scent. Minefields were the answer to these methods: mines attached by hair-thin wires to the fence, so that the slightest touch on it would cause them to explode. These were the fine wires which Stefan had cut. But we had still to cross over the buried mines. "Now the bridge," whispered Stefan.

The bridge was a device of his own invention, and we had brought it with us from the village. It consisted of two planks, two and a half yards long. As the guides raised it, I saw it silhouetted for a moment like some great black wing against the sky. I helped them to lower it into position until a faint grinding sound told us that its far end rested on the opposite fence. Then, with a movement of great precision, the near end, made with a space between the planks, was fixed over the nearest post: thus the bridge rested firmly on the topmost strands of barbed wire.

Helped by Paul and me, Stefan climbed upon it and crept across swiftly on all fours; a soft muffled sound told us when he reached the ground. Now Paul hoisted me up under the armpits. As I crawled along the shaking planks I had just time to think of what would happen if a searchlight were turned on that instant, or if I slipped and fell on to those damned mines. But the next moment I had jumped off safely on to Hungarian soil.

Paul joined us. We removed the bridge and quietly set off downhill.

Stefan walked about a hundred yards ahead of Paul and me. In case of danger he was to run away as noisily as possible, thus drawing off pursuit and warning us to scatter. He was completely swallowed by the darkness. Yet Paul followed in his footsteps, guiding me as surely as a well-set compass. He and I carried the bridge: we could not leave it behind, both because it was essential to leave no trace of our crossing, and also because the guides would need it for their journey back.

As we moved on through the night, on this unfriendly soil which was completely unfamiliar to me, I blessed Stefan and Paul for having been so faithful to me. How easily they could have got their pay, then stabbed me and left me in a ditch, instead of taking all these further risks for me. Such things did occasionally happen in these gruesome regions where good and evil, cruelty and kindness, existed so closely side by side.

We walked quickly. The dark outline of a wood appeared on our right. Very cautiously, and only after pausing a few moments to make sure the guards were out of earshot, we crossed a highway.

About midnight we stopped on the top of a hill among leafless orchards, silent and abandoned in their winter sleep. To the east the sky was growing lighter: it would soon be moonrise.

## Introductory Scene

Going on again into a valley, we soon came to the outskirts of the village we were making for. Like shadows, we slipped into a garden surrounded by a wattle fence, and past a low shed into a yard. The moon had risen over the horizon; it lit up a white-washed church with a tall sharp spire which stood, looking like a sentry, on a nearby hill.

Paul, who knew the place well, opened the door of a barn and signed us to go in. When the door closed behind us, we found ourselves in pitch darkness. I flashed my electric torch and saw two cows and a white goat lying on the straw: their bright, friendly eyes looked at us in astonishment. We also saw a corner banked with hay: worn out, we collapsed on to this soft bed. Groping in the darkness, I pressed a bar of chocolate into a hand of each of the two guides. One of them took my hand and whispered: "We're over the worst difficulty. I feel sure now that you will succeed."

I was grateful for his encouragement, and glad that Paul and Stefan too would soon be able to fulfil their dreams. The money I had paid them for their services would make it possible for Stefan to emigrate to Canada, where he would join his brothers and buy a farm, while Paul would rent the inn for which his pretty red-haired, green-eyed wife had been hankering for so long.

Soon I heard them breathing deeply in their sleep; apparently they felt as safe as if they were at home in their own beds. After a while, sleep overcame me too.

Suddenly we were all woken up by a cold rush of air and a dim yellow light from a smoky lantern directed on to our faces. The lantern was held by a tall old man who stood peering in at us; he wore a pointed fur hat and a coarse, reddish suit of home-spun. Gazing at us in terror, he exclaimed: "God, who's here—who are you? What are you doing in my barn?" As he bent down to get a better look at us, his long thin nose seemed to grow even sharper and I noticed that the twisted ends of his moustache were twitching.

"Good morning, Janos *Baci*, we've come," said Paul, as he and Stefan jumped up and shook hands with the old man.

"Were you parachuted here?" asked Janos in a trembling voice. He held the lantern close to my companions' faces, as if to make sure that they really were Paul and Stefan and not ghosts.

They began to tell him how we had crossed the frontier and reached his garden, but without waiting for the end of their story he rushed out.

By now dawn was breaking; the goat and the cows got to their feet, waiting patiently for their food, and Paul grabbed armfuls of hay for each of them.

Then the door was opened cautiously and Janos came back, followed by a thin, bent, elderly woman who was evidently his wife, and a broad-shouldered young man and a shorter, slimmer boy whom I took to be his sons. Once again the old man raised his lantern.

" Don't you know what's going on!" wailed the woman. "At any moment, soldiers will be here, and they'll arrest the lot of us, and they'll take everything we have—it happens every day." Weeping, she went up to Paul and took his hand: "Quickly, go into the wood before it's too late. You too will be safer there. They'll kill you if they catch you here. Don't you know we can't as much as go into our fields or visit our relations in the next village without a written permit?"

Paul tried to reassure her but she would not be comforted and we had to listen silently to her complaint.

I was appalled to see the terror under which these people were now living. A year before, when I had made my way through the same village, fleeing to the West, the peasants had been more spirited and had stood up fearlessly to the Security Police.

"Lucky the neighbours' dogs didn't wake up," said Janos. "If they'd heard you and begun to bark, the Security Police would have been here already, turning the place upside down." Janos's eyes glistened feverishly as he spoke, and his fear was almost tangible. "Don't you know there are informers in the village? If they know that strangers are about, they tell the police, and soldiers are called in at once. Go off to the woods and hide until it's dark and then get back to Austria—it's your only hope."

Paul went up to the old people, put his arms around their shoulders and said gently: "We can't do that. It's already daylight. We would all be shot within five minutes. Remember, I'm your nephew. Would I come into your house to bring misfortune on you? In Austria there's peace. Don't you too want to escape this hell and join us? Unless we help each other, even at the price of danger, this evil will destroy us all."

There was a long silence, then the farmer's eldest son said: "Paul is right. Where could they possibly go now? Let's show them that we have some kindness left in us." He stepped towards us and shook us all three firmly by the hand.

The woman must have been moved by what her son had said, for she left the barn and came back with a large can of milk and a loaf of bread. As her fears were partially allayed, her natural curiosity revived and she began to question the young men. "How is life with you? How is the old man? Has Ferri gone to Canada..." Finally, after a lot of local news had been exchanged, came the inevitable question: "Who is this gentleman? Why did he come with you? Where is he going?"

"He is a doctor and he has to go to Budapest. He is a good man and he'll be very grateful to you. We wouldn't bring a stranger we weren't sure of into your barn."

Nothing more was asked; for about such journeys, no traveller ever tells the truth. In fact, though I completely trusted Paul and Stefan, I had not told them that my destination was Roumania. Although I knew that neither of them would ever voluntarily divulge the truth, still, to be on the safe side, I had said that I was on my way to Budapest to rescue some acquaintances. Thus, even if there were a leakage, it would only lead to a false rumour as to my whereabouts.

Our hosts now told us, for greater safety, to move out of the barn into a large shed at the bottom of the garden, where they hid us in the dry hay. This done, they went about their daily tasks, glad perhaps that kindness and courage had triumphed in their hearts, although I knew that, underneath their outward calm, each was thinking of the help they would still have to give me in my preparations for going deeper into Hungary.

The first stage of my journey into danger was accomplished. This book tells about what happened to me when I reached Roumania, but, in order to explain why I was returning to my country, I must go back three years, to 1947, and give an account of how and why I came to be in the free world in 1950.

# Background

—⁂—

## 1947 - 1950

# CHAPTER I

IT WAS the spring of 1947 and together with Commander Teodoru, an expert on airfields, I had spent three days in the Candrelu Mountains looking for a place where a twin-engined plane could land and take off secretly. We had been unsuccessful.

Our object was to get the President of the National Peasant Party safely out of the country.

Iuliu Maniu was one of the founders of greater Roumania. He was a statesman and a man dedicated to the fighting of injustice. Now he had become the symbol of the struggle against Russian tyranny, and because of this the Russians had begun a full-scale press campaign against him.

I had known him since my childhood when I had met him through an uncle who was one of his devoted followers. Though I was only ten, he made a deep impression on me, and much later, in 1942, I joined his secret organisation,[1] which was planning Roumania's withdrawal from the Axis and seemed to me the one best fitted to protect our country from the cruel consequences of the war and the likelihood of Russian domination. Maniu fully realised what this event would mean in terms of loss of lives and liberties, and when, in 1944, it came about, his prophecies of ruin and destruction were more than justified. Experience had led me to take this step. As a student I had been for four years a member of the Iron Guard, like many other idealistic young men. I saw it as a Christian and patriotic movement and a spearhead against Communism—a movement which between 1933 and 1937 had won over a great majority of the university students in Roumania. Gradually I realised that it was totalitarian and facist and that its methods were dictatorial and dangerous to human rights and

[1] Maniu's National Peasant Party had been banned during Marshal Antonescu's wartime dictatorship.

liberties. This discovery led me to resign from the Iron Guard in 1940; it then took me two years of reflection to see that the fulfilment of my ideals lay in historic democracy.

For some time I had been lying low in Sibiu: it had been necessary for me to disappear because I had helped some friends who were in danger to escape across the border. It was here that Commander Teodoru, a friend of Maniu's, who knew that I had had experience in organising escape routes, found me and asked for my help in planning the President's secret departure for the West. In view of his age and failing health, we thought it best for him to go by air. But since we had found no airfield this appeared impossible and we had to plan another route.

I had not so far discussed these schemes with Maniu himself. The next step was to get an interview with him, discover his own views and make sure of his co-operation. To see him proved no easy matter. Six months earlier the Minister of the Interior had informed him that a plot against his life had been discovered and that a special guard had been appointed to "protect" him from now on. This guard, consisting of four Communist agents, followed his every step and reported on his every movement and on all his conversations.

I asked a Sibiu doctor, who was at that time treating Maniu in his clinic, for an appointment, and went to see him as an ordinary patient. Once in his consulting room I used the password Maniu's friend had given me and asked him to arrange the interview.

The following afternoon he brought me to his clinic as though I were a colleague of his. I was given a white overall and we walked down the long corridor to the patient's room. Luckily the guards, who should have been patrolling up and down the passage, had got bored and gone into the courtyard to enjoy the sun. We found Maniu sitting in an armchair before the window, a black coat with a fur collar draped about his shoulders, for at the age of seventy he was very susceptible to draughts. He looked calm and ten years younger than his age; he seemed content in this white room with its bare boards and iron bedstead.

He was expecting us; he greeted us, smiling, and asked us to sit down where we could not be seen by anyone from the court-yard. We had a long talk. I pressed the urgency of his escape to the free world where, I believed, he could best serve our country's interests; I argued that, unarmed and getting only verbal support from the West, we could do nothing from inside Roumania against the régime based on Russian military strength, and I assured him that the Communists were getting ready for a mortal blow against his party and himself as the chief obstacles to their final triumph. "Believe me, Mr. President," I said, "they will not rest until they have got rid of you."

The old man listened attentively. He asked me by what means I thought he could escape: he was followed everywhere. "Think of all the cunning you have had to use merely to see me." He remained calm but his eyes were brilliant and he paused questioningly.

I told him that though we had discarded the idea of an escape by air, he could go by land; this would be less dangerous than an attempt to leave by sea, for while airfields, ships and ports were closely guarded, even an army could not man our frontiers all along their enormous length; there were gaps and with trusty guides it was still possible to get through. Finally I suggested that he should go and stay with his sister at Badacin (a village only two hours' drive from the border), promising that, were he willing, we would undertake to deal one evening with his guards, and the next day he would find himself in safety in another country.

He heard me with great attention but I did not convince him. He answered that there were two great obstacles to my plan; one was his age, the other his prestige. He pointed out that it would be a splendid triumph for the Communists if he were caught by them red-handed; that they would tell the whole world that they had caught him like a thief, ready to desert his country. It would be the end of his life's work and of all the moral good he had achieved. "I would be extinguished as a symbol of resistance and much harm would come to many people," he concluded.

I still believed that we could get him out successfully, and that at present he could do more good to Roumania abroad than at home. His next remark convinced me that he did not fully realise the dangers of his situation. He said that he did not believe that they would dare to harm his person or our party, because the whole of the free world supported us. He was convinced that they would not use violence; deceit, lies, yes, but not open force. He thought they would be too afraid of intervention from abroad.

I urged my view that the Communists would stop at nothing, since violence and destruction were the very means they used to sweep whatever and whoever hindered them out of the way.

The President drew his coat-tails over his knees; very calm, he gazed out of the window at the lilac trees. He seemed lost in thought.

I waited in silence. Then he said that the terrible plight of our country was partly due to its geographical position: it was caught at the cross-roads between the German and Slav areas of expansion and in case of a struggle between them they would try to force us to take sides: out of this sprang our historical passion for independence, our desire to lead a life of our own.

"I have decided to stay here, to continue the fight, to defend whatever can be defended from within. It will not be easy. You must help me, all of you."

These were his last words to me.

Two months later Iuliu Maniu was arrested. He was accused not only by his open enemies but by some of those who had been closest to him and whom the Communists had forced to turn against him. The blow must have been appalling. He lived out the rest of his life in a prison cell, yet he kept his word and continued his resistance even in captivity, setting an example to all of us.

Immediately after Maniu's arrest a wave of terror swept over the country. One of those in imminent danger of arrest was Dr. Alexander Moga, Director of the Institute of Hygiene and a close friend and supporter of Maniu. After the Armistice, when Maniu, who was attempting to prevent Roumania's further occupation by the Russians, had held secret meetings with the representatives of Britain, U.S.A. and France, Moga had been his interpreter. Moga knew that whatever Maniu might be made to suffer he would not betray him, but in the course of the investigations his anti-Communist activities could come to light in other ways. He left his home and went into hiding with friends. At first he was buoyed up by hopes of early intervention by the West; later, when this appeared unlikely, he decided to escape. He had been long in touch with Patrascanu, then Minister of Justice and a prominent member of the Roumanian Politburo, and he believed that Patrascanu wanted to come with him.

Patrascanu had been several times in Moscow, where he had had abundant evidence of the pan-Slav policy of the Soviet Union; as a result, though still a Communist, he was now violently anti-Russian, and his ambition was to found a Roumanian Communist party wholly independent of Russia. He had gradually become convinced that he could not achieve this without foreign help; he thought that there were movements in the West which might support him, and he wished to go abroad and get in touch with them. He relied on Dr. Moga, who was on good terms with certain Western diplomats, to prepare the way for his arrival in their country. Moga, for his part, hoped that Patrascanu might become the pioneer of some new political solution which would eclipse Communism and avoid the chaos and destruction which followed in its wake; for Patrascanu was a widely cultured man, admirably suited to absorb the Western concepts of democracy. In any case, from Dr. Moga's point of view, the flight of so eminent a Communist was bound in itself to have a good effect.

Having come to this decision, Dr. Moga made the first attempt to arrange their escape by air on 16th October 1947 with the help of Mircea Mohan, Inspector of the Roumanian-Soviet Airways, who was to be on duty on that date.

As inspector he was responsible for the airworthiness of the planes as well as the efficiency of the pilots. So, one afternoon, on the pretext of checking the condition of the engines, he took over the controls of a plane leaving on its scheduled flight to Jassy, a town not far from the new Soviet frontier. Since it was flying towards Russia, he knew that no one would attribute an ulterior motive to his action. A few days later, using the same pretext, he piloted a plane to Oradea, close to the Hungarian border. After these rehearsals, which had caused no comment, he thought it safe to ask to pilot the Timisoara-Arad plane on its return flight to Bucharest on the 16th.

Eight places were reserved on it for Dr. Moga's party, and eight for Patrascanu's. For greater safety, the reservations were not made in Bucharest, but some in Arad, others in Timisoara, both over three hundred miles distant from the capital and close to Hungary. The plan was that after flying for ten minutes on its scheduled course, the plane would change direction and make for Austria or Jugoslavia. A longer journey was impossible, for one of the precautions which the Russians used against attempts to leave the country illegally was fuel-rationing: they knew that on a plane destined for Bucharest there would be fuel only for a two and a half hours' flight. Such rationing was not, of course, the only safety measure used by the Government; every plane carried two armed guards, and there were radar stations all along the Western frontier, ready to send up fighters in pursuit of an escaping plane. These risks were inevitable; in spite of them they felt their plan had a good chance of success.

A very trivial action of Mohan's was to ruin the scheme. On Tuesday the 13th, perhaps from fear of being searched, he tried to send out of the country an envelope which contained dollars. These were his savings. He gave them to a pilot friend of his who was flying an important Communist delegation to Paris, and whose plane was, therefore, unlikely to be searched. Unluckily, it was, and the dollars were discovered. To save himself, the pilot gave away the sender's name and Mohan was arrested there and then. Since the incident seemed to relate to no more than an attempted breach of currency laws, he was taken to the Headquarters of the Economic Police. Under interrogation he volunteered that he had changed his money into dollars and tried to send it abroad because the consequences of a currency reform had made him frightened of inflation. A report was made and Mohan signed it. By then it was lunch-time. The typist went off, and the interrogating officer picked up his file and went into the next room to hand it over to his chief.

The officer must have felt certain that Mohan could not escape: the room was on the fifth floor and the window had steel bars to prevent detainees from attempting suicide. Left alone, Mohan considered his prospects: he would be locked up in a cell pending his trial; should the investigations bring to light what lay behind the currency offence, this would mean his death.

He put on his cap and walked out into the passage filled with employees hurrying to their lunch. His uniform commanded respect; the lift attendant motioned others to make room for this high-ranking officer. Within a matter of minutes he was in the crowded street.

He knew that the Communist police never looked for a man in a crowd; they would wait, and then search for him at home, or at his friends', or wherever else they thought he might be hiding.

Outwardly calm, he walked along no faster than the lunch-time throng. He was happy to be free but appalled to think that he could give no warning to his friends, for in his present circumstances he could make no use of the secret channels by which they were accustomed to communicate. His only comfort lay in his belief that Patrascanu, as Minister of Justice, would quickly learn of his arrest through the official channels. Unluckily, this hope was not fulfilled and his friends were soon in trouble.

That same evening Dr. Moga was walking slowly down the Ardeal Boulevard with one of Patrascanu's close associates. As they passed the Faculty of Medicine, the headlights of a car lit up the darkness underneath the chestnut-trees. They blinked three times, then the car slowed down and stopped. The lights were the signal which Moga had agreed with a Western diplomat whom he was to meet in order to confirm the date of the escape; the diplomat was then to arrange that the fugitives should be met on landing at the foreign airport.

Moga and his friend got into the car which drove away at once. Seconds later two cars with very powerful headlights shot out of the darkness, chased them at full speed and, after overtaking them, slowed down, one on either side. While the three cars were running abreast, agents armed with automatics jumped on to the running boards and shouted to the diplomat to stop.

Moga and his companion acted quickly: by forcing the doors open they flung the policemen to the ground; next moment they heard the screaming of brakes as the police cars pulled up behind to pick up the injured men. But the respite was not long enough to enable them to vanish down a side-street into the safety of the damp autumn night: as ill-luck would have it, the Embassy car was not run in and could not reach its maximum speed.

Looking through the back window Moga and his friend saw the great headlights approaching and again enveloping them in their glare. When the police cars were within yards, the diplomat braked sharply, forcing them to do the same. Armed agents poured into the street; they must have thought the fugitives had recognised the hopelessness of their position and were giving themselves up. But before they could reach their car, it shot forward and swerved round a corner to avoid the murderous fusillade which broke out behind it.

As they raced round corners, glimpses of street lamps, buildings, trees, railings lit up by headlights, gave the fugitives a drunkard's vision of a fleeing town.

The diplomat remained calm. He had his plan. He meant to drive straight into the courtyard of the Embassy: once inside, he could rely on extra-territorial rights for his companions and himself. His pursuers must have guessed this, for they did their utmost to overtake and pass him and block the way. Tearing down one street and up another, to the terrified amazement of the passers-by, they finally reached the main thoroughfare of the city, Calea Victoriei; here the crowds forced them to slow down. But as they turned into the Strada Lahovari, one of the police cars caught up with them, mounted the pavement, struck a lamp-post and knocked it down. It had achieved its aim: the road was blocked. Before their car came to a standstill, Moga and his friend leapt out and streaked into the Calea Victoriei. They knew that the police would not fire at them through the crowd and they were soon lost in the mass of the pedestrians. The agents ran to the accompaniment of complaints: "Get off my toes!" "What d'you think you're doing?" Only after some minutes did they feel safe enough to slow down, and a little later they separated, each making for a different hiding-place.

Dr. Moga found his way to the building of the Petrosani Society, entered it as though he were one of the tenants and hid in the basement, where he spent the night.

At eight o'clock the next morning, when he knew that the streets would again be crammed with people, he came out and took a roundabout way to the house of a devoted employee, Georgetta Popovici, who lived in the Strada St. Dionisie. Here he hoped that he could stay as long as it would be necessary.

He had no idea when he rang the bell that the Popovicis were already harbouring three other friends of ours, who were also on the run from the police. They were in trouble because they were associated with the incident at Tamadau, where the Communists had laid a trap and captured the two planes that were to take to safety abroad some important members of the Peasant Party; and this had served as a pretext for the arrest of Iuliu Maniu who was accused of having planned it.

His fellow fugitives gave Dr. Moga a warm welcome. Up till now he had, of course, no knowledge of the misfortune which had befallen Mircea Mohan. Soon, however, he learned of it through a secret message and realised that his hopes of leaving Roumania by plane were over. But Mohan's story had another implication for him; it explained the happenings of the previous night. By an odd coincidence, he had chosen the very street in which the airman lived, for his own meeting with the Western diplomat. Clearly, the police were watching it in order to catch Mircea Mohan should he return home. When they saw the Embassy car blink its headlights and pick up two men, they must have thought that one of them was their quarry; the mistake was the easier to make since in build and looks Dr. Moga was rather like the pilot.

Unlike many others, Dr. Moga's story had a happy ending: after this first unsuccessful attempt, he asked for my help in arranging his escape by land to Vienna, with Mohan and other friends; in time he reached Canada.

The next five months passed very quickly for me as I was travelling between the capital and various towns in the frontier zone, supervising various departures in groups of four, and making sure everyone had the services of the best guides.

# CHAPTER II

In 1947, national disasters came one after another. The Resistance Movement lost half its strength through mass arrests, and it was obvious the Russians were planning to strike new blows in order to hasten the destruction of our institutions and our way of life.

My organising of escape routes ran into difficulties in the spring of '48. A group who should have crossed the south-west frontier failed to do so owing to the imprudence of two of its members. This passage now became unusable and we were forced to open up a new route through the north-west. There were still several people—and in particular a party of five—whom I was determined to get out; after that I hoped to make my own escape.

The two guides who were to be in charge of this party had arrived in Bucharest. They had been engaged in Hungary through a trusted agent of mine, Leon Pótócki, who had assured me that they were reliable and had given them a telephone number and a password so that they could contact me.

My first meeting with them was near the Abattoir Bridge; we discussed the proposed route through Satu Mare. But I realised at once that there was a weak link in the chain: the chief guide was Fekete, the famous Roumanian international footballer, a former employee of the Columbia Gramophone and Radio Company in Bucharest, and a well-known figure in the city. A Hungarian by birth, he had escaped to Budapest two years earlier and had since devoted himself to organising clandestine crossings in the hope of making enough money to emigrate to Canada. Plainly his reappearance in Bucharest was extremely risky, for he might be recognised at any moment and arrested on the spot. I made him promise never to go out by daylight, and not even to leave his house at night if he could possibly avoid it. In spite of this assurance, I was not at all happy and, as a precaution, I did not tell him the names of those who were to leave, although this was my usual practice when I got in touch with the chief guide. Instead, I arranged a second meeting for the next day, to be followed by still a third, at which the guides would meet "Miss Muresanu," who was to take the refugees as far as Satu Mare. My plan was that the whole party should go by the same night train but in different compartments. In Satu Mare the fugitives would meet in the market square behind the railway station; "Miss Muresanu" would then take them to another place nearby, where the guides would meet them for the first time and take over. After a day's rest at the home of a trustworthy woman, they would set out for the frontier that same evening.

No "Miss Muresanu" existed. This was a cover name for Georgetta Popovici, the girl who had hidden Dr. Moga and had helped many others to escape. I did not give her real name because of my fear that Fekete might be arrested: in case he were interrogated under torture, the less he knew the better.

The guides agreed to carry out my plan but asked for an advance payment of a hundred dollars each per refugee. I agreed to hand over the money at our second meeting.

The following afternoon (it was a Saturday in the middle of March) I went at four o'clock to the appointed place in the Strada Vulturilor. I had not been to the house before but I had had sufficient information to behave as though I knew it. There was a low building on the left side of the courtyard, with a door which had a top panel made of glass. I knocked and, without waiting for an answer, entered. I found myself in a small kitchen; it had a stuffy, musty smell. A frail little old man sat with his hat on his head, warming himself by the fire.

"Good afternoon," I said. "I have come for the football. Can I have it, please, as soon as possible?" (This was the password.)

"Please sit down and wait a moment," he replied. He looked at me anxiously, his black eyes darting away from mine, and exchanged a few words with an old woman in the corner of the

room. She looked as frail as he was, and as anxious. I had a feeling
that something was wrong—though in 1948 when everyone was
in constant danger the nervousness of an old couple was not
surprising.

The woman left the room and it was five or six minutes before
she returned; then she took me to a two-storey house across the
yard, pointed to the stairs and told me: "Go up to the top and
knock on the door. They're expecting you."

I found the door open and walked in; I was in a narrow room
with a single window looking out on the yard. Fekete was alone;
he motioned me with a friendly smile to sit down at a table placed
against the wall.

He was a tall man with a strong, athletic body; the collar of his
khaki woollen shirt was open and I noticed that he wore a thin
gold chain round his neck. I told him that I had brought the
money and added that I hoped he had not changed his mind and
was ready to leave that night. He said he was, and that indeed he
felt he had already been too long in Bucharest. Once again, I ran
over the details of the plan, mentioning "Miss Muresanu." I
looked him straight in the eyes, but I felt that his thoughts were
elsewhere and he was not paying attention. I ended by saying that
I hoped everything was clear; he echoed my words: "Everything
is clear."

At that moment a small door on my right burst open and a man
shouted: "Hands up! Don't move or I'll shoot."

Instinctively I turned to see who it was and the command was
shouted again, still more angrily; but by then I had caught sight
of a well-dressed man of medium height, evidently an agent in
plain clothes. He was wearing the Order of Michael the Brave, a
decoration awarded only to officers and only for exceptional acts of
gallantry. He stood two paces away and covered me with two
revolvers; I held up my hands.

"Your identity card."

From my breast-pocket I took out the forged identity card
which had protected me for the last two years.

"You are Ion Saiu?"

35

"Yes."

Still covering me with one of his revolvers, the man looked at the packet of dollars on the table—a piece of glaring evidence against me—and told me that he had arrested Fekete the night before. The footballer, he said, had been reasonable, and he advised me to follow his example by making a full confession. Now that he, the agent, had overheard us, my only chance was to supply the names of those who were intending to escape.

I said that I didn't know their names, that I was only a poor man who had agreed to act as go-between to make a little extra money for my family, and that only Miss Muresanu, whom he had heard me mention to Fekete, knew the fugitives.

This evidently seemed a likely story to the agent, for he went on to ask me who Miss Muresanu was. I replied that I had only met her once, by chance, in a café, but that I thought she worked in the Ministry of National Economy, for she had given me its telephone number in case I needed to get in touch with her. As it was Saturday and the Ministry was closed, this part of my story could not be checked till Monday. This point must also have occurred to the policeman, for he asked me angrily how, in that case, I had intended to report to her after my conversation with Fekete, and threatened to break my neck if I misled him. I said that we had arranged to meet at five o'clock that afternoon.

"Where?" he asked.

I had to think quickly. It was now four-thirty; I hoped that in his eagerness to find out the names of the refugees the agent would tell me to keep the appointment—accompanied by him of course, but even so, I felt that in the street I might have some chance of escape. What place should I choose? The whole city rose in my imagination—its avenues, its squares, streets and connecting alley-ways; the crowded cinemas, and a café which, I knew, had a back and a front entrance. Suddenly I thought of the Church "Biserica Alba", near which Dr. Moga had managed to make his escape not long ago.

Probably the agent interpreted my silence as a last effort at resistance, for he did not hurry me. Finally I said that I was to meet Miss Muresanu in the Strada Lahovary, at the corner of the Calea Victoriei, opposite the Church "Biserica Alba".

As I expected, he said that he would go with me, for he was "anxious to meet the lady."

While this was going on, Fekete stood with a smug smile on his healthy face: evidently he believed that by betraying me he had saved himself and his companion.

A tired-looking plain-clothes man in a black suit came from the adjoining room, and handed the officer his hat and his trench-coat. I was ordered to go ahead and the two men followed me. No doubt, Fekete was left in the charge of still other agents hidden in the next room.

I glanced at my watch; it seemed impossible that only half an hour had passed since I had entered, a free man. We came out into the warm spring day, golden from the setting sun. A police car stood a few yards from the house. I got in, followed by the two agents who sat down on either side of me, and we drove away through streets filled with people going about their ordinary business.

Within an hour at most, the agents would know that my appointment with Miss Muresanu was a fake; then would come the drive to police headquarters, the checking of my statements, the establishment of my real identity, an underground cell, torture . . .

I had been on the black list of the Security Police for years. Only a few months after the Russian occupation they had searched for me and, not finding me at home, arrested my father. Later I had used the papers of a friend who had died, and thanks to these, though at much risk and expense, I acquired the false identity card to which I had owed my freedom until now. It would no longer serve me. I felt as if a bottomless pit had opened before me, yet at the same time an instinct told me to keep calm, to think clearly and, above all, not to despair. But how I wished I were in Canada with Dr. Moga!

The car drew up about fifty yards from the supposed meeting-place, but the engine was kept running. The senior agent gave me his instructions: I was to get out, walk up and down the street in front of the chemist's shop but not as far as the Calea Victoriei; above all, I was to "look natural," and when Miss Muresanu came, I was to keep her talking.

"Don't pretend not to recognise her, and don't try to give her any sign. If you do, we'll shoot you. But if you play your part, I promise that I'll help you."

I said I understood and would do as I was told; I tried to look submissive and resigned. We got out. The car moved off to park round the corner.

For some minutes the agents followed close behind me, then they took up their position in a nearby archway, talking casually as though they were acquaintances who had met by chance.

I walked up and down my beat, my hands in my pockets; my heart was beating so violently that my neck must have swelled, for I felt my collar strangling me. I glanced at my watch; there were still twelve minutes to go before the "meeting" and I reckoned that I could count on perhaps fifteen more, since the agents would allow for some unpunctuality on Miss Muresanu's part.

At one end of my beat I was within ten paces of them, at the other within twenty. There were hardly any passers-by in the little street, though, within only a few yards, the evening crowds were already thickening in the Calea Victoriei. But I realised that to reach it was impossible. The agents' hands were in the pockets of their trench-coats, their fingers on the triggers of their guns. Besides, the light was too good. Late on a damp autumn evening, Moga had had the advantage of the darkness and of the milling crowd, but these were denied me; and I had no plan; I could only try to keep calm, and I cheered myself by thinking that I had, at least, achieved one of my aims: I was still walking in the open street instead of being locked up in some basement prison.

I looked at the Church of Biserica Alba only a few steps away; every few minutes someone entered it to pray. Suddenly I was reminded of a prayer I had been taught as a child, for those in sickness or in danger or who had no one to pray for their salvation, and I wondered whether, at this moment, anyone was saying this prayer for those in mortal peril.

My attention was attracted to a seven-storey block of flats with a large entrance which I passed on my beat. If the agents' eyes left me for a moment, I could vanish into it. But where would I hide? With whom? I knew nobody who lived there. Now I noticed a three-storey house next to the block: only my paralysing tension could explain why I had not seen it earlier. In it Professor Ovid Teodorescu, the brother of a friend of mine, had his flat. Not only this, but the house contained an excellent hiding-place which had been used by my friend not so long ago. The trouble was that the Professor might have left the city, for many thousands had been recently evacuated. Then I remembered that I also knew Teodorescu's neighbours—an engineer, Mircea Nacescu, and his wife who was a doctor. I prayed to God that one or other family might still be there.

Now I had a plan, but how to put it into action? The agents watched me ceaselessly, and time was flying; already it was five o'clock.

The pavement was about three and a half yards wide. Gradually it filled up and I was able to edge up against the window of the chemist's shop and thus, as I walked on, to pass close to the entrance of the flats. Yet however tempting it might seem, I knew I must on no account try to escape while my back was turned to the agents. My only chance would come if they glanced away at a moment when I was facing them as I passed the door.

It was five past five and when our eyes met I saw that they were scowling: they were beginning to be angry at Miss Muresanu's lateness. Just then a badly dressed old man with a dilapidated suitcase crossed to our side of the road and shuffled on, peering at the numbers of the houses. Evidently looking for an address, he stopped in front of the agents (he must have taken them for local men) and showing them a piece of paper, asked them something. I was outside the block of flats, but the agents, though they spoke to the old man, cast quick glances at me; so I had to pass the gateway of salvation and go on to the flower shop next door, where

39

the white lilac seemed to mock me. Then I turned and, very slowly, retraced my steps. To my relief, the old man was still talking and gesticulating nervously. As I approached the doorway —there were only two or three steps left to go—one of the agents stretched out a hand and pointed to a street alongside the Biserica Alba; the other glanced at me and, seeming to be satisfied by my slow pace, also turned towards the church. It was at this second that I arrived before the door of the three-storey house.

One step hid me from the street, then I hurled myself along the corridor towards the staircase. Up I tore, three steps at a time, until I reached the top floor. There two doors faced me, with a bell push on each. I put my fingers on both buttons and kept on ringing.

Every second was vital to me. I could not tell if the policemen had seen me going in, or had been left to suppose that the earth had swallowed me. Everything depended on that.

No one answered either bell. I looked at the unyielding doors, and as I heard footsteps hurrying up and the creaking of the stair-boards, I nearly gave way to despair. Mercifully, they stopped on the floor below, but they had made me terribly aware of my predicament, trapped on the narrow landing with no possible retreat should anyone come up the stairs.

Silently, the door on the right opened and a bent, wry-necked old woman looked out questioningly, keeping her hand on the latch. As she recognised me her face cleared: "Come in. The Professor's not at home. Madame is also out, but would you like to come inside and wait for her?"

"Yes, yes," I said as I hurried past her into the passage. I asked her if I could make a telephone call. She led me to the bedroom, pointed to a telephone next to the bed and left the room, moving noiselessly in her felt slippers. I dialled Georgetta's number; she recognised my voice. "It's you, Grigore—good. Mother and I are waiting supper for you. Is everything all right?"

"Don't wait for me," I said. "Something I ate in the canteen must have disagreed with me. I felt so faint that I only just managed to get to the doctor." I told her not to tell her mother, who would worry, but to go and wait for me at Marcel's, though I might be some time. And I asked her to let Marcel and his family know that I couldn't go to the cinema with them that evening.

There was a long silence, as though the heart of the human being at the other end of the line had ceased to beat. Then in a subdued voice Georgetta said: "I am sorry you don't feel well. Take care of yourself and don't worry. I'll do everything you've told me to." The receiver was replaced.

I was not particularly afraid that this call might have been tapped. In theory, in Bucharest, they all were, but in practice it would have needed an army of monitors and innumerable recorders to do so. To be on the safe side, however, everyone spoke in a sort of pidgin language.

I could only hope that Georgetta had understood me and would immediately let the fugitives who were to leave with Fekete know that the plan was off.

Having done what I could I lay down on the bed, exhausted. Although the house was in the centre of the town, the silence in this bedroom was complete. At first it calmed me, but soon my imagination turned to what the agents might be doing. If they believed that I was in the building or the adjoining block of flats, they must by now have sent for reinforcements; in ten minutes at most the police cars would be there; they would surround the two buildings and search every corner. I began to hate this belfry where I was shut in between four walls and which offered no hope of escape. I longed to be outside again, in the open street.

The key turned in the lock of the front door and light footsteps approached the bedroom. Madame Teodorescu came in. I jumped off the bed and asked her to forgive me for frightening her, explaining that I had no choice. . . . Her bright blue eyes looked at me in astonishment. I asked her if she remembered the last time I had been in her flat when we had sat up talking into the early hours.

Of course she remembered that evening. She had asked me to dinner with Cesar Daponte and her brother-in-law, Ionel Teodorescu. Cesar Daponte was the Director of the Creditul Minier, one of the most important industrial concerns in Roumania. Madame Teodorescu was his secretary and enjoyed his confidence. Daponte wanted to leave the country, so did Ionel whom the police were hounding as an associate of Maniu. We had been asked to meet so that I should offer to get Daponte out on condition that he paid the guides for both of them.

Now I told her that I had in fact prepared Daponte's and Ionel's escape but that another party had been waiting longer and had been about to leave tonight; then I went on to explain how this plan had miscarried and I had been arrested but had given the police the slip.

Madame Teodorescu became very pale and asked: "Where did this happen?"

"In front of the 'Biserica Alba'."

"Where are they now?"

"Down below in the street."

"Oh, my God!"

I told her I was terribly sorry to have involved her in this, but that I thought they must have lost the scent, for if they had seen me come in they would have been there before now. I had to keep out of the way for a few hours, in case they picked it up again. Then I asked if I could go into the hiding-place Ionel had used that time when the police made a surprise raid.

This appalled her and I soon understood why. It happened that she had not the key of the room in which the hideout had been made. This room was an office belonging to Daponte and usually he left the key with her, but just that day he had taken it with him, and it was hopeless to try to find him on a Saturday afternoon—he might be anywhere in the town.

Madame Teodorescu suggested that perhaps the best thing would be to see her neighbour, Nina Nacescu, and ask her if she knew of any place where I could hide. She went out at once, locking the front door behind her. When she returned five minutes later, she looked more cheerful. Nina Nacescu was at home; she was in bed with phlebitis, but she was horrified to learn of the trouble I was in and would gladly see me. We went across to her flat.

Nina Nacescu was a doctor and even in a crisis she had a calm manner. Presently she thought of a plan for me: I was to leave the house by the back door, and climb over the wall into the next yard which belonged to the Alcohol Monopoly: from there I could reach the Calea Victoriei. To give me an excuse for climbing over she would tell her housekeeper to throw the turkey they were fattening over the wall.

It sounded perfect but when, at her suggestion, Madame Teodorescu and I went to look out of the window, we saw a large black car standing in the neighbouring yard and men tinkering with the engine. So that way was cut off.

Disappointed, we returned to Nina's bedside. We could think of nothing else and the police might come at any moment. Finally Madame Teodorescu decided after all to go in search of Daponte.

While I waited for her, I looked round the room. Woollen rugs in our traditional black and red patterns hung on the walls, the oak furniture had carved motifs, and there were net curtains over the window. Noticing that they had a very close mesh, I came to within a yard of the window, so that I could see into the street.

Opposite was the Biserica Alba and, next to it, a delicatessen shop with the curious name "La Elevii lui Pescaru." I could also see a short stretch of the Calea Victoriei with its hurrying passers-by.

I watched them carefully, trying to judge by their expressions if anything unusual were going on, such as the arrival of police-vans; but they merely looked preoccupied like any passers-by hurrying about their own business. Then I noticed my two policemen: they were standing with their backs to the delicatessen shop, watching our block of flats; they looked bored.

I told Nina. She struggled off the bed and came up to the window. After a moment she told me that she knew the one in the trench-coat very well indeed.

It seemed that my captor was a police-inspector, Talangeanu by name, the son of a Colonel who had received the Order of

Michael the Brave in the First World War. Nina had seen him only a week before and he had then complained to her that he had just been transferred from the special corps and posted to a unit of the Economic Police; he had added that as so many inspectors had recently been purged, he was lucky to have been kept on at all.

So it seemed that the agents who had pounced first on Fekete and then on me had only been after dollars!

Nina and I talked it over. We asked ourselves why no police cars or reinforcements had arrived since my get-away. I thought that the two agents were perhaps ashamed or afraid of admitting that they had allowed me to escape, and were hoping to catch me first.

Nina suggested another possibility. Talangeanu had never been decorated; for that matter he had never been in the Army. She thought that he belonged to a new type of agent: these men knew that their turn would soon come to be purged and, in the meantime, used their position to blackmail those whom they arrested in the hope of putting by some money for a rainy day.

I realised that if she was right, this might mean my salvation: for it was possible that Talangeanu would not bother to search for me and had not even reported my arrest, hoping to induce me to pay my way out.

Since there was nothing to be done at the moment, we sat in the kitchen talking. Nina told me of cases of blackmail on a much grander scale than Talangeanu was likely to have in mind—people who had been kept in cells beneath the Ministry of the Interior until they handed over such jewellery and foreign assets as they still had; some of them, on their release, had been given visas for South America, to prevent their spreading rumours about the way in which they had regained their freedom. This was the more necessary since the blackmailer-in-chief was thought to be the Minister of the Interior, Teohari Georgescu, who used his staff to carry out such operations. Some people believed that the funds were used to finance the Communist International in the West.

I looked again out of the windows. In the backyard the mechanics were still working on the limousine, and the two policemen were still in front of the delicatessen shop. But it was after seven and the early darkness of the March evening had fallen over the city. The streets were lit. Presently, the iron shutters of the delicatessen shop were pulled down. Inspector Talangeanu and his subordinate patrolled in front of it for some ten minutes more; then they walked off in the direction of the Calea Victoriei and were swallowed in the crowd.

Had they gone for good, or was this a trick to get me out of hiding? To escape the net which was closing round me, it was essential to know.

Nina put on her coat and hat and, in spite of her phlebitis, limped out of the house. She was out for half an hour; when she came back she said: "They seem to have gone for good."

She had walked along the Calea Victoriei, where she had bought some cakes in order to have a reason for being out, and had looked round corners and into doors and archways. She felt sure that had the agents still been about she would have seen them.

I watched out of the bedroom window for another half hour; there was still no sign of them. Then Nina lent me a hat and trench-coat of her husband's; they were very unlike my own and when I looked in the mirror it seemed to me that, even if anyone had seen me coming in, I was unlikely to be recognised.

Together we went slowly down the stairs which I had raced up only three hours earlier. I had a moment of sadness at leaving this house which had welcomed and hidden me, and of dread at whatever might be lying in wait for me outside.

Downstairs, I stood in the gloomy entrance hall while Nina went out; two or three minutes later a taxi drew up outside the door; I gritted my teeth, hurried across the pavement, and joined her in the car. Its engine was running and we started off at once for the Strada St. Apostoli, a good distance away in the direction of the Patriarchate.

As we drove past the great building of the Royal Palace—it was in darkness as though uninhabited—the memory came to me of that December evening in 1947 when the King was forced to sign his abdication. Tonight there were no palace guards magnificent in gold helmets and patent-leather boots. The sentry-boxes were deserted; the palace had been turned into a gigantic museum. Across the square stood the re-built "Roumanian Athenæum," intended as a stone symbol of the traditions, history and culture of Roumania, a country which had beaten back so many invasions before it could take its place on the political map of Europe. Its cupola and its Doric columns were floodlit. So far the Communists had not dared to touch it; instead they had occupied a brand-new palace on the same side of the square. This was now the Ministry of the Interior and the home of the Security Police—in fact the citadel of Communist Government in Bucharest.

We turned into a street where, at that hour, private cars were rare. Looking out of the back window, I was relieved to see that we were not being followed. After ten minutes we reached our destination and there I thanked my benefactress for all that she had done for me, and went away.

Though it was only half-past eight, the streets here were nearly empty. I walked for some time, then took another taxi and drove for about a quarter of an hour to the Lemaître Bridge which crosses the Dambovitza. I got out a little beyond the slaughter-house and dived into a maze of narrow alleys.

# CHAPTER III

"THANK GOD you're safe. What happened? We were terribly worried about you."

Friendly voices greeted me as I entered the little house in Strada Salcamilor where I had asked Georgetta to wait for me. She had not, in fact, expected to see me, but had come to warn the owner, an Italian master builder, that I was in trouble. The whole family were there—the builder, his wife, his daughter, his son-in-law, his little grandson. Lydia Faur, who lived at Georgetta's, had also come, hoping to get news of me.

I told them my story as quickly as I could and said that I must move on, for the telephone number of the house was known to Fekete: it was the one at which he had rung me up when he arrived in Bucharest. This fact was not in itself dangerous to the builder so long as no other connection could be proved between him and myself.

"What shall we do if they take us away and question us?" his daughter asked me.

"Deny that you ever got a telephone call for Grigore," (this was the name by which Fekete knew me). "Say that you have no idea who Grigore is." And I pointed out that Fekete couldn't prove to the police that it was their number he had rung up. He didn't know any of them. I stressed that above all they must all say the same thing.

I went upstairs; some time before I had left a suitcase with the builder and I was now able to change my shirt which was soaked with sweat. After cleaning myself up, I came down, thanked my hosts and left with Lydia and Georgetta at whose house there was a hiding-place I could use in case of a police raid.

We went out into the calm night and hurried on, choosing back

47

streets where we were unlikely to meet anyone. As we walked along Georgetta told me that she had had a strange dream the night before. She and I were walking in some unfamiliar place, through gardens full of fruit trees in blossom, and fields bright with flowers. On each blade of grass there was a dewdrop shining with all the colours of the rainbow. There were many people about but they took no notice of us. Then, quite suddenly, it had all changed. We were in a desolate field and then starting to cross a dark, wide swamp. I had stepped so lightly that my feet hardly seemed to touch the ground and my shoes stayed clean, but Georgetta sank deeper and deeper into the slime and cried out. At that moment I gave a great leap into the air and vanished, but the swamp sucked her down till only her arms were free. She had woken up terrified. "I wonder what it all means?" she asked. Was it the good spirits who watch over us giving her a warning, or was the dream sent by evil spirits who intended our destruction? "Anyway, you're out of the swamp," she said, "but what will happen to me? I feel as if some evil were approaching me."

I was silent, amazed at the sensitivity of the human soul. I had no doubt that in her dream Georgetta had been made aware of the danger which was hovering around us. I looked at her as she walked beside me. She had a pretty figure and one of the most beautiful voices I have ever known, but her features were homely and she knew it; her face was small and pointed like a squirrel's, her eyes sad, and her hair pulled into a tight little bun. I told her that although of course it was possible that spirits had tried to warn us, I believed that sensitive people, like wild animals, develop a kind of radar which tells them of the approach of evil or danger. I said that my experiences that afternoon had convinced me that we must stop our risky work, that after the two groups I had still to help were safely gone I would try to escape to Vienna, and that she must not involve herself any more on such activities. She should stay at home and look after her mother, and I would do my best to send her something from time to time, to help them to scrape through.

She looked up sadly and said: "It's good of you." Then she

told me how she had lost her job because "they" knew that Dr. Moga had relied on her. She was devoted to him. She said that I had always done so much for them and that it would be difficult for them when I went away. She thanked me for saying that I would try to go on helping them from abroad.

We walked on in silence until we reached the gate of Georgetta's house. The garden was full of lilac trees. The friendly hall was warmly lit by a five-branched candelabrum. I hung up the hat and coat Nina had lent me—I intended to return them very soon—and we went into the living-room with its rosewood piano and the table at which Georgetta earned her living by making leather pocket-books.

Her mother welcomed me, made the sign of the cross on my forehead and thanked God for my escape. I felt very tired. Madame Popovici quickly prepared a meal and we sat round the table feeling unusually relaxed after the anxious hours we had lived through and talking without restraint. Then we went up to our rooms. I could still hear the three women talking as they got ready for bed in the room next to mine.

I had just undone my tie when there was a ring at the front door; then the bell rang again and again.

The next moment, Georgetta and I were on the landing. The bell was pealing ceaselessly now as if it were out of order. She started down the dimly-lit staircase and I was following her on tiptoe, when Lydia pulled me back: "Don't go down. I saw a man climb over the railings and there are five or six others moving about in the bushes. I looked out of the bathroom window. It must be the police."

I knew she was right.

"Quick!" I said. "I'll get into the hiding-place. Deny that you've ever heard of me. Be brave. You must brazen it out."

In a second we had drawn up the heavy wooden panel half-way down the staircase and I dived into the deep black opening behind it. Lydia and Georgetta pulled it back into place without a sound. Groping in the dark, I found the bolt which kept the panel as firm as the other steps, and pushed it home. This emergency hide-out had been constructed by friends who had formerly taken refuge in the house.

By now the men were beating on the front door with their fists. Up above I could hear the movements of the women. I guessed that they were folding away my bedclothes to remove all traces of a visitor in the house.

Next I heard Georgetta's light steps going hesitantly down the stairs, across the living-room into the hall. There she paused a moment before opening the door.

Now the house was filled with loud, coarse, angry voices. I lay on my back, motionless. Not a gleam of light entered my hide-out, but I could hear every sound; indeed the dry wooden staircase and the walls of the cupboard had such resonance that I felt as though I were inside a huge violin.

"Why didn't you open the door at once?" bawled one voice.

"We were in bed—we had to put some clothes on."

"Where is George Bolintineanu?" asked another, nasal and arrogant.

"I don't know—I don't know him," answered Georgetta.

"You're lying. Dr. Brancovici told us that you know him. Come on now! You'll only make things worse for yourselves by lying."

"I can't tell you because I don't know the man."

Then the angry voice asked why she had rung up Dr. Brancovici yesterday? And why she had given a false name when he answered the telephone? The voice explained that it was he who had answered and that he had recognised her voice, so it was no use her denying that she had made the call.

Georgetta replied that she had rung him up to make an appointment because a fortnight ago she had been bitten by a cat which had died a few hours later. Afterwards she had been afraid that it had rabies. She had asked Dr. Brancovici's advice and he had sent her to a hospital to have some injections. She had had the last one the day before yesterday and wanted to have a check-up. Usually the doctor or his secretary answered the telephone. So yesterday, when she heard a strange voice and the speaker insisted that she should give her name, she instinctively gave a false one. Her last words were: "With all the strange things happening these days, it seemed the natural thing to do."

This reply made Georgetta's interrogator furious.

"Dr. Brancovici is a radiologist—what's he got to do with rabies! It's a pack of lies and on top of that you have the nerve to talk about 'these days.' We'll soon teach you. . . ."

One of the women shrieked, there was a noise of scuffling and of chairs crashing, then Madame Popovici cried out: "Don't kill her . . . you're strangling her . . . I beg you on my knees . . ."

"Stop it, you old bitch!"

But he must have relaxed his grip on Georgetta, for all I heard in the next few minutes was excited conversation and the stamping of feet as the police began to search the house. Then the same voice went on again, telling them that they would not do themselves a lot of good by giving the police all this trouble.

"You've all been mad since the spring hoping your allies would start a war. But before they'd ever get here, we'd have wiped out the lot of you. Now! Have you decided to tell us where Bolintineanu is?"

Georgetta answered: "Throttling me again won't make me tell you, because I don't know him."

Heavy boots tramped up the stairs and it must have been an hour before I heard them coming down again. Judging by the sounds, the police were searching every nook and cranny of the top floor. Then they searched downstairs and in the cellar and came up again. They seemed to tramp endlessly over my hiding-place and each time the catch moved very slightly.

When I heard Bolintineanu's name I breathed more easily; it was not for me that they were looking, and I guessed exactly what had happened. Bolintineanu was a lecturer at the Faculty of Science and an old friend of mine. Since 1946 he had been an active worker in the Resistance Movement. The Russians and the Roumanian Communists knew this and had been searching for him for years but, thanks to his false papers and devoted friends, he had managed to avoid arrest. Recently, believing that capture was inevitable, he had decided to escape and had set out with the unlucky party which had failed to cross the frontier owing to the imprudence of two of the fugitives.

Bolintineanu, who had been hiding in a room in Dr. Brancovici's house in Bucharest, rang him up to say that he was coming back, and to make sure that nothing had happened to his friend since he had last seen him. To his surprise, a polite but strange voice answered him, asked for his name and suggested that he should leave a message for the doctor who was expected back shortly from his clinic. Without a word he put down the receiver, convinced that the doctor was in the hands of the police. Soon afterwards he sent me a message begging me to find out the facts.

Since Georgetta was already in touch with Dr. Brancovici because of her cat-bite, she was the obvious person to ring up his house: she too had been answered by an unfamiliar voice. It was then that I decided to include Bolintineanu in Fekete's party, and he was one of those whom Georgetta, when she heard I was in trouble, warned of the miscarriage of this plan. Bolintineanu left at once to go to some friends of his near Prahova; even we did not know their names, but in the meantime Brancovici must have admitted everything he knew about Bolintineanu and his contacts. Probably he did this under torture.

I thought how odd it was that all the trouble we were in would never have arisen if Georgetta had not been bitten by her dying cat, for it was only when she consulted Brancovici as a patient that she gave him her real name and her address. It was terrifying to think that such a small event could have induced one of us to disregard the prudent laws of conspiracy by which we had lived for so long.

But I had more immediate grounds for fear. Every time the men went up the stairs my step squeaked slightly, and I couldn't rid my mind of the idea that at any moment one of them might notice it, realise that the step had moved and try to pull it up.

I was stretched at full length in my cupboard, my head pressed against the rough boards and my neck cramped. All my joints ached and I had a bad pain half-way down my spine.

## Background

Very carefully I got out the razor-blade I always carried in my pocket and managed to unfold the paper wrapping without a rustle. My fingers, moving up and down as do a surgeon's before he makes a first incision, found my carotid artery. I had made up my mind to cut it if an attempt were made to raise the panel. My blood would flow so quickly that there would not be time to save me in order to drag information out of me by torture, and once my heart had ceased to beat, all that was in my mind would become inaccessible to men.

I had decided long ago to do this if I were caught, but now that I seemed within seconds of carrying my resolution out I was troubled to the depths of my being. I was young and I wanted to go on living, and I thought: "O God, is this where I've got to die —alone in this black hole?" My mind filled with bitter regrets, I saw myself as a child running barefoot in the grass towards a clear blue lake. Willows and acacias grew in the thick mud along its edge. One great willow was my favourite; its branches stretched far out and I used to climb along them, enchanted by the sensation of floating above the water. Sometimes I would bend down and pretend to catch the little gold and silver fishes I could see below. The leaves rustled around me, and bees and hornets hummed among the clusters of white acacia.

Astride my tree, I dreamed of travelling to distant countries, of discovering everything that had not already been discovered, of doing good, of flying to great heights, of writing a book full of extraordinary happenings. I wanted to know all there was to know of life, and men, and everything in the universe.

The lake was a kind of Eden in which bees and birds, red and yellow butterflies, fishes and insects, nettles and forget-me-nots, willows and acacias lived in perfect harmony.

Sometimes I walked along the shore to where a small stream flowed out of the lake and fell cascading down a terraced slope into a wide valley where it joined a river. When there were storms in the mountains the river rose and its angry waters frightened me. They could smash bridges, flood villages and in a single night destroy what had taken many years and patient efforts to build up. I kept away from the river when it was in spate. In the same way, for a long time after I grew up, I instinctively avoided the troubled waters of life. Now I thought back to the events which, against my natural inclinations, had forced me into the muddy current and brought me where I was now, so close to death that I was already lying in my coffin. "O Lord, help me," I prayed.

After many years of effort I had found a meaning to the life I was now to lose. I felt sad that I would not die, like my brother, at home, surrounded by those I loved, and with a lighted candle at my head, a symbol of the survival of the soul.

I spent several hours in a state of fearful tension; in my right hand I held the razor blade and every time the policemen stopped on the stairs I felt with my left hand for the artery I had to cut.

All at once I heard a babble of voices coming from the hall which was only a few yards below me. Then one of the men shouted: "Who do the hat and trench-coat belong to?"

There was a long silence.

"Whose are they?" took up the nasal voice of the man I took to be the leader of the squad. "Now I've got you. Where is Bolintineanu? We'll find him anyway, if we have to pull the walls down and tear up the floorboards. But I'll give you two minutes to tell me. If you don't, we'll shoot you one by one, beginning with the old lady. Perhaps that'll decide Miss Georgetta to speak."

"The hat and coat belong to my husband," said Lydia. She said he was an engineer and worked outside Bucharest but had been at home last week. She told them that they must have seen his suitcases when they searched the attic—indeed she had pointed them out. He had stored them with Georgetta when he was sacked from the Electrotechnic Factory and they had lost the flat that went with the job.

"All right, we'll check your statements," the man said crossly. "Give me your bags, we'll see what's in them."

There was a pause, then: "What's this return ticket to Timisoara? Used two days ago. Why did you go there?"

I was horrified. Lydia had gone to Timisoara with Bolintineanu

54

and his party when they made their abortive attempt to escape; she was to hand them over to the guides I had provided.

She spoke calmly: "I visited my uncle, Ion Filip, the lawyer. I only spent one day there."

It was true that she had used her uncle's house as cover and had actually been to see him. All the same, I wished she had remembered to throw away her ticket.

"That'll do, we'll check on that too," said the agent. "Now get your coats: you're coming with us. The old woman can stay here."

There was another scuffle, and Madame Popovici begged the agents not to knock the girls about and not to take them away, but evidently no notice was taken of her appeal and Lydia and Georgetta were removed by the police squad. At least one man was left on guard, for I heard him giving orders to Madame Popovici: "Go to your room but leave the door open and the light on." She was told that she could lie down but was not to go out of her room without permission. "Do you understand me?" he shouted.

"Yes," whispered the old lady. I heard her stumbling up the stairs, followed by the man.

Soon afterwards the policeman turned on the powerful radio which some friends who had escaped had left with Georgetta, and the house was flooded with South American music.

Later on he came downstairs. Following his movements, I could almost see him sitting by the table in the living-room, probably facing the hall and with his back towards me.

I looked at my luminous wristwatch. It was 3 a.m. My cramped position and the nervous tension were consuming my strength of will.

Would Georgetta and Lydia keep silent? And what would happen to them if they did? And what would happen to Georgetta's mother if they did not return? The house, no doubt, would remain occupied by the police. They would answer the telephone and keep the callers talking while the Exchange identified the numbers they were speaking from. If anyone came to the door, they would invite him in, arrest him and interrogate him. This would go on for a week or even two—until friends, relations and acquaintances

55

had had time to spread the news. After that, nobody would ring or
call, the place would be avoided like a pest-house. The usual procedure was then to confiscate the house and hand it over to some
police agent as a reward. But even then the trouble would continue
to spread in ever-widening circles, for all the relations of the
arrested person would eventually be rounded up and evacuated,
each with only one small bag containing necessities.

I lay exhausted and half-asleep when I was startled by a loud
snore. The policeman, I thought, tired out and lulled by the slow
rhythm of Argentine tangoes, must be sleeping with his head on
the table. Then I realised with horror that the snorer was myself:
I must have dropped off for a few seconds and, as I was lying on
my back, my mouth had fallen open. If the policeman had recognised the sound, he would already have telephoned to headquarters.

Silently I repeated prayers I had been taught as a child and
never since said; I thought of all those who were dear to me, and
of incidents in my past life—anything to keep myself awake. For
a time I resisted sleep by sheer will-power, then again I dropped
off and once more my snoring woke me up.

The only way to prevent myself from snoring was to turn over,
but it was almost impossible to do so without making a sound.
To twist my body round and settle on my right side, facing the
wall, took me a whole hour, but at least the effort overcame my
drowsiness, and any slight noises I had made were fortunately
covered by the unseen orchestra.

When I looked at my watch again it was six o'clock. The music
from the air had vanished. A sad, heavy silence hung over the
house and filled my vault.

Suddenly the door-bell rang; it rang several times in sharp
nervous peals. The policeman rose and opened the door, and a
second later I again heard voices in the living-room.

"Madame, we've brought your girls back. We haven't killed
them. You see we've got hearts, we aren't as black as you paint us."
The nasal tone was quite friendly.

"Thank you, thank you." Then to the girls: "Oh, how cold
your hands are. I'll make some tea at once to warm you up."

# Background

"We're off," said the agent. "Go to bed and forget everything. If you say one word about last night, we'll be back for you. You understand?"

"We won't say anything," Georgetta said meekly.

When the men had gone she came up the stairs and spoke to me.

"Not now," I whispered. "This may be a trick." I told her to go to her room, lie down, and not get up till eight. If they were watching, this would seem natural. "Thank you for all you've done," I said.

"Thank God they didn't find you," she whispered back. "I know now you'll be safe. But I think the swamp is going to get me."

A deep stillness settled over the house; I dropped off into a dreamless sleep and woke up an hour later, feeling refreshed.

I thought about the situation. I was convinced that the apparent kindness of the agents was a trick. The house was certain to be watched by at least enough police to follow the two girls and identify their contacts; I realised that their freedom still hung by a thread. The police would use the next few days to check Dr. Brancovici's statements and decide whether he had told the truth in the hope of mitigating his own punishment or lied in order to give Bolintineanu time to get away. They would also check the other clues: the coat and hat, and the railway ticket.

At about eight o'clock I heard the women move about the house, opening the windows, cleaning the rooms and apparently behaving as on any other morning.

When they had finished, the two girls sat down side by side on one of the steps, as if to take a rest and to have a chat, and Georgetta whispered to me:

"If we sit here, even if the police are watching the windows through field-glasses, it won't look odd to them." Then she told me what had happened to them during the night. There were six men in the squad. They had searched every corner of the house; they even went up on the roof to see if anyone could have escaped into the neighbours' yard while they were ringing at the door. Then, as I knew, they had taken the girls away. They went by car—not knowing where because their eyes were bandaged. When they got out they went into a building and down into the basement. Then they were questioned separately. At first the agents were polite and promised all sorts of things—the girls couldn't believe they were the same people. But when they refused to speak, the men changed. They began on Georgetta. They took her into a small room with padded walls, stretched her on a table and tied her up so that she couldn't move an inch. They beat her on the soles of her feet and on her thighs. They left the door open for Lydia to hear her screams and be frightened into speaking, but she still refused to say anything. They kept on asking her where Bolintineanu was, and she went on saying that she didn't know him. They had never once mentioned my name, so it looked as if they didn't suspect that the girls knew me.

She paused and I tried to thank her for all she had endured; but she said: "Don't thank me," adding that I had been so kind to them and that they were glad to be able to repay a little of my kindness. She pointed out that these men were young, well-dressed and very brutal; they had two brand-new Fords. She was sure they were the secret police, and much more dangerous than the blackmailers of the Economic Police who had been after me yesterday. However, as they had not found me in the house, and as the girls had not told them anything about Bolintineanu, there was some hope of being left in peace. "But what about you?" Georgetta asked. "And what shall we do now?"

"Dress and go into town," I replied. I told her that the police would surely follow them. I suggested that they should look at the shops, go into a church, make one or two innocent telephone calls, go to a cinema. Then, after a while, separate and go in different directions. Ten minutes after they left the house I would come out and we'd see what happened. "If I succeed in planning my escape to the West, you'll both have to come with me," I said. "You can't stay here. The police are sure to come back and they will use even more cruel methods to make you talk. We'll arrange to meet somewhere, and I'll take you to a place where they'll never find you."

There was a silence, then Georgetta said: "We'll go into town, and we'll draw the agents after us, but as for escaping, I can't leave my mother—it's out of the question. We've come to the cross-roads . . ."

When the two girls cautiously pulled back the panel and I crawled out of my cupboard, we were so disfigured by strain that we hardly knew each other. Georgetta's lips were bloodless, her eyelids swollen and her eyes feverish; Lydia too was completely changed. They had returned to the light and life of every day, but it seemed as if they had brought back with them the darkness of that subterranean world which they had visited. Lydia exclaimed: "How drawn and grey you look, and you're covered with dust. It's a wonder you didn't go mad, shut up in that vault. Come and wash."

They took me to the bathroom where Georgetta found an old razor of her father's. Two days earlier I had taken my clothes from the Popovicis' house and left them with a student friend of mine so that, should there be a raid, there would be nothing to betray my presence. So now, in order to go out looking like a carefree citizen, I could only brush the clothes I had spent the night in.

Soon Georgetta and Lydia were dressed and ready to go out. They looked quite elegant, but pale and sad and we had little to say to one another. I made one last effort to persuade them to leave.

"I can't leave Mother—whatever happens. Perhaps they won't come back." But I could see that she had little hope of such a miracle.

Lydia would not leave Emile, her husband. I realised how they felt but I made one last effort. "If they arrest you, you might be in gaol for years, so you would still be separated from your mother and from Emile. While, if you escape, it's true you won't be with them, but think how happy they will be to know that you are free and safe."

But I could not move them. Finally I told them how much I admired their courage and that I could never thank them for all they had done. "Let's promise never to forget each other," I said.

# The Lost Footsteps

"Perhaps some day we'll meet again, and live in peace, and talk about these times as if they'd only been a nightmare."

These were my last words to Lydia, though Georgetta I was to meet again.

They left at once, doing their best to hold their heads high and look unconcerned. I watched them from behind a curtain. About two minutes later a car cruised slowly in the direction they had taken.

After waiting ten minutes I said good-bye to Madame Popovici; then I went down to the kitchen, opened the back door and went quickly down the steps into the yard. Standing behind a clump of lilac trees I watched the wattle fence between our garden and the neighbours' and found a small gap where it had broken down. Through it I slipped into the next garden. Voices and a broadcast song came from the windows as I walked down the path, looking as confident, I hoped, as if I were the owner, though I glanced anxiously at the gate, wondering what I would do if it were locked. It wasn't, and in a second I was out in the street.

I knew that it would not be easy to recognise police agents among the passers-by. In any case I must not show any hesitation in my movements, so I turned at once to the right without even looking round.

At the end of the street there was a little church. I mixed with people going in and found a place at the back. Facing the altar and crossing myself from time to time, I watched the congregation. It was Sunday and the Feast of the Annunciation. The golden flames of candles burning before the ikons and the smell of incense added to the peace which always seems to descend from the Pantecrator[1]. The priest was asking God's forgiveness for our sins, and for peace to all men of good will. His voice seemed to be a long way off.

I could not concentrate on the Liturgy, nor was I able to offer a prayer of praise and thanks to God, for my mind was paralysed by the thought of the police agents. I felt certain that they were in the church with me.

[1] A symbol of the Holy Ghost above the choir in an Orthodox church.

60

## Background

When the service was nearly over I left the building and walked down street after street, never once looking back but feeling all the while that I was surely being followed. I told myself that I was not of the same build as Bolintineanu, yet all the same I felt that the police must almost certainly be on my track.

The day was cold and I kept to the sunny side of the street, for my suit was very light for the season, and my thick overcoat was at Nina's. After a long time, when I found myself in a deserted side-street and there was no sound of a footstep behind me, I turned round for the first time. The street was empty. I could hardly believe my luck.

# CHAPTER IV

LATE THAT afternoon, still confident that I was not followed, I reached the shore of Lake Floreasca, on the outskirts of the city. Here Ionel Teodorescu (the brother of Professor Ovid Teodorescu, to whose flat I had gone the day before) had been living in hiding for some months. He greeted me with pleasure, and I felt intense relief at being in another friendly house.

I told him all that I had been through and I ended up by saying that the night before I had been nearer to death than I had ever been and that this morning, while I was looking at the candles in the church where I had taken refuge, I had made the resolution that, no matter what should happen to me, I would resist so long as I had breath left in my body.

We sat in Ionel's room and talked until the evening, discussing our country's situation and the ways of helping to keep alive that spirit of independence by which alone she could survive into a happier future.

I left at eight o'clock. We shook hands warmly and wished each other well. I had the feeling that this was our last meeting and so it proved to be, for a few weeks later Ionel was caught by the Security Police and never heard of again.

During the afternoon I had arranged by telephone to meet Commander Teodoru (the airman who had asked for my help in planning the escape of Iuliu Maniu). I found him waiting at the appointed place and he took me to a house where I could stay in hiding for a while.

He had been lucky to be able to arrange this hiding-place at such short notice, for although Bucharest is a large town and, as one walked along its streets one passed many doors, most of them were barred and bolted against a fugitive. Everyone's life hung on a thread; no one knew when it might be his turn to hear a midnight knock which heralded an arrest. And so the number of one's friends grew ever smaller and to a hunted man this city of one and a half million souls was like a wilderness.

Whilst I was in this hiding-place I heard that two days after we had parted Lydia and Georgetta had been taken away by the police. Madame Popovici ran to everyone she knew and to every Government office, in utter despair, trying to get news of them, but in vain.

Realising that the girls might be tortured into giving information, I began moving from house to house, going only to places which were unknown to them.

The general situation in the spring of 1948 was more tense than ever. The evolution of the Civil War in China and the Communist *coups d'état* in Hungary and Czechoslovakia had given rise to rumours of an imminent war between the East and West; many people in the captive countries argued that the Western Powers would not put up with such aggressive acts and that "something would happen which would bring about our liberation."

The Communists reacted vigorously and, while I was moving from one refuge to another, I heard of a new wave of arrests and of powerful Security units, each said to be composed of five to six thousand armed men, surrounding district after district and searching every house and every room. It was clearly time for me to get out of the city, which had become a death-trap.

Fortunately I had foreseen this possibility years before, and had prepared a hiding-place in a mountain village far from Bucharest. Forged papers and the kindness of a lorry driver who was going in my direction enabled me to leave the capital.

After two risky days of travelling I reached the village after nightfall. By then the country people were asleep, so no one saw me slip into a house. My friend, a peasant, welcomed me as if I were his brother, saying: "It's good that God has brought you to our house. Don't be afraid. We'll hide you in the rafters of the barn, and no one will find you." And all through the rest of the night he worked to make a hide-out for me in his byre.

This was an excellent hiding-place, for my hosts, Petrus and his family, went in and out to look after their cows and so their visits to me caused no comment. In this eyrie I spent the summer, waiting endlessly. Petrus never tired in his devotion, although he knew that the least he risked by sheltering me was the confiscation of all his goods.

With the cooler autumn weather my life among the rafters became more difficult and I realised that it would be impossible to stay on through the winter: not only would I be exposed to the bitter cold, but in the long winter evenings the peasants spent more time in one another's houses, and sooner or later one of them would sense the presence of a stranger. The Communists had their informers in the village and I did not want to put my hosts in greater danger than I had already. I saw that I must either join the partisans in the mountains or escape abroad.

I went to the partisans and stayed with them for several weeks before I finally decided to do my utmost to get out of the country.

This meant first returning to Bucharest in order to reopen one of my clandestine routes. Unfortunately for many months now I had been out of touch with those engaged in operations of this kind. I arrived in Bucharest at the end of November.

When I had first come down from my rafters, after seven months of immobility and darkness, pale and with a long beard rather like a rabbi's, I could hardly bear the sunshine—indeed it seemed to me that I was going blind—and I moved as stiffly as if all my joints were locked. But I was young and a few weeks out of doors restored my strength.

In Bucharest I hid in the house of Alice Zamfirescu. She was the wife of an old friend of mine, a doctor who had been chief medical officer at the Malaxa Factories and who had been accused of industrial sabotage and arrested in November 1947. His wife, his two daughters and his mother had been allowed to stay on in the flat. The building had two entrances, and a friendly engineer who lived above the Zamfirescus was willing to take me in should there be a police raid.

After my months of isolation I needed to learn how conditions in the capital had changed, and I was lucky in that Alice Zamfirescu, who still had many friends, was well informed. Through her I got very different news from the information published in the newspapers. I realised how greatly the difficulties facing members of resistance movements had increased. For anyone to shelter a fugitive had become almost impossible, partly because living space had been so reduced that a single room was often shared by four or five people and there was nowhere for a visitor to sleep, even on the floor; partly because the price of food was now so exorbitant that the hosts had not enough to keep their own families alive. In addition, it was harder to obtain false documents because the old identity cards had been withdrawn and replaced by new ones of a different kind.

Nevertheless, resistance was continuing, but had moved more and more from the towns into the mountains, where many people had joined with the partisans in acts of sabotage. The Communists hoped either to starve them out by isolating certain areas or to destroy them after locating them by air reconnaissance.

I was particularly interested in these groups and felt more convinced than ever, now that I had stayed among them, that they were vital nuclei capable of attracting the support of thousands. Their very existence was a symbol of defiance and of optimism. But they needed help and I determined that if I ever reached the West I would try to get it for them.

Alice also gave me personal news connected with the aftermath of my escape which caused me great anxiety.

One night towards the end of April, Georgetta had been taken from her prison to a large convent in Moldavia. The police, keeping their cars out of sight, had crept up to the convent and surrounded it, to make sure that no one left the building unobserved.

In the morning Georgetta was sent in alone. She had been ordered to go into the chapel and pretend she was a Christian who had come on a pilgrimage, then to ask for one of my relations, Mother Mary Magdalen, and get news of me. She obeyed the first part of her orders and was made welcome by my cousin, but as soon as they were alone, she told her that she had been brought by the police and in tears begged the nun to warn me to get away at once. She told her that she had broken down under continued beatings and given away all she knew about me, including the fact that I might, as a last resort, take refuge in the catacombs underneath the convent; indeed she was terrified that I might be there at this very moment.

To prove that she was telling the truth, she raised her skirt and showed the nun her purple, swollen legs. My cousin had been much moved and had assured her that I was not in the catacombs and that indeed she had no idea where I might be. A quarter of an hour later the police had entered the convent and made a thorough and of course unsuccessful search. I was greatly touched by Georgetta's devotion.

After this the police tried still another way of tracing me. Lydia was released and forced to travel about the country, visiting our mutual friends and my relations on the pretext that she wished to warn me of the efforts made by the police to track me down. No doubt they hoped that she would thus get news of me and that they would be able to extract it from her by torture.

Georgetta and Lydia were not the only ones amongst my friends who were suffering because of me. Both Nina and Madame Teodorescu, who had sheltered me on the afternoon of my escape, had been arrested. I cursed my tongue—because in my relief that evening at Georgetta's house I had mentioned them. Fortunately, they had both succeeded in convincing the police that they knew nothing of my activities, and had been released.

It was Christmas before my plans for crossing into Hungary matured. By then a friend had managed to establish contact with a guide from Oradea, a large town situated near the Western frontier. The further journey, from Budapest to Austria, was more difficult to organise because Leon Pótócki and his brother Alexander, on whose help I had relied, had been obliged to flee to Austria to avoid arrest. Luckily I heard that Leon was still in correspondence with his sister-in-law, Marie, Alexander's wife, who lived in Satu Mare. I saw her and she very kindly wrote a letter to Leon in which she mentioned that I was "going to Aunt

Ethel's," adding that the old lady was not well and needed certain medicines.

Aunt Ethel was an aunt of Leon's who had always lived in Budapest. I was sure that he would guess that I was setting out for the Hungarian capital and needed guides to take me on from there to Vienna. Towards the end of January 1949 Leon wrote that he would send the "medicine."

My final preparations took another couple of weeks. By now I looked more like a rabbi than ever: I had kept my beard and I wore black-rimmed glasses, a blue overcoat and a wide felt hat. Alexander's wife, who wished to join her husband, decided to make the journey with me and to take her little daughter. I was delighted with their company, and though a child of two would slow us down a little, the disadvantage was outweighed by the disarmingly domestic picture we presented. Nobody who saw us travelling by day—I was carrying the child and a string bag full of dolls and teddy-bears—was likely to imagine that at night we streaked across the fields at the risk of being shot at any moment.

One moonless night we met our guide and he took us across the border by a path known only to himself. We had given the little girl a narcotic; she slept soundly in my arms and woke up only when we were in the fast train carrying us into the centre of Hungary.

Sitting with my eyes closed, like an ordinary weary traveller, I felt infinitely relieved and yet sad at leaving the places which I loved and at the thought of facing the future as a refugee.

It was noon on the 20th of February when we arrived in Budapest and went to Aunt Ethel's; she lived in a three-storey building not far from the centre of the town. Though she had never seen me before and was surprised by our unannounced arrival, she received us warmly, sheltered us in her one room and cared for us like a mother.

That evening we wrote a postcard to Leon Pótócki: the Budapest postmark would tell him that we had arrived safely and were waiting for the promised guides to take us into Austria.

The conditions in Hungary at this time were as bad as in

Roumania. The trial of Cardinal Mindszenty had just ended. There were frequent searches and thousands of arrests including, recently, those of two Communist Ministers.[1] Our own position as fugitive guests was particularly irksome. In Roumania I still had a few devoted friends and I knew my way about the country; here except for Aunt Ethel I had nobody. But this woman had the heart of a lion. Ill, lame and very poor, she never showed the least anxiety. She found us a safer refuge than her room and put us in touch with connections of her nephew's.

For two weeks we heard nothing from Leon; then a letter came, saying that he had posted several parcels of medicines which, he had no doubt, would arrive in a day or two, but that he would not be able to send more, since he was hoping in a week to emigrate to Canada with his wife and daughter.

This letter raised our hopes, but as the days and weeks passed and the guides did not arrive, our anxiety became intolerable. Assuming that they would never come, I got in touch with the Chief Rabbi, who offered us the chance to cross the frontier by one of the secret routes used by Jewish refugees going to Israel. We got as far as fixing the day of our departure and discussing the fee we were to pay the guides, when Pótócki's men arrived.

Our stay in Budapest had lasted thirty-five interminable days. It ended one bright morning towards the end of March, when we boarded an express train to Szombathely, a town which lies about twelve miles from the Austrian frontier.

After dark the following evening, our guides led us through muddy fields and woods to a small village a mile from the border. Here for an hour we rested lying on the straw in a barn. Our party had been joined by three Hungarian peasants who hoped to get to Canada, a Jewish girl who wished to join her fiancé in Israel, and a seminarist whom the police were hunting for his connection with Mindszenty.

[1] The Foreign Minister, Rajk, and General Palffy, Minister of War. They were later accused of plotting with Marshal Tito to assassinate Rakosi, the Secretary of the Hungarian Communist Party, and other members of the Government.

## Background

We set out in silence, walking in single file. At about two o'clock we reached the frontier. The guides produced steel cutters and cleared an opening in the barbed wire through which we passed.

We were on Austrian soil but we would not be safe until we reached first Vienna, and then one of the Western occupation zones.

Avoiding the Soviet control posts, our guides took us along unfrequented paths until, four days after we had left Budapest, we arrived in Vienna. Here we parted from the two devoted men to whom we owed so much.

I had dreamed of Vienna as of an oasis. All the friends whom I had helped to leave Roumania had stopped here on their way and each had given me some sign of life. Because of this, and although the city was unknown to me, I did not feel the same anxiety as I had felt in Budapest.

I went to see an old school friend. He had been in Vienna eighteen months and had decided to stay on in order to make good a gap which had existed until then in the chain of hide-outs available to refugees. He was now able to get us false identity papers and advise us about our further journey.

I arranged for Marie Pótócki and her child to be conducted safely through the Soviet Zone. As she could not speak German she went with a Viennese woman and arrived safely in Western Austria; on learning that her husband had been transferred to Italy, she joined him in his D.P. camp near Milan.

On a wet evening in mid-May I at last boarded the Arlberg Express. According to my passport I was a Viennese business man. A four-hour journey took us to the demarcation line and we drew up in the dark, small station of Enns where our passports were to be examined. Immediately a group of Soviet subalterns jumped into each coach. Two Mongolians in brand-new uniforms appeared in my compartment. This was the critical moment for me, cooped up in a small space and knowing that the train was surrounded by armed guards. Stretched out on my bunk, I tried to look indifferent and sleepy as they checked my papers. These were

69

written in German, English, French and Russian and stamped by all the four authorities. The subalterns peered attentively at the photograph and then at me, studied the description of my identity, and finally returned the passport and turned to go on to the next compartment.

Suddenly from the platform came the sound of shots followed by the chattering of machine-guns. The subalterns slipped out their pistols and leaned out of the window to see what was going on. The sinister calm which till now had brooded over the train gave way to pandemonium. Orders were shouted in Russian and broken German that no one should attempt to leave the train. For several moments the staccato bursts of machine-gun fire went on, then a silence, more ominous than before, settled on the waiting train and the inspection continued.

A quarter of an hour later we rumbled out of the station and over a long iron bridge, and halted at another station on the far side of the river Enns. Here American military police boarded the train and moved down the corridors, briefly flashing their electric torches in the faces of the passengers but not so much as glancing at the papers which every traveller held open in his hand.

It was not until the morning that we found out from the train guard what had caused the incident at Enns. It seemed that during the inspection the Soviet military police had become suspicious of a passenger and arrested him. While they were taking him along the platform to their headquarters he bolted, jumped into the river which marked the frontier of the Soviet Zone and swam towards the far bank. He vanished in the darkness; no one knew whether he had reached safety or had been shot or sucked under by the current.

My journey through the American and French Zones was pleasant; for the first time in many years I was in a friendly world, no longer threatened with arrest. Innsbruck received me hospitably. The mountains, valleys, fields by which it was surrounded, the rare beauty of the Alps and the rustle of the pine-woods filled me with serenity and new life and vigour.

I wanted, however, to reach Paris as soon as possible, there to join the friends who had arrived a year earlier, but three long months of patient waiting were needed before I could obtain a passport and a visa. I wanted this time to travel with genuine papers in my own name, and from now on to bury all memories of the clandestine life I had been leading for so long.

I first saw Paris beneath a mid-August sun; it charmed me at once and won my heart for ever. I was met by many friends. Now most of them were living in narrow little streets in the Latin Quarter. They would have liked to give a banquet for me, but in fact we each had a cutlet and a potato cooked over a spirit lamp; all the same, the meal was festive.

Afterwards they took me to see the city. We walked for half an hour until we reached the smoothly flowing Seine, its surface puckered with greenish ripples in which the lights that festooned the quayside sparkled. We crossed the bridge into the Place de la Concorde, deeply moved to be again together, in one of the most beautiful squares in the world. The years seemed to have dropped off our shoulders, we felt young and high-spirited. Like stage managers who had put on a splendid show and were quite certain of its reception, my friends took me to the Champs Élysées and the Place de l'Étoile. Indeed, the city with its neon lights and street lamps, its shadows and half-shadows, looked like a stage setting. Perhaps with the coming daylight the fantastic vision would disappear and the façade would show cracks and signs of wear and tear. But for the moment there was nothing around us but magnificence, kindness and gaiety.

"Can all this be real?" I asked my friends. "These cafés packed with laughing crowds and the language which sounds so musical to me? Can you assure me that I am not asleep among the rafters?"

They understood what I was feeling and assured me that this really was the heart of Paris, and I was safe and free to enjoy its beauty. And so, with time, it began to seem to me that, on the contrary, it was the rafters and the hide-outs beneath stairs that were unreal and part of a grotesque nightmare from which I had woken up.

# The Lost Footsteps

But in the early hours, when I was back in my small hotel, very different thoughts came to me. I was now in the position in which all my friends had been when they had first arrived. I would have endless trouble getting the labour permit which I needed in order to earn my living. Some of my friends were still without one. And meanwhile there was only enough money for the scrappy meals in the solitude of our bedrooms with a newspaper for tablecloth, and often not enough left over from the food and rent even for a Métro ticket.

Like all other emigrants I felt homesick. Some had improvised a day-to-day existence founded on the hope of some day going home. Others were awaiting permission to emigrate to the New World. But most of them, whether temporarily settled or merely birds of passage, were determined to go on working for our country.

Paris was now the European centre for exiles from Roumania. A group which represented Maniu's Peasant Party had been formed. I was asked to join it, and was then made a member of the Executive Committee.

At the same time a Roumanian National Committee was formed in New York from representatives of several democratic parties and various independent personalities in exile.

My friends warned me of the difficulties we would meet in putting forward our views and projects, for the Western countries were preoccupied with re-establishing their pre-war economic standards and for that reason were inclined to overlook the meaning of events in Asia and in Eastern Europe.

Nevertheless, my friends believed that the Atlantic Powers, even if they preferred to disregard it at the moment, were in fact aware of the threat which Russia's power position represented, and that America intended to erect a barrier to Soviet expansion by means of the combined armed forces of the West. Though it would come too late to save positions already lost, this policy would be, at any rate, more realistic than the one that had preceded it.

Personally, I saw it as our duty to unite the exiles from the Sovietised countries and urge them to persist in bearing witness to the danger. I was sure that the first arm of the West must be awareness of its peril, while the second should be sufficient strength to command respect and act as a deterrent; the third necessity, I thought, was that the unity enforced upon the Soviet bloc should be opposed by moral unity in the Free World, based upon reciprocal consent and the determination to preserve a social system which upholds the freedom, rights and dignity of individuals.

The Roumanian National Committee was in touch with influential circles in the Atlantic countries, interested in ensuring that the Free World should act in concert with the millions who, from the far side of the Iron Curtain, were carrying on the struggle against Communist dictatorship.

It was clear by now that the Red front extended round the world, and also that the Soviet leaders had taken Lenin's theories to heart: their strategy was to deliver separate local blows, giving particular attention to those backward countries which he had called "the weaker links of Capitalism."

Early in October 1949 I got a message from a friend who was responsible to the Committee for direct action in our country. He solicited my help and asked me to return to Roumania for an important undertaking, stressing that I was one of the few people left who had clandestine routes at their disposal and that my previous experience of resistance would be useful in view of certain projects.

I found it very difficult to accept. For one thing, I had only just recovered my health; for another, after the strain of the past years, I felt reluctant to face fresh danger. I consulted two friends; who were members of the National Committee and both advised me to go back. All of us wished to earn the moral right to speak for our country and we believed that to do our utmost to halt Communism was the way to earn it. We were acutely conscious that for the second time in a decade Roumania had been forced against her will into the camp hostile to the West and we wanted to show how unwillingly she accepted this position. Of course I knew that whatever action I took would only be one drop in the sea, but one drop can colour a great deal of water.

My strongest reason for wishing to remain in Paris was a personal one.

My experience of the last two years had left their mark on me; I was more and more aware of a deep feeling of loneliness. By a strange coincidence I met Alba the very day of my arrival in Paris. I was fascinated from the moment our eyes met. She had spent part of her youth in my home town and I immediately sensed the intensity of her interest in everything concerning Roumania. Her deep bright eyes reflected not only the nostalgia of a girl dreaming of the country she had left, but also the longing to help those who had lost their freedom. It was as if we had both come a very long way to find each other in order to share our joys and sorrows. I discovered in our long talks together in the wonderful Paris gardens her keen spirit and wonderful heart and we both grew so fond of each other that we knew of no other wish than to spend the rest of our lives together—working for the fulfilment of our ideals.

Perhaps it was because of this happiness that I was at moments tempted to adopt an attitude of resignation to the evil which had overcome my country, but then I would feel very strongly that it was better, or at least more dignified, to confront it. Finally I decided to accept the mission.

It remained for me to tell the person to whom, besides myself, my decision was of most concern.

I said what I had to say in the Jardin du Luxembourg. I remember that we were standing among flowers, and that near to us there was a sculptured group: two lovers who looked so happy in their secret world of feeling and imagination that they were lost to everything around them, and certainly unaware of the dreadful beast poised on the rock above them and ready to hurl a huge boulder down on their heads.

Alba made no attempt to dissuade me and only said how much she dreaded our parting and the risks I would have to take.

Soon afterwards I left Paris and set out for Roumania by paths so dangerous that my heart shrank at each new stage of my journey.

But behind me I left someone who, as it proved, kept me ever present in her heart and who, in my darkest moments, summoned me back to life. And here I must mention that when I was in Paris I used to give Alba three white carnations; much later, at a time when all my other friends had given up all hope of my return, this gift became the sign which made it possible for me, from far away, to tell her that I was alive.

# *The*
# *Lost Footsteps*

1950 - 1957

## CHAPTER V

IN THE first chapter of this book I told how my two guides, Paul and Stefan, took me across the frontier into Hungary, and how we found ourselves in hiding in a shed on a small farm.

As I waited for the evening, nerves tense and ears strained to interpret the slightest sound, my imagination became vaguely disquieted by several incidents of my journey from Paris which now seemed to me ill-omened.

To begin with, in Vienna I had missed a train for the first time in my life; then there was the heavy fall of snow which had forced us to delay crossing the frontier, and, later, the curious luminosity of the night we finally chose, instead of the leaden rain-clouds which had masked the moonlight the night before. And there was the arrest a few days earlier, in the very village in which I was now hiding, of the man who was to have been my guide.

Now I wondered if it was only superstition that made me feel as if these happenings had been meant as warnings. However, there could be no question, at this stage, of turning back. Indeed it was almost time for me to brace myself for the next stage of my journey.

We checked the plan for my return to Austria in three or four months' time. They believed that I would spend these months in Hungary. "Don't stay too long in Budapest," Paul said. "But whatever happens we'll be waiting for you here, even if we have to blow up all the mines to reach you."

After dark we left the shed and saw that low clouds overcast the sky and a fine drizzle was falling. Silently we made our way across the orchard, through a little gate into a field; here we took our leave of each other; a long time afterwards I felt the sting on my shoulders from Paul's and Stefan's brawny hands as they wished

# The Lost Footsteps

me luck. They turned right and set off towards the frontier, while Paul's cousin Endre, his friend Janos and I turned to the left along a slippery path which led into the heart of Hungary. There were twenty miles of frontier zone between us and the town of Sarvar which we had to reach by dawn. Sarvar lay outside the zone and was therefore subject to fewer controls; there I meant to get into a train for Budapest.

Half an hour later we entered a forest and stumbled through it for five endless miles. We walked fast, so fast that our throats were dry, while our clothing, soaked by rain and sweat, seemed to weigh more and more heavily upon us.

At last we were through the forest and after tramping for about four hours, we saw lights in the distance and calculated that they must be six to ten miles ahead. A little later we noticed that the lights came from three separate places. I stopped the guides and asked them if they knew which of the three was Sarvar. Without the slightest hesitation they replied: "On the right is Szombathely, on the left is Celldömölk; Sarvar is in the middle." This worried me: I had studied the map for days and according to my bump of locality, which is a good one, Sarvar was on the left. I told them what I thought but it annoyed them that I should set my book knowledge against their local experience and, as they were so sure of themselves, I followed them obediently.

Making for the middle cluster of lights we moved across flat country covered with dry rustling grass and withered maize stalks; canals, three or four yards wide, and a few roads were the only risks in our path; we had to cross them with great caution for fear of sentries who might be patrolling there.

Although we were advancing steadily towards the lights, they seemed to become less distinct, as if they were receding from us. It took us a little time to realise that a thick ground mist had arisen. Soon we could only walk in the general direction in which we had last seen our landmark.

Suddenly we noticed a white streak on the ground; almost feeling our way to it, we discovered the sleepers and girders of a railway line. We decided to walk along the track for, though it

80

might be guarded, at least by following it we were sure to reach the town.

After a long while it led us to where we could again see lights. We had arrived somewhere—but was it Sarvar? On the left were the high walls of some factory and ahead of us a barrier, down over a level-crossing, and a wooden shack. We crept up to it; from inside came loud snores. This was reassuring, so, like phantoms floating in the mist, we made our way across the lines and came into the outskirts of the town, walking down one deserted street after another, until Endre stopped and said: "We're in Szombathely. I'm afraid you were right."

This was disappointing, for though we were a dozen miles inside the frontier, we were still within the frontier zone.

There was too much danger of patrols and check-points for us to hang about the streets till morning and Endre, anxious to make amends for his mistake, suggested taking us to his uncle.

We accepted gratefully and he led us to a dilapidated house inside a yard with a ramshackle barn. Here we waited while he scratched gently on the door. After a moment, it was pushed ajar; warm stuffy air puffed out at us; finally a mat of hair showed in the opening followed by a bewhiskered face.

"Uncle Gabor! It's Endre. Can we come in?"

"Yes, yes, come in quickly, all of you," answered a friendly voice.

Gabor was a carter and he and his family lived in one room about nine feet square, lit by a small oil lamp standing in a corner of the floor. To the left of the door was a wooden bed on which lay an old lady with two long thick plaits, who looked at us with great curiosity. Gabor now resumed his place beside his wife, while at their feet a sleepy little girl sat up, astonished by our entry. Another bed across the tiny room was occupied by Gabor's daughter, her husband and their baby. The room also had an iron stove and one chair on which I was invited to sit. On the floor beside me a boy of about fourteen slept on a sack of straw. My guides pulled out stools from beneath the beds and sat down in the remaining space.

## The Lost Footsteps

After he had told his uncle of our night's adventures, Endre questioned him about conditions in the town and our chances of leaving by train for Budapest. The old man said that since the autumn there had not been many check-ups at the station and that there was a train at six and another at nine. Until then he could keep us in his room, but it would not be wise for us to stay much longer, since there were many poor families living in the house and someone might be tempted to denounce us in the hope of a reward.

I was impressed, however, by the fact that Uncle Gabor and his family were much less terrified of the police than our hosts of the night before. Indeed he suggested taking me to Budapest himself, hidden in the hay in his covered waggon: this would be an easy way for me to get through the control points.

I was touched and a little tempted, as I had no Hungarian identity papers. But the journey would take two days instead of the six hours by train, and as I could speak Hungarian well, I thought that I could bluff my way through an inspection. My immediate aim was to get out of the frontier area with its close network of controls as quickly as I could. In Budapest there would be, of course, the usual problem of informers but I could rely on finding at least one or two safe places to hide.

Early in the morning I left Uncle Gabor's kind, smoky, poverty-stricken house. I had put on the clean shirt I had brought with me, polished my shoes and even managed to shave; after all this I felt that I looked like any local man setting out for the big city.

Uncle Gabor was delighted with the present which I gave him in token of my gratitude. He wished me a safe journey and invited me to come to his house again on my way back to Austria. As it turned out, years later this was to save my life.

Endre had been out early to check the time of the train and the conditions at the station and had come back with our tickets; he was going with me to Budapest, while Janos was returning to his village that night.

Now we made our way separately to the station; the train was already in; pretending not to know each other, we got into the same carriage.

As I sat in my corner, impatient for the train to leave, I scanned the platform. I saw many militiamen in their grey uniforms and I had no doubt that there were also plain-clothes men among what looked like ordinary citizens. But although the militiamen were clearly keeping a look-out for suspicious characters, they did not inspect the papers of the passengers.

On the other hand, as the train drew out, I recognised the shack beside the level-crossing we had passed the night before. The shack was in fact a check-point and sentries were examining the permits of the peasants who were coming into town to deliver milk. I realised how lucky we had been last night that the sentries had taken shelter from the rain and been lulled to sleep.

We arrived in Budapest punctually and stepped out on to the packed platform, keeping close together, but as we moved on with the crowd we were brought to a halt. Raising myself on tiptoe, I saw that, about twenty yards ahead, militiamen were examining the papers of the travellers. Endre made the same discovery and turned pale. Pretending that I had forgotten something in the train, I turned back and, followed by Endre, made my way with difficulty against the crowd. I hoped that the inspection was going on only at the main exit and that we might leave the station by some other way, but we soon realised that all the platforms were surrounded by armed militiamen. Back we went to the main hall, for the militia were already rounding up the stragglers.

I thought how stupid I had been not to have got out at a small station on the outskirts of the capital and continued my way by bus or tram.

But at least Endre's papers were in order and, as we were pushed towards the barrier by the pressure of the crowd, I decided to pretend that I had lost mine, though I had not much confidence in the success of such an old trick. It looked as if my journey was about to end, and in such a way that none of my friends in Paris would ever know what had happened to me.

I looked at Endre and saw his anxious face suddenly relax;

he nudged me, whispering: "That's luck! The militiaman on the left comes from my village, we're like brothers. Take my identity book, don't open it, just hold it in your hand."

I did as he said and, as we came up to the barrier, Endre called out: "Hallo, Sandor!"

The militiaman looked up, grinned and shook Endre's hand: "You here? Just arrived?"

"This moment. I'm going back tomorrow; your family will be glad I've seen you. Any messages?"

Sandor wished his parents to be told that he was well and would soon be writing.

Endre added: "I travelled up with our district vet; he's come to get a stock of medicines for the cows. That's him."

I held up his identity book as if expecting it to be examined; Sandor smiled, saluted and waved me on. I smiled back and hurried after Endre.

That afternoon Budapest was enveloped in a strange yellow glow, perhaps because the sunset was reflected in the fine sand which the wind had carried from the *Puszta*; it made the city look as if it had arisen in a desert.

We walked to Aunt Ethel's house. From the outside, it seemed unchanged from a year ago, when it had been my refuge. I went upstairs while Endre waited for me in the street. I had thought it safer not to get in touch with the old lady in advance, and I could only hope now, as I knocked at her door, that she was still alive, for she had been so very old and ill when I had last seen her.

But all was well; when the door opened, Aunt Ethel peered at me incredulously through her thick lenses, pressed the palms of her hands together as though she were praying and exclaimed: "Is it possible! You're back in Budapest! Come in at once."

When I came inside she told me that she had had news of Marie Pótócki and her little daughter: they and Alexander had joined Leon in Montreal. "I was sure that you too were safely in America by now," she added. "If you knew how much worse things have become here, you would never have returned."

I explained that I had come to help some other friends to

reach the West and appealed to her to help me. Without the slightest hesitation she promised to do everything she could.

I fetched Endre. Aunt Ethel's room was only about six feet wide; the walls were cracked and black with smoke, and the furniture—a bed, a small chest, a cupboard and two chairs—was hopelessly dilapidated. The place smelt as though it had a decomposing corpse in it, although in fact the stench came only from the little oil-stove on which Aunt Ethel was already cooking an omelette for us. While I was out she had spread a clean cloth on the chest and put out plates and forks ready for our meal. The miserable setting was soon forgotten in the atmosphere of kindness which emanated from her.

After her husband's death, she had concentrated her love on her five nephews; now that all of them had left the country with their families, she lived only to help others who were in misfortune and this activity had brought her happiness. Indeed, she was one of the happiest people I have ever met.

Trust is as essential to those who are engaged in secret work as it is difficult for them to give and to inspire. It was because I wanted Endre and Aunt Ethel to trust each other that I had brought him to Budapest. Endre was to help me to return to Austria when my mission had been completed.

This was my scheme: a postcard from "Norbert and Mariette" would reach Stefan and Paul in Vienna and bring them to the village of Peressny, where Paul's uncle, Janos, lived. Janos would tell Endre in the next village, and Endre would go to Budapest where, through Aunt Ethel, he would get in touch with me. He and I would then travel together by night to Szombathely and thence on to Peressny where the two guides would be waiting for me. The plan was complicated, but in clandestine movements complication can be a safeguard.

When all these details had been settled, Endre set out for home. As soon as it was dark that evening, I went out with Aunt Ethel, slipped a picture-postcard into a letter box and said good-bye to the old lady at a tram stop. She was to be my post office, but beyond this I would not involve her.

## The Lost Footsteps

My postcard was for Professor Georgescu who lived in the Roumanian town of Cluj. It was to let him know that I had got as far as Budapest and was waiting for a guide to take me to Roumania.

The year before, I had discussed with him the need for a well-established secret route both to and from the West, which would enable us to help the partisans and to rescue friends who were in danger of their lives. He had been enthusiastic and we had worked out a relatively simple and safe plan.

Now, sitting in my tram, I felt elated for I had got to Budapest in record time, but although in this big city I was less a target for suspicion than I had been in the frontier zone, it was prudent to find a refuge as quickly as possible.

I got out at the terminus and walked through badly lit suburban streets. I was making for the house of an old engineer named Andrassy. His sister-in-law Mathilde, a Roumanian and a friend of Marie Pótócki's mother, had fled to Hungary and lived with her sister. I had met her through Marie the year before, and she had soon become "Aunt Mathilde" to me. At that time she had had to have a major operation and I was able to help the family with the expenses; the Andrassys were grateful to me and had begged me to come to them if I ever needed a refuge. Now they welcomed me and were most willing that I should stay for as long as I needed.

I kept away from Aunt Ethel for eight days. When I finally visited her I found two postcards for me. Her address was an ideal poste restante: for years she had been corresponding with her many nephews and, now that they were scattered, the hawk-eyed censors were accustomed to her getting letters from all over the world.

One of my postcards brought me greetings from Vienna and took a weight off my mind for it meant that Paul and Stefan had got home safely. The other, from Professor Georgescu, said: "Istvan's wife has had a boy. The christening is on the 20th of March." This told me that, four days later, my guide would wait for me in the village of Biharkeresztes, a place near the Roumanian border which I had passed through on my way to Austria in 1949.

## The Lost Footsteps

So on March 20th a van, driven by Andrassy's son-in-law, set me down outside the village; I walked across a field to a small hut belonging to a railway worker who had sheltered me the year before, and found the guide waiting for me.

The frontier defences were different from those dividing Hungary from Austria, but almost as effective.

On the Hungarian side, there were few patrols but many informers in the villages, who kept a look-out for clandestine travellers. On the Roumanian side there was first a strip of earth about three yards wide, ploughed and raked smooth, so that its surface would show the lightest footprints; then fine wires, attached to rockets, hidden in the grass bordering the ploughed strip. The two frontier commands were in touch by radio and telephone, and ready at the first signal to organise a search of roads, villages and trains throughout the neighbourhood.

We crossed the ploughed strip by a light plywood "bridge" we had brought with us, and hoped that by morning the wind and dew would have erased the slight imprint left by the slats.

We walked throughout the night; by dawn we reached Oradea, a town still within the frontier zone. All that day I sheltered in the house of an old Jewish watchmaker; then, during the hours of darkness, I managed by various means to travel to Cluj, a hundred and fifty miles inside Roumania. Here I spent ten days with one of my confidential agents, a chauffeur called Axente. I wanted to be sure that the secret police had no suspicion of my being back; I was also waiting for messages from Georgescu and from another friend with whom I had got in touch on entering Roumania.

These ten days were a strange experience. I had been a student in Cluj, so I knew it very well indeed. I still had many friends there and, strangest of all, at that very moment my parents were living within twenty minutes of my hide-out. How gladly they would have welcomed me, and how glad I would have been to join them in their warm family atmosphere and tell them about all that I had been through in the many years since I had seen them. But I was no longer "their child": I was a man who brought fear and danger into any house he entered. Indeed, if the police had any inkling of my return, theirs would have been the first house they would have visited.

Only very occasionally did I venture into the town at night. On one such evening I at last set out to see a friend; I had sent him a message that afternoon. Not a soul was about when I entered his orchard and stopped a moment in the twisted shadows of the budding apricots. I walked up to the door and rang the bell. Hesitant footsteps sounded in the hall; they were inconsistent with my memory of Professor Popovici, but to my relief the door opened and there he stood, his hand nervously on the latch, and his brown eyes staring at me in astonishment. He exclaimed: "Come in," but his voice belied the invitation.

All the same, I followed him into the comfortable living-room with its Persian rugs, gleaming piano, blue velvet-covered sofa, and the books and magazines.

He twisted his moustache and said that he had just returned from his laboratory and had not expected visitors at such an hour. I explained my situation, and observing his increasing nervousness, said: "I am sorry to be so unpleasant a surprise for you!"

Popovici protested: of course I was always welcome; only he had heard that I had fled abroad, so no wonder he had been bewildered when he saw me. In fact, when the young man I had sent round that afternoon had given him my message and the password we had used three years before, his first thought had been that this was an *agent provocateur*. The Security Police, he thought, had come to know the password and were using it to trick him into an admission that he and I had been connected in the past. This had frightened him so much that he had been about to make a full confession to their Headquarters.

"It seemed the only way to save myself," he said, "and I was lifting the receiver to ask for an appointment when it occurred to me that you might really be in Cluj: in that case a confession would be disastrous to us both."

How old he looks, I thought, as he stroked the top of his bald head; yet he was only forty-three.

He ended irritably: "Why did you come back? You were safe in

Paris. There have been thousands of arrests in the past year. For God's sake, go before the agents get you or you'll bring misfortune to everyone with whom you come in touch."

Suddenly I felt very angry. I said: "Yes, life in Paris was very pleasant. I came back to bring encouragement to you and others like you—to tell you that you are not forgotten—and to help some of our friends to escape abroad. You know how many resistance fighters have been condemned to death but have not yet been caught—isn't it worth a risk to save some of them, after they have done so much for their country?"

Popovici remained silent. I glanced round the handsome room and asked him: "What would your life be like without your Chair, your salary and your flat? What would you feel like if you were living underground, knowing that at any moment you might be caught, tortured and killed?"

I felt calmer now but I went on talking. I reminded him of our youth and of our devotion to social justice. How could we, who knew what gave a meaning to life better than so many of our fellow-countrymen, give up the struggle for liberty of thought and of expression for ever? How could we allow it to die and then face our children?

His reaction, when it came, was completely unexpected. Popovici got up and went over to the piano. "Let me show you something," he said. He handed me a photograph of a little girl of about ten. When I looked up, tears were streaming down his face. "She died three weeks ago of pneumonia; I can't get over it. Perhaps you remember her? . . . And my wife and I are divorced. Did you know that?"

He had taken me utterly by surprise. He went on a little wildly: "The terror here is suffocating . . . We've lost our bearings, we're just turning helplessly round and round . . . Of course you're right, we ought to set an example, but how can we? You've no idea of the number of secret agents—they know everything . . . I don't see what good you can do. You really ought to go away before it's too late."

So that was that. I could only sympathise with his loss and

assure him that he had convinced me, that I would go that very night. At least if he were questioned, he could honestly say that he believed I was no longer in the country.

He gave me his solemn promise not to breathe a word about our meeting and for the first time that evening his face relaxed. We talked for a little longer—about his research work and about our mutual friends, hoping that our parting would not leave too painful an impression in our minds.

This visit upset all my plans. Although on balance I thought Popovici unlikely to inform against me, I could not be sure of his reactions. It was better to leave Cluj that night. But I still had to see Professor Georgescu.

As I walked to Georgescu's house, I reflected that on one point at least Popovici had convinced me: the necessity to take more careful soundings before I went on with my mission. If Roumanian morale had suffered so radical a change, if other friends had altered as much as Popovici, then I was in for some dangerous surprises. Apart from this, the enormous number of recent arrests must have given the Security Police more information about the underground than they had ever had before; they would know enough about my contacts to set an efficient trap for me: to act hastily in these conditions would mean digging my own grave.

Georgescu was not expecting me but his greeting was extremely friendly. My story alarmed him and he agreed that I had better get out of Cluj at once and if possible lie low in Bucharest. We arranged a way in which I could communicate with him when I felt it was safe to surface again. I left his house very late without any presentiment that this had been our last meeting.

An hour later I reached Axente's home; he was waiting for me, alarmed that my "evening walk" had been so long. Although we had known each other for ten years (he had been my driver whenever I had travelled in Transylvania) he knew nothing about my activities and thought that the Communist Police were after me only because of my Nationalist past.

Axente was a good Roumanian as well as a good friend. I asked him now to drive me in his taxi the three hundred miles to Bucharest, offering him a handsome fee in consideration of the risk: at that time taxis were not allowed to carry passengers outside the area for which they held a licence. I felt that travelling by train would be far more risky, especially for someone like me who had no identification papers whatsoever. We started out at 4 a.m. and in spite of lack of sleep and worry I think we both enjoyed our drive. It took us across a lovely part of the Carpathians. The damp, early morning smell of earth and grass poured in through the windows and we saw the peasants in white homespun shirts working in the fields. Later on, we crossed the oilfield region of the Prahova valley, and finally, at the end of almost fifteen hours, we approached the capital by a little-used side road. Axente parked his ancient taxi in a small square where I could meet him if I had to call on him again that day. Here we shook hands and parted.

## CHAPTER VI

I HAD not yet managed to obtain a false identity card, and this proved much more difficult than it had been in the past. And, in addition, all the way to Bucharest, I had wondered where to find a safe refuge: some of my friends might have been arrested, others evacuated to the country, as often happened. I decided to take a chance and indeed I was lucky to find a refuge at once. I had only to knock on Mihai Prodan's door and tell him that I was in danger of arrest for him to offer me the shelter of his house. This was a one-roomed attic over a garage at the back of a yard near the Polytechnic School, and he lived in it with his wife and their baby daughter. I was the more grateful to him when I learned that he risked a five-year sentence merely by not declaring the arrival of a visitor.

I spent a fortnight at the Prodans'; then I moved, for fear that neighbours might have noticed my presence, and went to the home of Nicu Petrescu and his wife, a kind poor couple who were once caretakers in the office building of a firm of which I had been a director. They still had a room in the same basement, although the building had become a block of tenements. Here I also remained a fortnight, and from then on I continued shuttling between these two families.

The spring was beautiful but all I saw of it was a small patch of blue sky and a few branches of blossoming apricots, for nothing else was visible from either of the two rooms, and I went out only after dark, and then only to move house or to send a postcard to my friends abroad.

Then one evening in early June I went to a small post office and booked a telephone call to a nurse in Cluj, and the next night, at the same hour, I was put through, not to the nurse but to Professor Georgescu; our three-minute conversation would have conveyed

92

nothing to anyone else, but it told me all I needed to know. The news was good: Popovici had kept his word, and the police had not been to my parents' house—proof that my presence in the country was unsuspected. I could now get on with my mission.

During the past three months I had heard and thought a lot about the situation and what people felt about it. The Communists were trying, by every form of intimidation, to forge a collective society at the cost of the individual. As a result, everyone lived two lives: an inner life of personal desires, ambitions, hopes and tastes, and an outer life of ever harder work for ever smaller pay, which frustrated every hope of these desires and ambitions ever being satisfied. This frustration, growing in proportion to the pressure exerted by the dictatorship, sought an outlet in resistance. Some people came into open conflict with the authorities and were either arrested or driven underground; others joined the partisans, while many others lived in an increasing state of bitterness to which they dared not give expression. All of them listened to foreign broadcasts in Roumanian, especially to the news, and to comments on international events. Authentic news helped to keep alive the people's hope, and their longing for freedom took an almost Biblical form, like the longing of the Jews to be rid of the yoke of the Egyptians. But although these broadcasts could maintain a climate of resistance, they could not do more: to become effective the resistance movement needed to be led and organised. My mission was partly, as I had told Popovici, to rescue certain people, but partly to study the co-ordination of resistance groups.

Two theories about this problem were held abroad.

One was that the Headquarters should be abroad and that every group should be in touch with it by its own secret route. The advantage of this plan, which appealed to the majority, was that if any group were destroyed and, with it, its channels of communication, there were always others to fall back on, and resistance operations could continue without interruption.

But there was the immense practical difficulty of establishing a sufficient number of routes. The Black Sea was unusable, for the whole of the coast was mined and patrolled as well as protected by searchlights, anti-aircraft guns, speed-boats and seaplanes. The Danube was equally difficult, for Security Force motor-boats speeded up and down the river day and night, observing the shipping, while the shore bristled with sentries.

As for liaison by air, radar stations and a system of defence posts were on the alert to send up spotter planes and fighters, should the air space be infringed: a foreign aircraft would be chased into the heart of the interior, there to be brought down. And for every plane that tried to reach the partisans to drop supplies, the partisans had to be warned by radio or messenger and a party had to wait at the appointed place: a risk made deadly for them if the plane did manage to get through, because the radar posts could pinpoint the place where the aircraft had reduced its revolutions, and mounted patrols were sent to search the neighbourhood; the only result of the plane trying to confuse the radar by dropping packages in several places was that the patrols would go to all of them.

Besides, contact with partisans was difficult even for the local villagers and how much more so for people coming from abroad. The Security Force and the militia guarded every mountain path in regions where the partisans were known to operate; and on their side, the partisans feared *agents provocateurs* and were therefore suspicious of all attempts to get in touch with them.

The other view, which had few supporters, was that the Headquarters should be inside Roumania and keep in touch with the Free World by a single route while two others were held in reserve. Such a centre would have at its disposal all the latest local information on the continually changing tactics of the Communists, and could make immediate use of it in its organisation of resistance, though this would be subordinated to an overall plan. The danger was, of course, that the discovery of such an H.Q. would be a heavy blow to the resistance movement as a whole; for this reason it had not so far been attempted.

My own plan was an adaptation of this second view. I envisaged two leading groups inside the country, one for the mountains, the

other for the towns. The mountain H.Q., centred on the most
effective unit of the partisans, would keep in touch with all the
other units scattered throughout the huge Carpathian range which
stretched across the country.

The centre of the urban group, which would eventually link
all the towns, would be in Bucharest. Some members of this group
would inevitably be living underground but a high proportion
would lead normal lives; as many as possible would have posts in
state departments, and would therefore be unsuspected, free to
move about, and well informed about the moves of the Government.

I had expected Professor Popovici to join this urban group, and
I still intended to approach three other lecturers in Cluj, as well as
to be put in touch with several professors and academicians in the
capital—I believed that leaders would emerge from these two
universities. Many professors, especially of medicine and science,
were disaffected and had only been allowed to keep their posts
because of the shortage of specialists, while most students hated
Communist ideology and longed to demonstrate their belief in
liberty in an effective way.

The two essential problems were to recruit potential leaders
and to establish adequate routes both between the two leading
groups and between each of them and the West.

Secret agents, spies, traitors and weak men would be our
greatest danger. The leading group in Bucharest would have to be
kept small and based on people of the highest character. Their task
would be first to think out the framework of resistance, then to
maintain and to provide its spirit, but without drawing attention
to themselves.

It was impossible to foresee when the moment propitious for
an armed struggle against Communism and the overthrow of the
régime would come. It might take years before the 17 millions of
Roumanians were able to decide on their own way of life, or the
time might come unexpectedly soon. It seemed to me that it could
only come in one of two ways: as a result either of some internal
crisis in the Communist leadership (perhaps in a conflict between

## The Lost Footsteps

personalities) or of intervention by armed forces from outside. In either case we had to be prepared. A permanent organisation would both build up morale, and train cadres whom the leading groups could use, when the occasion came to direct the masses. Their desire for freedom made the masses long for this moment.

After my conversation with Professor Georgescu I decided to make the first move in my campaign on the following evening.

The elderly tobacconist pointed to the public telephone fixed to the grimy wall and went on reading his newspaper. I looked up the number in the directory, got through to Leontin, the friendly engineer who lived over Alice Zamfirescu's flat, and asked for "Jeanette." He said that she was in the kitchen washing up; I heard him tap four times on his floor and, a few moments later, Alice's voice saying Hullo.

"This is Nicol."

There was a pause, then: "How nice! You're in Bucharest!"

"Yes, I'm just back from the Danube Canal. I've got a new job now in the central office of the Sovrom Constructia. I'd love to see you again; perhaps if you're free we could go to a cinema tomorrow night. There are two good films—'Ivan the Terrible' and 'Far from Moscow'."

She replied with spirit that she'd love to see "As far as possible from Moscow" and we arranged to meet "outside the Scala Cinema."

The next evening I set out for one of the meeting places arranged between us long before and which the "Scala" designated. Dressed in my grey denims, with a cloth cap on my head, I looked like any ordinary workman. The June evening was hot and the air heavy with the scent of lime trees.

Alice, cool in her white summer dress, was waiting for me. "I can't believe it," she whispered. We discussed in low voices where we could go and talk for an hour and, deciding on her house, walked towards it by a roundabout way. She still lived in her flat with her mother and her two daughters, but it was shortly to be requisitioned for a Communist and they would have to move out.

## The Lost Footsteps

Her husband had now been in prison for three years. Although she was devoted to her children, her love for him and her desire to help him filled all her thoughts and took up all her energies. I had once made a desperate attempt to rescue him but had failed.

He was now in a prison for political prisoners: Aiud, she said. A friend of hers had put her into touch with an innkeeper in Aiud, who was friendly with one of the gaolers and in this way she had news of him. Her husband had kidney trouble and acute rheumatism. She had tried sending him parcels but they had always been returned to her.

Recently she had met a man who had been released after a two-year sentence in the same prison and who had been employed in the same workshop as her husband. He told her that the prison death rate had increased alarmingly because of cold, damp, undernourishment and overwork, and said many other things which her husband dared not write for fear the gaoler, though she paid him well, might show his letter to the authorities.

Now Zamfirescu only put hope in a new war. His message to Alice was that, if a war was likely, she should speak of something "white" in writing to him, and if it wasn't, of something "blue." "You've been abroad," she said to me. "What shall I tell him?"

"Speak of something white," I answered. "It isn't true, but you mustn't kill his remaining hope."

I told her why a way of liberation was so unlikely. I reminded her of all the millions of people throughout the world who so vividly remembered the evils and the agonies of the last war. I said that the attitude of the free peoples was profoundly pacifist and that no government could defy it. Only if their very existence was threatened would they rise up as one man to defend their way of life.

Alice agreed with my view, but she was in tears.

"Forgive me, I've upset you," I said. "But I know that you hate illusions as much as I do. And there are some things we can do ourselves: we can keep alive the spirit of resistance, so that when our Communist dictators are off guard, we can act effectively." I said that when that moment came, we would raid the prisons and free the prisoners.

We were sitting in Mihai Zamfirescu's study; I looked hopelessly at the rows of books lining the walls, dusty and abandoned as if their owner were already dead.

Afterwards we talked of other things. Alice said how happy she had been to get my card from Paris. She told me about her life: she worked eight hours a day in a tailoring co-operative, but the pay was not enough to keep her family, so she had also taken on an evening job as a waitress in a boarding-house.

There she had come across Dan Grecu, a lawyer who had been her husband's counsel at his trial and who, so Alice said, had told her something that concerned me. He had recently heard that a secret trial had been held: twenty people were sent to prison for ten to fifteen years, and several, myself included, were sentenced, *in absentia*, to twenty-five.

Her news did not greatly surprise me. I now told her some of the reasons which had brought me back to Roumania. It was better, and fairer to her, that she should not know the whole truth, so I only said that I had come to get some friends out of the country, and asked her if she would help me. Her reply was characteristic: "Mihai would be so glad that you had not avoided me. Tell me what I can do."

My immediate need was to re-establish contact with several people, but only after making sure that they were not under suspicion. Alice said that she would get the information for me, and we arranged to meet again in a fortnight. It was time for me to go, so that I could mix with the crowds leaving the cinemas on my way back.

Professor Mironescu, whom I went to see two evenings later, was an engineer by profession, but his interests were very wide and included art, literature and philosophy. Surprised but not in the least put out at seeing me, he took me into his study; it held such peace and charm that I could not help exclaiming: "How good to see you here, as serene and confident as ever!"

He smiled sadly. "That's not the whole truth. I'm lucky

because they need my knowledge, so I've still got my job at the Polytechnic and my flat—but not, I think, for long."

We talked about what had been happening in Roumania and he added to what I knew already. Like so many of my friends, he ended up by saying: "As for the future, it largely depends on what news you've brought us from the West."

I told him what I had told Alice about the atmosphere in the Free World, but a great deal more about my projects and I asked him if he wanted to take part in them.

"You don't even need to ask me," he replied.

My plan filled him with enthusiasm and we discussed it at length. He felt sure that I could count on the few close friends he still had at the University and the Academy, as well as on the support and the integrity of many students. He confirmed my view that the majority of the intellectuals in the Universities resented interference in the domain of thought, science and art even more than in that of economics.

He also gave me some advice about the partisans. He had recent news of Colonel Mihaileanu who commanded an important unit in the Campulung–Muscel region of the Carpathians. The Colonel had been seriously wounded in a clash with the militia. Rather than call in a doctor from a near-by village, he had sent a message (through a member of one of the resistance groups, whose brother was a student at the University) to Dr. Nestor, a nephew of Professor Mironescu's. Dr. Nestor was led by mountain paths to the cave in which the Colonel was lying, and operated on the spot; this and penicillin saved the patient's life. The doctor was filled with admiration for the partisans' morale, despite the terrible conditions in which they lived; not one of them, he said to Mironescu, dreamed of surrender.

Mironescu thought that the mountain Headquarters I had in mind should be based on Colonel Mihaileanu's partisans, and that contact should be established between them and the West.

As we discussed the prospects of resistance, and Mironescu walked up and down the room excitedly, his whole appearance spelt action and energy. If such plans in Russia, he said, had little chance of success today, it was because the Russian Communists had been in power so long, and as many of the older people had been removed from positions of responsibility, those who ran the country now were ignorant of any other system. In fifteen or twenty years, Roumania would be in a similar position. Yet the number of convinced Communists in Roumania was very small, and the opportunists who surrounded them would be the first to rat in a moment of crisis. As for the mass of the workers, the régime would be unconquerable if they were on its side; but what the workers wanted was a social system tending towards a higher living standard, shorter hours and better pay—the natural and steady progress towards maximum returns for the minimum expenditure of energy; whereas those who ruled them were interested in using the inhuman labour exacted of the workers to preserve their own high standard of living, and not in wasting it on raising that of others. The Roumanian proletariat, Mironescu believed, were conscious of their position, and ready to revolt if the opportunity arose.

"But forgive me, I have preached a sermon. I have been longing to discuss this with someone I could trust."

I thanked him for sharing his ideas with me; I agreed that Colonel Mihaileanu was the obvious Commander for the H.Q. in the mountains, "and you," I added, "are the obvious man to start the other leading group in Bucharest." We decided upon a definite plan of action in both fields. He was the first person whom I took into my complete confidence and I talked to him about the final objectives of my mission.

We parted after arranging to meet in July.

Anxious to make up for lost time and to report as soon as possible to the West, I went out evening after evening, widening my contacts. Many of my friends I could not reach: some were in prison, others underground or with the partisans; many had been forced to give up their professions and were working as navvies, scattered throughout the country. But I learned a great deal from those whom I did find at home, and I now decided to extend my activities to other towns: Timisoara near the frontiers of both

Hungary and Yugoslavia, Jassy near the Russian border (both are university cities), and Constanza and Turnu Severin—two ports, one on the Black Sea, the other on the Danube.

First, however, I needed to see one more person whom I could only meet in Cluj, and I sent for Axente to drive me back to my hiding-place.

The outbreak of the Korean war was interpreted as a sign that further Communist expansion would be actively resisted by the West; and this created an atmosphere favourable to my activities.

# CHAPTER VII

Ion Motru, whom I met one night in his cousin's house on the outskirts of Cluj, was the son of a peasant from the Bistritza-Nasaud region of Eastern Transylvania.

The peasants of this part of Roumania have a peculiar history. They had long held this land in joint ownership under an Austrian Imperial Decree which obliged them, in return, to maintain a locally recruited regiment for the defence of the Eastern frontiers of the Empire—a task for which they were well fitted by their local patriotism. Their tradition of relative independence had rooted in their hearts a strong devotion to freedom.

These peasants used part of their common funds to build schools and hospitals and to endow scholarships. Thanks to one of these Ion Motru was able to go to College in Bucharest and became a Doctor of Economics. Later he passed brilliantly into the civil service, and the Ministry of Social Insurance sent him to Cluj as Director of Social Services. Under the new régime, however, he lost both his job in Cluj and his house in Bucharest.

We had last met just after the arrest of Maniu. Ion had tried to help some members of the Peasant Party to escape the country and as a result had only eluded the Security Police by climbing on the neighbouring roof as they were knocking on his door. Disguised by heavy spectacles and a false moustache, he came to ask me for my help. I provided him with false documents and money and drove him in my car to his own village where he hoped to find a hide-out.

Now, as we sat in a downstairs room with wide-open windows through which the summer air brought the sound of crickets and the smell of roses and carnations, Ion brought me up to date on his adventures.

After lying low for some weeks in the autumn of 1947, he felt that the police had lost their interest in him and he went back to Cluj. Here he rented a mill which belonged to the Greek-Catholic Episcopate, and kept himself and his family by running it until June 1948, when the mill was taken over by the State. At the same time the Episcopate was abolished and the Bishop was arrested together with most of his entourage. Ion fled to Bucharest. He was on his way to see a priest, Father Matei, when, as he approached the church, a woman warned him that the priest had been arrested and the church was full of agents. He tried other friends, but found the same story everywhere: police visits, searches, and arrests.

A gigantic purge was going on; army officers, managers of mines, factories and workshops were being swept away to be replaced by Communists. Nearly all the leaders of the Greek-Catholic Uniate Church, starting with the Metropolitan, were put in prison. Lucretiu Patrascanu, whose escape was planned before I fell into Fekete's trap, was arrested at his mountain villa. More surprising were the arrests of Admiral Macelaru and of Alexander Pop, a key figure in industry.

Ion hid in his brother's house, though it was hardly a safe refuge if the police were looking for him. Then he had a stroke of luck: a friend of his in the Ministry of Education got his wife a post as teacher in a girls' school at Caransebes, a small mountain town in the district of Banat, adjoining Jugoslavia. There Ion was unknown and they settled down in a furnished room to a fairly normal life. One day, as Ion was looking for a job, he ran into a school friend whom he had not met since childhood and who was teaching in a local school. From then on they saw each other often throughout the autumn and the winter until finally, in the spring, Ion's friend felt sufficiently sure of him to tell him that preparations were being made for a revolt in the Caransebes mountains.

Ion stopped talking. The night was completely still, except that I remember an owl screeched loudly. Ion rose, scooped up the moths which had flown into the lamplight, threw them out of the window and stood looking at the starlit sky. Then he came back to his chair and went on.

## The Lost Footsteps

"I decided to join the partisans. My friend and I set out on just such a summer night as this. It took us three nights of difficult climbing to get to the camp. In the week that followed several hundred men joined us from nearby villages. The same thing was happening in other camps, all along the chain. Colonel Pompilian, our Commander, had planned the operation down to the last detail. On the chosen night each group was to go to an appointed town or village, collecting loyal peasants from the villages through which they passed.

"Meantime the resistance groups in towns were to seize the railway stations, telephone exchanges and main public buildings. An identical operation, under General Dabija, was to be launched from the mountains in Central Transylvania.

"Once we had seized the Banat, it was to be declared autonomous; a National Government would be set up, and would appeal to the Free World for military and political support.

"At that time Tito was on bad terms with the U.S.S.R.: we hoped that the revolt would bring about a complete break, so that the West could send us help by air through Jugoslavia. The freeing of the Banat, we thought, would lead to the liberation of the whole of Roumania, though how—and how long it would take—we could not yet tell.

"We all had arms. The partisans had got them by raiding arms dumps in the neighbouring towns, but, chiefly, by digging up the dumps the Germans had left buried during their retreat. Colonel Pompilian knew where they were because he was at G.H.Q. in 1944 and saw the declarations made by German prisoners.

"Well, at last the day for the attack was fixed. The night before, we began to move down to our appointed villages at the foot of the mountain. But instead of meeting friendly villagers, anxious to join us, we ran straight into the Security Police and the militia. They opened fire with their machine-guns and we had to retreat. Up among the peaks we were on our own ground. But the militia called up reinforcements and the fighting became desperate. There were heavy losses on both sides. But we began to run short of ammunition and food, and the appeals for help we broadcast over Colonel Pompilian's radio brought no response. So finally, we had to split up into small groups and try to save ourselves as best we could."

It was not until the rising was over, said Ion, that they understood why it had failed. The state of tension between Russia and Jugoslavia, on which they had relied, had in fact served them badly, for because of it the Russians had massed troops along the Jugoslav border, and they were able quickly to divert them against the rebels.

In Paris I had read brief newspaper accounts of the fighting in the Banat, but only as an isolated incident, and I had not known the real story behind it. The failure of the rebellion was a severe blow to the partisans, many of whom were killed or captured, and only small and scattered groups continued their precarious existence in the mountains.

While he was away, Ion's wife had fallen ill and had lost her job, so when she was discharged from hospital they went back to Ion's village, both of them unemployed. They could find no work and that winter they went really short of food. Ion had applied for the post of book-keeper at a local co-operative but when at last, in March 1950, he was called to an interview to the office of the Mayor, he found a stranger waiting for him, a young man sent by the Party Branch to discover what he, Motru, was doing in the village, and to order him out as an undesirable character.

Ion pleaded that he had nowhere else to go and insisted that, by law, those who had lost their posts could go back to their native villages. The Party officer grudgingly agreed that he should stay until his case had been discussed in Nasaud, but a couple of days later Ion was warned by the Mayor, his cousin, that the local agents had been told to watch him.

"Now I sleep in a friend's hayloft," Ion concluded his story, "so if they come for me at home I'll have a few moments' start to get out of the village and up into the mountains, to join my friends."

It was beginning to get light, but there was still a little time left before he had to catch the train back to his village. I asked him to tell me more about resistance and the spirit in the country.

He told me of the curious events which had led up to the trial of Alexander Pop. I knew Pop well; he was the Managing Director of the huge Resita foundries which used scrap iron from all over the country. Some of it came from army depots and included obsolete shells; these were checked in the control-room at the foundry, to make sure that there was no explosive in them before they went into the furnaces. Yet explosions did occasionally occur, putting the furnace in which they happened out of action. These genuine accidents gave Pop his idea for sabotage. An excellent mathematician, he worked out the odds in favour of a live shell escaping detection. Then he greatly increased the intake of obsolete missiles by buying up two concerns which specialised in collecting and disposing of them, and made sure that a suitable proportion of those reaching the foundry should be live. Now, every month or two a furnace would explode.

The foundries employed 20,000 workers and turned out most of the steel, iron castings and sheet iron which other factories needed for the production of machines, tools and consumer goods. As a result of the stoppages production dropped, causing shortages and a rise in prices, and leading to general economic instability.

Pop was determined that the workers of Resita should not suffer by his action. Luckily the foundries, like other industries still in private hands, were obliged by law to provide for all their workers' needs. Pop sent out into the country to buy up necessities, especially food, and he started a system of credits for the workers. The workers bought, and asked for more credits. Pop sent out for more goods. As prices rose the workers asked for a rise in pay and Pop granted it. Once again the price of all Resita products went up and this was ultimately reflected in the price of most consumer goods. Unfortunately, the rising chaos was eventually traced to Pop and though he made a splendid fight before the military court, he and several of his friends were sentenced to hard labour for life.

I had known Pop as an exceptionally brilliant and creative man.

# The Lost Footsteps

That he had used his talents to a destructive end, however admirably, made me sad. Ion did not share this feeling. He told me another story.

In the autumn of 1946, a lorry-load of Communist propagandists arrived in Merisor, a village near his home. The peasants listened to the speeches, then they overturned the lorry, set it on fire and drove out the speakers with sticks and stones. The Security Police swooped down on the village, but four of the trouble-makers escaped into the mountains. Now, four years later, they were still there and had become legendary characters. Last Christmas, Ion's nephew had taken him to see them.

Living in isolation in their cave, they had learned to meditate and had grown wise; they were regarded almost as prophets. Ion had felt that there was something apocalyptic about them. They encouraged the peasants who visited them to defend their freedom and resist collectivisation, but, for the rest, to await with patience the day when a general rising might be possible.

They were not the only group of this sort, Ion told me. Others were scattered throughout the mountains: communities of four or five to a cave, keeping in touch but not combining for fear of adding to the danger of detection. Their purpose for the moment was to keep their influence over the villages and to hold themselves in readiness. Ion was full of admiration for their spirit.

He thought that in general the impulse to revolt was growing, partly because of the shortage of necessities and the everyday hardships, but also, he believed, springing out of a deep desire for a new way of life.

The Communists were aware of the growing discontent. They had recently undertaken some showy public works, such as the building of a huge canal between the Black Sea and the Danube, but this did not distract the people from their daily miseries.

It was almost time for Ion to go, and I had still not spoken of my own mission. I gave him an incomplete account of it and asked him to help me by gathering any information he could about several people whom I wished to contact in the hope that they would give me their support in my activities.

# The Lost Footsteps

He said that he would need to make inquiries in various towns: Cluj, Timisoara, Brasov, and certainly in Bucharest, and that his search for work might serve as cover for these journeys.

It was five o'clock in the morning when we rose to go. The sun was already slanting through the fruit trees in the orchard. It turned the dew to diamonds but was less kind to our tired faces. The sand squeaked under our feet as we walked down the path to the wattle fence; there I shielded my face with my hat and glanced down the street. A man and a woman had just passed; when they turned the corner, we shook hands and I made my way to Axente's house.

I stayed on a few days in Cluj and on another evening found myself in the house of an old friend, Dr. Borza. We sat in his surgery, talking about the situation with Andrei Loghin, professor of organic chemistry at Cluj.

Loghin, though he was ready to resist in any way, even to fighting in the mountains, believed that Roumania's only hope of liberation lay in U.N.O. If U.N.O., backed by an international military force, embodied in its Charter the principle of mediation and, if need be, active intervention in civil wars, then a civil war could end in free elections supervised by U.N.O. So long as the East and West were of equal strength, such a remedy was possible; unfortunately time was on the side of the Communists. He did not believe that freedom could be won from inside the country, nor that the West would fight unless its own existence were threatened.

Dr. Borza, however, favoured immediate and active resistance and he gave me several names of people on whom I could rely—a nephew who was in charge of minefields on the Black Sea coast, a friend who was a Wing-Commander at Someseni airfield . . .

This was my last evening in Cluj, and it left me depressed. There was so much to do and so little assurance of success. The most we could have faith in was that we would keep open the way by which others would reach firm ground.

Back in Bucharest I was delighted to find that my friends had kept their promise. They had made new contacts and had brought in some key men who would be invaluable to our activity.

Secret aerodromes and landing grounds for parachutists in the mountains had suddenly become a possibility. Thanks to a map of the minefields along the coast, the Black Sea was no longer impassable; a rubber dinghy launched from a submarine by night could pass between the mines and then be buried in the sand on the beach where the landing party would be met by guides.

After I had been three weeks in Bucharest Ion Motru came with the news he had collected. I went to meet him in the evening of the 15th of July at the shop of his father-in-law who was a tobacconist. It lay behind the Colentina hospital. The door was open and I could see two customers inside and the old shopkeeper counting out the change. I walked past slowly as far as the corner and then turned back—this time the old man was alone.

"Good evening," I said. "Have you any Mihai cigarettes?"

They were a very expensive brand, called after King Michael, and they had been withdrawn years ago.

The tobacconist pushed up his spectacles, wrinkled his greasy forehead and stroked his big, grey, stubbly head.

"Come into the inner room. I keep the best cigarettes in there."

He took me through a door behind the counter and down the passage to another door.

I found Ion standing in the middle of the small room, reading; I noticed that the book was the *Beveridge Report* in English.

We sat down to talk. What he told me was very interesting.

In Cluj he had been unlucky: Colonel Mura, the person whom he most wished to see, was away. A schoolfriend on whom he had counted had been arrested, and two professors were so busy with their lectures and their clinics that they were not prepared to take part in any resistance work.

But in Timisoara he had been received with open arms by Professor Alexandru Lupan, a famous surgeon, who had been hiding Canon Damian (of the diocese of the imprisoned Bishop) in his home since 1948. The Canon was a member of the Propaganda

Fidei in Rome and was anxious to get back to Italy as soon as he could.

Here Ion also met another old friend of ours, Remus Rosca, an engineer who was prepared to give us valuable help.

He then went on to Brasov where he learned the sad news that General Petre Dumitrescu, another mutual friend, had been arrested a year ago and was now in the large political prison at Aiud. The General had commanded the Alpine troops and such was his prestige among his officers that when a number of them had been purged it was feared that he might become the leader of an Army resistance group.

In Bucharest too Ion had already made several contacts. One was with a monk, in hiding with a train driver, who was in charge of the clandestine organisation of the Uniat Church which had been suppressed by the Communists. More interesting still, he had got in touch with two naval officers, Admiral Rik Negreanu and Commander Dragu.

Ion's information, added to what I had already, pretty well completed the first stage of my mission. I was now considering asking him to make himself responsible, together with Professor Mironescu, for the setting up of an embryo H.Q. They did not yet know each other; I would have to put them in touch as well as give them the means of communicating with other people who had offered to collaborate in our activities. This would complete my mission. I would provide Ion with details of my clandestine routes and he and Mironescu would take over the organisation of resistance.

Unfortunately, my best route into Hungary was now unusable because, while arranging the escape of a young Jew, Georgescu, who was in charge of the Roumanian end, had been arrested in the house of the boy's grandfather. But my agents in Baia Mare and Satu Mare thought that an escape route could be run from there. I decided to probe this route, by asking a peasant to use it on his way to Budapest where he was to deliver a letter from me to Aunt Ethel.

Two weeks later he was back and had brought me a reply, as

well as a card from Austria, from Stefan and Paul, who were anxious because they had expected to meet me long before this. They soon would, I thought, for I had asked Aunt Ethel to forward an enclosed letter announcing my return on one of the moonless nights between the 20th and 30th of September. I thought that this should give me time to complete my business and to get to Budapest.

After my meeting with Ion I left Bucharest for a month to work on the new escape route. I was back on the 20th of August.

That evening I sent a short letter to Ion written in a disguised hand on blue paper, and addressed to his mother's house. It told him that "his father-in-law was ill and asked him to come and see him," and it meant that I was back. According to our arrangement, I was to wait five days after posting it and then go to his father-in-law's shop to pick up his reply.

The five days passed slowly. When I went to the tobacconist's there was no reply from Ion. I returned four evenings later and found the tobacconist looking pale and anxious. He said: "He hasn't come yet, I don't understand it . . . Two neighbours from his village came in this evening—I'm sure they are reliable, I've known them for years—they said he had left home several days ago. I know," he went on, "that there is some secret between you and Ion. Have you any idea what might have happened to him? . . ."

I told him that I had in fact summoned Ion but I did not know what had happened to him. I begged him to tell Ion, when he arrived, to leave a message for me letting me know where we could meet and said that I would call again in a week or so. I left feeling very sorry for the old man, he looked so tired and dejected as he leaned against his counter.

As I hurried towards my hiding-place, the darkness and silence of the deserted streets closed in around me. I was oppressed by the one thought, "Oh God, what could have happened to Ion." I could not sleep that night for I kept trying to think of reasons, other than the obvious one, which might possibly explain his delay. Could he perhaps have gone to Timisoara to fetch Canon Damian with the idea that I should take him with me to Vienna? They were childhood friends and Ion might go to great lengths to help him.

But it was no good. I did not know and for the moment I must go underground and break off all relations with the outer world. It seemed ironical that when I posted my blue envelope to Ion I had also sent a postcard in code to the West announcing my return, for how could I tell now when I should be able to set off?

# CHAPTER VIII

I DID not go out again until the 18th of September. After several weeks in my hiding-place the freshness of the autumn evening was miraculous. As I wandered along the back-streets I noticed that most of the passers-by were hurrying along, although the night seemed perfect for a stroll or for a glass of wine in a café.

The streets and houses of Bucharest held many vivid memories for me, old and new, and I wished that I could walk openly, by daylight, in the squares and avenues which I loved.

The autumn was associated with many turning-points in my life and, as I made my way through the narrow alleys, scene after scene came into my mind.

In the autumn of 1940 my parents and I had had to leave our home because Cluj had been ceded to Hungary and we moved into the heart of the country.

In autumn, 1941, I came to Bucharest and got a post in the Industria Zaharului, which offered me good prospects.

A year later I was promoted Director.

The autumn of 1944—the time of the Armistice—had brought a radical change to the life of the country, and my own life changed completely as well.

By the autumn of 1946 I was in such deep waters that I began to think of escaping to the West.

During the autumn of 1947 I succeeded in getting the largest number of my friends to safety.

At the same season in 1948 I was getting ready for my own escape.

Then, in the autumn of 1949, I was on my way back from Paris to Roumania.

And now, in 1950, it was again autumn and I was again preparing to go to Paris. Only about forty days, I said to myself, and with any luck I'll be walking in broad daylight down the Champs Élysées. How many people in Bucharest tonight would give all they possessed to be coming with me?

I began to make plans. I imagined a summer holiday in the mountains; I saw myself visiting the capitals of Western Europe, or just sitting fearlessly with Alba in a café on the Boulevard St. Michel in Paris.

I was approaching the tobacconist's. It would have been more prudent to send someone else to ask for news of Ion, but as I did not want anyone to know that I was in touch with him, I had no choice but to go myself. In any case, as the shop had many customers I thought that I could drop in without arousing suspicion. I had to find out what had happened before I could tie up the loose ends of my scheme, and this had to be done in time to take advantage of the moonless nights at the end of September. By October, snowfalls might make my escape almost impossible.

As I was about to cross the Boulevard Stefan Cel Mare, two brightly lit trams passed in front of me and the large block of the Colentina hospital loomed up on the far side of the road. I was only three minutes' walk from the shop.

During all that afternoon, I had felt restless and impatient, as though I were waiting to go to some big ceremony, but towards evening a feeling of great calm came over me. Now I hoped that I would find some news which would clear up everything and make it possible for me to leave in a few days' time.

The little street behind the hospital was dimly lit; there was not a soul in sight. I passed the shop and looked in through the window; the old man was sitting beside the counter, his head in his hands. I walked on, then where the street takes a right-hand turn I searched my pockets like an absent-minded man who can't find his cigarettes, and walked back. The street was still deserted and utterly silent; I almost felt as if it held its breath.

When I opened the door and stood on the threshold the old man raised a sleepy head to see who was coming in. For a moment he seemed not to recognise me, then he whispered urgently: "Go away. Go away. Ion never turned up."

# The Lost Footsteps

Puzzled, I was about to ask him for more details but his agitation grew and he whispered again:

"Go away. Go away."

I went out quickly. To get out of the cul de sac, I had to go back to the Boulevard Stefan Cel Mare.

There was no sound of following steps. I walked calmly, at a normal pace, and at the end of about a hundred yards I took the first turning to the right. Now I was following the wall of the hospital garden; in another minute or two I should reach the tangle of dark and twisting alleys where I could vanish the more easily because a thin mist was beginning to fall.

Suddenly I noticed two figures coming towards me on the same side of the street. When they drew near I saw that they were two youths; one wore a cap, the other a hat. After they had passed me and when the clattering of their heavy shoes was dying away, I realised that there was nothing to fear from them.

Then all of a sudden I sensed rather than heard light, quick footsteps behind me; their sound until then must have been covered by the resounding steps of the two boys.

I went on at the same slow steady pace without looking round.

What followed probably took a matter of seconds. My arms were seized and twisted behind me, handcuffs clicked round my wrists. All this was done in a few movements, by experts.

I put up no resistance—it would have been useless. But in those few seconds my life was changed. I no longer belonged to myself, I belonged to *them*. They could do what they liked with me.

Taking me firmly by the arms, the two agents walked me towards the Boulevard Stefan Cel Mare; we crossed it quickly. A shiny new black Ford was waiting in a side street.

Before I was pushed into it I looked up at the sky: it was clear and full of stars. For a long time I had been deprived of sunlight; from now on starlight would also be denied me.

The two plain-clothes men sat down on either side of me and the car accelerated and moved off. "Get down and don't move," ordered the man on my right. He shoved my head against the cushions and pushed a leather mask over my head. With that I entered the world of darkness.

As we speeded through the city, I could hear the clanking of trams and the roar of traffic. Whenever the car pulled up at a crossroad the agents leaned over me as though to hide from the passers-by what was going on in this elegant automobile.

After about a quarter of an hour, the car slowed down and stopped. I heard the click of the headlights twice, then the noise of heavy iron gates opening. The car shot through and then pulled up with a jerk.

No one spoke, but I could sense the movements of several people around me; were they communicating by signs? Then I was dragged out of the car, led over the sandy surface of a path or a yard and pushed through a door.

One, two, three . . . automatically I counted the twenty-three steps down of a twisting stairway. Then a long walk, doors opening and shutting on the way, and at last a halt.

"Eyes front," somebody rapped out behind me. My handcuffs were removed. "Take off your coat." I took off my coat. Someone immediately took charge of it.

"Take off your trousers."

And so I was forced to take off all my clothes, piece by piece, and hand them to those around me, until I was standing naked in front of them, wearing only my mask.

After a few moments' silence: "Where are your poison phial and revolver?"

"I have neither."

"Where have you hidden them?" asked the same imperious voice.

Irritated by their insistence, I heard myself saying impatiently: "I have no weapons—only my spirit, will and patience—I believe them to be stronger than firearms."

"Our opinion is that you are mistaken . . ."

There was another pause; I thought that they continued to search my clothes, convinced that I had at least one of the famous "phials" on me. But indeed, after my experience of arrest and escape two years earlier, I had carried no weapons on me, either for attack or suicide, and since then I had read in the reports of trials at the Military Court in Bucharest that whatever arms the prisoners had on them at the time of their arrest, not one of them had a chance of using any.

A heavy door closed behind me and I heard the click of a bolt. Then a voice ordered me to take off my mask, hand it over, and put on my shirt. When I turned round, I saw a hand pushed through a square opening in the door, ready to take the mask.

I was in a cell four feet wide and seven feet long and high. My shirt was lying on an iron bedstead covered by a mattress and a thin coffee-coloured quilt. That was all there was in the room. My shoes and the rest of my clothes had been taken away by the police.

I lay down on the bed and tried to think. Although I had always tried to prepare myself for anything that might happen to me, this blow had stunned me. It was the more horrible because it had fallen at the very moment when my dream of returning to the West had been so close to being realised.

I tried to imagine how it had all come about. There was only one explanation. Ion Motru must have been arrested. The fact that I had been caught near his father-in-law's shop made this a certainty. He had never been arrested before, so it was impossible to tell how he would react in such circumstances. I wondered how long he had been able to hold out.

Probably Security agents, hidden in the passage at the back of the shop, had been waiting for me for a long time. The old man had tried to warn me, but the agents must have heard or seen him. Hesitating a moment, they had allowed me to leave and had then overtaken me in the almost empty street.

The silence was absolute and seemed to have frozen this underground world into a block of ice in which all movement and life had ceased. My very heart seemed to be growing cold.

About an hour had passed since I lay down; suddenly a voice from the corridor shouted: "Get up!" and a hand, thrust into the same square opening in the door, held out the leather mask. The bolt was drawn and the door opened wide. My arms were seized by warders; steel handcuffs immobilised my hands. As we went along the corridors, in front and behind me other warders stepped softly, with an almost imperceptible shuffle; probably they wore felt slippers, so that their movements should not be heard. I felt the cold cement under my bare feet. Above ground in the city many people must at that late hour be sleeping soundly, others perhaps reading, or leaving the theatre or the cinema, or talking over a glass of wine. I reflected that if by a miracle they could see the procession going along this underground corridor, they would be filled with astonishment: a man wearing only a shirt, barefooted, a leather mask over his eyes, his hands fastened by handcuffs, being led by armed and slippered guards, to be put on show before the masters.

I walked down three steps and stopped before a wall. Without seeing it, I could feel it looming in front of me.

"Eyes front, until you are told!" said the man who was holding my right arm.

I could hear rustling, as if other people had come in and were preparing something.

"Turn round. Take off your mask."

I turned round. What I saw astonished me. I was in a huge room, about 45 feet by 30. The walls and ceiling were white and spotless. The parquet was brightly polished and gleamed with yellowish wax, as in the drawing-room of any large house. But there were neither pictures nor candelabra in this room.

Before me, about ten yards off, stood a long table with several powerful reflectors, their beams trained on me.

"Sit down," snapped a voice. Beside me was a small pinewood chair; I sat down on it precariously. "Fill up the form on the table on your right and sign it."

On my right was a pinewood plank fixed to the wall. The form was headed "Police Report" and contained the usual formal questions concerning my identity: name, date and place of birth, education, profession, residence, etc. I filled it in, turned towards the lights and said that I had finished.

"Read out what you have written."

I read it out, put the form down on the plank and waited.

There was a quick movement on the far side of the table, as if a newcomer had arrived. I caught sight of a tall, burly silhouette; then some whispering, a cough, a chair squeaking, and silence, until a voice said: "At last we have succeeded in getting hold of you. We have been on your tracks for a long time. You've been remarkably lucky. But you know the saying: 'Every dog has its day.' So here we are at last—face to face. So far, we have had to fight each other unseen, now we can look each other in the eyes!"

The voice was pleasant, self-confident, authoritative. In spite of the blinding light I could just see five figures seated at the long table. The voice of the one I took to be the newcomer continued: "During the last few years our agents have compiled enough information about you to make a book. We wanted to make your acquaintance. Now we have you at our disposal. We know all about you and your activities. You are now facing a court which is empowered to try you, to pass sentence and to execute you for your anti-State activities. Take care how you answer our questions; every word will be recorded and you will not be able to alter your statements once they are made. Turn left!"

On my left there was a table with a single light on it, and I could see the outlines of a tape-recorder. A youth was seated beside it, ready to start it running. The microphone stood on the floor, about a yard away, and looked to me like a snake's head ready to strike.

"Before we open the proceedings," said the President, "I want to speak to you as man to man. I take it you realise that you have no way out? Of those who have passed through this room, who have sat on the chair on which you are sitting now, hardly anyone is alive today; those few who are have had their nerves ruined and are human wrecks."

He paused for a moment as if to allow me to take in the full implication of his words and then continued in the same calm tone: "Don't imagine that we are going to use old-fashioned methods either to make you talk or to dispose of you. We could, of course, put you alive into the crematorium; or we might try the interesting system of tying you, for a month or so, to a table beneath a bell, and keep it ringing. Or we might put an iron ring round your head and smash your skull, according to the method of Count Scarpia. Or make you lie on your stomach and place a glass cloche with a rat inside it over your kidneys. But no—we won't use any of those methods. We have others which are more effective, based on scientific discoveries. Before we try them, however, we want to give you a chance."

He paused and held a whispered conversation with one of his colleagues; then he said:

"We want your answers to two questions—but you must give them spontaneously, without hesitation: what were your motives in returning to Roumania? What foreign Power is behind you?"

"I'll answer the second question first: there is no foreign Power behind me. The first question, however, needs a longer, more detailed answer."

"We're listening! Go on!" said the President of the Court.

That I had come back to Roumania to fight the Communist régime was clearly known to the men in front of me. I emphasised the moral reasons for my actions, my conception of a just society and my desire to establish one in my own country. My answer was long and diffuse, partly because I was trying to give myself time to collect my thoughts at the beginning of this strange contest.

When I had finished the President addressed me: "You have made yourself quite plain. You are an exponent and a representative of a world based on individualism. We are the exponents and representatives of a world founded on collectivism. These two ways of life are poles apart, so are our philosophies. We are materialists. We believe that matter creates spirit and everything else in the universe. You are an idealist and believe the opposite. You believe in the supernatural and in ideals which are unattainable. We have an ideal which depends upon our senses and which therefore *can* be attained. Because it can be attained it is superior to yours. Our two philosophies have been in conflict for thousands of years, they are irreconcilable. That is why we confront each other today and that is why we will have to fight against you to the very end. Our ways of life exclude each other, so it is simply a question of 'You or Us'. In the past it was you that had the upper hand and we who ran the risk of destruction. Now, in this part of the world, the balance of power is reversed. We shall destroy you step by step . . . But before you, personally, are wiped off the face of the earth we shall find out everything that's hidden in your brain, everything you have set in motion against us. You did not come back to Roumania only out of home-sickness."

This first interrogation continued for about four hours and remained on a purely political level throughout; it was not until later that I understood the reason for this.

At the end of it there was another whispered conversation, then the President spoke again.

"The members of the fact-finding Commission, who are also your judges, have decided to give you a little time in which to think. We advise you not to miss this chance. In any case we know what you have been doing." He held up a bundle of files in the beam of the reflector. "Here is the record of your crimes against the State and the Party, but it will be on the basis of your motives that we shall decide whether you will spend your life in prison or lose it at once as a dangerous criminal."

As soon as he stopped speaking, the lights were extinguished. The change from the glare to complete darkness soothed my strained eyes a little, though now it seemed as if there were an enormous black screen in front of me with a dazzling square projected on it.

A voice ordered: "Get up! Turn to the wall! Put on your mask!"

Then, with the same care and ceremonial as had accompanied my journey from my cell, I was taken back to it. I had a strange feeling of tiredness all down my spine and it seemed as if a rusty nail had been driven into my brain.

Left alone, I lay down again. My thoughts were in a ferment. I felt utterly desolate, shut up in this hollow cube under the ground. Again and again, I went over the scenes of the past few hours and saw myself, alone and naked, confronting the judges. "An individual," I thought ironically, "faced with collective action."

I knew that the methods used by the police, the swift brutality of the arrest, the leather mask, the removal of my clothes, this bare, harsh room and the dramatic setting of the trial were all intended to increase the shock of capture, to stun the prisoner, to throw him off guard and make him feel paralysed and exposed even to his brain cells as he sat pinned by the reflector beams before his many, half-seen, self-assured enemies. But while knowing this, I had in fact been stunned and confused and it had needed all my strength merely to remain guarded, to try to gain time in my rambling answers to the Interrogator. I wished I had said more to him while we were on this moral plane. I should have said: "Other people have believed in the ideals you call unattainable. Icarus fell into the sea but other men have realised his dream. And my dreams too, the dream of a new humanism, of a life of dignity for every individual, will become reality, even if only after centuries have passed."

To give myself courage, I tried to think of all the noblest aims which human beings have pursued from the earliest times. Lying on my iron bed, I had a momentary vision of a crossroads in antiquity, thronged with suffering people, and of the hope of a few visionaries in those days that the law of "eye for eye and tooth for tooth" would be swept aside and replaced by the ideal: "Forgive us our trespasses as we forgive them that trespass against us." And in spite of persecution, faith had triumphed and had exercised its humanising influence for twenty centuries.

After a while I fell into a heavy troubled sleep in which I had a dream. I was in a large, grand house in Bucharest. The rooms were spacious, spotlessly clean, sparsely furnished—almost empty. Grave young officers with oddly cut black hair and in khaki uniforms decorated with gold braid were making ready for some reception. Then the doors were thrown wide open and a crowd poured in, of men and women dressed as for a ball. The room was lit by exquisite candelabra. The crowd parted to make way for three middle-aged men in white shirts and black bow-ties and identical, double-breasted, coffee-coloured suits of some expensive material. After them came two guards in top hats and grey frock coats in the fashion of the eighteen-twenties, and between them, supported by them and walking with bowed head, a tall handsome grey-haired old man. I was astonished at the fineness of his skin and the pallor of his face. An ample black cloak reached to his ankles and had wide, slashed and fur-lined sleeves like those worn in the sixteenth century. Two men in dinner jackets were standing next to me; one of them gazed at the old man as at some famous masterpiece and said: "He is exactly as Milton saw him. He is the one who cannot be destroyed." They went on talking but I no longer understood their words. I moved among the crowd as though I were invisible. Suddenly there was a whisper: "The Court is in session", and I saw that the three men in coffee-coloured suits were seated at a long table at one end of the room. The old man stood before them, looking dejected and trying to steady himself on his feet. I knew that a death sentence awaited him. The two guards shook his arms and said roughly: "Why are you so frightened? You won't be hanged yet," but he only stared vacantly in front of him. I knew that he was thinking: "What harm have I done to them? Why are they all against me?" Then, just as the Court was about to pass the sentence, there was a loud knocking. "Silence!" ordered the judge. He stood up and peered into the crowd as if he were looking for someone. Then, gesticulating violently, he shouted: "*That's* the enemy! Let the old man go!" and pointing straight at me, he ordered my arrest . . .

"Get up! Put on your mask!"

The knocking was at my door. I got up. The warder's hand pushed the mask at me through the opening. I thought that the interrogation was going to be continued, although it could not have been more than three hours since I was brought back to my cell.

This time, instead of turning to the right, the warders led me in the opposite direction. After about twenty paces, they halted, pushed me into a room and banged an iron door behind me. When I raised my mask I found myself in a brilliantly lit cell of the same size as the one I had just left, but quite empty. After standing for about an hour I grew tired and sat on the floor, but I had not been sitting for more than twenty seconds when someone hammered on the door of the cell.

"Stand up and face the light on the wall. You must stand without moving in that position. You are not allowed to sit down. Now, think over what the Commission said to you and if you have anything to say knock four times on the door."

Clearly my interrogators were beginning to apply their well-known methods. The warders moved so softly that I could not hear them but I knew that I was not left unsupervised for a second.

The time passed very slowly. The silence was unrelieved by the slightest sound, and the powerful light and my motionless position combined to make me very tired in mind and body. Slowly I understood the action of the light. The white beam of the incandescent filament passed through the optic nerve into my brain and even if I closed my eyes it still shone through my eyelids. At the same time the unrelenting force of gravity drew me towards the ground; resisting it exhausted my muscles and also my mind. And it would be with my mind in this exhausted state that I would have to stand before my judges.

I thought over the two questions the Commission had asked. My answers, if I gave in, could provide the Ministry of the Interior with a pretext to stage a sensational political trial. The publicity which they would give it would compromise the resistance movement, for one aim of the "stage managers" was to show that its members were characterless good-for-nothings, the kind of people who plead guilty and confess how wrong they were. After a preliminary "treatment" the culprit was brought into court and witnessed that he had been misled, that right was on the side of the Party, whose aims were lofty, whose object was the "good" of the whole community, and so on. This might well be the role they had in mind for me.

My eyelids closed to protect my eyes a little from the irritation of the powerful light. In my imagination I could see the Military Court, the judges, the reporters taking notes, the "public" composed of "intelligentsia" from the Security Police. I could see it all as in a newsreel: how the printing presses would roll out thousands

*The Lost Footsteps*

of copies of newspapers reporting the trial; how it would be broadcast by the radio; and how my friends, now scattered all over the
world, would get to hear of it. The nightmare of that public trial
was more terrible than anything that the secret "forum" who had
me at their disposal could do to me.

I knew that even a "conversion" and "confession" followed by
a public trial would not be likely to save me from death. The death-
sentence had been introduced by a Decree in December '48 and
was often passed, whether publicly or in secret. A recent example
was that of a man I knew. In June 1950 Nicolae Ciobanu, a pilot
of the T.A.R.S.[1], had been brought to trial and the official Communist newspaper, *Scanteia*, had printed the report. The prisoner
had appealed for clemency on the grounds that, from the very
beginning, he had confessed everything and thus helped the Court
in its investigation. Nonetheless he was condemned to death; and
his was only one case among hundreds.

Although I felt exhausted, I tried to go over my activities in the
past few months. The poor welcome which Professor Popovici had
given me had at least had the good effect of making me extremely
cautious. I had shared my plans only with Professor Mironescu
and even with him I had spoken of them only in general terms.
Ion Motru knew only the initial aims which were to be the
stepping-stones to further action. I was lucky (if such a word
could be used) that our final meeting had not taken place, for at
least he did not know the latest contacts I had made nor my final
objectives.

There was a great deal that the Commission could not know
and which I must not tell them. The only factual revelations I could
afford to make were of the kind that added nothing to their
knowledge and involved no fresh victims—and for this I would
need to know what they knew already. Their two questions—what
had been my aims in returning to Roumania and what Power had
backed me—were so general that they told me nothing and so wide
that a full answer would involve a full confession. Luckily I had
replied only by moral reasoning to the one and by a flat denial to

[1] Transporturi Aeriene Romano-Sovietice.

the other; anything else—the most trifling statement or unguarded word—would be an irreparable folly. A trifle added to other trifles from other sources could complete a pattern; in any case it would provide a lead for other, more specific questions and would certainly be used as a starting-point for extracting ever fuller declarations.

My only chance of saving my life would come if they supplied me with clues as to what I could say harmlessly and I could dribble out such statements over a very long time—simply on the principle that "while there's life, there's hope." Once they were convinced that I was not only unwilling but unable to tell them anything more they would certainly kill me. But would I have the strength to stick to such a policy, with all the drawn-out suffering it would involve, with nothing tangible to hope for?

Even now, in spite of my determination to keep silence and my belief that a betrayal would not save my life, I was repeatedly tempted to knock four times on the door and announce that I would make a full confession. Somewhere in the depths of my mind the strong instinct of self-preservation fought with my reason. It seemed intolerable to die "down here," though fortunately it would be even less tolerable to die "up there," in the glare of the publicity, judged not only by my enemies but also by my friends and knowing to what fate I had condemned them.

## CHAPTER IX

THE SILENCE of the secret prison weighed heavily upon me. I felt as if I were the only prisoner. I could not hear a door open or close, nor a bolt shot back, no murmur, no sound, only this deep silence and the sort of calm which portends a storm. Something was being prepared—I could sense it; it was as if the thoughts of the malevolent men who held me in their power were being transmitted to me.

Because of the silence and my weariness my notion of time was gradually fading, but a day and a night must have passed since I had been brought to this cell. Only once had the warder handed me an aluminium can of water and a thin slice of bread. I did not feel in the least hungry, nevertheless I ate and drank, to gain strength.

More hours passed. When the warder came to handcuff me once again I had no idea whether it was night or day. With the same caution as before, I was taken back to the white room.

The décor was unchanged, but the air seemed to be charged with suppressed anger. Once again I sat in the blinding light of the reflectors, with my back against the white wall. For a few moments the eyes of the five men on the far side of the table examined me. I was conscious that I must by now be looking troubled and exhausted, and I felt as if the piercing light were making me transparent. But I also knew that they relied on my exhaustion and I was determined to overcome my weakness. It was evident that they were now awaiting the result of the "time to think" which they had given me. In fact this "time for thought" had given me a precious respite: without it, I would not have been able to recover from the shock of my arrest sufficiently to plan the attitude I should adopt before them.

# The Lost Footsteps

The President sat up in his chair, adjusted one of the reflectors so that the beams shone straight into my eyes, coughed slightly and opened the session.

"The time we gave you to think things over is now up. Have you decided to give straight answers to the two questions we put to you at the first interrogation?"

I waited a moment before replying. On what I said now depended all that would follow . . .

"I have thought a great deal about what you said to me and about the consequences which I must expect. There is nothing I can do but stick to the declarations I made the first time."

My voice sounded strangled and my knees shook as if I had delirium tremens, but I had said what I had intended to say.

"We give you five minutes; if, after that, you continue to be obstinate, we will pass on to something which will make you change your mind." The President gave me this warning in a calm, almost encouraging tone.

A metronome began to beat a loud, regular tick-tock, and the tension in the room seemed to rise with every one of its beats.

"Three minutes are up!" the President announced gravely. "You have two more minutes." The vast room seemed to me a boundless wilderness filled with the dry, rhythmic beat of an invisible gong. "Twenty seconds more . . . make up your mind . . . Five seconds . . . Two seconds . . . The time is up."

There was a moment of dead silence, then he went on:

"By your obstinacy you force us to continue the investigation by other means. We are a State authority, empowered to use our discretion in choosing our approach to your case. We began by treating it politically, and only secondarily from the more narrow angle of the Security Police. We tried to appeal to you as man to man. Obviously you misunderstood this treatment and what lay behind it. Are you anxious to play the hero? You will find it very costly."

All the lights went out.

"Turn to the wall! Put on your mask!" someone ordered.

I heard whispers, shuffling feet, and the clink of metal in a nearby room. Then the warder led me out and through another door.

From somewhere behind me came the voice of the President: "Begin."

They seized me and doubled me up so that my cuffed hands were clasped round my ankles, my arms encircling my bent knees. Through the space between my knees and my elbows they thrust a thick iron pipe, about two yards long; then the warders raised me and rested each end of the pipe on an iron frame. I was now suspended about a yard above the floor, head down, unable to make the slightest movement. The soles of my feet were pointing upwards.

Someone sat down behind me and fixed my head between his knees; he bound my neck and mouth with a coarse towel, taking care to leave my nose free so that I could breathe. When this was over, there was a silence; I felt that there were many people around me in the room. .

"Begin!" again commanded the voice of the President.

I felt the first blow right in my brain; it caused a pain like that of a burn. Then there was a second's pause; a second blow followed, and the pain rushed through me from my toes to the crown of my head.

The warder who was beating me was an expert; every blow fell either on the balls of my toes or on the equally sensitive muscles of the heels. By constantly biting my tongue and lips I endured the burning pain of fifty blows. The first "expert" was now tired out and a new one took his place. The pain became so unbearable that I began to groan and shriek. A warder seized my jaws and stuffed the towel into my mouth. Obsessed by the pain I went on counting the blows, one after the other. At about the eightieth I lost consciousness. When I came round my head was soaking wet and my nose so full of water that I could hardly breathe.

"Well? Have you decided to talk? I'm asking you for the last time!"

The voice of the Interrogator was quite emotionless. Only by the utmost effort was I able to master the impulse to divulge everything that was in my mind. Hoping to break my will, he now alternated the most terrible threats with the most attractive promises.

"Carry on!" commanded the President in a voice which seemed to come from a long way off.

Again the blows began to rain down regularly and with ever-increasing force; this time they fell not on my heels but on the muscles of the lower part of my back and thighs. My sciatic nerve soon caused me unbearable suffering. Frequent fainting fits were my salvation for they carried me out of this nightmare world. Each time I regained consciousness the flogging began again and at each blow I felt the same stinging pain in my head, no doubt intended to make me talk by driving me to the verge of madness.

I could not see the faces of the men around me but I was under the impression that they were not unaffected by my suffering—only, I supposed, their consciences were too weak to make them give in to pity. As for the Interrogator, he was a good psychologist and excellently trained. "Why don't you give in?" he urged me between the beatings. "Don't you see that you have no hope? Your world is finished. Who is going to rescue you? Blood is pouring out of you, you can hardly even breathe, you have not much longer left to live. Come on—speak! Speak! Speak!"

Once when I came round after a long faint, he gave me a lecture along these lines:

"We are building a new world; in it all men will be equal. The factory is our church, the machine is our ikon; these are the foundations of our life. We are creating social wealth, the basis of our earthly paradise. All your church has to offer you is the hope of paradise after death. Ours will be on earth. It's only at the moment that we must be harsh. We suffer, but future generations will be happy . . . Damn!" he interrupted himself, for he had tripped up over the pail of water into which my head was dipped every time I fainted, then he went on in the same optimistic tone:

"We know that the mind of a small child is like wax on which nothing has yet been recorded. These are the minds we mould to our ideals: the younger generation will complete the task of building the new world. But before building comes destruction. For the new life to triumph, the old life, and every brain that works for it, must be destroyed. That is why you are now undergoing this operation."

The picture of this world and of the price of its construction made me shudder but I was certainly too exhausted to argue.

I was flogged again. The pain was by now so intolerable that I longed to shout that I was ready to make any statement they wanted. To control myself I bit the gag and counted the blows until another loss of consciousness gave me a few moments' respite.

After many hours I was at last unhooked. Presumably this technique for irritating the human brain had its limits, for if the brain were destroyed the secrets hidden in it would be lost.

The warders carried me back to the interrogation room. The interrogation began at once. For some reason, I was again asked formal questions about my origin, my parents and my grandparents, my education and my profession.

Then the Interrogator snapped: "Attention—give all your mind to what is going to happen now. A man will be brought in. You will state at once, without hesitation, whether you know him, and his name. You are not to say one word beyond that."

Soon I heard a distant mechanical hum, then a narrow door slid open in the wall on my right. All the lights in the room went out except for one focused on this opening. It revealed a lift closed by a grating. Inside this cage stood a man with bent head, hands hanging loosely by his sides, his whole bearing one of dejection and extreme suffering. He was wearing a suit of a cut and colour which was perfectly familiar to me.

"Do you know this man?"

The President hurled this question at me. His question also had an effect on the man behind the iron grating; he raised his head and our eyes met.

The scene had been so perfectly staged that a light inside the lift threw a bright beam on the space in which I sat. It also faintly lit the room and as I turned to answer the President's question and looked at the table with my eyes now wide open I noticed that each of the five men at it held a fan before his face to prevent my seeing him.

"Yes, I know the man."

Any hesitation or denial would have been senseless.

"Who is he?"

"He is Ion Motru, a friend of mine."

The reflectors were turned on again, the door in the wall closed and the sound of the lift told me that my friend had been taken away. It distressed me that our last meeting had taken place in such circumstances and I knew how painful it must have been for him to see me, sitting on this stool with my back leaning helplessly against the wall, with my soaked head and blood-stained shirt, exhausted and battered.

As I waited for the next question I tried to raise my feet off the floor to ease the pain a little, but I could only manage a few spasmodic movements and they only made the pain in my thighs worse.

I expected to be interrogated about Ion Motru, but what the President questioned me about were the secret frontier crossings which I had organised in 1947 and '48.

"How many people did you help to cross the frontier?"

"Fifteen."

"Scarlet Pimpernel—eh? You didn't even ask for cash—we know that. But false generosity is no excuse. Well, as you'll die in this basement, you won't have an opportunity to be so 'generous' again," said the President mockingly.

That the frontier crossings for which I had been responsible were already known to the Security Police I had realised before, when Alice Zamfirescu told me that a Military Court had condemned me *in absentia* last June to twenty-five years' hard labour.

The Interrogator told me about them and finally came to the period I had spent in Paris. What he wanted from me was a "confession" that my activities had been backed by France. This was untrue, but the Commission were evidently convinced of it and all my denials were swept aside.

132

My shirt was soaked with sweat and my whole body shook so that I could not control it, while to control my mind needed a supreme effort. I could hardly concentrate and often began to ramble.

The President was trying to find out what circles I had moved in among the Roumanians in Paris. His questions appeared general but were in fact very skilful. In spite of a blinding headache, I realised that agents who had found their way to France, disguised as refugees, could have collected a good deal of information about my movements, but that they were most unlikely to know much about my secret contacts or to have found out what had been planned and by whom. My replies were calculated to tell the Commission only what it already knew and amounted to something along these lines:

"I saw my close friends and some of those whom I had helped across the frontier; there were also some Roumanians whom I came across in the streets and cafés in Paris and got to know. We talked things over and decided that it was a good moment to help some of our mutual friends, who were in difficulties in Roumania, to escape abroad. I had experience of such work, so it was natural that I should undertake it once again."

What I had in mind in making these statements was firstly that I must have been seen daily in the company of my close friends—I hoped that this would serve as cover for my connections with the National Committee in exile; and secondly that since my past escape activities were known the Court might be persuaded that I had returned only to help more friends of mine to escape.

"Who were these 'friends' you intended to save?" asked the President.

"The engineer Chica, Duliu Stere, Dr. Iosif Costea, Dr. Vasile Tarta . . ." I replied without hesitation, knowing I would do them no harm.

"Did you manage to get in touch with them?"

"No. When I got here, I heard they had already been arrested."

"How did you find that out? Whom did you ask about them?"

"I didn't ask anybody directly; this is what I did: morning and evening, at the times at which I knew that my friends went to work or returned home, I waited for them near their houses. In the case of Chica, I saw his wife taking the children to school in the morning and coming home late at night alone. I avoided speaking to her, however, so that she should not know I was in Bucharest. After a few days I realised that, since he never appeared, her husband must either have been arrested or have died. I did the same with each in turn. However, to check my observations I looked up an old friend, Ion Motru, thinking that he might be able to tell me if I was right."

The Commission listened in silence. But when I reached this point, the President stopped me and asked several questions about my connections with Ion Motru. To these I answered that I had met him in his cousin's house in Cluj and had asked for information about our four missing friends. (It was quite true that they were our mutual friends and it was in fact Ion Motru who had told me that they were in prison.) Then I went on:

"When Ion Motru confirmed that these four had all been arrested, I asked him to try and find out something about other people who were in hiding, for I felt that, as I had made such a difficult journey to return to my country, I might as well try to help others who were in danger to escape to the West. I also hoped to be able to organise some means of helping those of them who remained in hiding in Roumania to live, and also to help families whose bread-winners are in prison."

I thought it useless to refuse to speak about these minor activities, after my confrontation with Ion Motru, for since he had been forced to give my name to the Security Police, he must also have given the names of those he had been trying to get in touch with. But I hoped that their punishment, if any, would be light since their guilt was only that we were trying to get in touch with them. In any case they were already known to the police and most of them were in hiding.

One difficult phase of the interrogation was over. But as I sat there, stiff with pain, I was seized with a kind of numbness of my body, heart and soul. I had an urge to say at once everything that could be said without harming my friends, to declare everything I had been concocting, to get it all over. I longed for the end—not to feel anything more, to end this shrinking of my heart. All I hoped for was that the Commission would get on with it and pronounce my sentence and carry out my execution.

But the Commission went on questioning me and this time others besides the President joined in.

"The Commission wishes to know by what means you left the country when you went to France?"

I had expected this question. I replied that as the guides from Arad and Satu Mare whom I had engaged had been arrested, I had organised my escape with the help of a Jewish acquaintance in Cluj, David Hersch. With a rich embroidery of detail I described how I had fled to Budapest and Vienna, guided by this man. I added that David Hersch—who was engaged in various kinds of smuggling—used secretly to go to Vienna about three times a year, having established a clandestine channel which was at that time relatively safe.

David Hersch really did exist. He had lived in Cluj and had carried out smuggling expeditions, but it was not he who had helped me to escape. I now made use of his name and the facts about him which he himself had told me as extra cover for my real connections in the towns and villages along the frontier and in Budapest. I felt able to do this because David Hersch was out of reach, waiting in a Jewish D.P. camp near Milan to emigrate to Australia.

"By what secret route did you come back to Roumania and who were your guides?" The President's voice was impatient, as if he wanted to get on to more important matters.

"David Hersch showed me all the landmarks when he travelled with me as far as Vienna, and while I was in Austria I succeeded in making the acquaintance of a confidential agent of his, a peasant named Blagus. On my way back I appealed to Blagus to help me over the minefields into Hungary. He got me in somewhere near Köszeg; we took advantage of the fact that there is a gap in the minefield where the railway goes through."

# The Lost Footsteps

I next described my journey by Szombathely to Budapest, pretending that I had made it alone. I purposely mentioned the names of several places on the way in order to convince the interrogators of my truthfulness by describing them in detail. I told them that I only spent an hour or two in Budapest, between trains, adding that my fluent Hungarian had made it easy for me to buy a ticket and set out for Püspökladány and Biharkeresztes. There, I said, I had left the train just after dark and disappeared into the fields; by following the railway line and heading eastwards, I succeeded in reaching Oradea by the following morning.

The declarations I made were so framed that the Commission would have no means of checking them. Nor would they be able to lay their hands on any of the people I had mentioned. My fate now depended on their acceptance or rejection of my statements.

I awaited their decision, feeling the salty taste of blood in my mouth and scarcely daring to touch the floor with my feet when I tried to change their position to reduce the pain.

"Some of your statements seem to be true," said the President. "Others, however, are a gross distortion of the facts. We order you to answer truthfully, within three minutes, the first two questions we are going to put to you. First: what were the motives which determined you to return to Roumania? Second: what foreign Power . . .? If you don't make up your mind to reply at once, we will be obliged to continue the treatment."

The ultimatum expired at the last beat of the metronome. Within a few minutes I was once more suspended from the iron bar. When fresh blows, more vicious than before, began to rain down on the raw flesh of my heels, the unbearable pain forced me to shout out: "I'll confess! I'll confess!" Delighted, the warders unhooked me at once and dragged me back into the court-room.

"Have you made up your mind to give us a true answer to each of the two questions?" asked the President incredulously. "It's useless to hold out—you do realise that? You can't escape from us and we know everything you have done. All we ask is that you should admit your actions sincerely, frankly, like a gentleman."

My body was shaking. But the fact that he had used the word

"gentleman" awoke me to reality. That a man sitting at that table behind the glare of the reflectors could use such a word to another who was leaning helplessly against the wall, bleeding and handcuffed—this gave me the strength to decide that I could bear more torture. With a supreme effort I pulled myself together and repeated, almost word for word, my earlier statement: no foreign Power stood behind me . . . I had not said more than four words in reply to the other question about my "motives," when the lights were extinguished. In the darkness the warders set on me, put the leather mask over my eyes, and dragged me again to the torture chamber. A cruel flogging followed. Though I yelled: "I'll confess! I'll confess everything!" the blows went on until I lost consciousness. When this happened for the second time, I did not come round again in that room.

## CHAPTER X

I HAVE no idea how long I was unconscious, but when I opened my eyes I realised that I was on the bed in my cell. I woke with the feeling that I was drowning in a shoreless sea, my mind obsessed with some dream I had had which I could not shake off . . . I was on the bank of a very broad river which flowed down a valley in some beautiful tropical place, between banks of giant trees hung with tufts of exquisitely coloured blossoms. I had been watching it a long time when the tall grass along the edge swayed gently as if a wave had stirred it. The wave broke on the gravel of a watering place. Then, from amongst the grasses, a tiger's head rose with majesty and he slowly looked about him. He bent down, tasted the clear water and, moving forward into the pool, drank contentedly. Now and then he stopped and gazed at the strong current. Coming out of his dark jungle he seemed to be enchanted by the bright horizon, the level expanse of river and the immense sky. Suddenly a thin wave sliced the surface of the water and advanced rapidly, not down-stream but cutting across it.

I sat perched on the branch of a tree, where I was out of danger of being scented by the tiger, and I saw the narrow wave speeding towards him. He had satisfied his thirst and was about to turn back into the concealing grass when a crocodile shot out of the water. The tiger stood stock-still as if petrified. During that fatal pause the crocodile sank his teeth in the tiger's breast.

A wind lifted me from my safe seat on the branch and bore me above the river. I was filled with terror. With great effort I stretched out my arms and flapping them like wings, succeeded in keeping myself airborne and flying in wide circles. I could see the tiger digging his hind legs firmly into the damp gravel to steady himself while he struggled, head held high, striking at the crocodile again and again with his steely claws. I could see scales and pieces of the monster's head flying into the air, an eye was torn out at one blow, but still the crocodile held on to his prey. He lashed the water with his tail as if it were an enormous oar and shook and dragged the tiger to and fro, trying to dislodge him from his firm hold on the damp gravel. At every movement made by the two wild beasts fresh patches of blood spread on the water and the sand.

As time passed the current gradually washed the gravel from beneath the tiger's feet and he began to slip forward slowly step by step . . . Then the crocodile snatched him and carried him into the stream. For a moment I saw the tiger's head above the surface; he looked resigned as if knowing that further struggle would be useless. His eyes gazed at the broad expanse of river and sky, then he disappeared below the waves.

Horrified, I felt my arms beginning to weaken and my aching body no longer able to sustain their flapping. Soon I fell helplessly down into the middle of the current. The water was boundless, turbid and full of blood and it was drawing me into its depths.

At this point I had awakened, stiff with pain. I have no idea how long I lay there motionless, staring at a point on the wall in front of me, which seemed to be somewhere far away in space.

"Turn your face to the wall! Shut your eyes and don't move."

With great difficulty I succeeded in obeying. The bolt was shot back and the door banged against the wall. There were sounds of something being brought into the cell and the door closed again. From outside it, the warder said: "The Commission wants you to write down, word for word, everything you declared in the last session. You are not to leave out the smallest detail or you will be punished again. Get up and write . . . Get on with it."

I sat up on the edge of the bed and tried to concentrate, resting my head on the small table which had just been put into the cell. I had to put down in writing every word which had been registered on the tape-recorder. Luckily I have an excellent memory and so I was able to reconstruct my statements and not to contradict myself; but it was difficult, for I was overwhelmed by weakness and suffering, and it took me about ten hours to write my declaration, perhaps longer. I often had to lean my head on the table in order to collect myself though I realised that every gesture I made, every sign of weakness, was being noted by the warders and reported to the Commission: it was well known that the psychological reactions of the prisoners were watched and followed with the greatest attention.

When I had finished writing and handed the sheets of paper to the impatient warder they were no doubt taken to the President of the Commission. I only hoped that the proceedings would not drag on much longer. I wanted them to sentence me and shoot me soon, so that I should stop suffering and have peace. I hoped that I would behave properly when they came to fetch me and that that would be the only thing I still had to do. "Bullets don't hurt." A friend of mine, wounded by machine-gun fire during the war, had told me that when the bullet struck his leg it had been no worse than a blow; it was only after he had taken a few steps that he felt the pain. If they shot me through the head, it would all be over in a second. Already I felt as if my soul had left my body and was floating about somewhere in a corner of the cell. Indeed, from that point I could see my body quite clearly: it was lying motionless on the bed, clothed only in its soiled, bloodstained shirt; the feet were swollen and deformed, the hands clasped on the breast, the eyes open. I said to myself: "That body carried my soul through my earthly life; now the moment has come to part from it."

Once again I was filled with a calm feeling of expectation, as though some great ceremony were about to take place—and this was what had happened on that afternoon of the 18th of September before my arrest.

"Get up!"

I got up.

This time they did not hand me the mask but threw the door wide open and came into the cell. There were four of them. They wore long black cloaks, and hoods with two openings for the eyes over their heads. When they had handcuffed me they put the leather mask over my face and we set off. After a walk down subterranean corridors which seemed as if it would never end, we halted. They took off my mask and I saw that I was standing in front of a wall. It blocked the end of a corridor about seven feet wide, and fastened to it was a wooden crate, a little taller and broader than a man. Five powerful electric bulbs were fixed to a bar on the ceiling above the crate; there were bullet holes in the wood and a little rust-stained sand had spilled between the boards.

The warders had retired behind me. Something was pushed about and put into position with a metallic clink. I tried to stop my knees shaking by gritting my teeth and clenching my fists, driving my nails into the palms of my hands. About three minutes passed; then a warder ordered me to begin moving from left to right. I could not understand what he wanted but I did as he said. I was sure that they were going to fire into my back.

"Not like that! Not like that!" they shouted.

One of them came up to me and, taking me by the arm, showed me how I was to move in a circle in that narrow space at the end of the passage. Then stepping back to join the others, he ordered me to begin. About five yards away from where I was turning round and round, the warders had placed a table with powerful reflectors on it. Behind it, shielded from the light, they shouted: "Faster! Faster!" beating time on the table with a stick in ever quicker rhythm. I moved faster and faster in that closed circle without a second's intermission. It seemed at every step as if my feet were treading on the points of knives; I could feel the blades striking through my heels; through the small bones in my feet; through my ankles and knees. I could not understand what these men wanted of me, why they were delaying the execution. The pain of my swollen feet was unbearable.

After about half an hour of running round I asked: "Why don't you shoot? Why do you go on with this senseless torture?"

"Shut up! Run! You thought you'd get out of it as easily as that! No! No! You have a lot more to suffer—very much more—

before we condescend to put a bullet into you. You don't deserve
that yet. Faster! Faster!"

Thoughts went round and round in my mind in a never-ending
circle like the one in which my body was forced to turn without
a respite and with ever gathering speed. Whenever I slowed down
the warders threatened me with a beating. The memory of their
stinging blows made me shudder, so in terror of them I resumed
my pace.

After a long time a warder brought in lunch for the men behind
the table, or perhaps it was supper; I heard the clink of glasses,
plates and cutlery. A few hours later I heard a movement which
made me realise that a new shift had come on duty. They too were
served a meal after another long interval, and all the while I still
continued to turn round and round. Every time I raised my foot
the pain in it was lightened for the tenth of a second, but when I
had again to lean my weight on it, the knife-points jabbed at me.
I do not know how many hours passed—it seemed an eternity—
before a voice from the table behind the lights ordered:

"Sit down!"

I sat down on the cold cement, leaning against the wall; I
could have stayed there for ever. One of the warders—his hood
drawn over his head and wearing his long black cloak—brought
a piece of bread and a mug of water and set them down beside
me.

"Eat!" he ordered.

My throat was quite dry but I forced myself to eat a little and
I drank to quench the thirst which I felt throughout my whole
body. However, the amount I was given seemed only about as
much as a nutshell would hold. I had hardly set the mug down on
the floor when one of the warders tapped the table with his stick
and shouted at me:

"Get up! Carry on! Run!"

The wall beside me seemed like the face of a mountain, its
summit hidden somewhere in the clouds. Getting up was like
trying to climb a vertical precipice and groping blindly for a ledge
of rock to which to cling. But the threats and shouts of the warders

and the tapping of the stick gave me the strength to drag myself up. I rose and continued my circular march, revolving with ever increasing speed in time to the tapping on the table. For the first ten minutes the pain caused by the wounds on my feet was even worse than before I had sat down.

Warders replaced each other, lunches and suppers were served at the table behind the lights while I ran . . . ran . . . without ceasing. "Oh God, when will it end?" I thought. "Shall I smash my head against the wall?" I knew that there is a part of the skull which is very thin—it should be easy to smash it and to die. But I realised that I was now too weak to make the effort and there wasn't a nail or a lump or a corner anywhere to make it easier; the wall was completely smooth.

At the end of twenty-four hours—or perhaps it was thirty-six hours, or even longer—I had reached my limit. I could hardly drag my legs, swollen to the dimensions of tree-trunks. I was no longer running, but only tottering, dragging one foot after the other and supported by my hands against the wall. By now I was heedless of the warders, I scarcely heard their shouts. Finally, my hands slipped slowly down the wall and my body crumpled up on the floor. After this I dragged myself round on all fours, in a slow, agonising movement. Now and then I rested my forehead on the cold cement to gain a little strength—my forehead touched the floor as if in a gesture of supreme humility, or a silent prayer which I was unable, even in my thoughts, to formulate and raise to God.

I regained consciousness; the warders had dipped my head in a basin of water and when they saw my eyes open, they carried me to my cell and flung me down on the bed. I fell asleep at once. My sleep lasted perhaps an hour, at the most two. I was then awakened and again taken to the same place at the end of the corridor. The short rest I had been given was actually to my disadvantage for my swollen joints and muscles had stiffened.

It was only by the change of warders and by their meals that I was able to gauge that several days and nights had passed since the beginning of this punishment. My only food was the piece of bread and can of water which I was given once a day. By now I was unable to eat the bread except for a little bit of the soft centre. Water—that was what obsessed me. My lips were cracked with thirst; my saliva had dried up and my body was becoming dehydrated. The faster I was forced to run, the more the force of gravity wore me out. My whole organism was out of gear and its slow destruction was much harder to bear than the kind of death I had expected.

I became delirious. Feeling the invisible knives going through my muscles, bones and nerves, I could no longer run for more than a few hours before I began clinging to the walls and, soon after, slipped down on all fours. My horizon grew narrower and darker till it was limited to the ashen cement floor polished by my footsteps. Then suddenly the floor became transformed. On its surface flickered the tiny golden flames of candles like those before the altar in a church. I wanted to pray, but it seemed that my lips and indeed my very soul were sealed. Then in my delirium I saw myself lying on bleached rocks flooded by sunlight, with white ferns growing in the crevices. All at once black vipers which had been sleeping in the sun awoke, roused by my presence, and reared their heads to strike at me. To escape them I dragged myself in terror faster and faster, until I banged my head against the wall of the corridor. The vipers followed me; I broke a twig off a hazel-nut tree which grew in my path and with this little rod I tried to keep them at bay. I tried to hit them on the head, but the twig bent and I could never reach them. So I continued to run over the sharp stones until suddenly, there was a pool beside a water-mill, half-hidden in the shadow of great trees. With my last ounce of strength I threw myself into the ice-cold water and lowering my head beneath its surface, watched the vipers waiting for me to reappear.

I realised that the warders had been plunging me in and out of a bath of water, waiting for me to come round. When I had recovered a little the vicious circle began again—running, slipping down and falling and dragging myself round on all fours . . . Now I was on a flying carpet, borne over fields and hills and villages to the edge of the familiar lake where the willow tree awaited me, and I gazed down from its branches at the clear water—until a cloudburst filled the valley with noise and swept me off my willow branch . . .

The worst moments began when the warders were taking their meals. I heard the cork popping at their table and the clink of bottle on glass; the warders talked loudly about their tasty food or exclaimed: "What nice cold mineral water!" or "How about a little white wine and soda water?" I swallowed the little saliva I could secrete and tried to fight my obsession and the warders' sadism, but soon I was again hovering over an expanse of water, or plunging into a world of sea-weeds and exotic trees at the bottom of the ocean, or swimming among monsters, octopuses and huge sharks, until a sound—the clinking of glasses or a voice—brought me back again to my endless race under the glare of the reflectors.

The walls changed into windows; clear streams of mineral water flowed behind them and air bubbled out of its depths illuminated from within by neon-lighting. I pressed my lips to the glass, but not a mouthful of that water reached me. I struck the window with my fist but it would not break. I prayed for a glass of water and there was a miracle. Through the window I could see my friends coming towards me, carrying golden trays set with crystal goblets filled with water. They shouted to me from the distance to be patient until they reached me with the living water to quench my thirst. But from the left came soldiers in cloaks of green and gold brocade and shining breast-plates of some green metal, with round shields in their left hands and, in their right, short swords like enormous scalpels; and from the right, a second line of soldiers, identically clothed and armed but in vivid red. The two lines advanced, converging on my friends and, when they reached them, cut off their hands bearing the golden trays. The water broke up into darkness and flashing lights and the warriors rushed at me with their swords.

These hallucinations were caused by the progressive dehydration of my body. The little water I was given seemed a divine gift. I begged the warder for a drop more but he would only say: "As soon as you are ready to talk to the Commission you will be given anything you want."

Every time I regained consciousness in the bath I tried to drink, but the warders kept their hands over my mouth and immediately I opened my eyes they dragged me out. I was taken very rarely to the lavatory, but now I planned to take advantage of the moment when I had pulled the chain to take a little water into the palm of my hand. I was trembling with impatience when the warders led me along the corridors and pushed me into the little lavatory. "Now I'll pull the chain and drink to my heart's content ... water ... water ... all that comes out of the cistern." But when I reached up for the chain I was overcome by faintness. I pressed my forehead to the wall and in that moment a sudden courage welled up in me. I leaned against the wall for a second more, then I pulled the chain and looked calmly and somehow indifferently at the precious stream of clear water. I said to myself: "I'll keep my human dignity." Just then the warders pushed the door open violently and led me away. Probably they had expected to catch me drinking. They knew to what humiliating solutions men driven to the verge of madness can have recourse. Once that human dignity was lost, they knew that the prisoner was on the way to capitulation.

And all this was happening to me not in a desert, or on a boundless ocean, where ship-wrecked men are sometimes driven to bestial actions. Above me was a large city full of people who were powerless to prevent what was going on beneath their feet and could not even give a glass of water to a man dying of thirst.

The act of self-control which had prevented me from humiliating myself in the eyes of my gaolers had a decisive effect on me —it changed the whole trend of my thoughts and did something to wake me up from my delirium. The polished circle which my steps had made in the dead end of the corridor was, after all, a kind of lasting imprint of the events in that cramped space—I existed somewhere on the earth, somewhere in the universe.

I knew that I could stop my circular torment at any moment

if I said: "I am ready to make the declarations asked by the Commission." The warders would then take me to the white room; the tape-recorder would register my statements; the paper would afterwards unfeelingly receive the names of my friends, and the shining black Ford cars would set off to tear them from their homes. In my imagination I could see them being pushed about by the police, brought here one after another, kept in solitary confinement, made to play their part in the drama staged in the white room, until finally they would end up revolving in an eternal circle, phantoms clothed only in shirts stained with their own blood. I could bring them here or keep them out.

I was now in a strange state of mind. The thought of water worried me less for my exhaustion had reached a point at which it paralysed even sufferings. I hardly noticed the shouts of the warders and the tapping of their stick. My heart and the upper part of my body seemed extraordinarily light; I felt convinced that if I were to stretch out my hands I could fly up into the air. But the earth was holding me down, as if blocks of concrete were fastened to my feet.

My body was revolving endlessly in the glare of the lights, parched, feverish, tousled, with a long black beard and filthy with blood and with dust gathered from so much crawling on the floor. If only I could get rid of it! Only the thought of my approaching death gave me a feeling of blessedness, of exaltation. I awaited it with intense joy. But how to reach it?

The final separation of my soul and body depended on the will of the Commission. My last journey must be made by way of the white room, and they would hold it up until they got a full confession from me.

The sound of voices broke into my thoughts. There seemed to be some sort of discussion going on at the warders' table.

Someone asked:

"Is he still putting up a fight? Still running round?"

"Yes. He's stubborn, he's giving us a lot of trouble. Look at him trailing himself round on all fours, he's at the end of his tether again. Sometimes he starts shouting, 'Black vipers, black

## The Lost Footsteps

vipers, sharks . . .' Or he mutters to himself, but you can't tell what he's saying . . . It's seven days now since we brought him in here. We don't know what to do with him next. Perhaps you should try to find out what's going on in his head? We've told him dozens of times that there's no escape for him unless he tells everything he knows."

Two warders in their hoods and black cloaks came over to me and lifted me to my feet, supporting me with my face turned towards the lights. The President himself addressed me.

"Listen to what I am saying: if you think you will hold out for ever, you are mistaken. You are also mistaken if you hope to die here and take your secrets to the grave with you. If necessary, we will keep you alive for a year and force you to go on running round and round, day and night. Sooner or later you'll go down on your bended knees and ask us to listen to your confession. But by then it will be too late. By then you'll have missed your chance, and you will only have to suffer more and more, without being allowed to die, as punishment for your crimes. Now are you going to talk?"

I tried to look in the direction from which his voice was coming, but the lights forced me to lower my eyes.

"I have made up my mind!"

"We expect you to make fresh declarations—under no circumstances a repetition of the old ones . . ."

"I will make fresh declarations."

Supporting me by the arms, the warders brought me to the cell and laid me on the bed. A few minutes later I was given a glass of milk and left alone.

About an hour passed, then the warders came for me again.

After staggering about at the end of that corridor for a week, the immensity of the interrogation room and its white walls made me feel that I had been transported into some ancient temple and the long table was an altar erected by sun-worshippers. The room was full of a ritual silence and tension.

The President made a short speech ending with these words: "The State Commission, in whose presence you are, is awaiting

148

your full confession. Weigh your words carefully. Everything you say will be recorded."

"I came to Roumania to make preparations for an attempt on the life of Gheorghiu-Dej, the General Secretary of the Communist Party."

My words came clearly and unhesitatingly, in spite of the extreme weakness of my body. The silence which followed was portentous.

"My idea was to buy a motor-bicycle in the *Talcioc*[1] and intercept Gheorghiu-Dej's Buick when he was on his way to the palace of the President of the Council of Ministers, on the Calea Victoriei. I meant to do this at the moment when the car slowed down to cross the Strada General Manu, two hundred yards before it turned into the courtyard of the Old Palace. I intended to intercept the car on that short stretch of road, and riddle Gheorghiu-Dej with bullets from a Mauser revolver."

For a few moments no further question was put to me. I heard agitated whisperings.

The session lasted about two hours. The Commission, in its eagerness to find out every detail, hurled dozens of questions at me. Guided by their questions, I tried to build up a convincing picture. I felt, however, that although the prevailing mood was one of satisfaction, the investigators still had moments of doubt and wavered between the two opinions.

When I had been led back to my cell, I was ordered to put down my declarations on paper so that they could be checked with the tape-recording. I took care to mention the Mauser and the box of ammunition which, as I had told them, were hidden in a hollow tree in a park. I hoped that this would prove that my story was more than the imaginings of a man worn out by torture, for in fact I had hidden a Mauser in the hollow of a tree-trunk in the park some years ago.

As the light in my cell was left on all the time I had no way of telling exactly how many hours or days passed but, judging by the intervals at which I was given a little food, I thought that about

[1] *Talcioc*—an official barter market on the outskirts of the capital.

149

ten days must have gone by. This fact strengthened my hope that my "final confession" had been accepted. My physical suffering was now almost bearable though my discomfort was great. Since my arrest I had not once been allowed to wash my face or hands, and I was still clothed only in the shirt I had been wearing then. I lived in complete silence.

# CHAPTER XI

"GET UP! Put your mask on!"

The cell door was thrown open, my arms were pulled roughly behind my back and my wrists handcuffed.

Presently we came to some steps. Instinctively I counted one, two, three . . . we climbed up twenty-three steps and I took a deep draught of cool, damp, life-giving air.

I was pushed into a car and doubled up on the floor at the back. A rug was thrown over me. The guards got into their seats and rested their booted feet on top of my body. Before we set off someone whispered: "If you make the slightest move you'll be shot."

The noise of the trams, the hum of the traffic and the nearness of movements of people going about their daily tasks seemed unreal.

After a fast drive through the streets of the city the car slowed down and braked abruptly. Heavy iron doors were opened noisily and I heard the hoarse bark of an Alsatian as we drove into a courtyard. A few minutes later, I was pushed into a cell, the mask snatched from my face by someone behind me and the door banged and locked.

The cell was about as wide and long as the one I had left, but its height—about twelve feet—astonished me. Exhausted and giddy, I made for the bed, but a warder immediately opened the door and told me that I had been deprived of the privilege of lying or sitting on the bed.

"You can sit on the chair or walk up and down as much as you like."

Sitting on the hard chair revived the pain in my flogged body and the cold of the cement floor numbed my feet. My legs were still so swollen that the three steps up and down, which the length of the cell allowed, were hardly less difficult, nevertheless, I tried to walk. In this way hour after hour dragged silently by.

Some time during the night the warder opened the door and ordered me to go to bed. It was a great relief to be able to lie down on the rough, straw-filled mattress and pull the blanket over me. I fell asleep at once.

"Turn your face towards the light! You are not allowed to sleep facing the wall!"

The warder woke me up and stood in the open door waiting for me to carry out his order. I had been sleeping for perhaps an hour or two, and now, with my face turned towards the light I tried to doze off again, but my brain, refreshed by a little sleep, began to work feverishly; questions, contradictory answers and regrets tortured my mind as my body had been tortured earlier. Through half-open eyelids I could see the warder's eye fixed on me through the peep-hole in the door. At length, worn out, I fell into a troubled sleep.

"Wake up! Get up! You can walk about or sit on the chair, but you are not to go to sleep."

I did not know how long I had slept, certainly it was not for long. The warder, in the khaki uniform with blue pips and epaulettes of the Security Police, waited for me to get up, and took me to the lavatory. The wide corridor was thickly carpeted to deaden the sound of footsteps. On the right I counted the doors of twenty-four cells and there was a warder to every four doors. That meant six warders to guard the passage in addition to an extra one outside my door. There was something uncanny about the silence of their movements and the speed and precision with which they pushed aside the metal discs of the peep-holes to spy for a few seconds on the inmates of the cells.

Outside, dawn was beginning to break. After the weeks spent in an underground prison, I saw daylight filtering in thin, weak gleams through a small window in my cell. Suddenly I became aware of a sound like someone singing far away. Standing close to the radiator I realised that the water in the pipes was making a curious sound like the note of a flute or of a shepherd's horn heard a long way off in the mountains. The pipe gave off some warmth, so I pulled my chair over and settled myself with my back to it. A pleasant drowsiness crept over me from top to toe; my hands felt like lead and kept falling by my sides; my eyelids kept closing and my head nodding on to my chest; my will power could not keep me awake. A powerful banging on the cell door made me start.

"You are not allowed to sleep. Hold your head up and keep your eyes open! If you feel sleepy get up and walk about the cell till it passes off! Don't forget to keep your mind on what the Interrogating Commission asked you!"

The warder, a tall slim youth with dark, wavy hair parted in the middle and combed down each side, emphasised each word by a menacing gesture. He had opened the door so quietly that I had heard nothing until his brutal knocking startled me. The other warder who had been in charge during the night had gone off duty. He also was a youth, but fair, green-eyed and with a cold, weak expression in which I sensed a successful but not effortless mastery over pity.

The warmth from the radiator lasted only about an hour. Towards midday the cell became so cold that I was forced to keep moving almost without a pause. I had been given nothing to eat during the morning. Judging by the sounds coming from outside the other prisoners had been given food in cans or on enamel plates. In order to keep account of the passage of time—now that I was able to see light dawning and darkness falling—I drew a thin line with my nail in a corner of the wall; to this I added another thin line to mark the day before—the day of my arrival.

In the late afternoon I was given my ration of food: a little soup, a few potatoes and about five ounces of bread. My sleepless night and the continuous pacing to and fro had made me very hungry. But instead of strengthening me, it seemed as if the food had weakened me still more. I sat down and leaned my head against the wall, then closed my eyes and hoped that the warder would not notice me. But my sleep never lasted more than thirty seconds before he woke me up by knocking loudly on the door.

"Don't you know that you are not allowed to sleep?" he said

angrily. "You must stay awake and think without ceasing about the questions put to you by the Commission. If you try to doze, let me tell you there is always the 'training ring' and a flogging to wake you up. Don't forget that!"

The hardest part of the day began—instead of ending—at nightfall. It must have been about seven o'clock when I was given a second meal, identical with the first. The radiator had been turned on again a short time before and the flow of water in its pipes resumed its plaintive song. It was agonising to look at my bed while struggling with the desire to sleep, increased by the warmth of the radiator and the efforts to digest my food. Infuriated, the warder opened the door and shouted at me that if he caught me dozing again I would have to stand facing the strong light with my arms above my head.

"Come on, walk! Get off that chair!"

I looked him straight in the eyes and without saying a word I began my walk: three steps forward, three steps back . . . It seemed that time had stopped; the few sounds which suggested any activity inside the prison had ceased.

Some time late in the night the order which I had awaited in a frenzy came at last: "Lie down!" As I was very hungry I could not resist the temptation of biting off a corner of the piece of bread I had kept back to allay my hunger the following morning. Chewing it slowly, so as to enjoy the wonderful taste of every crumb, I lay down. My bruised body experienced a sensation of extraordinary relaxation, but the strange thing was that, instead of falling asleep at once as I had hoped, I lay awake for a long time. I wondered if some stimulant had been mixed with the soup I had had that evening. I tried to blot all images from my mind by counting from one to a thousand; I recited the alphabet and tried other means of conjuring up sleep, but in vain. I felt a sharp pain in my scalp, as though flames were searing me and thought I might be going to have meningitis. At last I did fall asleep but my sleep, instead of being healing and restful, was filled with nightmares and full of exhausting emotions. As on the previous night the warder woke me up every hour or so.

# The Lost Footsteps

Then came the order: "Wake up! Tidy your bed! Get ready to be taken to the lavatory!" It was morning.

My second day was identical with the first, but still more tiring: a struggle with sleep, with cold, with hunger and with my own spirit. In order to avoid trouble with the warders I succeeded by an enormous effort in keeping my eyes open.

One evening, ten days later, I was taken by two warders to a room of the same size as my cell, where I found a barber. The mirror showed me a pale, thin face: could I really be that wild-looking man with matted hair and a long, curling black beard streaked with grey? When my beard had been shaved off and my hair cut short, my face remained unfamiliar. In the mirror, above my head, the light fell on a slogan in large red letters: "Show no mercy to the enemies of the people! Death to them!" I thought to myself that I had probably been confronted with this mirror in order that I should see into what a stage of degradation I had fallen. It never happened again. After this one time the barber came to my cell, accompanied by two warders who supervised the proceedings with great care. The barber shaved me with a safety razor but, even so, it was held by one of the warders while the barber soaped my face, in case I should snatch it from his hand and attempt to commit suicide.

The lines by which I recorded the passing of the days were accumulating on the wall in groups of ten; they were very lightly scratched so that they remained unobserved by the duty officer who searched my cell from time to time. On the morning on which I had just drawn the sixtieth line on my secret calendar, a Security subaltern led me to one of the interrogation offices of the prison, first having taken care to prevent me from learning the topography of that part of the building by putting metal shields over my eyes.

"Sit down, please."

In a polite and friendly tone the Interrogator invited me to sit down on a low stool before a table. Leaning comfortably against the back of his own chair behind his desk, he gave me a long look, as though he wanted to create an impression of understanding and

155

The Lost Footsteps

compassion. After a few unimportant questions about how I had
crossed the frontier—to which he noted my replies with apparent
indifference—he addressed me in a warm, paternal voice.

"In the opinion of the Interrogating Commission you have
realised that you will die only when it decides to let you, even if
you long for the end to come. We are perfectly aware of everything
that is going on in your mind and soul. It is just because we have
great experience of this that we are leaving you in your present
situation and giving you the chance to reflect without interruption
on your past—on every act, on every detail. In this way you will
recognise your faults and form conclusions. The only wise thing
is to capitulate—that is the only way to have the peace you
long for."

The Interrogator drummed lightly with his fingers and stared
abstractedly at some point on the carpet which seemed visible only
to him. He was wearing a brown suit of good material; his high
forehead and rich chestnut hair, streaked with grey and brushed to
the back of his head, made him look like a professor or a philo-
sopher. He did not appear to be more than fifty.

"I want to say something else before we part," he continued,
still in a friendly voice. "You must realise that we are in no hurry.
We are patient; we give a man just as much time to think as he
wants. We can wait for a month, a year, five years, or even longer.
The longer you take to make your decision to talk, the greater and
the more intense your suffering will be. We regret this, but your
own behaviour warrants this procedure. As for going on living—
we will see that you do this in any case, even if your resistance
should last a hundred years!"

With a calm gesture, he pressed a bell on the wall beside him.
When the warder was about to place the metal shade over my eyes,
the man who had just given me this fatherly advice saluted me as
though confirming the impression of good will. I returned the
salute though spiritually I was far away and indifferent to him.

The fact that I had hardly been allowed to sleep since I had
come to this new prison made me believe that the Commission
were not satisfied with my final declaration. No doubt the heads of

the Security Police, having examined it and compared it with information gathered by their agents, had come to the conclusion that many secrets were still hidden in my brain. Probably it had not taken them very long to find out that, driven to the verge of insanity, I had invented a plot which had led them on a wild goose chase, and they had therefore decided to continue to exert pressure on my mind by a new method. The régime of sleeplessness which I had undergone almost without interruption for about two months (as far as I could judge) had prevented me from recovering my mental powers and had also given rise to excessive irritability and a psychological upheaval of terrifying dimension. There was little I could do about it, however hard I tried. I felt as though I were on a huge merry-go-round which revolved by day and by night at the speed of thought and caused a continual state of giddiness, an emptiness in the stomach, a light-headedness, an unimaginable mass of confused hallucinations.

The first team of warders had been replaced by fresh, young recruits and I had not a moment's respite from their relentless supervision. I had become a victim of the earth's gravity, of the winter's cold, of the radiator's heat, of the stimulant which drove away sleep, of the warders who kept me awake—all these were part of the net which entangled me.

The memory of the floggings and of running round in that eternal circle still terrorised me and to avoid these tortures I used all my strength in fighting sleep. For hours on end as I took three paces to and from the door (which, like the doors of burial vaults, was without a knob or handle on the inside) I repeated a kind of incantation I had made up. It was based on an old legend about a sculptor who had begged God to transmute his being into some other form and had become a tree with golden leaves, then the sun, then a cloud, a rock . . . "Lord, change me into a rock," I prayed, "help me to stand up to these frightening storms; make me strong, so that they cannot break me."

Repeating these words thousands of times, I began to imagine that I had indeed been changed into a rock. The rock was lashed by breakers and struck by lightning, apocalyptic monsters flew towards it through the crests of giant waves; but only small fragments were torn away from it—its rocky substance resisted the claws of the wild beasts and its head remained above the swirling waters.

The spy-hole opened softly and I could see the warder's eye through the round opening in the door. I could see his long, black eyelashes, the whites of the eyes, the iris with its golden specks, the pupil trying to discover what was going on inside my soul. After a long, fixed look, he shouted: "Come on! Walk! Don't stand still!" As I went on walking, I repeated another prayer: "Oh Lord! Keep me from dying under the gaze of this inhuman, hating eye. Nothing has ever filled me with so much dread as its watchfulness, its lack of pity."

I longed for a different death and my mind was filled with visions which I could hardly distinguish from reality.

I saw a region of great beauty in the Fagaras mountains. The rocky peaks were sharp against a clear sky; forests of oak, beech and fir sloped into a valley with its grasslands and its fields of silvery maize. Winding along a narrow path came a long procession of men in white homespun shirts and trousers, the bright embroidery on their wide belts coloured like the flowers in the fields. These men were followed by old priests whose long white beards and hair made them look like patriarchs. Their copes of ivory brocade stitched with gold gleamed in the summer sun, and from their hands swung chased silver censers spreading the smell of incense over the fields. At the head of the procession, four youths carried a pine-wood catafalque on which my body rested. The priests chanted the funeral dirge—"Lord deliver him! Lord, receive him into his eternal resting-place where there is neither sadness nor torment but everlasting peace"—and the *contakion* was taken up by the whole procession. They came to a wide river flowing between old willows and tall grasses which bowed to the reflections of the sun and the white clouds. The youths laid my body down on a white stone block and the priests blessed it with sacramental gestures. At that moment a white flame burst from the sun, enveloped the block of stone and turned it into pure crystal. The procession, still chanting, slowly withdrew. Left alone, fixed in the block of crystal, I gazed at the setting sun, the fall of twilight, the beauty of the summer night with its millions of stars, daybreak and sunrise—the universe was displayed before my wide-open eyes; I gazed at it, eternally awake, safe . . .

I led a fantastic life dominated by hallucinations which I could no longer resist. In the evening, the water singing in the radiator pipes conjured up an Indian town and an exotic orchestra. Hundreds of musicians stood in an enormous amphitheatre—with flutes, pipes, gold and silver trumpets, clarinets, and string instruments which were unknown to me. I was the conductor and stood on a raised platform. On my right a choir of young boys and girls dressed in white saris were waiting for me to begin. When I gave the signal the music rose in a plaintive, meditative overture; it gradually increased in volume until it became a great outburst of swelling, protesting sound. Another movement of my baton and the choir took up the melody, their pure voices rising in perfect unison and faithfully interpreting my every gesture. Now they raised their arms and I could hear their words:

"Gods of light, turn away from the abominations of the earth!"

"Dark gods, why do you still suffer men to destroy each other?"

Suddenly, choir and orchestra started to revolve in an immense spiral, and finally vanished though I could still hear the melody, from a long way off, and now returning to the plaintive opening theme.

Then, as from an abyss, rose another music, made up of the screams of millions of tortured men. The vision broke up into many horrible scenes—aeroplanes, hit by missiles, crashed in flames and smoke exploding as they hit the earth; giant tanks crashed into each other, becoming incandescent like lamps . . . Millions of tracer bullets tore through the darkness. . . .

With each of the thin lines by which I marked the passing of the days I knew that I was nearer to madness.

# The Lost Footsteps

For about two weeks now I had been woken by a scream com
ing from a cell which must have been about ten yards from mine.
It was a woman's voice and the scream held a note of indescribable
terror. I concluded that this woman, waking up in her narrow cell
with no human being to offer her the slightest consolation, was
screaming to relieve her nightmare existence. When this happened, the officer in charge and the warders rushed to her cell
and tried to muffle the shrieks. I could hear her quite clearly
crying out, struggling, groaning, begging for human company.
Finally her voice would dwindle to an almost inaudible murmur
and die away. Probably an injection of some strong drug made her
fall into a heavy sleep.

One afternoon a man's voice called out:

"Ortansa! Ortansaaa . a . . a . . . a! Do you hear me? I was taken
from Jassy to the prison at Ocnele Mari; I am in cell number four.
I implore you! Send the car this evening to bring me home . . . I
can't bear to stay here any longer—please bring me home! I
implore you . . . I implo . . o . . ore you!"

Jassy is a university town near the Russian frontier. Ocnele
Mari is about 200 miles from it and is famous for its salt-mines
which are worked by convicts.

From this man's voice I took him for an intellectual in his
fifties, a professor or a doctor perhaps. In his frenzy, he hammered
on the door of his cell calling to his wife, apparently unaware that
the secret prison where he was detained was in Bucharest. The
officer on duty and the warders rushed to his cell and set upon
him:

"What's all the row about? If you've got anything to say, call
for your warder and ask him to bring the officer in charge. If you
go on shouting you'll be whipped to the bone . . ."

"Please let me go home. Ortansa, my wife, is waiting for me, so
are my children. They're worried, they don't know where I've
disappeared to. I know how worried they must be, they'll go mad
if they don't get news of me."

"You'll have to settle that with the Commission," replied the
voice of the officer on duty. "It's asked you for a declaration and

## The Lost Footsteps

you'll go home to your wife and family as soon as you've made it.
Until then, we must keep you here, so it's no use shouting. You
understand?"

"I understand," replied a resigned, stifled voice.

But a few minutes later he was shouting again:

"Ortansa-a-a-a-a! Ortansa-a-a-a-a! Do you hear me? I was
taken away . . ."

Again the warders and the officer on duty hurried to his cell
but the prisoner struggled and, instead of calming down, shrieked
with all his might.

"Ortansa-a-a-a . . .! Ortansa-a-a-a! Come and rescue me from
these Communist vipers. They know I'm a Social-Democrat and
they want to bite me, to kill me with their fangs!"

He got more and more excited; he fought, howled, groaned,
swore. At last he was taken away, down the corridor in the direction of the interrogation rooms. About an hour later he was
brought back. I could hear him stumbling and muttering:

"The Communist vipers have kidnapped me. Death to them!
The Communist vipers have kidnapped me . . . have kidnapped
me . . . have kidnapped me . . .! Death to them . . . death . . .
death . . .! Ortansa, save me . . .!"

He was not the only prisoner whose mind was beyond control.
Every morning, in a cell somewhere to my right, I heard the voice
of a young man shouting: "I am not General Fanfani; I am
Captain Giuliano, his adjutant. There has been a mistake, I am
not guilty."

When the warders came near him Captain Giuliano would
shriek and howl like a wounded animal.

Then, in the silence of the night, a young woman would start
pleading: "Have pity on me. I am pregnant. I am expecting a
baby. Please let me go home so that my child will not be born
here . . ."

She never spoke very loudly. She pleaded, implored her
gaolers to be human, to understand, to have pity. I could hear the
warders trying to calm her by all kinds of arguments. Several hours
would pass, and then again she would beg for compassion. I could

hear her retching at meal times, when the smell of the food always
made her vomit.

Every day at about lunch-time an old man in a cell about half
way down the corridor would beg: "I'm hungry! I'm hungry!
Send me a piece of bread, mother dear!"

Sometimes he recited verses about a matter which apparently
obsessed him:

> *"I have no savings in Beirut!*
> *In Beirut I sold my daughter's body.*
> *That's how I earned my bread!*
> *In Beirut I had no money.*
> *I sold my daughter's body.*
> *That's how I earned my money!"*

I imagined that he was an Armenian or a Greek who had
perhaps once been a rich merchant. Probably he had been locked
up to make him hand over his assets abroad or the gold which he
may have buried somewhere.

Sometimes in the evening a young man woke the whole prison
with his cries: "I am innocent! I am innocent! I have not betrayed
the Party. I have not given in to the Enemies of the People nor to
the Imperialists! I have not made any concessions in the class
struggle! I am devoted to the Party. Why am I being kept locked
up?"

Another, with a high-pitched voice, chanted:

> *"Come, angel of the Lord,*
> *With a flaming sword in your hand.*
> *Come and break down the walls,*
> *Come and break down the door!*
> *Angel of the Lord, deliver me."*

The cries were stifled by threats or by the bedclothes or, when
this had no effect, by an injection or a drug.

Those who had gone out of their minds were left in their cells
for about a fortnight. Then, when the gaolers were satisfied that

their madness was genuine and not a pretence, they were taken away, presumably to an asylum.

The behaviour of those who had lost control over their minds frightened me, for I realised how over-strained I was myself. I had another hallucination, of madmen crowding an immense cavern lit by blazing pine-trees which crackled as the flames rose high into the darkness of the roof. From time to time warders, dressed in the khaki uniforms of the Security Police, seized one of the men and dragged him shrieking and struggling to a river on which a boat shaped like a gondola awaited him. The boatman, in a black cloak with a hood, had the features of my last interrogator, the one whose tone had been so fatherly. The warders forced their captive down on his knees and dragged his head back so that his eyes looked straight into those of the boatman. Then, after a moment, the kneeling man rose to his feet, apparently conscious and master of himself; the warders wrapped him in a white, hooded cloak; serenely he stepped into the prow and standing up, his arms crossed on his breast, looked ahead while the boatman pushed the boat into the middle of the river where an unseen current bore it swiftly down-stream. Only then did the other madmen catch sight of the gondola floating majestically onward with its two upright figures at the prow and at the stern. Seizing torches of burning pine they rushed down to the river bank and there they began to turn round and round as if directed by a ballet master, spinning faster and faster while the gondola vanished through a pointed opening as high as a church steeple. Then the madmen suddenly became aware of my presence and invited me by gestures to join their dancing. "Come, dance with us," they seemed to say. "Come, shout and howl with us. It's the only way to stop thinking and when you have stopped thinking you will know the rare happiness which is our lot!" And such was the strength of their appeal that I could feel a scream forming in me and rising to my lips and it was all I could do to silence it by clutching at my throat and stopping my mouth with the palm of my hand. I felt that the moment I screamed something in my brain would snap. I strove desperately to master the impulse towards lunacy, to throw off my hallu-

cinations and to come back to the world of reality; but I knew
that only a small incident was needed to release the suppressed
scream.

"Doctor, please don't go without helping me. I am an old, sick
woman, please help me to be taken to hospital."

The plea was made in a gentle voice which seemed very
familiar to me. Where had I heard that voice before and that sad
restrained sobbing which seemed to come from the cell two doors
away? Then I remembered: the voice reminded me of my mother
at my brother's funeral when she had cried in just that same
gentle, pitiful way.

Next day the same scene was repeated, but this time I could
hear more clearly. A man whom I took to be the prison doctor was
saying: "I am sorry, it doesn't rest with me. It's true, you are ill
and you ought to be in hospital. But only the Interrogator in
charge of your case can let you go."

"Please, doctor! Do something to help me! Don't leave me in
this state . . ."

Surely the voice was my mother's. Surely I couldn't be
mistaken. Since the day before I had been obsessed by it and now
I was almost certain that it was my mother who was in the nearby
cell though I argued with myself that that was impossible. But on
the ninetieth day of my imprisonment I had been taken to the
interrogator who, perhaps to assess my psychological condition,
had briefly questioned me and then given me a little talk: "Your
mother will be held responsible for not having denounced you to
the authorities when you came back from abroad. We know for
certain that you met after your return . . ."

I had in fact carefully avoided seeing anyone belonging to me
—but clearly the Interrogator had kept his word all the same.
And what was I to do now?

The régime which the Interrogators imposed on me had, as it
were, caught my mind and soul in a vice and this new agony far
surpassed the pain of flogging.

It was about this time that I became obsessed with the idea of suicide. I was convinced that only my death would save my family and those whom I protected by my silence. But how was I to die ?

For months I had scrutinised every detail of my cell, hoping to find a means of taking my life. The walls were absolutely smooth; the radiator pipes were encased in wood; the window had a close-meshed wire netting between the glass and the bars. I had no hope of getting hold of a cord and still less of finding anything on which to hang it. And even if I had such things, the warder's visits at thirty-second intervals gave me no time to prepare my suicide. In the lavatories the cisterns were fixed so high that they were out of reach and even the chains were encased in pipes cemented into the wall.

In one corner of a lavatory I did find a thick cast-iron pipe—it was part of the drain—fixed to the wall at a height of about ten feet by a large iron ring at each end. It must have escaped the notice of the warders and here it would be possible to suspend a rope.

But where could I find a rope?

While I was trying desperately to find a solution the cell door opened and the officer on duty threw a pair of thin pyjamas on my bed and ordered me to hand over the filthy, evil-smelling shirt which by now had almost rotted away on me. Putting on the clean pyjamas was a pleasant experience; it reminded me of a far-distant life . . . Next day I noticed that one of the mother-of-pearl buttons on the trousers had cracked down the middle, and I managed to break off a sharp splinter, about three-quarters of an inch long.

I intended to cut the veins of my left wrist. First I thought of doing it when I lay down at night—I would have a chance to hide my hand under the quilt and the blood would flow into the mattress; then in an hour or so my heart would stop beating without the warder having noticed anything. But, on second thoughts, what would happen if he ordered me, as he often did,to keep both hands outside the quilt or to turn to face the light? He would certainly notice my increasing pallor, or bloodstains on the bedclothes.

## The Lost Footsteps

My mind then fixed itself on a single problem: how to get hold of a cord. After several days I discovered that there was a thin piping-cord in each of the outside leg-seams of my pyjama-trousers. I could not undo the seams while I was in the cell for the warder would have noticed my movements, but in the lavatory I should have two-and-a-half minutes to myself. I would take my splinter with me and cut the seams just below the waist; then I could pull the cords out with my fingers.

I spent two days and nights going over the time I would need to slit the seams, pull the cord out, tie it to the iron ring in the wall and put my head into the noose . . . I believed that I could do it in sixty seconds; but I thought that the other minute and a half would not be enough to kill me. Each morning I counted the number of seconds I was allowed to remain in the lavatory. When I got to about a hundred and fifty, the warder knocked loudly and ordered me to come out. If after that I delayed a moment he pushed the door open and ordered me to leave. I believed that in order to be sure that I would not survive I needed at least two hundred and forty seconds. A lot would depend on which of the warders was in charge of me when I went to the lavatory.

These young Security men were between twenty and twenty-five years old; judging by their features, speech and manners, most of them came from the suburban slums of Bucharest while some were peasants. Their discipline was perfect. They never entered into conversation with a prisoner; their only answer to a request was "Yes," "No," or "Wait." All these young men lived under the pressure of a stern rule and of perpetual fear of punishment. Even to attempt to get into communication with them was virtually impossible. Yet one of them—I think he was of peasant origin—seemed more tolerant than the others. On one occasion he had allowed me an extra sixty seconds in the lavatory; on these extra seconds I based my hope of committing suicide. But I would have to wait another five days before this "kind" warder was on duty.

Then two days before the moment which I was awaiting so feverishly, the whole team of warders was replaced by a new one and I had to give up my plan. I was overwhelmed by frustration, I felt as if I had been crushed by an avalanche and buried under the debris so that I could scarcely breathe.

After this my hallucinations became very frequent.

One evening, when the radiator had begun its mournful music, the wall in front of me rolled back and a chain of snowy mountains gleamed in the rising sun. In the foreground was a little Indian temple dedicated to the goddess Kali. A tall tree shaded it. At its foot an old man sat with his legs tucked under him and his hands resting on his knees in Brahmin fashion. He had a long and very thin white beard. His ascetic face had the same serenity as the blue sky stretching over the dazzling peaks. As I gazed at him he bowed his head slightly, smiled and said: "I can see you have forgotten me. Don't you remember Aurobin Dogos, the Brahmin?"

I heard myself replying: "You have no idea how long I have been looking for you and calling you . . ."

"I had to make a long journey to get here," he said. "It took me sixty years."

For months after this I lived in the company of the "Brahmin" whom I believed at the time to be a real person other than myself. But these visions were different in character from the nightmare hallucinations I had had before. It seemed that, somehow, I had reached a deeper level of my being and these new experiences, instead of helping my enemies, marked the beginning of a period of spiritual integration.

I held long conversations with the "hermit" and it was "he" who argued me out of committing suicide, persuading me that life was sacred and must be lived to the last breath.

I complained to him that, locked inside these walls and thinking ceaselessly night and day without a moment's respite, I had reached the limits of my endurance. "Tell me," I begged him, "am I the victim of these men who hold me captive, or at the mercy of some harsh, blind laws of nature?"

He explained to me his view of suffering. "Some people it destroys," he said, "other are challenged by it to resist some evil or to undertake some positive, creative act; some are corrupted, lose control over themselves and become cruel and vengeful, others grow in strength and grace."

"But what can a man do alone, armed with nothing but his free will, against an overwhelming evil?" I asked him.

In answer, he told me a story.

Two swallows nested under the eaves of a fisherman's hut near the sea-shore. Teaching their young to fly, they took them out over the sea, gradually training them to cross long distances and to face the hardships they would have to undergo during their migration. The fledgelings shot into the air, exulting in the joy of flight and freedom, but a gust of wind caught one of them and flung it down upon the surface of the waves. The small bird kept its wings outstretched so that it did not sink, but neither could it rise; floating like a leaf, it called piteously to its parents as they circled over it. The parent swallows did their best to calm and to encourage it, then they flew back to the shore and made innumerable journeys to the water's edge, each time carrying a drop of water in their beaks and pouring it into the sand. Thus they hoped to empty the ocean and to save their young.

"Their heroic effort is a lesson to us," the "Brahmin" went on. "The human will and spirit must also not be resigned at moments of crisis; it must go on looking for a solution, however overwhelming the odds. You must not accept defeat, you must not believe your efforts to be in vain. If you have the blind courage to continue to endure and to struggle, you will find a new beginning in your life."

My conversations with the hermit living in solitude near the temple to the goddess Kali had lasted several months. Outside spring was appearing; the strength of the light and a suspicion of warmth in the air were the first signs. Who was the "Brahmin"? Why was he trying to give me precious support? Understanding my perplexity, he gently held out a pale, skeleton-like hand and stroked my forehead with his cold fingers. Somehow transfigured, he said to me with emotion:

"You want to know who I am? I am your spirit; your reason! You appealed to me in a moment of abject despair. In your isolation and helplessness, only I am capable of encouraging you to bolster your morale and strengthen your will; apart from me, there is no one who is able to come to your aid. Put your trust in my strength and you will never regret it!"

This encounter was indeed a turning point in my existence. Gradually my nightmares left me and I discovered an inner calm and balance and achieved control over my mind and body.

After days and weeks of practice I found that I could sit motionless on my chair for hours, my head leaning gently against the wall and my eyes open. I breathed deeply and quietly, my will controlling my heart-beats and keeping them steady. Hunger and fatigue took less toll of my strength than when I had dissipated it in pacing up and down my cell, fighting against drowsiness. My small ration of food and the two or three hours' sleep I was allowed out of the twenty-four were now sufficient for my bodily needs.

To detach my mind totally from my surroundings took more time and effort. At first I told myself that I was a spectator in a darkened room: my prison life was nothing but a film projected on a screen, which I trained myself to interrupt at will. At a later stage I succeeded in looking upon my body, sitting motionless in the chair, as though it were a photograph. Still later I felt my spirit able to escape the prison walls and undertake long journeys.

The warders were puzzled by the transformation which had taken place before their eyes: a man who had been frantic, driven to the verge of madness by lack of sleep, now sat calm and as still as a statue. From time to time they knocked on the door and ordered me to move my head or blink my eyes, to make sure that I was still alive and lucid. Inwardly I had reached a peace and a serenity which I had never known before.

Time no longer dragged; solitude was not a hardship, it was the opportunity for ceaseless contemplation. Freed from its anxieties, my mind devoted itself passionately to pure thought. I now longed to survive—even, if need be, in prison—for I was enchanted by the happiness of my new spiritual freedom. I longed to encompass the universe, to search its mysteries, as inexhaustible as infinity. At the same time this transformation made available to me a source of energy which enormously increased my powers of resistance to my adversaries. This triumph of reason over madness radically changed my whole life. I believe now that, through the discipline of contemplation, I did in fact arrive at a new philosophy based on the values of humanism and the laws of concord. Freeing myself from theories and beliefs, I became conversant with the laws of the universe and developed a new understanding of suffering, freedom, discord and harmony, revolution and evolution.

In this book of factual events there is no place for a philosophical treatise. I mention it only because it was the development of these ideas which gave me the will to stay alive in order to pass them on to the West.

The young Security Lieutenant who sat behind the desk in the interrogation room was unknown to me. He looked at me for a moment with an expression of curiosity. The strong daylight falling straight on his head from a window high up in the wall brought out the red tints in his wavy hair. Without any preamble he began to tell me about a wolf-hunt he had taken part in the day before (it was a Sunday). His story was full of detail: the journey to the Danube Delta with two other officers, keen huntsmen; the night spent in a fisherman's cottage; the lying in wait; the beaters, the wolves coming out of their lairs among the reeds; the joy of being free, active, and able to enjoy the beauty of the spring landscape; the return to Bucharest.

"But although I was out of town I was thinking a great deal about you," he went on in a friendly voice. "We are much concerned about those who have been overwhelmed by the exceptional circumstances of our time. The historical process we are living through is not only hard for those who have misunderstood it and opposed it but for those of us who have brought it about and are carrying it through. The difference between us is that because dialectical materialism is a science we can see our way clearly ahead and achieve success after success. The Party makes no mistakes. Such small errors as happen are made by individual institutions or individual members, and they are soon put right.

"But this is not what I meant to talk to you about. The Comrade Attorney has asked me to see you and find out about your health. Have you any complaints about your food or the warders in attendance on your cell? Today it is exactly two hundred and twenty days since your arrest, and it is our duty to make a check-up after such a time. Have you any requests you wish to make?"

The envoy of the Comrade Attorney brought me back into a world from which I had become estranged. His polite message from a high-ranking authority was a great surprise to me. I replied dryly: "Thank you for your interest in my lot. My health is all right. I have no complaints about my warders and my food is satisfactory."

"Would you like an extra slice of bread?" he interrupted. "The Comrade Attorney would be willing to grant such a request."

"Thank you, but the food ration I am getting is enough. Please ask the Attorney, however, if I could have a few books, and permission to send a few lines to my family."

The young officer—he could not have been more than twenty-five—reddened with anger at my refusing the Attorney's generous offer of a piece of bread. He said sarcastically: "At the moment that's impossible. You must first answer the questions put to you by the Commission . . . Perhaps, after a few more years you'll have learned how to behave in a prison, and then you'll be allowed to read and to write home."

Dissatisfaction was written all over his face when he rang for the warder.

That same evening I was taken before another officer, this time a Captain.

He proudly told me of his proletarian origin and his record as a Communist. The old régime had given him a ten-year sentence for his underground activities; the Party, in recognition of his services, had appointed him Interrogator, thus giving him an opportunity to play his part in the campaign against the "enemies of the people."

He interrogated me on and off for nearly forty-eight hours and ended with an outburst of horrible threats. Most of his questions concerned my helping people to escape abroad and were a repetition of those put to me by the Commission seven months earlier. They were skilful and probing, though as usual, to avoid giving me a clue as to how much was already known to the Commission, they remained fairly general.

Afterwards, once again enclosed in my cold cell under the unsleeping eye of the warder on duty, I sat motionless on my chair, trying to regain my calm. But I was shivering violently and I felt a pain in my kidneys as if they had been caught and squeezed by forceps.

The prison was a strange institute of psychiatric research, in which the research workers tried to read the thoughts of men shut up in cages and constrained by every means to offer themselves for experiment; but I for my part could study these experts, down to the smallest detail of their science. Only those within its walls could understand its secrets, and as few of them emerged into the light of day the secrets remained locked within its dungeons. But as a human guinea-pig I was one of those who had the chance of studying them closely.

It was a paradox that prison life was calculated and built up to appear as harmonious and as inevitable as the stars in their courses.

The impression created was that of a small collective society whose life was based on harmony. But happiness and contentment, the fruits of harmony, were absent; instead were hatred, unhappiness, cruelty, slow destruction and despair. In this struggle of opposites the victors imprisoned the conquered and created a strange relationship. The harmony was not true harmony, but a kind of concord imposed by force.

The vanquished were forced to live a life which was mercilessly imposed upon them by a power which had absolute dominion over them. There was no other power to appeal to, no one to defend them or to judge them impartially.

Moreover this forced concord now constituted one of the basic laws of the "New World" built by the victorious Communists. The "New Society" was divided into two classes, the leaders and the warders (the Security Police); these compelled the mass of the people to live according to their model of collective life.

The only difference between the forced concord within the prison and the forced concord imposed on the millions outside was the degree of constraint and the method of its application, and the resultant difference in degree of suffering and of despair. In essence the two ways of life were the same.

It was true that Communist theoreticians held out the ideal of a classless society and of the "withering of the State"—of a society without injustice or compulsion. But this was to be reached at the end of a ruthless "dialectical" struggle of opposites, and it was clear to me that it was quite impossible for this to be a means to such an end.

Sitting in my cell, I had a vision of our century in which the soul and spirit of man were going through a decisive test. Not only social systems but religions and philosophies were passing through the fire of a terrestrial purgatory. The fate of millions of human beings in centuries to come depended on the triumph or defeat of positive, eternal values, and on every man's capacity to understand and to defend them.

## CHAPTER XII

THE BELLS of a nearby church were announcing urgently that the day was Sunday. They brought me a memory of an Easter Sunday in my childhood, early in May, and I saw myself, after the Liturgy, running about in the long grass of the churchyard in our village under the blossoming cherry and plum trees. It seemed now a vision of a world in which only angels dwelled.

"Put your spectacles on," said the warder. "First get into these." The pale young subaltern who was on duty held out the usual dirty metal eyeshades, but this time also a cloth jacket and a pair of cotton trousers. I put them on over my pyjamas.

A few moments later he opened a door at the end of a passage and banged it behind me. I was in a cell of the same size as my own but with two bunks, one above the other. A man with a very pale round face was sitting by the radiator. He had a thatch of silvery hair and a beard reaching to his chest. He looked about sixty. Seeing me, he got up with a surprised, questioning smile.

"I am Stelian Ionescu," he said. To look into my face he had to raise his head as he was much shorter than I am. For the first time in all these months a man had smiled at me.

"Don't confuse me with Ionescu, the painter," he went on quickly. "He's famous, and he's much older than I am. I was a teacher at the Lazar grammar school. Then in 1941 an influential friend offered me a job at the Central Statistical Institute and by an unfortunate chain of events this led to my arrest. But who are you? How did you get here? When were you arrested? Do you know what prison we are in? Do you know the date? Have you any news from outside?"

He spoke in a very low whisper—he reminded me that this was the only way prisoners were allowed to communicate with each other. I told him my name, the date of my arrest and, briefly, how

174

# The Lost Footsteps

I had returned from Paris in order to save some of my friends, only to find that they had been arrested already.

"Ah, wonderful Paris! I know it from my student days; I spent a month there one summer long ago . . . What a splendid city! What parks and gardens, and what art treasures! What a pity you didn't stay there . . . I'd be so happy to live even under the stairs in a house in Paris—if only I could walk about in freedom in its streets and parks and palaces and museums . . . But I see you don't know what date it is today! It's the 5th of May, 1951. And this is the secret prison by the Malmaison barracks, kept for the investigation of special cases. Once, when I was taken out for exercise in the prison yard, I caught sight of a cornice of the barracks where, in my youth, I did my military service, and the bells of the little church next door gave me another clue."

From the 18th of September, 1950—the date of my arrest—to the 5th of May, 1951, two hundred and twenty-seven days and nights had passed. The presence of another human being and the chance to talk put me in a state of over-excitement and well-being. The first day in my new cell passed like a flash.

Stelian Ionescu had been arrested on a charge of having connived in the repatriation of some 20,000 Roumanians who had lived for several generations in Transnistria, in Western Ukraine. During the war this territory had come under Roumanian Military Command and the repatriation of our nationals was organised by the Statistical Institute. Ionescu had been inspector-general of the commission sent to carry out the scheme. After the Armistice, however, the Soviet Military Command in Bucharest had ordered the 20,000 Roumanian repatriates to be sent back at once to Transnistria, and the repatriation scheme was declared to have been a war crime. When this became known, fear of arrest had determined Stelian Ionescu to try, together with some friends, to escape to Paris. After February 1948, when the Communists launched their campaign against the Social-Democrats, an anti-Communist and anti-Russian party, Ionescu who for years had been an active member of it became still more anxious to get away, but he was unsuccessful, for the friends he hoped would help him

175

had disappeared. He was arrested in January 1950. Now he had been waiting for over a year for his interrogations to end; when they did, he would be sent for trial by the Military Court.

After two days, a warder told me that I could now lie down whenever I wished and, to make my happiness complete, I was taken out with my fellow-prisoner into the yard for ten minutes' exercise.

It was eight months since I had felt the warm rays of the sun, and the cloudless day filled me with a painful longing. We were in a prison yard, guarded by armed soldiers, but the air was full of spring and a plum-tree, heavy with blossom, leaned over the back wall. A few tufts of straggling grass and three stalks of shepherd's purse grew between the flagstones. After the winter frost, new sap was rising from the thin roots which clung to the crumbs of earth between the stones—it seemed to me a symbol and an encouragement.

We did not go out again for three months. In the meantime, cells roofed with wire-netting had been put up in the yard, so we no longer had the feeling of being almost in the outside world, but even so the ten minutes' fresh air we were allowed was a blessing.

The alleviation in my conditions was an immense relief to me. On the other hand, I found that I had lost something of the serenity which I had achieved in solitary confinement. I was not sufficiently established in the way of contemplation for the peace it gave me to be proof against distractions and, now that my outward circumstances were a little more normal, I realised once again how severely my nervous system had been strained. I was allowed more sleep and I tried to take advantage of the permission, but the creaking of my cell-mate's bed or the slight sound of the metal disc over the peephole being moved now woke me up and gave me palpitations; however hard I tried, I could not succeed in sleeping soundly and continuously, without nightmares.

Our life, lived slowly, moment by moment, in the narrow cell, was naturally favourable to friendship. My companion proved to be a well-read man, sensitive, attentive and cultured, and our conversations were a real joy to me. Gradually we came to talk about our memories, and fragmentary though our stories were, we could soon have reconstructed many periods of each other's lives. I, however, remained permanently on guard and allowed no detail to pass my lips which could give a clue to the interrogators. Not that I had any reason to be suspicious. Ionescu's attitude was beyond reproach; his questions were never pressing and we were never taken separately out of the cell. Our treatment was identical except that he received five cigarettes a day. Still, I thought it better to be prudent.

One day, as he was shuffling up and down in his felt slippers, talking about the causes of our misfortunes and whether we could ever become free of them, he stopped, pointed a finger at me and, looking at me searchingly with his green eyes, said: "You'd be horrified if you could see yourself—pale and thin and bent as if you had a millstone round your neck. As for me, how old do you think I am? Fifty? Sixty? In a few months I'll be forty! That surprises you? And well it may: even my mother wouldn't recognise me. You know, I was arrested before her eyes . . ."

His father was dead; he had kept a hairdresser's establishment in Bucharest but, as he wanted something better for his only son, he made many sacrifices in order to send Stelian to the University. As the months passed, Ionescu told me many stories about his childhood and adolescence.

His closest friends when he was a student were Mendel Mendelovici and Ion Dumitrescu. Together they went to concerts, plays and operas—in the gallery of course. They also visited the Morgue and watched the dissection of corpses, in order to experience "the stark realities of life." Sometimes they attended lectures on psychiatry, at others they did the rounds of the notorious night-clubs of the Crucea de Piatra quarter. They were all voracious readers and spent the little money they had on books.

All three were in love with Liliana, a girl of their own age. But Liliana would pay no attention to Dumitrescu; he became increasingly wretched and, one day during the summer holidays, he shot himself beneath her window. He died in hospital after two days of agony. "Lord!" commented Stelian Ionescu now. "Why didn't I know then what prison life was like? If I had, I guarantee I could have cured him of his love! I'd have locked him up and kept him on a little bread and water for six months . . . Left alone with his soul, my poor friend would soon have realised how pointless it is to sacrifice one's life for someone else's whims!"

His reminiscences followed one upon another like the tales in the *Arabian Nights*.

"My childhood and youth were not as innocent as yours," he said with a note of sadness in his voice. "I never knew the joy of swinging on the branch of a willow tree on the edge of a blue lake . . . I did not spend my holidays with kind grandparents, or eat honey from the comb, gathered by the bees from mountain flowers." He was silent for a while, then he continued: "I went on seeing Liliana after Ion's death, for by that time she had settled her affections on me."

One evening he had taken Liliana home; they had found themselves alone in the house and, one thing leading to another, had ended up under the dining-room table. At the height of their passion they were surprised by the girl's parents who had come in quietly. Naturally there was a scene; they refused to let her marry him because his father was a hairdresser and also because they were orthodox Jews. They sent her to Paris; with her went another girl, a cousin who wanted to continue an affair with a distant relation of hers who had married and settled in France. Two months later they were followed by Mendel Mendelovici, the third friend, who by then had become home-news editor on the newspaper *Timpul*. Before leaving Bucharest Mendel handed over his job to Stelian; they parted on the best of terms, although Mendel knew what had happened between Liliana and Stelian.

This long story, filled with farcical incidents, ended in a tragedy. Liliana decided to bestow her love on Mendelovici and they planned to spend the summer on the Côte d'Azur. But the German advance overtook them. Liliana, her cousin and her cousin's lover were arrested by the Gestapo and taken to Auschwitz where they were gassed. Mendel alone escaped. He enlisted in the French army and was on active service when he fell into the hands of the Germans. Since he was a prisoner of war his life was spared, and after his release at the end of hostilities he was awarded the Legion of Honour and granted citizenship by the French in recognition of his services. The last news Stelian Ionescu had of him was that he was a successful journalist, married to the daughter of a rich English industrialist and had become an active member of the French Socialist Party.

Liliana was not the only girl in Ionescu's youth. After she had left for Paris he became attracted to a fellow-student of his at the University. "Indeed," he told me, "I was very much in love with her, and she reciprocated my feelings."

Stelian took his degree and became a schoolmaster while still keeping his job on the *Timpul*. His liaison continued until one day, as they were strolling under the blossoming lime trees in a quiet street, the girl told him her parents were pressing her to marry a rich old man, an Academician, who had asked them for her hand. Her parents were poor and she had four sisters, all as yet unmarried. They urged her to make this sacrifice in order to restore the family fortunes and to make it easier for the other girls to marry. She felt it was her duty to consent.

Ionescu fell into a fury, snatched the felt hat from the young woman's head and tore it into shreds; he told her she had only refused his repeated proposals of marriage because she liked to live in the fine surroundings she had known before her parents lost their money.

"She married the old man," Stelian said bitterly. "And now, at this very moment, while I'm locked up in this filthy cell, she's living in the Palace of the Diplomatic Mission in Ankara where her husband is Ambassador. I'm sure it was the influence of her family that made him join the Party in power, for he could not have been sympathetic to Communism . . . Still, I've never succeeded in getting her out of my mind and heart, and who knows, perhaps she too thinks about me sometimes."

I was fascinated by Ionescu's stories and by his state of mind. He told me he felt deep remorse for what he called his past mistakes. One of them was his unkindness to his mother. He kept a *garçonnière* and took advantage of his mother's fondness for him to make her do his housework. "Think of it," he now exclaimed, "she was old and ill, and I made her go out every morning to do my shopping and clean my flat! I even let her make the very bed which I had shared with Angela the night before! And I spent five thousand *lei* a month on that girl and I never gave my mother more than twenty!"

While he was still a student he had become an atheist. In his despondency at the thought that God did not exist he decided to do good to people so that their gratitude should comfort him in his despair. His thirsty soul was longing to be loved, if only for his generosity. For much the same reason he became a Social Democrat.

He gave up his flat and went back to live in his parents' house. They kept him and asked for nothing but a little kindness in return, while he distributed his salary (which was quite respectable by now) to all and sundry and thus won admiration and praise.

"It's only now I've realised," he said, "that I had no idea what goodness means. I ought before all else to have given my affection to my parents, to my sister and, when I married, to my wife. But their love got on my nerves and so I spent my money, time and energy on total strangers."

When his father died, Stelian, grudging the money for a hearse, borrowed a lorry from the Statistical Institute. According to his outlook at that time, a funeral meant no more than that a body on the point of decomposing should be put into the ground.

"I stood on the step of the lorry," he continued, "and kept telling the driver to go a little faster. It was raining. All the prayers and halts on the way to the churchyard which the ritual prescribed seemed to me a frightful waste of time. When we came home, a few friends came in with us to eat the dinner which my mother had prepared. One of them had brought the Banner of the Guild of Hairdressers. It had a symbolic razor, scissors and brushes painted on it . . . All the guests ate heartily. They laughed and talked about my father. I realised how much they had in

common with him and it put me in a rage. When they asked for
still another little glass of brandy to drink in memory of the
deceased, I hid the bottle so that they should go."

Ionescu passed his fingers wearily through his hair and pressed
his palms to his greying temples. His eyes were full of tears when
he looked up.

"When I think of my indifference towards my father all those
years when he was ill and could not leave the house, I feel as if my
head would burst with pain. He wanted me to sit and talk with
him a little, but I never had a moment, I was always rushing off to
see to someone else. The memory of his expression haunts me to
this day. And my stinginess at his funeral! And my contempt
towards his friends! I realise now that by their stories and their
talk about him they were keeping him alive.

"Now I live only for the day when I'll be free of these accursed
walls—I cannot wait to make up for my past mistakes. I'll never
come to terms with myself till I have started a new life."

The hope he clung to was that his mother was still living in
their little house in the Strada Foisorul de Foc. There he would
find his room, peace, his books. He wanted to be present at the
seventh anniversary of his father's death when, according to the
Orthodox ritual, the remains would be exhumed. He would dig up
the earth with his own hands; kneeling and praying, he would
wash the bones in holy water and would bury them again in a small
casket in the same earth—all except the skull: this he would bring
home and keep under a glass dome on his desk, so that every day
for the remainder of his life he could go down on his knees before
it and beg his father's forgiveness at sunrise and at sunset, at
midnight and when the clock struck three in the morning.

His other ambition was to be reunited to his wife, Marguerita,
though it seemed to me that his feelings towards her were confused
and he told the strangest stories about her. He suspected her of
bringing him ill-luck. When I looked surprised he told me she
had been engaged three times before he met her. Her first fiancé
had gone to study law at the Sorbonne and after taking his degree
had come home by steamer along the Danube. Marguerita waved

## The Lost Footsteps

to him from the harbour and, before her very eyes, he slipped, fell and was crushed to death between the boat and the quay. The second man Marguerita had loved was an airman whose plane crashed into a lake. The third was drowned in his bath; he was an officer in the Security Police and it was never established whether his death was due to accident or to foul play.

"And I'm the fourth man in her life!" sighed Ionescu. "And here you see me, buried in this tomb, not quite dead and not quite alive. Still, to be quite honest," he added, "I'd had plenty of bad luck before I met her."

He and Marguerita had refused to marry in church and had thereby much upset their parents. Nagged by remorse, he now cherished a dream: One evening he would be taken out of the cell, the metal shade over his eyes, put into a car and dropped somewhere on the outskirts of the city—free. (This was the normal method used by the Security Police when they released a prisoner; the object was to make him lose his sense of direction so that he should not learn what prison he had been kept in.) As soon as possible after his release he and Marguerita would be married in church with no one present but the priest. He saw himself in his black suit, white waistcoat and patent-leather shoes, a thin gold chain reaching from one waistcoat pocket to the other. Marguerita would wear a simple, elegant black gown, a single orchid pinned to the *corsage*.

Outside a handsome carriage drawn by two white horses would be waiting for them. It would drive them to the entrance of a park and they would walk along a peaceful alley to a certain bench, for it was there that on a summer evening long ago he had kissed Marguerita for the first time and asked her to be his wife. Then the carriage would drive them at the same unhurried, aristocratic pace back to the centre of the town. He hoped that a sudden shower would drench the streets so that, from the warm, comfortable interior of the carriage, they could admire the play of street lights on the glistening pavements.

They would dine alone in a private room at the best restaurant in town. The table would be covered by white damask and set with

182

## The Lost Footsteps

porcelain, silver plate and crystal goblets—not to mention excellent food and wines served by an elderly, white-haired waiter in tails. Afterwards they would go home on foot, arm-in-arm, chatting and joking. His parents' house would be awaiting their return, its windows brightly lit and the din of many cheerful voices reaching them as they crossed the yard. The rooms would be full of guests, invited in advance but ignorant as yet of the occasion of the party. Ionescu and his bride would take their places in the middle of the room; surrounded by his friends and relations he would announce his news: he had come back to the Faith! His church wedding was the token of his pact with God.

The family would shed tears of joy, congratulations would be poured upon him, and there would follow a festive supper which his mother had prepared. But the clearest image in Ionescu's mind was that of an old fiddler who would play romantic music and songs handed down from princely weddings, some gay, others recalling tales of tragic love.

Ionescu's reparation for his past mistakes was, however, to go still further. Across the street from his parents' house stood the Radu Voda church; its walls were defaced by age and almost crumbling. Stelian would offer his and Marguerita's services to renovate and paint the building (she had studied at an art-school and was a gifted painter). Together they would paint the walls with frescoes like those on monastery churches built under Stefan cel Mare, ruler of Moldavia, centuries ago. In return, their names would be engraved among the donors and the founders on the plaque in the church porch. As donors they would be entitled to be buried at the foot of the church walls—and this Ionescu passionately wanted, for his childhood with its unforgettable Christmas and Easter holidays was bound up with this little church, its churchyard and its garden. His humble wish was that his body, after death, should lie in the patch of hallowed soil which, for a quarter of a century, he had avoided as if it were cursed.

Ionescu's grief over his errors was only equalled by his resentment at the ill-luck which, he assured me, had dogged him persistently ever since his student days.

## The Lost Footsteps

Motivated by the loftiest ideals, he and a group of his student friends had founded a review with Leftist tendencies. It continued publication for some years, then the little group disbanded, some of its members going over to the Communists while others remained Social Democrats.

"You'll find it hard to believe," he said, "how unlucky I have been. One of the students with whom I founded the review became a journalist. In 1935 he was sentenced to a ten-month term in prison for a so-called violation of the press-laws: he had written a few clever articles in which he criticised the King and some of the politicians. Every week I took him a little food and a small sum of money to the prison. Ten years later he became a Communist and his prison sentence ensured his membership of the Academy under the new régime. Several others of my friends joined the Communists when the Social-Democratic Party was dissolved— today they are all Ministers or university professors. If only I had known the turning I should take at certain crossroads of my life, I too could have had at least a Chair at the University. But I was led astray by my idealism ..."

When he left prison he meant to isolate himself from the world, which now disgusted him.

"But what will you live on?" I asked him. "From what you've told me, you have no private means ..."

"I've thought about that," he smiled. "I'll become a calligrapher."

"But what would be the use of that in our times?" I asked, surprised.

We were talking, as we always did, in whispers. We sat on either side of the little table in our cell, our heads bent over it to hear as well as possible. Ionescu's eyes shone with an inner happiness as he described his future profession.

"I'll go out into the street in front of our house, and there I'll sit on a chair with its back to our fence. Some old woman or other will go by: I'll stop her and ask her about her family. If by any chance she has a son who is away somewhere—doing his military service or working in another town—I'll offer to write him a nice

letter from his mother. It will be enough for her to give me an idea
of what she wants to say, and I will write a letter in the style of the
old craftsmen, with illuminations and flourishes such as only too
few people know today."

The old woman, he thought, would give him a little money, or
perhaps an egg or a piece of bread for his pains. But he was even
ready to exercise the profession of calligrapher free of charge, only
to be able to sit on the chair, against the fence of his parents' house,
in the street which he had known for forty years. He longed to see
people coming and going, to greet them, to exchange a friendly
word with them, to be appreciated for the modest services he
would be rendering them. In his humble situation nobody would
envy him, no one would do him any harm; and so his life would go
on, year by year, until the hour of his death, serene and innocent of
any further misfortunes.

Ionescu had forgotten, of course, that his native street was by
now paved and lit by electricity, and that the town was ruled by a
dictatorship which planned the life of every single citizen. The
calligraphers who wrote letters, protests, or petitions—some of
them perhaps in that very street—had lived a hundred years ago,
when few of the common people in the city could read or write.

To Ionescu his family house was an ivory tower. He hoped he
would still find in it his library, a collection of some four thousand
five hundred volumes, which he had put together at great sacrifice
over more than twenty years. The idea that the Security Police
might have confiscated these treasures, or that the State might in
the meantime have decreed that all such libraries would be
nationalised, drove him to the depths of despair. "Ah, my books!"
he would exclaim. "If only I find them intact! If they are not on
their shelves, I shall take my life!" They were catalogued in his
memory, and he would recite the titles, authors' names, editions,
dates of publication, sizes, sometimes even to the number of pages,
with an ease which was astounding to me. Yet he complained that
his many and varied occupations had prevented him from reading
as much as he would have liked. Even of his own books he had read
only about as many as took up five out of his seventy yards of

bookshelves. He hoped that in his retirement he would read a yard of books each year . . .

"According to your calculations that would mean," I said, "that you'll have to go on reading your own books for another sixty years or so. You'll have to live to be at least a hundred to read them all."

"Don't imagine I haven't already worked that out," replied my cell-mate rather crossly. "I shall try to read as much as possible!"

He was obviously enchanted by the idea that most of his time would be spent in the company of the greatest human minds —thinkers, philosophers, poets—in an atmosphere of spiritual communion and great serenity of spirit. He called this last phase of his existence his "Retreat to Olympus."

He had, in the past, himself written several books of poetry, and a provincial publisher had brought them out, at the rate of one a year, in five small volumes. From poetry he had passed on to literary criticism, and in prison he had written a historical novel about the life of a family of Roumanian aristocrats during the last three centuries. But one day his manuscript of more than seven hundred pages had been taken away by the warder on the pretext that it had to be "checked."

In his more optimistic moods he hoped that it would some day reappear. He said that in his will he had left his writings to certain cultural institutions; his nephew or his nephew's heirs would hand them over to them when the Communist régime had ended. The Academy would then decide their fate.

It would be hard for anyone to imagine how interminable were our days. Stelian Ionescu's tales filled the blank to some extent. His remorse, his longing to survive, his hope that the twenty-first century would bring him back into the limelight moved me. My liking for him grew, but the suspicion and prudence which had guided me in our first weeks together continued to direct me, though I had indeed come to believe that my cautiousness was morbidly exaggerated.

Six months had now passed and never once had my cell-mate

# The Lost Footsteps

been taken separately from our cell. Nevertheless, reason still warned me not to tell him any incidents from my past which could bring harm either to others or to myself.

Nearly every Sunday Stelian gave a musical recital for my benefit. His musical memory was excellent. Once he had wanted to be a conductor and in order to learn this art he had spent hours on end in front of a large mirror, conducting an imaginary orchestra. In the performances he gave in our cell he softly whistled melodies which only I could hear. The programme always began with the Pilgrims' March from *Tannhäuser*; then conductor and orchestra passed on to motifs from *Lohengrin, Parsifal, Siegfried* and the *Meistersingers*. Sometimes he enchanted me with fragments from Beethoven's symphonies, or arias from the operas of Verdi, Rossini, Donizetti or Leoncavallo. The concert always ended with either Chopin's or Beethoven's funeral march. His gestures as he conducted his invisible orchestra were impeccable, impressive. Locks of hair fell over his forehead and he sweated with enthusiasm.

At other times we would spend the evening on an imaginary crawl round the once-famous pubs of Bucharest. We would sample the sparkling wines and feel their strength intoxicating us and evoking buried memories. A band of fiddlers played Roumanian songs (Ionescu softly whistled them) and the words and tunes which had a special charm and meaning for us made us forget our cell.

The summer went by. The October chill was already creeping in. I was afraid that the day of our parting might be drawing near: one or other of us might be transferred to another cell, or even to another prison. This almost made me overcome my wavering doubts and decide to tell Ionescu about that part of my life which I had not so far revealed to him. His case was less serious than mine; he had a chance of being, if not released, at least transferred to an ordinary prison and from there he could smuggle out a message to the outside world. My idea was that, through him, I might be able to send my friend Professor Mironescu some news of my fate, and perhaps even give him the necessary instructions so

187

that he could let my friends in the West know what had become of me.

"What is the date?" I asked Ionescu on the morning of the day which I had chosen for my confidences.

"I think it's the 13th of October," he replied.

I had only said a few words to prepare the ground when I heard the grating of the iron bolt and the door opening. I was surprised, for it was not the usual time for the warder to take us to the ventilated cell in the yard. It was the officer on duty who appeared and handed me the metal eyeshades, which meant that I was to be taken along to be interrogated.

When I sat down in front of the low table in the Interrogator's office my knees began to shake with cold, weakness and nervousness. As always the Interrogator examined me silently for a few minutes before speaking. He did not ask about my health, nor about my diet. Abruptly he informed me that I was to write a declaration describing my whole life from birth to the date of my arrest, without leaving out a single detail and including the names of everyone I had ever known. He stressed that the declaration was asked for by the "office of the Comrade Minister," and, as such, it must be written urgently and with special care. While he spoke I looked at him curiously, struck by his haggard, pale, weak face. He looked a sick man; only his dark, shining eyes and his greying temples gave some life and a certain distinction to his appearance.

The duty officer took me to a cell in which a chair and table with pen and paper on it had been set ready. The whole day passed as I wrote page after page. Obviously, it was a new trap. At short intervals, through the peephole, the attentive gaze of the warder took stock of my movements. In the evening the duty officer came back and silently took the sheets of paper from the table, without giving me time to sign them or even to finish the sentence which he had interrupted.

When I got back to my cell, my friend was already tucked up in his blanket. I was shaken by this new development and I lay awake for hours. Exactly a year had passed since I had been flogged and forced to revolve in that interminable circle, and I tried to guess what new attack the Interrogators were preparing. In the morning my cell-mate asked me anxiously what had happened. He seemed worried and ill at ease.

"They took *you* out for another interrogation, although only six months have passed since the last one!" he said. "But they keep *me* here, buried alive. It's fourteen months now since I've set eyes on an interrogator."

He seemed envious of my "luck." Sitting in his usual place by the radiator, he spent several hours in silent thought. Stretched out on the upper bunk, I awaited the officer on duty in a state of overwhelming tension. The Interrogator had spoken of my declaration as urgent; I was sure that I would be taken out again to go on writing it.

The day dragged by. The night, the morning and the whole of the next day lagged with the same oppressiveness, and still the officer did not appear.

More days and nights passed, and after a time my anxiety abated. Life in the cell resumed its normal course, enlivened by long conversations on various topics. I waited, however, for some inkling as to what lay in store for me before giving Ionescu a message for my friends in the world outside.

About the end of October the door opened and the duty officer took me straight to the cell with the writing-table. "The Comrade Major orders you to go on with your declaration from the point at which you left off three weeks ago." He banged the door and shot the bolt, leaving me alone with my thoughts and the white paper on the table. Covering page after page, I went on writing until I was again taken back to my cell at bed-time. There was only one interruption, when a barber was brought in to cut my hair and shave me.

I realised that the interrogating commission wanted this declaration in order to compare it with the one I had made a year before. The three weeks' interval between October 13th and now was no doubt intended to confuse me by making me forget the details I had written down at the beginning of this new statement and the point at which I had left off. Obviously, the Commission hoped to catch me out contradicting myself. I had to use my memory. My brain, however, was in great need of rest.

Just then something happened which disturbed me profoundly. In the morning Ionescu looked at my shaved face and asked me excitedly if I had noticed anything special about the barber.

"Of course!" I said. "It was a different barber!"

"Do you know who he is? It's Nicu!"

"Nicu?"

"Nicu is a friend of mine!"

Ionescu then told me that Nicu had been his father's apprentice and had then worked for him for fifteen years. Stelian and Nicu had become good friends and were almost like brothers—especially in later years when the apprentice actually lived with them as one of the family. But that wasn't the greatest piece of news: Ionescu, who had also been shaved the day before, had taken advantage of a moment's inattention on the part of the warder to whisper a short message to Nicu for his mother and his wife. He was now greatly agitated as he waited for a reply. Curiosity provoked a state of impatience in me too; the coincidence of the arrival of a barber who was a friend of Ionescu's seemed so surprising as to be almost unbelievable.

After four days Nicu kept his word and brought a reply. He had gone to see his friend's mother and his wife; they were still living in the same house; each had a job and earned a small salary; his library was intact and well cared for!

Another week passed; then my cell-mate offered to share with me this means of communication with the outside world. He assured me that Nicu was a man in whom I could have complete confidence. It was a very tempting opportunity, but it would have to be used soon, for Nicu might at any moment be replaced as prison barber. But what if Nicu should tell the prison authorities about my message and show them the address to which I wanted it delivered? He would be given an award, perhaps even a decoration. No! Better to be prudent and give up the idea! So I told Ionescu that I did not want to put Nicu in a situation which

## The Lost Footsteps

would cause him to risk his life and that of his family for the sake of doing me a good turn. He did not insist, but continued to profit by his friend's kindness and sent two other messages to his family.

Christmas was approaching and my heart was heavy with memories of happy Christmas holidays long ago. The cold in the cell became hard to endure. Ionescu had a fur-lined coat which he wore day and night and which made the winter frost easier for him to bear. He was happy to have had encouraging news from his mother, though saddened by the cruel fate which forced him to spend a second Christmas in prison.

When the cell door was thrown open I was sure that I would again be taken to continue my endless declaration. But the duty officer, without opening his mouth, pointed at Stelian Ionescu and handed the metal eyeshades to him.

Two hours passed in silence. When he was brought back he sat down in his corner and remained deep in thought for a long time. I did not disturb him by asking him anything. Towards evening, he walked up and down the cell a little, with short, tottering steps, his fur collar drawn closely round his neck and his hands thrust deep in his pockets. I lay on the upper bunk, with my eyes closed and my arms stretched along the sides of my body in one of the positions which I found conducive to the practice of yoga. Suddenly he said: "You'll never guess why I was taken to the interrogating room today!"

I opened my eyes and looked at him, waiting for him to continue. Very agitated, he told me a piece of news which had greatly raised his hopes: the Prosecutor had read out his indictment and informed him that he would shortly be sent for trial to the Military Court, and that the Act applying to his case provided for a sentence of two years only!

"If I am lucky enough to get all these months of detention taken into account—and the Prosecutor told me this was possible—I might be discharged at once! In January it will be exactly twenty-four months since I was arrested."

Tears shone in his eyes at the thought of seeing his wife and his mother. The whole evening he talked about his books and the new life he would lead after his release.

His impatience, however, became unbearable as the days dragged slowly by. Eventually the first week of January 1952 came round. Then one morning Stelian Ionescu said to me: "My dear friend, I realise that your return from the West has put you in a very difficult situation, and Heaven only knows when you will get out of it. For the last few days I have been racking my brains to think of some way of helping you. Perhaps, when I've been home for a month or two, I could send a message for you to someone? I would take it myself, or send it by my nephew who is devoted to me—and of course I'm ready to do anything else you'd like me to. In all these months together, in this cell, I have got to know you and appreciate you, and now that the day of parting is near, I should like to feel that I can do you a good turn."

Ionescu's words both moved and disturbed me. It seemed as if a guardian angel had walked in and offered me a messenger. Ionescu could not only send a few words to a friend: in the remaining days we had together I could tell him all that had happened, and also my new conceptions, and as soon as he got home he could write it all down. And everything he had written could be sent to the West through Professor Mironescu. Stelian Ionescu was an educated man, it would be easy for him to do it. This was very different from using Nicu the barber!

His trial had been fixed for January 1952, though Ionescu had not yet been told the exact date. Any day now he might be transferred to the prison of the Military Court. I had to make up my mind.

The decision was a frightful strain. Supposing Ionescu was not, after all, to be trusted? Once I was no longer the sole guardian of my secrets, how could I be absolutely certain that they would not ultimately fall into the wrong hands? Again and again I asked myself what I was to do.

What troubled me was the appearance of Nicu the barber and the coincidence of his old friendship with Stelian. This could easily have been a trap set by the Commission for Ionescu and through him for me. It occurred to me that my cell-mate might even be released—provisionally—and then watched in the hope of intercepting some message I had given him. Ionescu might himself be innocent, but too naïve to see the role which was intended for him.

After several days and nights of mental turmoil, I hit upon a plan which, if Ionescu were kept on a string, could not do any harm to anyone.

"If you are released soon and go home—as God grant you may—I should be very grateful if you would do me the good turn you offered to, the other day," I told him. "This is how you could be useful to me . . ."

I asked him to visit a relative of mine—an old man living in a far-away village in Moldavia. I told him how to find the village and the old man's house. Through this intermediary my message would be passed on to my parents in Cluj, some 250 miles distant from his village. My message was very simple: that I had come back to Roumania against their advice and that the inevitable had happened—I had been arrested. I wanted them to know I was alive, and that I could feel in my heart that their love would protect me from all evil.

Ionescu promised that he would carry out my wish as soon as he was sure that he wasn't being followed and could undertake the journey to Moldavia.

"But perhaps you'd like me to see some friend of yours in Bucharest? It would be easier and quicker. Though, of course, I'm ready to do anything you wish . . ."

I thanked him but explained that the few friends I had had in Bucharest had either been arrested or had escaped abroad, so that there was no one to whom I could send a message. Ionescu did not insist further.

After this, our life continued in the same rhythm as before. There was so little room that when one of us wanted to walk about, the other had to lie down on his bed. Our conversations were just as friendly as ever. The officer on duty appeared at long intervals and took me to another cell, sometimes for a day, sometimes only for an hour or so, to go on writing my declaration. All this time I was waiting for some clue which would make it possible for me to decide whether I could put my complete confidence in Stelian Ionescu.

Since the autumn of 1951 my health had deteriorated: I could no longer digest the half-cooked grains of buckwheat or the hard leaves of sour cabbage which were our daily food. I suffered from terrible pains in my bowels, while the foul air had given me some nasal infection. I spat up a lot of green slime, especially at night, and I thought that my lungs and bronchial tubes had been affected. In conformity with the rules written up on the door of the cell, I asked to see the prison doctor. The Security sergeant who acted as sanitary inspector told me that my request had first to be approved by the Commission. My application was refused.

I had to face the question of how long I could hold out physically, and the decreasing chances of my survival strengthened my wish to take advantage of Ionescu's offer.

The month of January 1952 passed, and still my cell-mate was not transferred to the prison of the Military Court. This fact was the first step towards my enlightenment: the Interrogators were not interested in releasing Ionescu just for the sake of delivering a sentimental message to my parents.

Silence began to reign in the cell. Most of the time I lay on my upper bunk with my eyes closed but wide awake, my mind occupied with dozens of problems. Ionescu lay on the lower bunk, sad and depressed. He complained that he had caught a cold.

Indeed, he was ill. About the middle of February, a swelling appeared on the right side of his head. The prison doctor prescribed some tablets. Sometimes the swelling diminished, but a few days later it would flare up with renewed virulence, causing him much pain. Day by day his head became more swollen, deforming him grotesquely. He had bouts of fever. The doctor ordered penicillin and injections of his own blood, but the infection did not respond. The only hope now was surgery.

Ionescu could no longer get out of bed; he had grown very

weak. He could not even eat or perform the simple necessities of life without my help. He sweated all the time. I helped him to change his damp shirt and washed him gently. The prison doctor, accompanied by the director, visited him every day. Ionescu begged them to send him to hospital.

"We have reported your state of health to the Interrogating Commission. Until we have their approval, we can do nothing further. We are empowered only to give you medical treatment in the cell; obviously, the conditions are not favourable, but that's the best we can do . . ."

His head had become unrecognisable; he had been ill for two months.

The thin but strong daylight announced the beginning of spring. I sat on the chair in the corner by the radiator (Ionescu's favourite seat) so that I could give him the small attentions which he needed all the time. But the greatest service I could do him was to talk to him and try to cheer him up. I spoke to him in whispers for hours on end, even repeating some of his own stories about the life awaiting him at home after his release, and reminding him of his wife and of his mother.

"My dear friend, I feel I'll never see them again," moaned the sick man. "Something tells me I have nothing more to hope for; death is waiting for me in this cell. Then all will be at peace: my mind, my heart, my soul. I am not a good man, as you know. I have made too many mistakes . . . Indeed, my last crime was against yourself! I am afraid the moment has come for me to pay for all my sins."

Stelian Ionescu held out his pale hand and tried to grasp mine. I wiped his sweating forehead and wrapped his blanket closer round him.

"You won't end your days here. I am convinced you will go home," I told him. "You must have the will to live; you must make your body react to your mind, to your spirit, to the dream of returning to your dear ones who are waiting for you."

"Before I die I owe you a confession," he said, his eyes full of tears.

He could hardly speak. I did not interrupt him in the course of his staggering confession, which came so unexpectedly.

During the previous spring he had been taken to one of the interrogating rooms. There, to his great surprise, instead of an interrogator he found George Bogza, the Academician who had been a journalist and a friend of his student days. The conversation began on a friendly note; they spoke of the review they had once published together, then about their later social evolution and the very different paths which they followed. "If only you had taken the same road as I did," said Bogza, "if you had taken the advice I gave you long ago! How dearly you are paying for it now!" Then he told Ionescu that, out of gratitude for his kindness to him when he was in prison fifteen years ago, he had intervened for him with someone in the Politburo. As a great favour, Bogza had obtained a promise that Ionescu should be released, on condition that he made amends for his "political mistakes." By way of reparation for them, and to prove his devotion to the Party which he had once opposed, he must carry out a mission which George Bogza now explained. It involved playing the role of *agent provocateur* in the case of a stubborn prisoner who was causing trouble to his Interrogators. The prisoner had evidence, which he refused to give, in connection with an important action plotted in the West. Bogza assured Ionescu that if he succeeded in this matter which interested even the Minister of the Interior, his dossier would be closed and his trial annulled; not only would he be released, but he would return unblemished to the ranks of society. Bogza convinced him that the Communist régime would last for decades and this decided Ionescu to agree.

For a whole week he had been instructed by a major of the Security Police on the tactics to be used in dealing with the prisoner. He knew that he must not make the slightest mistake, for his own fate depended wholly on his success.

When he had thus opened his heart to me, he grew a little calmer.

"We have lived together in this cell for almost a year. It was inevitable that we should get to know each other well," he said.

## The Lost Footsteps

"Your patience and strength of will in a situation ten times worse than mine, have won my respect. What a pity that I only realised too late how rotten were the means by which I tried to save myself! I am sure that the day will come when you will get your own release honourably from these walls. Please believe me! I bear no grudge against you for my failure; I blame only myself. How could I have been so naïve as to let myself be taken in by what Bogza said? The suffering I endured in solitary confinement last year served as an expiation of my past sins; I felt I was being purified. How then could I have made this last great mistake of trying to save my own life at the price of another man's ruin? O Lord God, how could I have so profaned my soul?"

Ionescu wept weakly, tears and sweat running together down his cheeks. He continued to talk, but the fever made him transfigure his inner conflict and give it a strange turn.

"It pains me terribly to think that I have defiled the memories of my past by turning them into a play which I then acted for your benefit. I hoped to influence you by my acting so that you would give me confidence for confidence." He turned to me with a gleam of his old jauntiness. "Did I tell you?—I studied acting in my youth."

Then he said, as though he were delirious: "At the end of the last act, at the drop of the curtain, the spectator's head was meant to fall under the guillotine. But something dreadful has happened; the stage manager has made a mistake and it's the actor's head that's going to explode! His pus and splinters of his skull will smear the walls. Well! I don't deserve a better fate! It's my own fault! I've always been unlucky! I die hating myself. Instead of retiring to Olympus, I'll retire into the earth! The book I wanted so much to write about my life—what a sinister end it would have had!"

Although Ionescu was exhausted by his frightful remorse, he became lucid enough to point out that his illness and suffering had failed to awaken the slightest human compassion in the hearts of the authorities, and that it was only I—for whose destruction he had worked—who had shown him sympathy and understanding, even though he believed that I had probably suspected his inten-

197

tions. He clutched my arm with feverish, sweating hands and warned me to be on my guard against some other trick of the same kind. "It's the only kindness I can do you before I die," he whispered. He thought that the Security Police had an ulterior motive in refusing to let him go to hospital: as he had failed to trap me they were trying to make sure that I had no suspicion that he was their tool.

"Would it be possible," he concluded, "for you to forgive me; not to hate me? I should like to die reconciled to myself, to you and to all those whom I have wronged."

I replied: "I don't know what will happen either to you or me. But whatever does, let's shake hands and hope that we'll continue to be human beings, not monsters. I don't hate you. You have my sympathy. You are the least to blame; those who bear the greatest guilt are the men in the shadows who have made use of you."

The confessions of Ionescu were a prelude to an attack of meningitis, which in the first week of May 1952 proved fatal. He regained consciousness for a moment before the end, then, as if he had had an electric shock, he gave a great shudder and lay rigid, his mouth and eyes open. He was dead.

# CHAPTER XIII

THE BODY was taken away. Only the pungent smell of the sick man's bedclothes was left to remind me of Stelian Ionescu. After about three weeks, another prisoner was brought in. With Ionescu in mind, I wondered who this tall, thin, white-haired man could be. As the days passed he told me his story; it was weird, romantic, tragic. Three years earlier he had been attached to the Israeli Embassy and had become adviser to the Ambassador. He was closely watched by the Security Police, for the Ambassador was known to have secret contacts with Ana Pauker who, as Foreign Minister, had facilitated the emigration of more than seventy thousand Jews to Israel. Finally he was arrested; now his interrogator wanted not only the names of the intermediaries but those of a number of rich Jews whose gold, jewellery and other assets had been smuggled out by diplomatic bag. The old man had so far managed to resist the pressure put on him by the Commission, and he hoped that he would be ransomed by the World Jewish Congress in Switzerland. His dream was to join his family in Tel-Aviv, where he hoped to write a book of memoirs to be called *The Cell*.

During the time we spent together this old Jew told me about five hundred good jokes; he disappeared one afternoon, just as suddenly as he had appeared.

By now the warm air reminded me that outside it was summer. About this time I was transferred to another cell, of which the occupant was another Jew, a man in his thirties. His blue eyes were a little mad. Solitary confinement and the other methods used by the interrogators had induced him to "confess" to all sorts of fantastic acts of espionage, supposed to have been carried out on the instructions of the Israeli Ambassador.

After he was removed, four other prisoners took his place in

quick succession: an engineer accused of spying on behalf of
Germany and Austria; a lawyer charged with obtaining military
information from his brother and passing it on to Switzerland; an
old businessman—the interrogators wanted him to say where he
had hidden his ten thousand dollars worth of savings; and a
student from the Polytechnic, arrested as a member of a students'
resistance group. The life-stories of these men were deeply moving
and interesting. In the course of our conversations I also learned
some news of the outside world. The Korean war had become
localised. And there was no sign of an anti-Communist revolution.

One morning in April '53—nearly a year after my last interrogation—I was taken into the presence of the same Security officer
whose pale and haggard face had so much impressed me when
I first saw him. He fixed his curious, searching gaze on me and sat
biting a nail on his left hand; his right hand, in a leather glove, lay
on the table and I now realised that it was a wooden one.

After about two minutes' silence he rose and placed a bundle of
about eighty sheets of paper on the table in front of me.

"You know what this is, don't you?" he asked. "You recognise
your own handwriting? This is the declaration you have been
writing at intervals over the last year and a half. You will now
sign it."

Looking me straight in the face, he went on: "You look pleased!
Perhaps you're gloating because we haven't found any important
contradictions between your earlier and your later statements?
Well, don't imagine that your memory can serve you in the end.
We have at our disposal witnesses and documents which tell us
absolutely everything about you. So let me remind you: he laughs
longest who laughs last."

While he spoke, I signed the pile of papers on the table beginning with the usual formula "I, the undersigned, have made the
above declaration of my own free will, without any compulsion..."

"Believe me, there is no way out for you. It seems to me that
you are trying to ape the fervour of the Communists who, even
before the open door of the incinerator, prefer to burn alive rather
than betray their comrades. But their moral strength springs from

their vision of a new world—it's this that gives them their supreme courage. Can you really hope to draw the sap of resistance from the foul swamps of the rotten world to which you cling? Believe me, we are stronger than you are."

The Interrogator then told me a legend which he had found in the writings of some old Roman historian.

"At the time when Italy was divided into small kingdoms, the King of Rome unleashed a war against one of his neighbours, with whom he had an old and bitter quarrel, and sent his son to invade his lands. On the day of the decisive battle the gods weighed the balance in his favour. Delighted, the young Prince despatched a messenger to Rome to announce the news and to ask his father what should be his policy towards the vanquished. The aged King's reply was: 'You have two courses open to you. One is to hand over the city to your soldiers for three days and let them pillage and rape as they please; then bring the conquered people and their King to Rome as slaves and raze the city to the ground, brick by brick, so that no building can ever rise again upon its ruins. The alternative is to respect the city, its inhabitants and the conquered army, free the captured King, give him your trust and friendship and offer him a treaty of alliance and eternal peace. . . But avoid the middle way as you would the plague!' The Prince, wishing to please his soldiers, handed the city over to them for three days. Then, wishing also to please his father, he offered the conquered kingdom a treaty of alliance and friendship. They accepted. Five years went by in apparent peace. But all the time the vanquished people were planning to avenge their humiliation and make good their losses. One night, they attacked Rome, while the Romans were sound asleep, and mowed them down by fire and sword . . ."

The Communists, concluded the Interrogator, had learned their lessons from history and knew how to treat their conquered enemies. I replied: "Don't forget that the reaction to the brutal Roman ways you have just described was one of the causes of the destruction of the Roman Empire. Today, the circumstances are different but the reactions are the same . . ."

He dismissed me in some annoyance, saying that we would

meet again soon. In fact, I was brought back to the same interrogation room two days later, but this time there were two other officers besides the major with the wooden hand. A colonel presided; the major sat on his right and a captain on his left. A prisoner whom I did not recognise sat at a small table on one side of the room and I was placed at another, opposite him.

"Do you know this man?" the colonel asked me, looking me straight in the eyes. "Think well before you answer."

"I don't know him and I don't remember ever seeing him before."

The colonel put the same question to the other prisoner.

"Yes, I know him," he answered with assurance. "He is Dr. Silviu Craciunas."

"In what circumstances did you come to know him?"

"It was in the spring of 1948 . . . I was sitting in the Café Franklin on Boulevard Bratianu with General Bistritzeanu, who had brought me news of the conspiracy in which we were engaged. We were just about to go to a safer place where we could discuss it when the General whispered to me: 'Look! You see that tall young man in a blue coat hurrying past the window? He is one of the initiators of the plot. He is known as Engineer Grigori.' The young man was the prisoner I see before me. I was told nothing more about him at the time, but I discovered his identity later, when I was confronted with the General in the course of the investigation of my case."

He explained that he had served under General Bistritzeanu in the old Roumanian army. When the Army was purged, he was kept on as a specialist in tank warfare, with the rank of major, and transferred to an officers' training school in Bucharest. But he had continued his friendship with the General and, influenced by nationalist feeling, had responded to the General's call for a military *coup d'état*. This was to be brought off on the 1st of May.

"I was in command of a tank which was taking part in the May-Day military parade. I induced my crew to join in the conspiracy and had the tank loaded with ammunition. As we passed the grandstand we were to fire and wipe out the members of the Government

202

## The Lost Footsteps

and of the Central Committee of the Party who were taking the salute. Then a group of former army officers led by General Bistritzeanu was to seize power and form a new government."

According to the prisoner, everything was ready on the morning of May Day, but there had been a leakage, and an armed detachment of Security Police had appeared in the barracks and arrested him and his crew.

"Do you admit to having planned and organised this criminal attempt against the Government of the Roumanian People's Republic?" the colonel asked me gravely.

"No. I do not. This is the first time I have ever heard of such a plot."

The second part of my reply was untrue. But I greatly doubted if the General had in fact revealed my name, and I felt sure that in presenting me with this bomb-shell the Commission hoped, not merely to induce me to admit my participation in the plot, but to get further confessions from me including full replies to the two fundamental questions which I had still not answered since the night of my arrest.

"It's useless to deny it," the colonel said roughly. "Any man in his senses would plead guilty."

He pressed the bell-button beside him twice. After a few moments' wait in tense silence General Bistritzeanu was brought in. He could scarcely drag one foot after the other and was supported by two warders. He had grown completely bald and he looked at least ninety. A low table and a chair were brought for him.

"Mr. Bistritzeanu," said the colonel, "will you tell the Commission the names of these two prisoners and the circumstances in which you came to know them?"

In spite of his exhausted appearance, the General answered with assurance.

"This is my former adjutant, Major Vasiliu, and this is Dr. Silviu Craciunas."

When he had given an account of how he had first met us, the colonel said: "And now tell us all you know about the attempt

203

against the Government of the Roumanian People's Republic planned for May 1st, 1948."

General Bistritzeanu hesitated. The presence of Major Vasiliu and myself had no doubt made him suppose that we had both admitted our part in the conspiracy.

"This is what happened," he replied, this time less confidently and with a hint of suppressed emotion. He remained silent for some time, leaning his elbows on the table in front of him and rubbing his hands together; then, apparently making up his mind, he gave substantially the same account of the events as Major Vasiliu. As soon as he had finished, the colonel addressed me with a note of irony: "It seems that you did not expect us to know so much about your actions, Mr. Craciunas. Do you now admit to having been an instigator of this plot?"

"I am afraid I don't. It is true that I have known the General for a long time, but never once did we discuss anything connected with this alleged plot. Here, in this room, I have heard about it for the first time. I can assume no responsibility, as I was not in any way involved in it."

"You dare to deny a fact which has been proved here in our presence by the two chief witnesses!" The colonel banged his fists on the table. "I warn you that you will regret your attitude."

At this point Major Vasiliu got up angrily and addressed me without asking the interrogators' permission (prisoners were strictly forbidden to speak to one another during an interrogation).

"Why don't you have the courage to own up? Can't you realise the situation we are in? Don't you see that you are aggravating our position as well as yours? It would be more dignified to confess the truth." He went on attacking me violently.

Suddenly the General lifted his hand and interrupted him: "Mr. President, I am sorry I cannot rise to speak. You know that the régime imposed on me for the last five years has given me thrombosis. I wish to tell you that I withdraw my former statements which were made under pressure. I alone was the instigator and the organiser of the attempted *coup d'état* of the 1st of May,

1948, and I accept full responsibility for what I did. Mr. Craciunas had absolutely nothing to do with it."

"You have no idea, Mr. Bistritzeanu, how dearly you will pay for your change of attitude," said the President sharply. "Nor will you save your friend by your naïve tactics. He is a known criminal. His part in this plot is not the only, nor the worst charge we have against him."

The General, in a voice full of passion, went on: "I do not think my friend Silviu Craciunas can be called a criminal simply because he threw himself with all his heart into the struggle for an ideal which means more to him than his own life. Can you tell me what *you* would call a devoted Communist who, falling into the hands of the Imperialists, kept silent, denied all accusations, and was ready, if necessary, to give his life to defend his cause? No doubt you would put up a statue to him. I regret that I myself have not the strength to deny everything. It would have been much better both for myself and for others. My declarations did nothing to ease my situation; on the contrary . . ."

The President of the Commission banged his fists on the table and ordered the General to be taken out. The confrontation had lasted a long time and was heading in a direction which the interrogators had not intended.

Before the day was over I learned the reaction of the Commission. A duty officer informed me that the "Comrade Prosecutor" had withdrawn his permission for me to lie down during the daytime and had reduced my seven hours' sleep at night to five; I was again put into solitary confinement and my ten minutes of fresh air were cancelled.

Undernourishment and lack of vitamins had given me a hæmorrhage of the intestines; this had begun about a month before. I had had bronchitis throughout the winter and now my fits of coughing sometimes lasted for hours. I found it much more difficult to keep awake than I had in the first months after my arrest; two years of this life had inevitably weakened my resistance. Sitting on the hard chair aggravated the old lesions of nerves and tissues brought on by the flogging and sometimes I had a pain in the small of my back followed by a sensation of paralysis. The warders sedulously woke me up whenever I dozed off. After a month of continual practice, however, I again succeeded in sitting motionless and wide awake.

But the inner peace I had again achieved was shattered one day at the beginning of June. This time I was confronted with Georgetta. She looked profoundly shocked when she saw me brought into the room. She must have believed that I had successfully reached Paris . . .

The Commission had raked up the long-forgotten incident of my arrest by Inspector Talangeanu of the Economic Police and of the night I had spent in hiding under the stairs in Georgetta's house in 1948. They now claimed that my reason for helping people to escape to the West had not been friendship but the fact that some were leading members of the former democratic parties who would help to organise an anti-Communist campaign in exile. Georgetta had learned from Dr. Alexander Moga and others to whom she had given refuge that this was their intention on leaving the country. She revealed this under torture, as well as the links between myself and Professor Bolintineanu, a leader of the old Command of the Resistance Movement.

She also gave away the fact that one of the people I tried to help was Lucretiu Patrascanu, the former Minister of Justice. The Commission deduced from this that my aim in coming back might be to contact some of Patrascanu's followers, many of whom continued to be known as Communists, but who were secretly on his side, and to persuade them to join the Resistance. To support Georgetta's statements a new character was brought in and confronted with me, a doctor who had acted as go-between for Lucretiu Patrascanu and Alexander Moga.

Some of the conclusions arrived at by the Commission were accurate, others false. My denial of all of them infuriated the colonel. Knowing that I was ill, he warned me that I would get no medical attention until I changed my attitude.

About a fortnight after this confrontation an unusually violent coughing fit ended in a hæmorrhage. My request to see the prison doctor was again refused. Day after day, fits of coughing brought up more blood. It seemed that my survival now depended on the medical attention which I could not get. I clung to the hope of some miracle which would still save me if I held out as long as I could. But how long would my body last?

For eight months I was left in solitude and unattended, my health gradually deteriorating. Then in February 1954, there began a month of fresh interrogations which left me utterly exhausted.

New evidence had come to light concerning my escape activities six years earlier and I was confronted with five more witnesses. I had tried to organise the flight of several air, naval and artillery officers, among them General Oltescu of the Staff College. They had hoped to form a High Command somewhere in the West and then, by means of the secret routes at my disposal, to get in touch with disaffected officers at home. These included the thousands of victims of the purge of the Army, and a possibility would have thus arisen for an organised civil war.

My refusal to admit facts proved by witnesses threw the President of the Commission into a state of near-apoplexy at each session. Finally he gave the order to submit me to "electrical treatment." This operation was carried out in the lower basement of the prison. I was taken to a cell in which there was a dynamo, and strapped to a table. A warder pressed a lever. The electric shock was of a greater violence than my weakened organism could bear and, after a fainting fit of unusually long duration, the "treatment" was stopped.

I had always thought in spite of everything that the interrogators wanted me alive as long as they believed that I had information which they needed. This had encouraged me in my resistance all these years. So every morning I told myself that a fighter has a chance—and it's his only chance—if he can last out even a moment longer than his adversary. And each stage of my ordeal developed further my personal philosophy.

Since the spring the door had opened only to admit my wretched plate of food or for the warder to take me to the lavatory. Then one afternoon in August 1954, at the hour when a soft rustling and a nauseating smell of cabbage announced our meals, my ear, sharpened by so much silence, distinguished an unfamiliar footstep in the corridor. The door was flung open.

"Pick up your belongings," ordered an officer on duty.

"I have only this." I held up a rag which had once been a towel.

"Take it."

Two minutes later, when my eyeshades were removed, I found myself in the office of the Prison Governor, surrounded by four Security officers.

"Take off your clothes and leave them on the floor."

Everything I had on was filthy and in rags.

"Put these on."

On a chair lay a shirt, underclothing and a navy-blue suit, freshly pressed. It was only after I had put them on that I realised they were my own clothes. The metal shades were put back over my eyes and I was taken by the arms and led from the room. The fresh air and the squeak of sand under my feet told me that we walked across the yard. I was pushed into a car which started off immediately; I could not guess in what direction we were going.

There were sounds of traffic. Suddenly my eyeshades were slipped off. Instinctively, I closed my eyes to protect them from the sunlight pouring out of a cloudless sky. The streets were crowded with people in light summer clothes, wilting in the August heat. After four years inside a stone box 28 feet square, the sight was unbelievable.

The car drew up about thirty yards from the Gara de Nord. Walking between two guards who stuck closely to my sides, and handcuffed to one of them, I crossed the entrance hall without attracting much attention.

In about half an hour the train set off. The names of the towns pictured on the walls of the compartment led me to believe that we were travelling in the direction of Vatra Dornei, a terminus in the north, near the Soviet frontier. There were only the three of us in the compartment and I was still handcuffed to the lieutenant beside me. No one uttered a word.

At first I felt a terrible anxiety, for the direction in which we were going made it seem likely that I was being taken to Russia. But gradually I calmed down. The astonishing sight of hills and fields outside the train windows moved me so much that it almost drove away my terrors; and when I saw people at wayside stations —those free people whom I had so much longed to see again—I only wished I could fling out my arms and embrace every one of them.

The sun sank behind the hills and dusk veiled the splendour of the countryside. Soon only an occasional spark from the engine streaked in the darkness, or the black silhouette of a tree or a telegraph pole stood out against the night sky.

Towards morning we stopped at a large station; it was completely deserted. We had been travelling for fourteen hours towards the north—a distance of about 280 miles, I reckoned. As we got out into the chilly morning air, the outlines of the buildings seemed to me familiar. The station was Burdujeni; it served its own village as well as the town of Suceava, about four miles away. It was thirteen years since I had last been there.

A half-hour's drive brought us to Suceava prison, one of the largest in the country and known to be reserved by the Security Service for "criminals" whom they regarded as dangerous.

My new cell was about fifteen foot by six—enormous in comparison with the one I had come from.

The days went by without any indication as to what awaited me. No one spoke a word to me. Then, very late one night, I was taken to be interrogated.

The Interrogator, a major with a big round face, looked angry; he scowled at me for several minutes, leaning his elbow on the arm of his chair.

"Do you know Grigoras Suceveanu, formerly head of the legal department of the Archbishopric of Bucovina?"

"Yes."

"How did you get to know him and what were your relations with him?"

My account failed to satisfy the major and he accused me of evasiveness.

"We know that at the end of the war you founded a clandestine organisation with Grigoras Suceveanu, to oppose the 'liberating' Soviet armies. We have known for years that you were in touch with thousands of men in the north of the country. We now have indisputable proof that when you came back to Roumania in 1950 you intended to stir up revolt, making use of the network of conspirators in this region, which you believed to be less closely watched by the Security Services because of the proximity of the Soviet frontier."

"I declare categorically that I returned in order to help certain close friends of mine to escape to the West. I had no other motives."

The major was unimpressed.

"We will prove to you, for the last time, that we know what your motives were and what Power was backing you. You will be confronted with several people whom we kidnapped abroad and others who were parachuted into Roumania by foreign planes. *They* will tell you who sent you and for what purpose. Read this."

He handed me a copy of *Scanteia* and pointed to a front page article. This was an official statement that thirteen parachutists dropped by the Americans had been condemned to death by the Military Court in Bucharest.

The interrogation, begun in this menacing way, continued at intervals during the following days and nights. Sometimes the major was assisted by a captain who spoke Roumanian perfectly but with a Russian accent. They tried to force me to admit to plotting with Suceveanu and to reveal the names of our agents. In actual fact, resistance in those days had not had the unity they claimed, and by now those friends of mine who had organised local groups were dead, arrested, or had escaped abroad and were scattered all over the five continents. It was, however, possible that the Communists had kidnapped some of them and would be able to confront me with them. At this stage I realised that the interrogations were taking a much more dangerous course than I had expected, and my one desire now was to gain time, to avoid further questionings, until I was strong enough to build up a new defence.

I had bouts of fever and spat blood every day. There was no glass in the window of my cell and, after the warmer climate of the south, the cold night air coming through the grating set me shivering for hours. I determined to make a last attempt to get medical treatment. When I was taken to the interrogation room once again, I told the major that I was ill.

"I keep spitting blood. Look . . ." I spat out phlegm mixed with blood into the palm of my hand and held it out to him across the table. "I have not so far been condemned to death, and even if I had been I would still have the right to a minimum of medical treatment. If you refuse it, I refuse to answer any of your questions."

"You dare to impose conditions!" he shouted. "You have the insolence to talk of rights! Don't worry, you'll be shot before long. Medicine would be wasted on you."

He tried to carry on the interrogation but as I would not open my mouth to say a word he ordered me, furiously, to be taken back to my cell.

Next day, when the officer on duty came for me, I refused to leave the cell. Ten minutes later he came back with four warders. They fell on me, tied up my arms and legs, carried me to the Interrogator's office, set me down on a chair and left me alone with the major.

"Have you decided to answer your Interrogator?"

I remained silent.

His eyes blazing, he leapt at me and struck me again and again with his fists until the blood poured from my nose and lips. Then he summoned the warders to take me back.

Ten days dragged by. I was burning with fever and losing more and more weight. I could hardly swallow more than an ounce or two of my daily ration of half-cooked buckwheat. The water I was given was heavily chlorinated as a precaution against typhus, the chlorine gave me stomach cramps and I could not drink more than a few mouthfuls. I suffered an infernal and continuous thirst and felt as if I were a shipwrecked sailor surrounded by undrinkable water.

At last one morning the officer on duty took me to the prison infirmary. The doctor, who wore the uniform of a Security captain, questioned me about my health but made no attempt at an examination, and in the end offered me an aspirin and sent me back! After dark, however, the same doctor came with two junior officers to fetch me. My eyes as usual covered by eyeshades, I was led out to a car. We drove through paved streets, then over bumpy roads where the potholes obliged us to slow down. When my eyes were uncovered and we got out, weak electric lights shone in the darkness. We walked as through a tunnel under the low branches of overhanging trees towards the silhouette of a large white one-storey pavilion. The room to which I was taken contained three hospital beds, and a tiled stove stood in the corner. My clothes were taken away and I was given a hospital nightgown.

"Get into bed," the prison doctor said dryly. "You are not, of course, to leave the room and you are to speak to no one."

One of the two junior officers remained in the room with me and I could see the other standing outside the door, which was left wide open; during the night several Security men walked past it, up and down the corridor and I thought that there might be other sick prisoners in the pavilion.

The chief medical officer of the hospital came to my room in the morning, accompanied by two sisters. From the moment he looked at me through his gold-rimmed spectacles, I had an impression of kindness and compassion. He was a man in his sixties, with grey hair and a pale, deeply lined face.

"How long is it since you have been out in the fresh air?"

"About eighteen months."

"I can see that . . . You'll be taken out into the garden for an hour, and you'll have a diet of milk, eggs, sugar, fruit and vegetable soup . . . But I must warn you: you are only here for a medical examination. If we find a serious illness, you'll be able to stay on for several weeks, but if there's nothing badly wrong I haven't the authority to keep you for so much as a day."

That afternoon I sat on the freshly scythed lawn at the back of the pavilion. According to my calculations it was the 20th of September, 1954—I was entering on my fifth year of prison life. The autumn sun was still warm. Near the house were old apple trees laden with fruit.

From the conversation of the two guards, who sat watching me with sten-guns on their knees, I gathered that I was in a hospital for infectious diseases, not in Suceava but near Burdujeni where we had got out of the train a few weeks before. The ground sloped away towards the south, and the cupolas of Suceava and its old ruined fort gleamed in the distance on the brow of a hill. To my right, the towers of a monastery church rose above the tree tops. The hospital had five pavilions built at a distance of about fifty yards from one another.

That evening, after dark, the prison car came back and the officers were in a hurry to take me somewhere, but my clothes had been locked up and the storekeeper had gone home; it took an hour to get the keys. Then, accompanied by the two officers, the hospital doctor and the prison doctor, I was driven to a nearby clinic and X-rayed. The fact that I was in an isolation hospital and the measures taken to avoid my being seen suggested that there was to be no change in my status as a "dangerous" prisoner.

Next day samples of my blood, sputum, urine, etc., were taken for analysis. I noticed that the warders avoided being in my room and preferred to stay outside the open door. From their conversation with the nurse I discovered that someone had died of scarlatina in my bed the day before I had arrived, and that nothing had been done to disinfect the room, the bed or the bedclothes!

For the first time in over four years I was outside a prison. The idea of escape had never occurred to me since my arrest, for there had never been the glimmer of a hope. But now the possibility that there might be an infinitesimal chance entered my mind.

On my third morning in hospital the doctor told me that he

expected the results of the laboratory tests that day. He stood in his white overall, his hands deep in his pockets, looking down on me with pity.

"I wish I needn't say this, but I must tell you again that unless the result shows evidence of a grave infection, you will probably be taken back to prison tomorrow or even tonight. I have examined the X-rays—there is a shadow over your left lung. It may be a cavity caused by tuberculosis or it may be a thinning of the tissues, the result of lack of vitamins and fresh air; I am not yet sure. But in my experience the prison governors do not regard tuberculosis as a sufficient reason for leaving a patient in hospital. The most you can expect is medical treatment in your cell and eventually a pneumothorax."

I had thought all along that the only object of my being brought to the hospital was to let the interrogators know exactly how much pressure they could still subject me to without killing me outright. What the doctor said confirmed my view. I realised that my chances of staying on were very small, for it seemed improbable that I had any source of serious infection other than my lung. If so I was unlikely to stay longer than this one night.

# CHAPTER XIV

EVERY TWO minutes a warder looked in on me by the light of the corridor lamp which fell on my bed and walked back along the passage, his boots thumping on the stone floor. I had assessed the time between his visits by counting the seconds, and I did this again now.

At the end of an hour I asked to be taken to the lavatory. In silence the warder signed me to follow him. I got out of bed in my nightshirt and went barefoot into the corridor. The warder opened the door of a small bathroom opposite my room and switched on the light. He kept his eyes on me through the half-open door, waiting to see me back to bed. The room stank of urine, excrement and sweat, and a narrow window was kept open for ventilation. When I came out, I made as if to shut the door as I usually did, but instead of closing it properly, I only pulled it to; the warder did not seem to notice.

Back in bed, I pretended to go fast asleep. Now the warders made their visits at slightly longer intervals—about four minutes instead of two; probably, as on the previous nights when they thought I was asleep, they would settle down to a game of dice. I waited a little longer. It was about ten, I thought. I had to make up my mind, for when they finished playing they would resume their sentry-go outside my door. Next day I would be taken back to prison. My interrogation would no doubt begin again with increased severity, and I might be confronted with parachutists or with people who had been kidnapped abroad. There would be nothing more to hope for except death when the interrogators chose to allow me to die. Certainly if I were caught escaping, I would be shot, but there was a chance . . . The window of my room was nailed down, but the hospital building was not under heavy guard, for, as I had realised from the conversation of the warders, only one or two small rooms were reserved for political prisoners. I heard children's voices from the other wards.

When the warder's footsteps had died away, I slipped out of bed. The shock of the ice-cold floor to my bare feet helped to clear my brain. My clothes were lying on a table in the corner of the room; the storekeeper had been told to leave them out in case the prison car should come to fetch me before he was back. My heart was pounding so much that I pressed my hand over my chest as if to keep it in place. I crossed the room, whipped the clothes over my left arm and clutched my shoes in my left hand.

In front of the open door I stopped short, drew a deep breath and glanced to left and right. The man who had just looked in on me was leaning against the veranda door with his back to me; the voices of the other warders and the night-nurse came from the veranda at the other end of the passage. I took the three steps needed to cross the passage. The bathroom door gave way easily at a touch; its slight creak was drowned by the voices of the warders. I slipped through and took care to push the door back, so that it again looked closed.

The darkness was not total, for a small flame burned underneath the geyser. A pile of laundry, waiting to be washed, which I had noticed before, made a light patch in the corner. The rumbling of the water in the pipes was enough to cover the soft swish of my clothes as I slid through the narrow window.

The distance to the ground was about seven feet. My mind was on the movements which I had to make with speed and precision, for every second was precious. I had no thought for the risks I was running; I was only conscious of the passing of the seconds.

It took me about a minute and a half from when I left my bed to reach the shadow of the trees. The sky was overcast and as I leapt over the grass I heard the first raindrops on the leaves over my head. The white outlines of an old chapel next to the mortuary served me as a landmark to reach the garden fence. I threw my clothes and slippers into the road and climbed over. There were no street-lights but I could see the outlines of houses. I hurried

## The Lost Footsteps

feverishly as I put on my suit over my white hospital shirt. The three minutes on which I had counted were almost up: at any second now the warder would look into my room.

I had calculated every movement, but from now on the lie of the land was unknown to me. All I knew was that the hospital stood on a hill on the outskirts of the small town of Burdujeni; the best thing at the moment was to follow the line of the fence. I felt an extraordinary surge of strength and a few strides brought me to the corner of the garden; here the road turned westward and down hill. I had worked out that the railway line must run at the bottom of the valley, about a mile and a half away. As I passed the wall of the monastery church I had seen from the hospital garden, I heard the alarm being given in the hospital.

Out of the benevolent skies the autumn rain fell faster and faster; it would make it difficult for bloodhounds to pick up my scent. I also counted on the warders and the junior officers at the hospital to make a quick search of the garden first, in the hope of catching me before I got outside so as to have a better chance to cover up their negligence. But this would take them ten minutes or so at most.

Although I could hardly see the road I ran lightly and quickly. After four years of complete inaction this cost me a tremendous effort, but I had to get as far away as possible at once. Much depended on the strength of my heart and my reserves of energy, but I was worried about my infected lung and dreaded a hæmorrhage.

At the first turning I took a narrow path to the right and suspected that the road I had just left might be the only one by which a Security Police car from Suceava could approach the hospital. As it was unpaved and full of potholes, I reckoned that it would take them at least half an hour.

Fortunately I was running downhill; even so, the pain in my heart and lungs forced me to stop from time to time. But at the sound of a machine-gun somewhere near the hospital, my exhaustion vanished and I rushed through the blackness.

I had to reach some hiding-place where I could disappear

217

without a trace for several months. Hiding in the woods, in the hope of getting help later from peasants in the neighbourhood, was too risky. Unluckily the nearest place where I knew anyone was Roman, about sixty miles south of Suceava. I had only one advantage over my adversaries; they had to search a circle of 360° with my hospital room as its centre, while I was running steadily in one direction. If I were not picked up at once the circle would gradually be extended to a radius of perhaps 60 miles, but I thought it would take at least an hour before police on the perimeter of such an area would get instructions to check all transport on the roads and railway.

I had to catch a train at once and I had to get on it at Burdujeni, for although Burdujeni station would be the first to be alerted, I could not risk trying to get a lift by road out of the district, since nearly all the cars and lorries were State-owned and the few private cars were likely to be searched.

After about half an hour I saw the first green, red and yellow lights of railway signals.and I cut across the fields towards the station. By now the rain had soaked me to the skin and a cold wind from the east lashed at my sweating body. My throat parched with fever and thirst, I could feel the blood throbbing in the veins in my neck and I was shaken by great shudders like flashes of lightning. Stumbling and falling on the wet grass, and running on again, I reached the western outskirts of Burdujeni and saw the station buildings vaguely through the curtain of rain.

In the past this station had been the customs control point between Austria and Roumania: this explained the several customs sheds and the vast network of sidings where the trains used to wait for their freight to be examined.

I hid underneath a wagon on a side line and tried to see what was going on. My sight had been extremely keen but now it seemed to me that it was weaker, and the heavy rain blotted out the sounds which could perhaps have told me what measures had been taken since I had left the hospital.

Suddenly I heard the loud puffing of an engine nearby. Crawling beneath the wagons, I soon reached a goods train and.

in spite of the darkness and rain, discovered that it was loaded with timber; judging by the strong scent of resin, it was pine-wood; the train must have come from the big pine-forests in the north and must be moving south (for in this part of the country, timber never travels from south to north). Very cautiously I climbed on to a wagon and hid under the ends of the broad planks. Excitement, weakness, exhaustion and cold racked my body with a violent fit of shivering. I considered what I could do if the police found me, and was comforted by the thought that an attempt to run away would certainly end in a burst of machine-gun fire. In any case I was determined not to give myself up alive.

Ten minutes later the train moved off at a speed of about twenty miles an hour; it was going south. I felt a sudden happiness.

I think that at times, during the next few hours, I must have been delirious. Though I huddled up under the ends of the broad pine-planks, I could get little shelter from the torrential rain and the sharp gusts of wind; a kind of numbness took hold of my body.

The train halted at several small stations. It was only at the third of them that militiamen searched the wagons. Alerted by their voices and lanterns, I slipped out through the rainy darkness and hid in the guard's van of a solitary carriage which stood in a siding. The search lasted for about half an hour; then once again silence fell on the little station and I dodged back to my wagon of timber.

It was nearly dawn when the train drew up at the station of Roman. It took me a long time to slip through the groups of militiamen who patrolled the lines and to manœuvre my way out. Although it was thirteen years since I had last visited Roman, I remembered many of the landmarks. I found my way to a large, deserted park not far from the station, and there I crept into a wooden pavilion which was used in summer as a bandstand. Stretching myself on a bench, I tried to control my shivering. I could hardly believe that I had managed to get so far away in such a short time.

At daybreak I took off the hospital nightshirt I was still

wearing underneath my suit and put on my own shirt which I had
stuffed under my coat. With the nightshirt I wiped my face, dried
my hair and wiped the mud off my shoes. Soon it was broad daylight. The sky was still overcast and it was still raining though
less heavily than during the night. An occasional pedestrian
appeared in the street outside the park; this and the risk of being
seen by a park keeper meant that I could not stay where I was.
But neither could I roam the streets for long without attracting
attention by my pallor, my weakness, my soaked clothing and
my crumpled shirt. I had to find my friend's house as quickly as
possible.

The open entrance of a courtyard and a small veranda at the back
of it seemed familiar, so I tried my luck, though the dilapidated
look of things was a change from my last visit when everything
had been tidy and well kept. I knocked gently several times on the
door of the veranda, and was just turning away, for the house
looked uninhabited, when a woman of about forty in a flannel
dressing-gown opened the door.

"Who are you looking for at this hour of the morning? You
must have come to the wrong house."

I said that friends of mine, Mr. and Mrs. Filon, had once lived
here.

"Yes, they did, but Mr. Filon died of a heart attack, and soon
after, Mrs. Filon went to the south—it was during the war—the
front line wasn't far from this town. Since then I haven't heard
anything more of her."

I felt faint and dizzy; I knew no one else in the town.

"But who are you? "

"I am Brosteanu, an engineer. I haven't been in Roman for
thirteen years. I can't tell you how sorry I am not to have found
my friends," I said, turning away.

The woman hesitated a moment, then suddenly opened the
door with a friendly gesture.

"Do come in. You look exhausted. It's all right—I'm Mrs.
Filon's niece. She left the house in my charge when she went

away. But what has happened to you? How did you get in such a state?"

I sat watching her silently as she lit a wood fire in the kitchen and put a kettle on the hob. Should I trust her or go away at once? But I had nowhere to go and I was very ill.

Without giving her my real name or more than a few details about myself, I told her of my escape from the Security Police at Burdujeni. She took my story calmly, gave me some hot tea and two aspirins, then made up a bed on the divan in the adjoining room and pressed me to lie down and sleep for a few hours.

By the time I woke up Mrs. Istrati's husband had come home.

"You have no idea how glad I am that you got out of their clutches," he said warmly. "But I am afraid you won't be able to stay here more than one night." He looked at me kindly but anxiously.

He was in his late thirties, tall and well built but with greying hair and a lined face. He had been a lawyer but was now a lorry driver for a State-owned sugar firm.

After Mrs. Filon had gone, the police had raided the house several times. They were still looking for her because they had discovered—buried under the floorboards of the summer-house where they had been hidden in case the Russians occupied the town—the papers of an anti-Communist political organisation. Now the lodger who had the best room in the house was a Security Police officer, so my stay had inevitably to be very short. But the Istratis offered to help me to get to the nearest town, Bacau.

Early next morning, I left Roman in a sugar lorry driven by Ion Istrati; I was hidden in a narrow tunnel built between the crates at the bottom of the load. Bacau was only an hour's drive away, but during that short journey the police stopped and searched the lorry three times.

When I parted from my benefactor Bacau lay gleaming in the sunshine—not a trace was left of the clouds and rain of the night before. The windjacket, cap and gloves Istrati had given me altered my appearance though they were not a complete disguise. The Istratis had also pressed on me a packet of food and a hundred *lei*—the money could not get me through more than a few days but it was all the spare cash they had for a fortnight.

Yellowing leaves, blown down by the first cold winds of autumn lay on the grass in the garden of the house I knew in Bacau. Three little girls who looked like sisters poked their heads out of the window as I hurried up the path.

"Can you please tell me if Mrs. Carp is at home?"

"She's not at home," they replied in chorus.

"When will she be back?"

"At Christmas."

"That," I told myself, "is the last straw."

A woman who came out on to the veranda said, however, that Mrs. Carp might be back the following day—she had gone to stay with her married daughter in another town but had written that she was returning.

I had pinned my hopes on Mrs. Carp. She was an old lady without any political record. I could not stay out in the open, for by now my description must be in the pocket of every policeman in the street.

Fortunately Bacau had a Turkish bath. There I spent the afternoon, as welcome as the most honoured citizen in the town. A naked giant weighing at least twenty-two stone came every half-hour to throw five buckets of water on the heap of red-hot bricks. The heat and the steam perfumed by dried wild flowers had a salutary effect on me and I had a good sleep in the rest-room afterwards, lying on a divan with a corner of the blanket drawn over my face.

Where to stay the night was more of a problem. I spent it shivering in a little booth (cool drinks and sweets were sold in it in summer) on the edge of a large park on the outskirts of the town.

The next day Mrs. Carp came back. She welcomed me with kindness and sympathy. She could not hide me, however.

In 1948 the State had taken over her house leaving her only one room; the other seven were occupied by various workers and employees, and in the room opposite hers, sharing it with his wife, lived the house-manager who kept a record of the tenants and of all their visitors for the militia.

"But stay until it's dark, and don't be so downhearted, "Mrs. Carp encouraged me. "God will help us—we'll think of some-where for you to hide."

And indeed, by the evening, God had held out a slender straw. We walked for nearly an hour and a half to an orchard on the southern outskirts of the town. A scarcely visible track led from the gate to a little wooden hut, almost hidden under the branches of old trees. I had brought a sack, containing two blankets, a jug of water and food—enough to keep away cold, hunger and thirst for several days.

When Mrs. Carp left, hurrying to get back home, I groped about in the darkness, and made myself a bed in the dry hay. I was full of hope again: at last I had a shelter.

An identity check of everyone who happened to be in the street had been made while I was in the Turkish bath; I knew nothing of it but as happens in small towns, Mrs. Carp had heard of it as soon as she returned home. I had missed it by the skin of my teeth!

The smell of the wild flowers in the hay acted as a miraculous narcotic. I dreamed of my childhood and of my friends. I floated above an unfamiliar town and entered, like a puff of wind, a room in a strange house. It was my sister's dining-room, peaceful and well cared for. The white table-cloth was embroidered with arabesques, and on it—sunlight striking water and crystal—stood a vase holding white lilac. Then suddenly there was darkness and hard claws beating on the window-pane.

Heavy autumn raindrops falling on the wooden roof awoke me. I was again shivering with fever. It occurred to me that a serious illness in this abandoned orchard would probably finish me off and would certainly cause Mrs. Carp, the owner of the garden, much unpleasantness.

The days and nights passed slowly. I could not make a fire in the hut because of the dry hay, and because in any case the smoke might have attracted attention; so I could have no warm food or drink. Mrs. Carp only visited me rarely, for now that the fruit crops had been gathered in, she could not come often to the orchard without arousing the suspicions of the peasants in the neighbourhood. Winter would cause even greater complications.

Finally we made a plan. One clear frosty evening in October I went to the station accompanied by Mrs. Carp who had insisted on coming with me in order to help me. We got into a train.

"Is that your son?" asked a curious peasant who sat opposite us in our compartment. "He's very thin and he looks as if he had a fever. Has he got consumption? He looks young—it would be a pity for him to die."

"He's got a bad cold," my supposed mother said. "I'm taking him to Cluj, they've got very good doctors there . . ."

And indeed the University Hospitals in Cluj enjoyed great renown. People travelled from as far as Moldavia to consult them. I had wrapped a large brown scarf round my head, leaving little more than my eyes uncovered.

After two nights in the train, with a day in between spent at a small inn, we arrived at a junction on the outskirts of Cluj. Here I parted from kind Mrs. Carp for ever.

Helped by my friends and by luck, I had made the first step towards safety. The next step would be to arrange my flight across the frontier but this needed lengthy preparation. In the meanwhile, as my health forced me to seek the shelter of the town and I could not therefore join the partisans in the mountains, Cluj, however risky, at least offered the advantage of being within a hundred and fifty miles of Hungary. Above all it offered me a safe refuge while the hunt was at its height.

Dawn was breaking when I reached the eastern suburbs of the city. I sneaked down an empty street towards a house which I had only seen once. The large cobbled courtyard with its yellow walls looked unchanged; at the back of it stood a modest building of timber and unpainted brick. I knocked but no one replied. I tried the handle; it yielded and the door creaked open revealing a humble, untidy kitchen. A woman, woken by the noise, came out of the next room and stood in the doorway. Obviously alarmed by the appearance of a stranger at this early hour, she stared at me as though petrified.

"Don't you remember me, Veronica *Neni?*" I asked. I had recognised her at once. She was the mother of Maria Pótócki who had come with me to Austria in 1948.

"No, no! I don't know you. I've never seen you before," she stuttered nervously.

"Perhaps you'll recognise me now." I took off my cap and covered the lower part of my face with my hand.

"Five years ago, on the evening of the 18th of February, I set out from this very room with your daughter and granddaughter. I had a long black beard and you said it made me look like a rabbi. Your little granddaughter, Agnes, had been crying, but she stopped when I let her play with it."

"Oh! You are Lotzi *Baci*, now I recognise you! Come in."

Veronica lived with her younger sister, Magda, and their mother who was eighty. The two younger women fussed over me while I told them something of my story.

"Don't worry! We'll hide you," they exclaimed. "Thank goodness we can do something for you at last! If it hadn't been for you, Maria and Agnes would still be here. Look, we've got something to show you."

Veronica took some photographs from a drawer—a snapshot of Maria and her daughter, well dressed and in a comfortable, prosperous-looking room, and another of a little boy, Harry, born to Maria after her arrival in the States.

I spent that day in the room next to the kitchen. In the evening, after dark, Veronica took me up to the attic. It was cut off from the rest of the house, the only access to it being a narrow wooden ladder from the yard.

That attic was to be my home for three months. I was prevented from leaving by my ill-health, my lack of money, and the difficulties in the way of reaching friends who could have helped me to escape. Besides, the longer I remained in hiding the more discouraged my pursuers were likely to become.

## The Lost Footsteps

But my staying on was a great hardship for my hosts. Magda and Veronica worked in a restaurant co-operative. Their wages were wretched, and their mother and their jobless brother were dependent on them. To keep alive they sold whatever they could do without, in the local flea market which was held on Sundays, but the sums they got were negligible. With still another mouth to feed the situation became desperate.

Nevertheless, every evening Veronica when she came home brought me a bowl of soup hidden in a canvas bag, and sometimes a few scraps of cake which the chef had thrown away. She refused to talk about her difficulties. It was not until two months later that I discovered she had sold her sewing machine, her only remaining asset. No one in the family knew anything about me except that I had helped Maria; they thought vaguely that I was an engineer from Bucharest; yet they fed and sheltered me like true Samaritans.

In the morning, before the two women went to work at half-past six, they locked the attic door, so that no one should wander in out of curiosity. I lay on my bed, wrapped in a worn blanket and a few rags Veronica had found for me. There was always a small bunch of flowers on the shelf under the sky-light. They were real and they banished my feeling of loneliness. Between their stalks and leaves I caught glimpses of the sky—I was no longer looking at the sky through bars.

It grew colder. I moved as little as I could for fear of the floorboards creaking, and I dared not even cough, for only a thin wall separated me from the next room where I could hear a new-born baby crying and its mother crooning to it; this woman knew that Magda and Veronica were out all day and would become suspicious if she heard noises in the attic.

Although my fate was in the hands of three poor, elderly, helpless women, and I was wretched at the trouble I was giving them, the feeling that I had a chance, that I was my own master and could make decisions, filled me with an extraordinary exaltation. Gradually I regained vitality and strength; it was as if I were recovering after a serious operation.

I knew about outside events from newspapers which I read

from cover to cover, and from the gossip which Magda and Veronica brought me every evening: parachutists had been dropped by plane and captured . . . The body of a famous surgeon had been dug up by some poor people whose misery had driven them to do this in order to obtain his clothing, his gold teeth, his ring . . . A luxury shoe-shop was selling women's shoes at 500 *lei* a pair. Workers were indignant because 500 *lei* was their average monthly wage; Veronica earned only half this sum: she could have bought one shoe!

Even the house where I was hiding had its news. The tenants were a strange mixture: a young artillery lieutenant, so proud of his red motor-bicycle that he garaged it in his room; an old retired trooper who rented one of his two beds to a couple of beggars; a former Commander in the Air-Force who had become a ticket collector on a bus. In other rooms there lived a shoemaker; a tailor; several clerks; a student and his mistress; a militiaman and his family. A Turkish bath attendant with his wife and their twelve children occupied the basement. Last summer his eldest son, a boy of eighteen, had been drowned in a reservoir in the mountains; he had been one of a gang of workers who were employed on its construction. His workmates had refused to hand the body over to the parents and had buried him according to their own rites—no priest, no service, only the Red flag and a fanfare. Was it a sign that the "new religion" was taking root among young people?

One evening, as November was approaching, Veronica said to me: "You must forgive us, Lotzi dear—we'll have to leave you by yourself on the eve of All-Souls. We are going to the cemetery after dark, to visit our father's grave . . . When, by God's help, you get to the West, please don't tell Maria her grandfather is dead. She loved him so much that we haven't the heart to let her know. One day, when we too are gone, she'll understand . . ."

I looked at her. How bent and wrinkled she was with suffering and worry and work too heavy for her. Her sister looked less weighed down, though she was doomed by an incurable heart-disease.

## The Lost Footsteps

The approach of the eve of All-Souls impressed and troubled me. I might never again be in my home town for this festival. At length I decided to go to it, whatever the risk.

It was dark and cold outside. The worn overcoat borrowed from Veronica's modest wardrobe (it was destined for the flea market) was too thin to protect me from the evening frost. The streets were almost empty, for thousands of people had already gathered in the cemetery. A path parallel to the main road and lined with ancient walnut trees led uphill. I slipped in through a side gate, my cap over my eyes, muffled in my brown scarf and looking like any poor workman. There was no lighting on the paths but almost every grave had recently been tended and was covered with flowers and bright with dozens of lighted candles stuck into the earth. No one took any notice of me: those who came here were absorbed in their own memories. I heard soft sobbing sounds; I saw sad faces; many people were weeping tearlessly, perhaps not only for the dead but also for the tragedy of their own lives at this cruel time.

The sky was full of stars. The golden flames of thousands of lighted candles flickered on the tombs, small and helpless, easily snuffed out by the slightest breath of wind, like the fragile mortals who stood round them. I knew this cemetery—it covered many acres on the slope of a hill. Several generations of the city's inhabitants were hidden in its soil. The city, lying at the foot of the hill, blared music from loudspeakers at street-corners and in market squares invading the few moments of peace which the people had come to find among the tombstones.

I crept stealthily towards some abandoned Armenian tombs; the families of those who had been buried had died out and there was no longer anyone to light the candles for them. Hidden behind a stone carved with Arabic characters, I looked for my grandparents' grave and beside it, that of my brother. I found them. Candles lit the graves. Six beloved members of my family stood around them—their pale, sad faces lit up by the flames. I recognised my parents. I was about twenty yards away from them, but some hidden strength kept me from revealing myself or giving them any sign. It would have upset them too much and it might have endangered their lives.

The ceremony was nearly over when I arrived. The mourners began to file down the long alleys leading to the main entrance— each with a lighted candle in his hand. I remained for another quarter of an hour in the dark shadow of the Armenians' tombstone. Soon there was not a living soul in sight. Silence took possession of the cemetery and only an idle wind soughed through the leafless branches of the trees. In a few seconds I was standing before those two graves. I wept silently. It was the first and the last time I wept during those years. Sitting down at the edge of my brother's grave, I thought about his fate and mine and about our parents.

The flames were dying away on the guttering candles. I bade farewell to both the dead and living members of my family.

# CHAPTER XV

THERE WERE still ten days to go before Christmas. Since the ceremony in memory of the dead, I had not dared to leave my attic. But now necessity compelled me to end my isolation: the little store of firewood had been used up in the frosty evenings of an early winter; all the old clothing had been sold; the money received for the sewing machine had all been spent, and the provision of the bare necessities of life had become an almost insoluble problem for my hostesses.

So one cold, foggy evening about the middle of December, I sneaked through some back streets to the consulting-room of a doctor who was an old friend. This time I was wearing a more respectable overcoat, borrowed by Veronica from her brother-in-law, a chauffeur. At that hour—about 8 p.m.—there was only one other patient in the waiting-room. Dr. Tudor Farcasanu was a famous heart specialist. The casual glance he threw at me as he called the other patient into his consulting-room made me certain that he had not recognised me, worn out as he no doubt was by a heavy day.

The patient left. The door of the consulting-room remained open.

"Next patient please!" the doctor called out.

Sudden emotion made my temples throb.

"Please sit down, I won't be a moment." My friend stood with his back to me, washing his hands. "Tell me what's the matter with you. It's late; you must have seen the notice on the door—my consulting hours end at 7. What are your symptoms?"

"I am suffering from cold and hunger," I replied.

"Everyone is suffering from cold and hunger. I'm a heart specialist . . ."

# The Lost Footsteps

The doctor dried his hands, hung up the towel and looked at me for a few seconds. I had taken off my cap and looked at him, my face in the full glare of the light.

"Good Heavens! It's impossible!"

Quickly he closed the door and holding out his hand to me, said: "I can't believe my eyes! Someone told me you were dead; someone else that you had been sent to Russia; then a few days ago Doctor Mihail whispered as he passed me in the corridor at the clinic that he had heard you speaking on Brussels radio."

"There's so much to tell you, and I can't stay more than half an hour," I replied. "By a stroke of good luck someone who saw you buying a cake for your little daughter at a café happened to mention it in my presence. You see how famous you are! After that I found your address in a telephone book and that's how I'm here."

We had last met ten years ago in Bucharest, about the time of Roumania's capitulation. Soon afterwards my friend, largely influenced by me, had retired from politics and had devoted himself exclusively to his work as a doctor. It was the only way for him to keep out of the limelight and build up a reputation he could draw on when the necessity arose. All traces of our connection must by now have been wiped out, and I felt reasonably sure that the police could not involve him in setting any trap for me.

I told him my story. Tudor's face reflected his emotion. "Thank God you've escaped at least from prison . . . So few have managed it." He realised at once that I was in dire need of clothes and money, and also that I would need more money—a considerable sum—to pay for guides. It was four years and ten months since I had last set foot on the frontier-zone. No doubt the system of defences had been strengthened in that time. Only someone who had lived continuously in the area would know by what path I could slip through the barrage. Any attempt to cross the frontier alone would be tantamount to suicide.

"I know," I said, "that you can't provide me with the large sum I'll need for my escape; but could you sound your colleagues at the University?—Dr. Ion Borza and Professor Andrei Loghin.

Here's the password: 'The White Lilac isn't in blossom yet'; they know you well, so they won't suspect you of being an *agent-provocateur*. They'll believe you've come from me. Tell them what has happened to me in the last four years; they'll know that my resistance to the Interrogators saved their lives as well. Professor Loghin meant to come with me to the West when I was going back to Paris in 1950. At that time he spoke to me about some jewellery and a sum of five thousand dollars. Please remind him . . ." We arranged to meet again five evenings later, in a quiet street outside the Tower of Baba Novac.

Five days passed . . . The wall of the medieval tower where Baba Novac, one of Michael the Brave's generals, was hanged, loomed darkly against the sky. The cold was piercing as I walked up and down the narrow street. My friend came punctually.

"I've got some good news," he said. "I have some things for you—a new overcoat, cap, scarf, shirts, socks. You must be decently dressed, so that you don't look too much like a suspicious character to the police. And here are five thousand *lei*[1] to get you out of your immediate difficulties; we raised it between us, Borza, Loghin and I. Unfortunately, I have also some bad news . . ."

It was true that Professor Andrei Loghin had been in possession of five thousand dollars. But he walled up the bundle of hundred-dollar notes in the cellar of a friend's house and when he came to fetch them after some time he was horrified to find that the bank notes had rotted. The possession of foreign currency was strictly forbidden by the régime and anyone breaking this law was exposed to the most severe punishment.

He also had some jewellery. He adored his wife and had showered jewels on her for more than thirty years of a happily married life. For fear that, if he were arrested, the jewels would be confiscated, his wife had asked a niece of hers to keep them for her. Loghin's wife had since died and the niece had fallen under the spell of an actor from Jassy and had eloped with him taking the jewels with her.

---

[1] The sum was quite a large one at that time in Roumania, though its equivalent in foreign currency would only have been about £85.

"But don't despair," said Tudor. "Professor Loghin is determined to back you up at any cost!"

The professor's remaining asset was a small house consisting of two flats. By selling it, he could raise the sum I needed. But the house was occupied by civil servants whom the Government had installed in it and the few people who still had money tucked away would hardly wish to buy a house on such conditions—so the transaction might take months, perhaps even years! A vague idea of finding some other way out lingered in my mind, but it would now be too much to hope for a quick solution, and it was risky to remain in Cluj, even though my friend had found me an excellent hiding-place.

"Do you think," I asked him, "you could possibly borrow a car or a motor-bicycle and take me to the station at Mohu—it's about fifteen miles south of Sibiu? I'd like, if possible, to go on Christmas Eve."

"I'll do my best," he replied.

Then he went with me to a large Lutheran church, about two hundred yards from our meeting-place. Here in the dark porch he had hidden the suitcase with the clothes which he had bought for me.

Once again—on Christmas Eve—we met by the tower; it was only six but it was already very dark. Dr. Farcasanu had borrowed a small, rickety car from a friend. I had no luggage—only a few odds and ends stuffed in my overcoat pockets.

The air was frosty, but so far there had been no snow; the Feleac road wound upwards to a height of about 1,500 feet above the city in a southerly direction, towards Bucharest. Veronica and Magda would now be able to celebrate Christmas with easy minds: they need no longer fear a raid by the Security Police, and I had given them more than half the money.

Although the celebration of the birth of Christ had been struck off the calendar of the "new society," nevertheless on that evening everyone, young and old, was gathered round the table in almost every house. I had chosen this night to go to the capital in the hope that there would be little traffic on the roads and that the watchfulness of the Security Police would be relaxed, and indeed, on the journey of nearly 120 miles, we met less than a dozen cars.

We drove for five hours. This gave us a chance to talk, and to tell each other of our experiences in the past ten years. The clinics connected with the University were a meeting-place for doctors, nurses, students and patients from all parts of the country. As a result a great deal of news circulated among the doctors. Although Stalin was dead and his heirs were quarrelling, the dictatorship continued to keep a firm grip on its victims. As I had foreseen, the passive resistance movement had grown, but no one dared to bring the fight into the open, and active resistance had decreased year by year. Many groups of partisans and other anti-Communist organisations had been wiped out; they had been overwhelmed by numbers, for a new army of nearly half a million men had been built up, trained and armed on the Soviet model, and had succeeded in consolidating the Communist régime. The Air-Force also had been reinforced by hundreds of fighter planes and about ninety jet planes. Rumours told of a great wealth of uranium discovered in the western part of the Apuseni mountains and in those of Maramures; of colossal machines installed by Russian engineers to mine it, and of thousands of tons being extracted and transported under military guard to Russia. The Communists, however, had abandoned the half-built Danube-Black Sea canal, as well as their project for the construction of an underground railway in Bucharest. A hundred and fifty thousand workers had been sent to work on the canal, and of these, it was said, forty thousand—mostly professional men who were political prisoners—had died of hunger and exhaustion.

Tudor Farcasanu also told me about various measures the Security Police had taken after my escape. Under a number of pretexts and disguises they had planted agents in the house of my parents and in those of my relations. For about a week there had been frequent checks on trains and roads throughout the country. Dr. Ion Borza, our mutual friend, had been told by a Security officer (whose child's life he had saved from meningitis) that a "dangerous criminal" was on the run; but it was only when I visited Tudor Farcasanu that our friends put these various happenings together. What he told me now helped me to avoid the traps which might be set for me.

The rickety old car rattled along the highway over hill and dale never exceeding thirty miles an hour. My last drive along this road had been in Axente's taxi in 1950. We were numb with cold by the time we saw the lights of Sibiu shining on the crest of a hill and knew that in another hour we would reach Mohu.

"I didn't want to mention it until the last moment. We have a little Christmas present for you," said Tudor. "It's like this . . . While you were in prison and standing up to all that frightful pressure, we have led a much more bearable life; we put up only passive resistance to the Communists—unfortunately we haven't your pugnacious nature! Well, now Loghin has formed a group from among our friends, to back you up in your further ventures."

Then he told me that every month I would receive a sum of money through the medium of Dr. Mircea Vulcanescu, the head of one of the big hospitals in Bucharest. To get it I had only to ring him up from a public call-box. On the other hand, if I rang up Dr. Leonid Nicoara, a cancer specialist, it would mean that I had urgent need of a hiding-place. Both doctors were old friends of mine though in the last ten years we had completely lost touch. The plan was reasonably safe, as the telephone lines of hospitals and clinics were the least likely to be tapped by the police.

Tudor Farcasanu dropped me about half a mile from the station. My ticket was already in my pocket—he had bought it on our way through Sibiu. The red lights of his car grew smaller and smaller in the darkness until they vanished round a bend in the road: Farcasanu was hurrying back to Cluj so that he could be at his post at the clinic the next day. The small station, which served three or four neighbouring villages, stood in the open fields; there was not a single traveller that Christmas Eve.

Now the freshness of the night seemed to give me new life. The wind which had whistled among the peaks of the Carpathians and was filled with the smells of the pine-forests, blew about my ears. I no longer felt lonely. Kind, understanding friends were supporting me. The train arrived at two in the morning. As I gazed into the darkness through the carriage window, the sparks from the engine and the dim outlines of trees and telegraph poles made me think of my journey from gaol in Bucharest to gaol in Suceava. I looked down at my hands: they were free, unchained . . .

On the evening of Christmas Day, twenty-four hours after my departure from Cluj, I knocked on the door of a small house in the Grivitza district of Bucharest; it stood next to a bombed site overgrown with briars and long-stemmed thistles. I had managed to get a lift in a lorry for the last forty miles of my journey: to arrive by train at the Gara de Nord would have been too risky.

I would gladly have avoided Bucharest altogether. The knowledge that the police were still hunting me kept me in a constant state of tension, while the nearness of the prison where I had been tortured terrified me. But I had to find money to pay guides and work out my escape route, and since I had failed to do so at Cluj, Bucharest offered the best opportunity.

Sandu and Anthea had been warned of my arrival. Their tiny kitchen became my home. Sandu was studying engineering and Anthea medicine; they had only been married for six months.

The young couple occupied the adjoining room; it was miserably furnished with a dilapidated divan, a shabby wardrobe and a rickety table. Nevertheless, they made me feel welcome from the first moment and although I had never met Sandu before, and only remembered Anthea as a little girl with white ribbons at the ends of her long plaits, all three of us became friends at once.

Once again I lived indoors, without heating, without hot food, my movements restricted to the minimum. Anthea and Sandu were at the University all day. My only living companion was a bitch, Frunza, who was chained outside in the little garden and who barked furiously every time anyone approached the fence. As we could not tell whether she was barking at a passer-by or at a snooping Security agent, the noise she made at night put us all in a state of near-panic.

January passed in waiting. A small wireless-set brought me

news, music and the urge to set out on the long journey over the frontier.

On the last day of the month Anthea made up her mind to speak to me.

"I am terribly sorry but I've got to tell you something." She wrung her red, swollen frost-bitten hands. "I am four months pregnant: when Frunza barks at night, I wake up and I can't get to sleep again. It's not just that I'm afraid of the police, but I have the feeling that one more of these frights and I'll have a miscarriage. You know how fond we are of you, but we have to beg you to look for another hiding-place. After my baby is born, you'll be welcome back to stay with us for as long as you like."

"Of course. When would you like me to go?"

"As soon as you can."

I moved before the following evening. My new hide-out was in a large block of flats and there was always a porter in the entrance hall. But my host, Matei, had chosen a moment when the porter went down to the basement to see to the central heating and we were able to slip through. Matei was very agitated though he tried to look at ease. He was a young student of architecture who looked like a musician. We went up by lift to the sixth floor, climbed a metal staircase to the seventh floor and hurried along a passage to a door marked No. 4.

"Come in," he whispered, "and don't be surprised at what you'll find."

The room was less than seven feet by five. Matei's wife was waiting for us, sitting on a corner of the narrow divan covered by a red and white striped rug. She held out a small, pale hand, looking at me wonderingly with her dark eyes shaded by long lashes. Then, as if we had been old friends, she said: "Come and sit beside me. How do you like our home?"

The room was hardly bigger than my cell in Bucharest. Matei and Diana had been living in it ever since their marriage, more than two years ago. Both were going to be architects. They lived on an allowance of 10 *lei* a day from Matei's father who had been a naval commander and was now a carpenter. Diana's father, who had been a friend of mine, had died during the war. The young people lived on hopes and dreams rather than on food. One of Matei's dreams was of a large, luxurious house which he would present to his beloved wife; at the moment it lay, planned to the last detail, in his portfolio.

The attic walls were hung with linen towels embroidered with Roumanian motifs in black and red. A silver ikon hung on the wall, with a lighted candle before the image of the Virgin. Matei had fixed up some shelves in a corner; on them were arranged some cups and plates of fine porcelain and a few pieces of solid silver— all that remained of the family possessions.

It was midnight before we decided to go to bed. Matei and Diana lay down on their divan. My bed was a blanket on the only available floor-space, between the divan and the wall; it served as both mattress and covering, and I used my rolled-up scarf as a pillow. The youngsters, full of good spirits, whispered to each other before falling asleep. My view changed the moment I lay down, for under the divan were piles of books and note-books, a bag of potatoes, another of beans, jam jars, onions, footwear, brushes . . . The divan itself was made of two empty packing cases with some boards laid across the top.

In the morning Diana and Matei hurried off to their lectures. Then it was my turn to lie on the divan, but not to sleep—for a snore might betray my presence to the neighbours, or worse still, to the cleaning women who were known to spy for the Security Police.

In my isolation in the 7th floor attic, I often had the impression of being chained to the top of a tall rock. No vultures gnawed at my heart, but every step in the corridor outside gave me palpitations.

In the last week of February, Matei began to cough; it looked like an attack of bronchitis. He went to be examined by a doctor; two days later he heard the diagnosis: tubercular germs in the sputum, and the X-ray had revealed a cavity in the lung. Under-nourishment, lack of fresh air, cramped quarters, general misery, all had contributed to the onset of the disease. I also realised with horror that I myself might have given him the infection. During my rest in the attic in Cluj my diseased lung had healed to a certain extent, but the damp and bad ventilation in Anthea's kitchen had made me spit blood again.

Now I too began to cough. The cold draught between the space under the door and the tiny window, which had to be kept open if we were not to suffocate, went like a knife through my ribs every night as I lay on the floor.

One evening Matei came home with the news that he was being sent to a students' sanatorium for treatment.

Since my arrival in the attic there had been additions to the household. For two years Diana and Matei had been scrimping on the money for their food to give each other a surprise. Touched by their devotion to each other, I had made up the sum they needed and Matei had returned from town with two tiny green fish—no bigger than match-sticks—swimming in their bowl and Diana with two blue love-birds. Tonight the fish were swimming as usual among the aquatic plants, but the love-birds drooped dismally and no longer chattered, as if sharing the young people's sadness at their parting.

## CHAPTER XVI

IN THE beginning of March the last blast of winter had brought a heavy snowstorm—three feet of snow had fallen in a single night. My head was muffled in my scarf and my cap pulled down over my ears. The southern suburbs and the last electric street lamps were behind me. I crossed a rickety bridge over a stream into what officially was the country; but here too citizens of Bucharest were living, in little shacks which they had built themselves of timber and dried earth. They drew their water from a well and their oil lamps gave a weak golden glow, like the light painted by Rembrandt. My new host guided me through the dark lanes. Sever's house lay on the edge of a cemetery; on the other sides were open fields. Although I was a total stranger, his family welcomed me warmly and hospitably. My bed was a divan made up of boards and empty cases, and I shared it with an old woman of seventy. In one corner of the room slept the goat Stelutza; in another several moulting hens and a black dog huddled together for warmth. The smell of the animals, the stuffiness and the cold all contributed to the impression of living in a stable. Sever worked as a technician in the Radio-Popular factory and his wages did not run to any form of heating.

"Do you know whom I met today?" he asked me one evening when he came back from work. "Filimon. I hadn't seen him for ten years."

Filimon was a childhood friend of Sever's. They came from the same village in the Banat. Filimon's father was a poor peasant; Sever's was the parish priest. In the new society Filimon had risen to the rank of a militia lieutenant, while Sever, who had studied economics at the University of Bucharest, had become a simple electrician. Now their friendship had revived, and this inspired me to make an attempt to obtain a false identity card.

## The Lost Footsteps

This was in the spring of 1955; preparations for the Four Power meeting at Geneva created an extraordinary optimism in Roumania. Millions of people believed that by the autumn the Soviet armies would have been withdrawn, and that free elections would be held. Members of the Security Services, realising how unfortunate would be their plight in such a case, were panicking. As a result there was a relaxation of tension in Bucharest; people spoke more freely, their faces looked less strained.

Early in April, Sever brought me an identity book, complete with photograph. Filimon had obtained it, without any idea of the identity of the man for whom he was doing this good turn; he believed that he was helping a Roumanian from Bessarabia[1] to avoid "repatriation" to the Soviet Union. His reward was 2000 *lei* from me, and an oath from Sever to protect him, on the day that the régime changed, from retaliation for having worn the uniform of a militiaman. This money and Filimon's trust in the word of a priest's son solved my problem.

The request for a new identity card on the grounds that the old one had been lost had been made through Filimon! He had had to arrange for references, proofs, and publication of the loss in the *Monitor Official*. The file of an unsuspecting citizen, who of course had not lost his identity card, was used as the basis for mine; our ages and descriptions were the only things we had in common.

Now I possessed a paper of which the duplicate was in the files of the militia and, short of a thorough check-up, it should protect me in an emergency.

The moment had come to send an S O S to my friends abroad. I made my first attempt . . .

Could this deaf, decrepit old lady be the Mrs. Alexandrina Rossini who had once been lady-in-waiting to the Queen? She was now living in a bathroom and working as a caretaker in a block of

---

[1] Bessarabia: Roumanian province near the Soviet border, annexed by the U.S.S.R. after the conclusion of the Ribbentrop–Molotov Pact in 1940, against the will of the Roumanian nation.

flats. I could not believe that in the seven years since I had last seen her she could have changed so much.

She had been in touch with an engineer who was a member of the Israeli Embassy, but he had become *persona non grata* and had been ordered out of the country. Mrs. Rossini could no longer help me.

I made a second attempt. . .

". . . and so, after six months' detention in the prison at Jihlava, I was set free. I denied that I had ever known you," said Alice Zamfirescu, in her familiar friendly voice. "I still correspond with my brother in Frankfurt through the dressmaker whom I told you about. But I don't think that it would be wise for you to make use of her. I have the feeling that the Security Police are still keeping an eye on me."

After that evening I never saw her again. I did not wish her to suffer any more on my account.

I made a third attempt. . .

"My dear friend, I am at your disposal and ready to do anything you ask me," Dr. Nestor protested warmly. "As you know, my cousin is no longer in France; she has been working in a hospital in Milan for two years now, but she could send your message to Kostea in Paris. Let me have the text . . ."

I gave him the text: "Petre, by using autotherapy, has cured himself of tuberculosis; if his brother Gabriel would send him a tonic, now that he is convalescent, it would help him." A postcard with this message slipped in among the family mail would convey the news of my escape and an appeal for help. Kostea should receive it in Paris and pass it on to "Gabriel" who was in touch with those who had sent me back to Roumania. But this method was roundabout and uncertain.

It was a joy to see Dr. Nestor again. Not only he but his uncle, Professor Mironescu, remained free, and Colonel Mihaileanu and his partisans were still continuing their resistance in the mountains. My disappearance had worried them considerably. I had not turned up at the meetings we had planned in August 1950 and they had never known if I had left for Paris earlier than I had intended or been caught in Bucharest or on the way.

Getting in touch with them again meant that I learned more about what was happening in the country. The Russians had strengthened their military bases in Roumania. Large units of tanks and artillery were hidden in the forests of Muntenia, Oltenia and the Banat. A submarine harbour had been constructed at Mangalia. Secret aerodromes had been built at Caracal, Tecuci, Silistra and Apahida. In the hilly regions of the Campulung-Muscel and Arges there were stores of petrol and oil, equipment and food, to be used in case of emergency or open conflict. The air space was guarded from one end of the country to the other, and the Black Sea coast had a tight system of defences. Clearly the Russians valued the strategic importance of Roumania in case of war, both as a barrier and as a base for the invasion of Central and Western Europe.

My fourth attempt to send a message was more fortunate.

Old Jacob opened the door in answer to my ring. He bowed and, without uttering a word, motioned me to come in; he was overwhelmed with emotion. He had a weak heart and I had not really expected to find him alive.

His niece, Anne-Marie, was married to a Swiss and had been living in Montreux for over fifteen years. They wrote to one another every month and, on my return to Roumania in the summer of 1950, I had sometimes given him a message for Alba.

"You were fated to bear a heavy burden, but you see that our Heavenly Father has protected you from evil. My heart tells me that you will reach safety," old Jacob encouraged me. "But you must be impatient for news of Alba. For many months after you failed to return to Paris she kept writing through Anne-Marie, asking for news of you—sometimes long letters, at others only a line or two; since then she has never asked again. I don't know whether she still waits for a miracle or whether she has given up hope of ever seeing you again."

In my happiness I threw my arms round the old man; he promised that my message would go to his niece the very next day and from there to Paris. My hopes soared; Alba could not have forgotten me! Although nearly six years had passed since we parted in the Gare de l'Est in Paris, I felt that the web of love could never be unravelled.

I very rarely left my hiding-place. Few of my friends in Bucharest knew each other as they did in Cluj and, after a five-year silence, I realised that any messenger I sent might be taken for an *agent-provocateur*. Fear demoralised me: however I told myself it was absurd to think that any army of agents could lie in wait for me for hours, days, weeks and months on end in the streets of Bucharest. But the danger lay elsewhere, in the army of informers who did circulate throughout the city and who might be anywhere —in cinemas, trams, inns, in people's houses—even those of intimate friends. Experience had taught me that silence was still the safest course.

Late spring found me still in Sever's house; the apricot and peach trees were the first to flower; then came cherry, plum and apple blossoms. The animals had now been moved to a little outhouse in the yard. I avoided going out except by night. But my lungs were, all the same, filled with fresh country air and growing stronger. I had stopped spitting blood.

Gay winds scattered the early blossoms. Now the acacias decked themselves in long white pendants; the lime-trees, their sap warmed by the blazing June sunshine, opened their first flowers. The tropical heat hardly lessened with the approach of night, and I often remained awake until all hours. One night the suffocating heat was more than I could bear; as the cuckoo-clock struck three, I slipped softly outside, and sat down in a dark corner of the veranda. The moonless sky radiated a faint, bluish light.

I could hear the throbbing of aeroplane engines; they seemed to be circling over the city as if in search of something. The noise was sometimes clear, sometimes less distinct. Suddenly the beams of dozens of searchlights criss-crossed the night sky. Anti-aircraft guns went into action and red streaks of tracer bullets flashed upwards.

"The Communists must be trying out their air defences," I

said to myself. "Or perhaps it's a demonstration of force while another drama is being staged at Geneva." I was mistaken.

Pieces of shrapnel fell with a dull thud on the wooden roof of our house. Sever and his wife Ana rushed out on to the veranda; the old grandmother, scared out of her wits, remained huddled on the divan. The gunfire had been going on for about half an hour and a wan light had appeared on the horizon when there was a sound of splintering woodwork and falling plaster.

"Help! . . . h-e-e-elp!" the old woman wailed from inside the house.

We ran in and by the flickering light of a match saw that her head was covered with blood. A piece of shrapnel about eight inches long had gone through the thin, sun-dried timber of the roof and had wounded her. It was about two hours before the ambulance arrived to take her to the hospital. Hidden in the stable, behind the hoarding of the manger, I vaguely heard the agitation outside.

About lunch-time light footsteps approached the stable. I hoped that the commotion had died down and I could leave my hiding-place, which was no bigger than a coffin. Ana pretended to be talking as usual to the goat, Stelutza, and her kid, then she whispered the latest news: "I don't know what can have happened, but a militia officer came in to find out who the tall, fair young man is who is living unregistered in our house."

"What did you say?"

Ana had admitted that a tall, fair youth did indeed live there, but said that he was registered. She fetched the "house-book," stamped by the militia, and proved that the young man was her brother, a student. Refusing to believe her, the subaltern had insisted that Puiu Sangiorgio should stay at home that evening when he returned from his lectures, so that he could check up on him in person. It seemed that the information had been given him by one of the "kind" neighbours. But Puiu came home only on Sunday evenings; he was living temporarily with a friend so that I could have his share of the divan.

That afternoon was torture. Ana had to rush off to the University to warn her brother. I spent several hours moving about inside the stable watching the yard, the garden and the small stretch of the road I could see through a crack in the door.

It was growing dark. Ana was back accompanied by her brother, but Sever was late; he must have dropped in at the hospital to see how his mother-in-law was getting on.

I waited until it was dark before I left the stable. It seemed safest to cross the cemetery to the road which lay beyond it. There was not a sound except the occasional barking of a dog.

I had been walking for about ten minutes along one of the roads which led to the town; ahead of me were the red lights of a stationary car. Suddenly they went out. I walked on, keeping close to the hedge. Where the lights had been there was now the white glow of an electric torch. I stood stock still. A searchlight flashed on at the end of the street and swept the road. The sound of my footsteps on the cobbles must have given me away.

"Who's there? Come forward!" ordered a loud voice.

I made no reply. Someone tried to start up a motor-bicycle about a hundred yards away. The street was now as bright as daylight. I jumped over the fence into a garden and fled under the low trees. The motor-bicycle came throbbing down the road and there was a burst of firing from a machine-gun at the place where I had vanished through the fence. I jumped over another fence; crossed another garden; another yard and another street. My heart was pounding. Lights were coming on in the cottage windows. I could hear the motor-bicycle roaring in the surrounding streets. I was groping about in search of a hiding-place, but I had completely lost my bearings. For a moment the hue and cry seemed to move away. I crawled through a hedge on the right. I could just see the whitish outline of a tombstone. I was back in the cemetery.

Sever came out in answer to my light tap on his bedroom window. I was panting and sweating after racing desperately through the darkness. We both went into the stable.

"If you had only waited another five minutes I'd have been at home and I would never have allowed you to leave," he said with a shade of annoyance. "Of course, you couldn't know as you were alone all day. There were parachutists dropped last night, and so now the whole of this district is surrounded by thousands of troops and police. They'll make a house to house search in every street."

Sever had heard the news in full from Filimon, the militia lieutenant. The police believed that the parachutists had been dropped in our neighbourhood, and that members of the Resistance movement in Bucharest would try to get in touch with them in order to hide them; among them, they thought, might be a "dangerous political criminal" who was somewhere at large. Filimon, in charge of four men, had been given his description and photograph, and had realised with horror that they were those of the "Roumanian from Bessarabia."

It was impossible for Filimon to retrace his steps—the identity card, the money, the oath sworn by Sever to protect him opened an abyss under his feet. He could not save himself by a confession to his superiors. So he chose to play our game to the end. Fearing the effects of a Communist setback at the Geneva Conference he wanted to remain on safe ground; he preferred to be sure of the friendship of Sever but also of the "dangerous fugitive." That morning he had tried to warn Sever, but he could not find him till the evening.

"I'll make for the open country," I said. "I'll try to disappear among the vineyards."

"You won't have a chance," said Sever. "The hiding-place behind the manger is much safer."

"It's too dangerous for you," I said.

Without a word my friend drew back the hoarding and taking hold of my arm helped me to slip inside. Then he threw some dry hay in the manger in order to camouflage the hide-out more thoroughly.

"Sprinkle a little paraffin to destroy the scent round the stable and in front of the door," I whispered.

"Don't worry! I'll sprinkle the whole place!" he assured me.

Back in my airless coffin and worn out by the emotions of the

247

last twenty-four hours, I dozed off against my will. Heavy, hurried footsteps and coarse voices woke me. It was the turn of Sever's household to be searched by the Security men. In the confusion of sounds it was hard for me to tell how the operation was going. Nasturel, the black dog, gave the signal. He barked furiously, as if trying to break his chain, fastened to a hook in the wall of the stable. Someone opened the door. The goat and the kid jumped up uneasily and tried to rush out. A thin ray of light from an electric torch reached the hoarding behind the manger. Sever's dog continued to bark furiously, while the goat and her kid made off into the yard.

"Control that cur of yours!" ordered an angry, impatient voice. "Or our Alsatian will tear him to pieces!"

Ana was begging: "Please keep your Alsatian on the lead or he'll kill my kid. Oh, where has my kid gone . . .?"

"Come on! Don't you see the stable is empty? They haven't anything in it but that confounded goat!" said a bored voice. "There's no sense in going inside—the hens would only light on our heads . . .!"

Heavy footsteps came towards the manger. Someone shook the dry hay suspiciously with a pitchfork. The hens, roosting on a wooden beam, cackled noisily and two of them flew towards the open door. The nocturnal visitors withdrew, spreading themselves out over the orchard to look under the trees and among the raspberry and currant bushes. The squad were in a hurry; there were about a hundred thousand people in their district and the operation had to be completed before dawn.

Silence fell gradually on the house; on its inhabitants; on the garden. The "wolves" had got to within one step of my hiding-place, but good luck—or perhaps the unseen wing of my guardian angel—had protected me.

This intense activity on the part of the Security Police swept like a wave over the country, threatening to swamp anyone unlucky enough to stand in its way. But it lasted only twenty-four hours and was followed by a period of relative calm. I spent the summer in different hiding-places: one of my hosts was the director of a State bank; another, a well-known lawyer who was Counsellor at the Court of Appeal; still another, a surgeon who lived some seven miles outside the capital.

My existence was made up of patience and waiting. I reminded myself that my chances of escape were better than those of thousands of other people in hiding; their only hope lay in the outbreak of a war or of a revolution, whilst mine was pinned to the receipt of a message from the West. Letters did come, but they voiced astonishment and incredulity. Even Alba was unable to believe that I was alive, while the messages from my friends breathed suspicion in every line. "What diabolical net can the Roumanian Security Police be casting now? Who can guarantee that Silviu is alive and free? Supposing some agent has stepped into his shoes and is using his contacts and his name?"

At that moment it was not the seventeen hundred odd miles between Paris and Bucharest which mattered, but the Iron Curtain and the difficulty of finding out what was going on behind it. There *were* means, however, and one of them I used in my second message to Alba. The letter purported to be from old Jacob to his niece in Montreux: "Petre often thinks of the garden where you wandered together when you were young. He gave me a nostalgic description of your favourite meeting-place: a spring bubbling from beneath a rock; a white marble statue of two young lovers reclining on a green lawn, unaware in their happiness that a gigantic boulder above their heads threatened, at any moment, to fall and crush them. The waves of life have washed you up on different shores; you are far away but please don't forget him altogether. He once told me how much he wished he could send you three white carnations—your favourite flower—to remind you of him." The statue in the Luxembourg Gardens, the days spent in the alleys of that beautiful Parisian park and the three carnations I used to bring Alba were details known only to Alba and to me. When she received this letter she was at once convinced that I was alive. Her answering message was full of love, of hope and of optimism. From then onwards, in spite of the distance between us, we no longer felt cut off from each other: some hyper-sensitive form of telepathy kept us in touch; I had the impression that Alba's love was protecting me and fighting for me.

But the message that convinced Alba failed to convince my other friends in the West. They wanted more tangible proof. They wanted me to send a perfectly normal, undisguised specimen of my handwriting. The risk in doing this was very great: the censors were supposed to keep a file for everyone writing a letter abroad, in which the addresses of both sender and addressee were meticulously entered. If my handwriting aroused suspicion, nothing should be easier than to set a watch on the house and catch me when I came to collect the reply. Fortunately, the censors were hopelessly overworked, and no one in Roumania knew of my connection with old Jacob. The decision was not an easy one but finally, in August, another letter went off to Montreux, with several words in my own handwriting on the last page.

For over two months there was no reply. Then early one morning in October with a thin, fine rain falling from a leaden sky, I was outside old Jacob's house. The position of the flower-pot on the window-sill told me that it was safe to ring the bell.

"Welcome!" the old man greeted me. "I was beginning to feel anxious; it's nearly two and a half months since you've been to see me."

With a cheerful smile he invited me in, hurriedly opened the door of a cupboard, lifted the lid off a saucepan and took out a small packet wrapped in newspaper.

"I've been waiting impatiently! Look! I have a present for you!" he said, handing me the packet.

My surprise was great indeed: wrapped up in the sheet of newspaper was a bundle of ten thousand *lei* in hundred-*lei* notes. About two weeks earlier old Jacob had been visited by someone unknown to him, a man who looked about fifty. As an introduction, the stranger had produced a letter from Paris in which he was asked to inquire about old Jacob's health, and to take him a present for his niece. To confirm the receipt of the money the old man was to send a few commonplace words to someone in Paris and to mention the present to his niece "on the occasion of her tenth birthday."

A letter from Montreux was also waiting for me: in it Alba announced that the money had been sent and that my friends insisted that I should try to leave Roumania without delay. It seemed that their incredulity had been overcome.

The sum of money was a substantial one. It amounted to two years' income of an average worker, though its real value was only about £170. Yet in crossing the frontier in 1949 and 1950, I had had to pay much more, in dollars, to the guide.

Preparations for the journey absorbed my days: first, I must reach the frontier-zone, which meant a journey of some 450 miles to Satu Mare (a town ten miles from the frontier). I tried to find a way of sending somebody to Lotzi, the guide with whom I had planned my journey in the summer of 1950. He was extremely dependable and I wanted him to be my guide again. But, in case he had been arrested in the intervening years, I had two other men on whom I could fall back.

At the beginning of autumn (1955) I moved back to my first hiding-place in Bucharest—Sandu's house in the Grivitza quarter. Sandu offered to go to Satu Mare with a message to Lotzi. In June he had obtained his diploma as a constructional engineer, and he now happened to be on a few days' leave because the rain had interrupted the work on the gantry where he was gaining experience. The trouble as usual was that after five years' silence the guide might imagine that Sandu was an *agent provocateur*. Fortunately I remembered that Lotzi had a cousin who was a tailor in Bucharest, and it was through this contact that I communicated with the guide in 1950. I went to see him with Sandu, and he agreed to accompany Sandu on his journey.

The result of their visit was discouraging. The price for getting a fugitive as far as Budapest had risen to 20,000 *lei*—the equivalent of a thousand dollars. Sandu bargained with the guide, but Lotzi's attitude was understandable. He would be risking his life and he had a wife and child. They lived undisturbed in a little house which he had built himself on the outskirts of the town, and once in every year or two he acted as a guide, but he had to earn enough to make his family secure. Only his prudence and good luck had so far saved him from arrest.

I had only half the sum he asked for and I would still need money for my further journey from Budapest and to pay a guide across the frontier into Austria. To set out without the necessary sum would be hopeless. I had no alternative but to stay on, for the moment, in Roumania, supported by my friends.

Just at that time Roumania was caught in a tornado. The Four Power Conference of Foreign Ministers at Geneva had ended in failure. The continuation of "peaceful co-existence" seemed impossible. "But what," the Communist-dominated peoples asked themselves, "was to be the alternative?" Only a world war; and people actually longed for it—anything to put an end to the intolerable dictatorship and to achieve their liberation. Thousands of people, braving the rain and the frost, queued outside the shops. "If war is going to break out soon, we must lay in at least a small store of food, oil, matches, soap, sugar, some tinned meat and fat," they would say, remembering the experiences of the last world war.

A strange psychosis gripped the population. On the one hand, they imagined that the fighting would be short and might even pass over their heads. On the other, they felt that the Communist dictatorship which had now oppressed them for over ten years might, without a war, continue for a century.

At intervals I changed my hiding-place of my own accord because I wanted to spare the nerves of the kind-hearted people who gave me asylum, since the strain was perhaps even greater for them than for me.

One calm, clear, but very cold evening about the middle of November, I left Sandu's house. Anthea's baby, Justina, was about five months old and my presence in their modest home was bearable, but if I stayed too long the neighbours might notice some suspicious detail.

My destination was a building in Strada Semicercului where

the chemist, Melchior Karajan, was to wait for me in the street and smuggle me up to his one-roomed flat. I hoped that the round-about way I had chosen through deserted alleys would not take me longer than an hour. I had already covered most of the distance; now, with my heart in my mouth, I crossed the busy, brilliantly lit Basarab Boulevard—it took me about half a minute—and turned into another quiet side street. I had only gone a few steps when a car came round the corner and pulled up about thirty yards further on. Three people got out, two in civilian clothes and one in the khaki uniform of an officer; I could not see if he belonged to the Security Police or to some military unit. Instinctively I looked round for somewhere to vanish.

The wall on my left was that of an old one-storey building. It looked like a storehouse. At the end of it, about three yards ahead, there was a passage. I darted into it. I could hear footsteps ap-proaching in the street; I groped along the wall and came upon an open door with panels of broken glass; it seemed to lead into a courtyard, but when I slipped through a quick flash of my pocket torch showed me that I was in a room full of empty boxes and with no other exit.

The footsteps hesitated near the entrance to the passage, then turned into it, guided by a torch. Through a chink between the wooden crates I could now distinguish the blue pips and the four stars on the officer's uniform: he was a captain in the Security Service. Inwardly I counted my last seconds. But the light and the footsteps did not come any closer. There was a noise of splintering wood together with a tinny sound, somewhere nearby; it lasted for about three minutes; then the footsteps retreated and shortly afterwards I heard the car starting up its engine and moving away.

I came out of my hiding-place and from the dark entrance of the passage took a quick look to right and left. About twenty yards away I spotted the silhouettes of the two civilians standing on the edge of the pavement.

Hours passed; very occasionally some late-comer would hurry home along the street. But the two silhouettes remained; from time to time, they left their favourite vantage point and patrolled in front of the building or on the opposite pavement. Time dragged by; I could not think of any way out of the trap. I looked for an outlet in the room with the empty packing-cases, but the fear of overturning one by mistake and making a noise made me give up the search.

It was probably about three in the morning when I heard two cars pulling up at the corner and several pairs of footsteps coming down the passage. A voice asked: "Is everything ready?"

"Yes, Comrade Captain; everything is quite ready."

The officer and his companion went away. About two minutes later several more people entered the passage. I could hear the captain's voice addressing someone: "Do you understand? In a quarter of an hour you will be set free and you can return home to your family. For the last time I repeat my orders: you must not speak a single word to anyone about the prison where you were detained nor about the matters on which you were interrogated. You swear? "

A weak, emotional voice replied:

"I swear it!"

"We do not wish you to see the cars which brought you here. You will stand with your face to the wall, guarded by two militia-men until they remove your eyeshade. Then you will be free to go. You will find your own way out of the district and you will go straight home."

The officer went away and there was silence in the passage, broken only by the breathing of the three men. Round the corner in the street engines were started and gears changed: the cars were leaving as the captain had said. So I was to be an involuntary witness of a prisoner's liberation, in the manner often practised by the Security Police. I had not after all been followed down the side street as a suspect; the police had merely been in search of a quiet, unfrequented place in which to set the prisoner free.

I had just begun to count the seconds of the fifteenth minute since the cars had left. One of the two militiamen addressed the prisoner: "In a moment we will take off your eyeshade. But first we will move you one step to the right and you must promise that you will stay exactly where we leave you for another five minutes. You are not to see us going away."

"I promise," replied the man with a shade of happiness in his voice.

A torch lit up the passage once again. And so I was able to watch the whole scene: the man who was awaiting his liberty was seized and placed with his face towards the open door of the room in which I was hiding.

"Don't move!" he ordered curtly. "Now we'll take off your eye shade . . ."

He stepped back two paces, raised his right hand and fired a single bullet into the neck of the prisoner. By a reflex movement the victim made as if to raise his hands to his head, but the gesture was lost in the air. He gave a convulsive shudder and fell, face downwards, on the cement. He died without realising his fate, happy in the thought of being free and going home.

The militiamen at once ran out into the street. From there they fired a few bullets down the passage, which ricocheted off the walls. In a few moments the street was full of people who had rushed out of their houses at the sound of the shooting. The militiamen had their answers ready: they had caught a thief breaking into the warehouse *Alimentara*; ordered to give himself up, he had attacked them with a knife, so they had had to shoot him in self-defence.

The scene was lit by the militiamen's torch for curious on-lookers to see: the dead man lay, face downwards; on the ground beside him was an old leather bag, open and with various burglar's tools scattering from it; the vicious knife shone on the cement. On one side of the door the wooden wall was splintered and the metal casing damaged—proof of the thief's attempt to break and enter.

Soon the police cars came back and so did the captain—I recognised his voice. The stage manager of every detail of this gruesome drama now appeared in it as an actor. Fortunately for me the "investigation" was confined to the passage and only lasted two minutes; as a token gesture the captain flashed his torch over the crate in front of me, then he banged the door shut.

In the course of the day a continual stream of people passed along the street to look at the dead "bandit." A notice was put up at the corner and I heard someone read it aloud: "This is the punishment meted out to anyone who steals the Workers' property! Death to him!" Four Security men were left to guard the building; they patrolled up and down outside the entrance to the passage, thus allowing the dead man to be seen only from a distance. The warehouse was kept closed all day. Covered by the noise of trams and cars on the boulevard and the seething mob in the side street, I was able to move about a little and to take my bearings. I found that the hut was an outhouse built on at the back of the main building and used for storing old crates, barrels and bottles. Late that evening, the body was taken away. The notice, the evidence of the crime, the onlookers and the Security agents all disappeared. The drama was over.

The epilogue was left to me. The cursed place over which the soul of the murdered man still hovered was now carefully avoided by the passers-by. Waiting for a safe moment, I left it and disappeared into the night. Melchior Karajan, pacing up and down distractedly, was waiting for me at the appointed place. Our arrangement had been that if anything prevented me from coming on the first evening, he was to wait at the same place the following night.

The murder I had witnessed was not the only one of its kind. During the next fortnight some fifty people were shot under the pretext that they had tried to break into State shops. Corpses appeared in every district of the city—even in the central thoroughfares—and were left on view for twelve hours. These tactics were intended to spread terror, and to warn the public who, tired of standing in endless queues, were in a mood to raid the shops.

I believe that the Communist rulers, as well as the millions whom they terrorised, were by now suffering from grave mental unbalance. A decade of intense strain was giving rise to acts of sheer lunacy; it had produced a collective disease which it would be hard to cure. And instead of using humane methods to relieve this strain, the Communists applied measures which could only aggravate it.

## CHAPTER XVII

ESCAPE TO the West became every day more imperative. Andrei Loghin had not succeeded in selling his house in Cluj in spite of all the efforts he had made for almost a year. At Christmas fresh messages were sent off to my friends in Paris, telling them, in veiled terms, about my plight. I reckoned that a clandestine journey to Vienna now cost between four and five thousand dollars. I hoped that my friends, if they could not raise as much as this among themselves, would get assistance from the Western circles who had shown an interest in the resistance movement at the time of my return to Roumania in 1950.

Winter in cramped, unheated and ill-ventilated quarters was again straining my nerves and my physical condition. In February 1956 a reply from Alba, via Montreux, increased my anxiety: my friends asked me to review the expenses of my escape, and to let them know the minimum on which I could manage it. I begged them to send me whatever sum they could raise.

The confinement and monotony of my life tried my brain and my nerves, already worn by years of strain. Had I been stronger I would have joined the partisans in the Campulung-Muscel mountains, where the pure air, the beauty of the landscape and the interest of working with Colonel Mihaileanu would certainly have been good for me. But the condition of my spine and legs—still suffering from the effects of the thrashings and of running round that eternal circle—made it unlikely that I could live in the cold, damp caves of the mountains, without becoming a burden to my hosts.

Indeed I felt I had become a painful burden and a source of continual fear to all those who sheltered me. Suddenly a way was opened for me to a region about which I had long dreamed. An elderly lady from Bucharest, going on her yearly pilgrimage to the

Convent of the Dormition of the Virgin in the village of Vladimiresti, took a message from me to my cousin, Mother Mary
Magdalen, who was assistant to the Abbess.

The nun came to see me one day—it was the last day in
February—when heavy snow was falling. Her small slight figure
was unchanged. She might almost have been a young woman of
twenty-five, although she was twice that age; only her hands were
rough and worn, with swollen joints like those of a rheumaticky old
woman of seventy. We had scarcely heard of each other for about
eight years. Her last news of me had come through Georgetta,
whom the Security Police had sent to her in 1948. Without the
slightest hesitation she invited me to the convent.

"You can come to us without any fear! No one will know
except myself and Mother Marietta, the Abbess. I showed her
your letter. She gave me money for the journey and begged me to
set out at once; she has known about you for ten years or more
and she is delighted at the thought of being able to do you
a good turn. We will share with you our food, water and
fresh air, and you will be under the protection of our patron, the
Virgin."

And so one night about the middle of March, Sandu brought
me in a little Skoda car belonging to his firm to within a mile of
the village of Vladimiresti. He had a false permit in his pocket, in
the name of himself and his assistant, Mihai Lipaneanu, to go on
an urgent job to Tecuci and Galatz. The convent lay in the heart
of the country, but not far from the road which connected these
two towns. As we had arranged at our last meeting Mother Mary
Magdalen was waiting for me at a shrine by a crossroads at two in
the morning.

The warm March days had begun to melt the snow and the
earth was awakening to life; the snowdrops were nearly over, the
nun told me as we made our way over the fields, and grass and
violets were coming up. A half-hour's walk led us to the convent.
From a distance, the lighted windows of the church looked like
gold medallions in the dark. But instead of entering by the main
gate, Mother Mary Magdalen took me to a solitary, spreading tree

about a hundred yards within the walls of the convent grounds. Here she helped me down a few steps, switched on her electric torch, veiling the light with her handkerchief, and opened a wooden door into a small dug-out.

"This dug-out has precious memories for us," she whispered. "It was beside this tree that our Abbess had her visions twenty years ago. For us this is holy ground."

The dug-out was a small underground room. On one side of it was a wooden bed, on the other a bench. The bed was covered with hand-woven linen embroidered in peasant designs. The tidy cleanliness of the cell, faintly scented by the wild flowers in front of the ikon of the Virgin, had something festive about it.

The wall beside the bed was lined with smooth pine-boards, yellowish with age. The nun leaned against it, pressing gently to the right. The wall slid open about eighteen inches. We went through it into a narrow passage and, pushing the panel back into place, disappeared under the ground.

The short passage sloped gently upwards. At the end of it we climbed a ladder through a square shaft lined with planks into a space about five feet in length. My guide pushed back a panel on our left; beyond it was a cell as small and simple as the dug-out; on the right was another cell exactly like the first. Each had three plastered and whitewashed walls with a door at one end and a window at the other; the fourth wall—the one with the sliding panel—was made of wood and concealed the tiny passage between the two rooms. The first cell belonged to the Abbess, the second to my guide.

The Abbess blessed me and sprinkled me with holy water. She smiled happily, glad to be able to do a good turn to a man whose life was in danger.

Soon after I came in, the church bells announced the end of the midnight Liturgy which lasts till dawn; as their clear bronze and silver voices died away, a chant intoned by a choir could be heard as if at a great distance. Mother Mary Magdalen drew a corner of the curtain aside and beckoned me to the narrow window.

# The Lost Footsteps

"Look," she said, "you can see the whole of our community. There are two hundred of us."

A procession was leaving the church. The nuns, two by two, walked round the courtyard singing, each with a lighted candle in her hand. Their black robes flowed to the ground, but it seemed to me as if they floated above it, such was the peace and serenity of their movements and their faces in the candle-light; it seemed as if they were living in another world. The service over, the nuns vanished, one after another, to their cells.

Just before it grew light the Abbess, accompanied by Mother Mary Magdalen, led me to the catacombs underneath the convent. We slipped one by one through the opening in the wooden wall and climbed down the ladder; then, from the underground passage, we entered a labyrinth. This time our subterranean journey took us about ten minutes; at last we reached a little room, its floor and two of its walls covered with rush-matting. Ikons, with lights burning in front of them, hung on the other walls giving the room the air of a chapel. A mattress and some bedding had been laid on a mat in the corner.

I remained underground for three days, for I had to learn the exact topography of the catacombs or I would never find my way in case of danger. The nuns had given me wax candles, an electric torch with spare batteries, an oil lamp and a sketch-map of the corridors with their three exits, hundreds of yards outside the walls of the nunnery. The Abbess and Mother Mary Magdalen visited me often, and with their help I got to know every nook and every landmark.

According to the nuns, the layer of earth over our heads was about nine feet thick. The silence was of a depth I had never known before. Everything which existed in the world above seemed to take on another aspect.

As I sat talking with the Abbess and my cousin, the air was filled with the smell of pure wax candles. Our stories, and the way we sat in oriental fashion on rush mats, made me think of the *Thousand and One Nights*. The fantastic personages of the age-old tales joined me in my subterranean dwelling; indeed, the events

261

of their day could hardly surpass, in complexity and in drama, those of our own time.

I had long wanted to meet Mother Marietta. Her life had become a legend in many different parts of the country, and extraordinary things were told about her.

The Abbess was now thirty-five. She had lost her mother when she was two and her father had married again. Her stepmother was as wicked as in the fairy tales; for years the child was kept shut up in a hen-house without any windows; she lived like a little animal. Her father and stepmother intended her to die. But one summer morning—by then she was eight—Marietta escaped from her hen-coop and ran into the village. The children, then the peasants, surrounded her, horrified; she was filthy and in rags. Marietta showed them a small wooden ikon of the Virgin and stuttered a few unintelligible words. The ikon had been given her by her mother just before she died. In the end the child succeeded in explaining what she meant; her mother had left her in the care of her Heavenly Mother, the Mother of Jesus.

The priest and the village people looked after her until her mother's parents fetched her and took her to live with them. They were very poor. Marietta earned her keep by herding cattle in the neighbouring pastures. She suffered from the burning sun and the biting wind and the icy rain. She lived like a hermit, talking to the flowers and the grass. The falcon, the stork and the nightingale became her friends, as well as the gentle cows in her charge.

Years passed. At fifteen Marietta was still herding cattle and could neither read nor write. In the summer of 1936 there was a drought. The earth dried and cracked, the crops wilted and the animals began to die. On a white-hot day, when the air was dancing in the sun, Marietta came running down the village street, announcing a miracle: she had seen the Virgin, Jesus and an old man —perhaps it was God the Father? They had given her a command to pass on to the people: a convent must be built and dedicated to the "redemption of Roumania." Great trials, they had told her, would befall Roumania in the years to come; so the nuns in the convent were to pray for mercy unceasingly by day and by night. The nuns must never be more than two hundred, and the church, the cells and the rest of the convent were to be the work of their own hands.

The work began that very week. Marietta carved a cross on the bark of the old tree near the place where God had spoken to her, and a few steps from the tree she began to dig a dug-out. The news of her vision spread throughout the neighbourhood. Christians, impressed by it, came to see her and were touched by her spirituality. Gifts began to pour in, some very humble, others very rich. Girls flocked from the neighbouring villages to join Marietta. The peasants gave her the field with the tree.

Ten years had passed since then. The convent of two hundred nuns had come into being on the site chosen by God. The obstacles had seemed insurmountable, but year by year they were miraculously overcome.

In this decade waves of adversity had swept over Roumania— war, occupation, an apocalyptic revolution. Millions of its people had suffered untold misery. And throughout those years the prayers of the nuns had risen to Heaven by day and by night, begging for salvation from evil and remission of sins. Tens of thousands of the faithful had come from all parts of the country as pilgrims.

Much of this I had heard already. In the following weeks I was to see a little of the life of the convent. In our talks together the Abbess and Mother Mary Magdalen added to what I knew.

The Convent of the Dormition of the Virgin was an embarrassment to the Government and the Politburo. In 1948 Georghe Apostol, who was then Secretary of the Party, paid it a visit. He knew Mother Marietta very well, because twelve years earlier she had helped him to hide in a hut on the edge of a vineyard: Apostol, a Communist hunted by the police, had come to his native village of Vladimiresti in the hope of shaking off his pursuers, and Marietta, the cowgirl, had brought him food, water and news from the village. As she saw it, she was helping a neighbour who was

## The Lost Footsteps

being hounded for believing in the age-old dream: equality and fraternity.

When he came in 1948, Apostol was astonished at the buildings which had risen from the bare fields—a church and around it two hundred cells built in the shape of a horseshoe; refectory, kitchen, store-rooms, work-rooms, offices. In the outhouses were some twenty cows and dozens of pigs and poultry; a flock of three hundred merino sheep grazed in a neighbouring field. Fifty swarms of bees, housed in the apiary, provided honey as well as wax for the candles. There were orchards and corn-fields. All the work was done by the nuns. They ploughed, they sowed and they harvested; they spun and wove the wool and the hemp into carpets and linen. They were dressed exactly alike and they lived identical lives. They worked willingly, their effort limited only by their physical strength. Equality and fraternity reigned among them; willing concord gave them inner peace; their collective life was founded on freedom, and on the free acceptance of the moral principles which governed it.

The Secretary of the Party saw that in a field in his village a small Communist-Christian society of rare perfection had been created; not through dialectical materialism and dictatorship but through faith, charity and hope. But he had not come to admire the flourishing community. He had come to offer the Abbess on behalf of the Government more land, more cattle, more bees, as well as agricultural machinery and new equipment for the work-shops, so that the output could be doubled and the living standard of the community considerably increased—on certain conditions: the Abbess was henceforth to rule the convent in accordance with the directives of the Central Committee of the Party. She must stop preaching religious mysticism and nationalism. And there must be no more of the pilgrimages which involved the loss of many work-days to the State economy; and—Apostol gave Mother Marietta to understand—no more subversive activities. If these conditions were rejected the entire establishment would be wiped out.

The offer was refused . . . In fact the Abbess and the two

264

hundred nuns had been spending their time not on subversive activities but in practising their rule of prayer and charity. Four years earlier, however, when the Soviet armies had entered Roumanian soil, they had considered their predicament and unanimously decided that they would not renounce their life's work. With their strong hands they hollowed out subterranean galleries —rooms where they could live, store-rooms and safety exits.

The tide of war swept over the region. The Abbess ordered the nuns to hide in the catacombs, while only she herself and ten of the administrative staff remained in the church, in front of the Altar. The Red soldiers invaded the grounds and the buildings, but the nuns' courage, the significance of their naïve—yet essentially divine—gestures, commanded respect. The convent and the nuns were spared.

Later they offered shelter to Roumanian soldiers who had escaped and were in danger of being captured. The secret passages were thrown open to fugitives; some stayed for a few months, others for two or three years, until kind-hearted people helped them to escape across the frontier.

But the gun-barrels had hardly cooled when fresh troubles broke out and the Communist revolution drove other fugitives towards the convent's gates. So the nuns assumed responsibility for the salvation of these hunted people and hid them in their catacombs. Others, whom they could not rescue, fell into the hands of the Security Police. Even for them the nuns did what they could: by extraordinarily ingenious methods they managed to send consecrated hosts in tiny phials to the prisoners, so that those who were dying in agony might receive the last rites.

The misfortunes which the Abbess had seen in her visions and had prophesied had proved to be anything but figments of an exalted mind. Now, whatever the dangers which threatened them, the nuns were determined to stay in their convent and to carry on their work. There were eighty mounds in the cemetery: eighty nuns had given their lives carting bricks, cement, water in the burning sun and the lashing wind; tuberculosis, pneumonia and other diseases had struck them down. And the remaining nuns felt a profound devotion to the memory of their martyrs and to the task of the "redemption of Roumania" to which they were dedicated.

Georghe Apostol, as he rose in the Communist hierarchy, continued his attempts to win over the convent by various extravagant promises. He realised that to use its influence over the faithful for Communist aims would be much more profitable than to destroy it. But the Abbess, supported by the Council of the nuns, stolidly refused.

On my fourth night in the convent, when the nuns had retired to their cells after the midnight service, the Abbess took me up into the church. It was a monumental building. Candles burning day and night in massive silver candlesticks illuminated the interior, their lights flickering towards the great walls and domes. A single nun was praying to the Virgin and Child, her eyes fixed on the Altar in accordance with the Convent Rule. Painted Byzantine saints with long ascetic faces and clothed in blue, purple and gold, worshipped the Father, transfixed in eternal wonder. Woven rugs with Roumanian designs, spread on the mosaic floors, evoked memories of fields and meadows.

Passing through the church, we continued our journey. The Abbess led me to the church tower. We climbed its height of 60 feet by twisting wooden ladders and came at last to a little room. It was crammed with lumber—musty books and boxes of candlesticks and candle-stumps. Mother Marietta opened a large cupboard full of old and tattered clothes; vestments of tarnished blue and green brocade hung beside nuns' worn-out habits and cloaks. At a push of her hand, the back of the wardrobe opened, allowing us to pass through into the space behind. Here we climbed another, almost vertical, ladder and through a trap door into a room identical in size with the one below.

It was octagonal in shape and about seven feet across and in height. A faded yellow carpet with a black design covered the floor. In one corner there was a shake-down—a mattress, two blankets and a long-haired sheepskin. Books were piled against the wall and from a nail hung a pair of binoculars in their leather case.

# The Lost Footsteps

Water and other necessities had been provided. From that night I began my new existence, suspended between earth and sky.

I woke at dawn. I could see the horizon on all sides through the narrow windows in the eight walls. My prison dream of living inside a crystal cube seemed to have come true. I could watch the sun as it rose and progressed, the white clouds floating on the blue waters of space, the sunset and the twilight.

From my tower I also watched thousands of pilgrims arriving for the Feast of the Annunciation on the 25th of March. The crowds gathered from every direction, filled the church for the services, and spent the night under the open sky, sitting round camp-fires in the field below me. Next day they went back to their towns and villages.

I continued my strange existence in the eyrie. Now and then, Mother Marietta or Mother Mary Magdalen visited me. Below, the fields were growing green. The air, fragrant with the sap of growing things and the scent of freshly turned furrows, filled my lungs and restored my strength. I read books, reviews and newspapers, living in perfect tranquillity and coming to believe that evil was impotent against the peace which surrounded me.

Through my field-glasses I followed every detail of the life of the awakening countryside. Six years had passed since I had really seen the country in spring. It made me want to live for ever.

Easter was approaching. The first pilgrims appeared on Palm Sunday, and thousands arrived during Holy Week, some by train, others in carts drawn by horses or oxen. They brought their food and bedding with them; all were eager to attend the midnight service on Easter Sunday. Their gifts, left at the doors of the convent, were humble but given by generous hearts. Dozens of fires were lit up in the fields by night. By Saturday evening nearly forty thousand pilgrims had assembled.

The murmur of thousands of voices reached my windows like the sound of restless waves. At midnight, the Liturgy began inside the church. Later the doors were thrown open and twelve priests, robed in their copes and stoles embroidered with shining gold, came out, each carrying a book held up in his right hand. The procession moved towards an altar built on a raised platform in the middle of the field so that the huge crowds could all follow the sacred service of the Resurrection. The two hundred nuns followed the priests and stood in a long file two deep, in front of the altar. The priests opened their books and the service began. Half-an-hour later a happy peal of bells announced the Resurrection of Christ and the nuns took up the song of the bells, chanting the message of eternal hope:

> *Christ has risen from the dead*
> *And has abolished death*
> *And brought life and immortality to light . . .*

The hymn was taken up by the pilgrims and swelled in volume until it was intoned in unison by forty thousand voices.

The priests lit the candles of those who stood near them from the flames of the candles burning on the altar, and the light was passed from man to man until thousands of lit candles illuminated the darkness.

Then the priests moved in procession, followed by the nuns and by the endless stream of worshippers, each carrying his candle. They wound their way three times round the church, singing the joyful hymn.

The feast lasted for three days. On the fourth day not a soul remained in the field. The marks left by the fires of the pilgrims made it look as if a camp had been struck in great haste.

Soon the budding acacias and the sweet smell of the long clusters of blossoms announced the beginning of May. From Bucharest came the news that the Patriarch Justinian, head of the Roumanian Orthodox Church, was to visit the convent. He arrived one Wednesday towards evening, in a Cadillac of the latest model. The nuns who assembled at the gate did not know on which to bestow the greater attention—the splendid limousine, or their spiritual father robed in a cashmere cope with a massive gold cross hanging on his breast.

The Patriarch's visit lasted two days. Unfortunately he was

concerned neither with spiritual problems nor with the life of the community. His mission was of quite a different order. The Government and the Communist Party were increasingly alarmed at the growing influence throughout the country of the Abbess and of her Christian labours for the "redemption of Roumania." They considered that the time had come to put an end to it once and for all. The legend attached to the convent must be destroyed. It must be made clear that the Virgin had no power to redeem Roumania, and that the workers' everyday efforts in workshops and factories were the only force capable of ameliorating the lot of mankind. In this the Patriarch shared the opinion of the Politburo. He put his arguments, one by one, before the Abbess, not omitting the grave consequences for the convent if she disregarded his advice. He also reminded her of the phials containing the consecrated hosts, which he termed "ridiculous nonsense." Then the head of the church patiently explained the tenets of dialectical materialism in regard to the relation between body and soul, showing that death caused the destruction of both. So what was the use of Holy Communion? Those who were condemned to die might as well die without it . . . In addressing the Abbess the Patriarch stressed that he had come to see her both as her spiritual father, anxious about her fate, and also on behalf of his friends Gheorghiu-Dej and Georghe Apostol, now respectively Secretary of the Party and President of the General Confederation of Workers. He begged her to recognise the significance of his advice which amounted to an ultimatum.

That night, after the midnight service, Mother Marietta groped her way up the ladders to my room at the top of the tower.

"Black clouds are gathering over us," she said as she began her account of the Patriarch's visit. We discussed the position at length. "How can we give in!" she exclaimed. "What would the faithful think if we lacked the courage to defend our faith? Would it not be a prelude to total defeat?" Submission would save only the physical lives of her nuns. Resistance would make martyrs of them: the story of the Convent of the Dormition of the Virgin would become a legend and the spiritual achievement of the nuns could never be wiped out by the Communists—nor eaten by worms, nor swept away by floods, winds or rain.

The Patriarch Justinian went back to Bucharest, having failed to obtain the convent's submission. What would happen to us next? Our peace vanished. For me too, the spectre of the Security Police began to hover over the convent precincts.

The storm broke on the tenth night after the visit of the Patriarch. I had been lying on my bed on the floor, watching the rising moon. Suddenly the headlights of several cars appeared in the distance. I looked through my field-glasses; now I could see that a whole motorised column was advancing along the highway. About half a mile from the convent, it broke up into two parts, the one turning to the left, the other to the right with the obvious aim of surrounding the buildings. I had counted ten cars and about forty military lorries; it was unlikely that manœuvres would be taking place at this time of night.

When I came down, the Abbess was still awake and on her knees; I could see her dimly by the light of a single candle as I opened the door. "So it has come," she sighed. She got up and blessed me, making the sign of the cross over my head. "One thing I ask you," she said. "If by God's help you regain your freedom, I charge you with the responsibility of spreading the story of the convent—and of its end—throughout the world." She took down a little silver ikon from a nail over her bed and gave it to me: "May the Holy Virgin keep you in her care." We bade each other a hasty farewell.

I pushed back the sliding panel and stepped into the narrow passage from which I could climb down to the catacombs; but I wanted first to say good-bye to Mother Mary Magdalen. The sound of heavy footsteps caught my ear. I stood still and listened; three Security officers, conducted by the portress, came into the Abbess's cell.

"We have orders to inform you that the convent is to be closed down at once," one of them said. "You, as Abbess, the priest who acts as your chaplain and the ten nuns on the Council are under arrest; you will be taken to Bucharest tonight. I must warn you that any opposition would be useless. Two hundred yards from here, outside the walls, there is a cordon of machine-guns and artillery. Make no attempt to alarm the neighbouring villages . . ." The guns were not directed towards the convent but outwards, against anyone who might try to come to its help.

The rest of the nuns were to leave their cells and return to their homes, taking with them only their clothes. The entire property of the convent was to be requisitioned by the State. Finally the officer ordered the Abbess to take him to the administrative building and to hand over to him the inventory and the money and valuables belong to the convent.

"First I have something to say to you," said Mother Marietta. "You may not believe in the existence of God, but I dare say you believe in something that we can call a moral force. I assure you that one day this crime committed by the State against defenceless nuns will be avenged. Why didn't you have the courage to come by daylight? Why do you come in the darkness, like bandits, with your guns and rifles? . . ."

"You'd better change your tune or we'll smash your teeth in," said the officer. "We know that you hide criminals in your catacombs. We'll settle up with them as well as with you."

The Abbess called Mother Mary Magdalen and asked her, as her assistant, to accompany her in order to be present at the confiscation of the convent's property.

I heard the rustle of their footsteps along the corridor until it was obliterated by the heavy tread of the boots of the Security men.

In the meantime, as I was to learn, the rest of the nuns had assembled in the church. After the visit of the Patriarch, the community had decided that they would not, this time, hide in the catacombs but would remain at their post, before the Altar, and risk being arrested or killed rather than leave the convent. Only Mother Mary Magdalen had been ordered by the Abbess to try to escape and to reach a convent in the mountains, which had recently been founded by the same order, and where she could hide and carry on their work.

# The Lost Footsteps

The lights before the ikons in the room in the catacombs which had sheltered me for three nights were still burning. Now they were destined to be extinguished for ever.

The space in which the several subterranean corridors intersected was circular and about ten feet in diameter. It had taken me about seven minutes to reach it. Flashing my torch down the passage on my left, which led to one of the exits, I saw what I was looking for: a coil of strong rope, a wood-axe and a shovel lying against the earth-wall.

Suddenly I heard a thud and several muffled explosions, followed by the sound of a woman groaning in one of the other passages. I hurried in the direction of the sounds. A short distance away, the corridor was completely blocked by a fall of earth; lying on the ground with her legs buried in the rubble was Mother Mary Magdalen. I quickly freed her; she was badly shaken but she got up, supporting herself against the wall, and managed with my help to reach the circular chamber. There she collapsed.

As they were going towards Mother Marietta's office, she had succeeded for a moment in slipping away from the Security men on the pretext that she had to fetch an account book. She made for a room which had an entrance to this central part of the catacombs through a panel in the back of a cupboard, and had just pushed the panel into place behind her when she heard one of the agents who had followed her calling to her to come back. He had then fired through the boards of the panel and had wounded her in the chest. She had just enough strength left to shut and bolt the heavy iron trap-door of the shaft leading to the underground passage; then she fainted and rolled down the ladder to the floor below. Above her, the Security men tried to blow the trap-door open with hand grenades, but the explosions caused the soil beneath it to collapse, blocking the passage.

By now Mother Mary Magdalen was very weak. The bullet must have lodged in her lung and her breathing was extremely painful. She begged me, with tears in her eyes, to make my escape without losing a moment. The police would assume that she had intended to warn others who were hiding underground, so they would tear up the whole place in order to reach the catacombs, and if they found me, this would only worsen the position of the nuns. Although in great pain, she reasoned lucidly. But how could I leave her there alone?

Now there were more sounds of explosions and we heard men's voices calling in the distance. I half carried Mary Magdalen into the corridor which led to the exit, and putting my lighted torch on the ground, got down to a very difficult task.

The earth roof was supported by wooden struts, and the axe and the rope had been left for just such an emergency as we were facing now: if I could cut down several of the supports in time, the ceiling would collapse and block all the corridors at the point of their intersection. I chopped furiously and managed in the next few moments to bring down three of them, but the post at the centre of the room was thicker and had only moved a little when a shout came from the passage opposite:

"I heard blows in that direction! This way!"

In a nightmare of haste I fastened the rope to the base of the support and, rushing into the corridor in which Mary Magdalen was lying, tugged with all my strength. One of the policemen had already come into sight and fired a volley in our direction; hot on my track, he arrived at the crossroads when the ceiling crashed noisily down, burying him in a mound of earth and sand and separating us from the rest by a barrier several yards thick.

We advanced slowly. The wounded woman was utterly exhausted and could hardly move although I supported her. When we had crawled about a hundred yards, I cut down more struts with my axe and the sandy soil collapsed behind us, forming a second wall to protect us. But, for all we knew, the police might be waiting for us at the exit.

Our fate was in the hands of the Abbess and of those of the nuns who knew the plan of the catacombs. If they held out for an hour or two against threats and possibly torture, we might have a chance.

An hour passed. We were coming to the end of the passage and the air freshened. But Mother Mary Magdalen, her clothes soaked in blood, finally collapsed. I wanted to try to stop the bleeding with an improvised bandage and to carry her across the fields. But she could no longer make any movement and, looking at her face, I had to recognise the truth. A trickle of blood was dripping from the corner of her mouth and her forehead and temples were bathed in sweat. She pressed my hand gently and implored me to go—to go this moment.

"Follow the river Siret. Hide along its wooded banks," she whispered.

She was quiet; then summoning a little strength, she said: "My heart tells me that you will be free . . . As for me, for years I have longed for the end of my earthly journey. Only in the dominion of the Holy Virgin shall we have peace." In a few seconds she was dead.

The image of Mother Mary Magdalen and the memory of her goodness are imprinted for ever on my mind.

A few yards before the end of the passage I caused a part of the earth ceiling to collapse again. Her body was thus buried—safe from the hungry wolves and foxes.

Fortunately there was no one about as I emerged from the well-concealed exit and saw the calm waters of the Siret gleaming in front of me in the early light. The bank was steep at this point. Clinging to shrubs and roots, I followed Mother Mary Magdalen's advice and climbed down to the shallow pebbly edge of the stream. I waded in for a long time and then swam to the opposite shore, so that police-hounds should not be able to follow my scent.

It was not until noon that I heard the clatter of hooves on pebbles and saw a patrol approaching with two bloodhounds. I had hidden in a thicket of poplars and willows and was waiting until nightfall to continue my journey.

The branches overhung the river, and below me the current had hollowed out the bank, leaving the roots of the trees bare and depositing sand on the bottom of a deep pool.

I slipped quietly into the water, keeping only my head

above the surface in the shadow of the branches to which I clung.

A raft carrying pine logs moved slowly into sight round the bend of the river. The commander of the patrol called out to the raftsmen to draw closer to the bank; as the water was low, the raft went aground several yards from the shore.

"Have you seen a tall young man in a green jacket and black trousers walking along the river bank?"

"Certainly we did," replied the raftsmen in chorus, "a couple of miles upstream near the bridge at Cosmesti. Only he was not going anywhere, he was lying in a field near a clump of alder-bushes."

The patrol wheeled and set off at a gallop for Cosmesti, while the raft was steered back slowly into the current. Mother Mary Magdalen had done me a last good turn by advising me to hide in the thickets on the river bank.

At night I covered about twelve miles over meadows and fields of wheat and maize. Just before dawn I knocked on the window of Anton Iordan's house in the suburbs of Tecuci. The old cripple, with both legs amputated at the knees, hid me in a hen-house at the back of his yard. I had several friends in the town—elderly people who had not been uprooted by the tumult of revolution. At the end of ten days Sandu, to whom I had sent a few lines on a postcard, came to fetch me and we travelled back to Bucharest in the same rickety Skoda, protected by another faked permit. My stay in the Siret region was over.

I was told later that a notice was nailed to the convent door which read: "This building, which is the property of the Roumanian People's Republic, has been requisitioned for the use of Mental Hospital Number 10."

## CHAPTER XVIII

It was nearly two years since my escape and I had made no real progress in arranging my flight to Vienna. My hopes were pinned to my friends in the West. I waited impatiently for an answer to my last appeal which had been sent in February. Four months had gone by without a sign from them: I tried to encourage myself by the thought that they were trying to obtain the sum necessary for my escape and had probably turned for help to the influential Western circles who, before my return to Roumania, had shown interest in supporting resistance to Communism beyond the Iron Curtain.

At the end of July a reply arrived from Paris. It came in the pages of a letter from Alba. She wrote: "I am anxious and worried to death about the fate of my youngest child. He is ill. I have consulted all the best doctors. Their unanimous opinion is that nothing more can be done for him. They do not believe there is the slightest chance that he will survive."

This message voiced the stark reality: I had been wrong in thinking that my friends in the free world had been convinced of my survival; they refused to send me help because they did not believe I could possibly have escaped. The realisation that they had abandoned me to my fate was a terrible blow to me. The Iron Curtain now seemed to stretch from the earth into the sky.

Before returning to Roumania in 1950 I had left with my friends in Paris a list of twenty-six people in Roumania with whose help I planned to organise widespread action against the régime. By the summer of 1956, Ion Motru was the only one in prison; the other twenty-five were still at large, thanks to my silence. Also because I had held my tongue, the secret lines of communication between

Roumania and the free world had continued to function between 1950 and 1956. It was therefore possible for my friends in the West to discover the truth, but it seemed that they preferred to regard me with suspicion.

I could read between every line of Alba's letter how painful it had been for her to send me this discouraging message. In spite of the distance of both time and space which separated us, we knew that only in each other could we find true and enduring support. So I concentrated all my hopes on a last appeal which I sent her in August; I begged her to make one last attempt. Sixteen people had escaped from Roumania to other countries with my help; I hoped that at least one of them would remember.

Meanwhile, in September 1956, the Suez crisis caused universal tension and rumours that a war was imminent, whilst the current of liberalisation in Hungary had generated instability in Roumania.

I felt that this was not the time to sit with folded hands in my hiding-place. I was back in my attic home with Matei whose lungs had been cured of their infection. Dr. Nestor and Professor Mironescu met me secretly in the capital and together we agreed on the measures to be taken. In the same month I sent a message to Professor Andrei Loghin in Cluj.

In October the revolution broke out in Budapest and spread all over Hungary. News of the revolution, heard over the Western radio, was passed from man to man throughout the Communist world. Influenced by the example of Hungary, people began to say: "So revolt against even the most crushing dictatorship *is* possible . . .!" In Roumania students and workers were the first to raise their heads. The squares and avenues of Bucharest seethed with tens of thousands of restless inhabitants, and in other large towns—especially in the university centres—revolutionary passions were at boiling point. The peasants remained calm; they followed the march of events but, with their age-old prudence, waited patiently for some line of action to become more definite.

Even the Security Police and the Communists, from the topmost ranks to the last party member, experienced days of confusion and perplexity, not knowing what to expect from the development of events.

Those who unleash a revolution carry a terrible responsibility. Thousands of people were itching for the bitter struggle to begin. The international situation was critical; the armed conflict in Egypt had increased the tension even more and the opportunity, they felt, ought not to be lost; a decade, or even more, might pass before another such chance occurred.

Professor Mironescu's study became my new hiding-place. Colonel Mihaileanu—who had been expected since September—left the Carpathian Mountains and came secretly to Bucharest. He suggested a plan of action and we agreed at once to give him our support. The force we counted on above all else was the railway workers in the capital. This group of ten thousand men, compact and united, had served the Communist Party from 1933–45 in a series of successful *coups*. Eleven years of dictatorship had cured them, once and for all, of the illusion that their lot would change for the better in a Communist society; now they were its adversaries. They had replaced the famous slogan: "Proletarians of the world, unite!" by "Slaves, unite and let us rid ourselves of the tyrants!" Two young engineers, former pupils of Professor Mironescu at the Polytechnic, were working as overseers in the railway workshops and through them the Professor had made many important contacts.

We were also in touch with small but strong resistance groups formed by students, professors, Academicians, writers, artists and doctors.

The revolution in Budapest was going from strength to strength. Western European radio stations kept us accurately informed. We waited, keyed up, for a suitable moment to launch the attack. Colonel Mihaileanu's partisans had slipped into the capital. They were to seize the buildings of the University and of the School of Architecture where many of the students would certainly have joined them.

The railway workers were to occupy the Palace of the Premier and the key points in the city and, through couriers on the trains, to spread the revolution throughout the country . . . Cluj, as the centre of next importance, was preparing for similar action and was ready to back us up.

Colonel Mihaileanu insisted that we should give the signal for attack at once.

"I have been waiting ten years for a chance like this," he said, as he walked excitedly up and down Mironescu's study. "Under no circumstances must we allow this opportunity to slide."

I felt compelled to restrain him. First I thought that we must see what Russia's reaction was going to be. I considered that the Colonel had overlooked the fact that in Roumania neither the Communist Party nor the Government was collapsing as they were in Hungary. It was easy enough to give the signal for attack, but how would we ensure the continuance of the struggle? If the masses were intimidated by Russian military intervention, we would run the risk of being left in mid-air.

One of our greatest problems was the lack of shock troops. Whom could we use to lead the masses who were seething with impatience to begin the struggle? If in 1950 we had been able to organise cadres, they would now have proved of the utmost value. Six years had been lost and it was too late to make up for them.

Two days later the Colonel came in from the next room rubbing his hands and said in an excited stage whisper: "The Professor has just heard the news on the radio that the Russian Army of Occupation has given the order to withdraw from Hungary. You see! The Russians are frightened and are giving up their positions, just as I was informed they would. The moment has come! We must give the signal for attack."

"I agree," said Professor Mironescu.

A high-ranking Roumanian officer had secretly passed on to Mihaileanu a message received from a Russian general, which seemed to justify his optimism: the Soviet leaders were so impressed by American progress in rocket technique that they had decided to withdraw their forces from their advanced positions in Europe and keep them within the frontiers of the U.S.S.R.

# The Lost Footsteps

We fixed the 5th of November as the date of the attack. The plan for operations was agreed. The Professor sent off our instructions by couriers. We waited calmly, hoping that the time had come for our destiny to be determined. The initial action was to be based on a stratagem: three important leaders of the railway workers, with whom Professor Mironescu had kept closely in touch for several years, were to organise a "manifestation of sympathy" with the Government and the Communist Party. Under this pretext the ten thousand men were to leave work and march towards the Palace of the Premier in the Piata Victoriei.

The city was seething; optimism and hope of imminent liberation could be read in every eye.

On the morning of the day before the attack a courier arrived from Cluj with an extremely urgent message from Professor Loghin: it said that a Russian air officer, whose information had always proved reliable, stated that a group of Soviet jet planes from the air-base at Turda (twenty miles from Cluj) had been ordered to take off on the morning of November 4th, their destination Budapest.

Russia's armed interference in Hungary obliged us to call off the attack. Fighter planes based in Roumania were taking off for Hungary and within a few hours their crews had occupied many strategic positions. Simultaneously two thousand tanks came out from their hiding-places in the woods and invaded our neighbour. Long convoys of artillery and motorised infantry set out across the frontier in support of the Soviet occupation troops who in fact had never withdrawn from the country.

In Hungary the revolution ended in a blood bath. In Bucharest an uprising would have met the same fate. The information supplied by the Russian general was of course false. Such rumours were spread by agents of the Politburo and the Soviet General Staff to induce the anti-Communist forces to reveal themselves, and thus lay themselves open to elimination.

Soviet military patrols appeared in the streets of Bucharest and by night hundreds of armoured cars kept the city under tight control. The Communist Security Police resumed their threatening attitude. The Government took unusual steps in the hope of calming the spirit of revolt; prominent members of the Communist Politburo mingled with the workers and students, hoping to keep them under the control of the Party. The West European radio stations brought us daily accounts of the dying revolution; we learned of the exodus of thousands of refugees to Austria; of the bombardment of Budapest; of the last fighting along the barricades; of preparations for the military occupation of the whole of Hungary. For another week or so Colonel Mihaileanu and Professor Mironescu bolstered each other up with illusions, still hoping for a miracle: "It is unthinkable that after showing such courage the Hungarian revolutionaries should be left to their fate. The Western Powers are bound to intervene . . .!" The Colonel tried to establish contact by means of a radio transmitter with the interested circles in the Free World, but only a few radio amateurs picked up his messages.

Colonel Mihaileanu and his partisans retreated to their lairs in the Carpathian Mountains and I moved on to another hiding-place, in order to leave no trace of what had been going on in the past weeks. By now I had almost given up the idea of escaping to Austria; all the same, I awaited a reply from Alba to the message I had sent her in August. On the evening of the 13th of November I knocked at old Jacob's door.

"Welcome!" said the old man with a slight sigh. "Three months have passed since you were here. Come in! Sit down by the fire and tell me what has been keeping you away."

He opened a cupboard as he spoke and, exactly like the other time, took a small packet wrapped in newspaper out of a saucepan and handed it to me, smiling happily.

"Another present for you from Alba!"

The new "present" of twenty thousand *lei*, in notes of a hundred, had been brought by the same person. The ceremony of confirming its arrival followed the same ritual: a postcard was sent thanking the donor for a letter of congratulation on the occasion of the recipient's "twentieth wedding anniversary." My store of money had now risen to thirty thousand *lei*, for I had kept the last precious sum of ten thousand *lei* in reserve.

There were also two messages from Alba, sent as usual through Montreux. She had travelled through several countries in an attempt to collect money for my journey from people who were under an obligation to me. It was only in London that she found someone who understood the real significance of my gesture in leaving for Roumania in 1950. It was this generous patriot who had put at her disposal the sum which had recently been transferred to me. Alba warned me that it was the last on which I could count.

The end of November brought me another surprise: Professor Andrei Loghin sent me fifty thousand *lei* to Bucharest; after efforts lasting two years, he had at last succeeded in selling his house at Cluj and had put the entire sum at my disposal.

The psychosis caused by the thought of war and revolution had driven the population into a frenzy: everyone was obsessed by the idea of laying in reserves of food, oil and other necessities. The Security Police did not dare to shoot any more so-called "thieves of the workers' property"; indignation, tension, collective discontent, could only too easily have avenged such action by breaking out into open revolt. The great demand for food, in view of the small supply, had raised the price of a little sack of beans from one hundred to four hundred *lei* in the course of ten days, and the increase spread to every single basic necessity of life.

The situation became further aggravated. The peasants, terrified at the general insecurity, had lost faith in the Government bank-notes; they refused to sell their beans, maize or wheat, and instead stored them away. This was a signal for everyone to lose faith in the official currency, everyone avoided being paid in it or saving it up. It was in this mood that a peasant woman, alarmed at the economic chaos in Roumania, looked for an investment for the money she had hoarded and bought Professor Loghin's house.

So my stock of money had grown to eighty thousand *lei* in the course of a month—that is to just over thirteen hundred pounds.

But now that I had the necessary sum it looked as though it would be of no use to me.

A year earlier a clandestine journey through Hungary would have presented relatively few difficulties. But now, to get across that country, torn as it was by fighting over most of its territory and subjected to intense military occupation, seemed to have become an almost impossible task.

Nevertheless I had worked out a detailed plan which would take account of the new situation, though every move had to be made with the utmost caution.

During the first week of December, Sandu went to Satu Mare with a message to Lotzi the guide, asking him to get me a false identity card from Hungary. His brother lived in Rozsaly, a village about six miles across the frontier. The price for my secret journey was paid in a rather unusual coin: twenty wrist-watches made by Omega, Doxa, Longines and Movado. Lotzi would not accept payment either in Roumanian bank-notes or dollars. Watches, however, had a very high exchange value and were received everywhere with complete confidence. The State shops *Consignatia* had a good stock of these watches, for many people had been forced to sell jewellery, carpets, cameras and other valuables during the last few years, and these goods had piled up in the State repositories owing to lack of clients. Unlike the peasants, the employees of the State shops could not refuse either to sell the watches or to take official bank-notes in exchange. It was Sandu and his wife Anthea who had bought the twenty watches at different times and places, at prices varying from 1,500 to 2,500 *lei* apiece.

The first news came on Christmas Day; Sandu brought it from the tailor, Ion Damian. Lotzi had returned home after an absence of two weeks. He had not succeeded in getting the identity card; he had, however, handed over my photograph and five of the watches to his brother who would continue his efforts to obtain my document.

I was back again in Sandu's house. I followed the news of the events in Hungary on the radio and noted the number of refugees who were arriving each day in Austria. This gave me a fairly good idea of the chances of crossing Hungarian territory, as well as of the changing conditions in regard to frontier control. While waiting, I tried to ease my suspense by listening to music. For hours on end, while thousands of human beings were dying in its streets, Budapest transmitted disturbing gipsy music, played by its world-famous orchestras. Both Justina, the little daughter of Sandu and Anthea, and I were carried away by that music. By now I had become nurse to the little girl who had so nearly failed to come into the world because her mother had been terrified of a raid by the Security Police every time she heard a dog bark in the night. Frunza was no longer alive; the dog-catcher had caught her. The new dog was called Bodri.

Towards the end of January 1957 the eagerly-awaited news arrived: a false identity card had been obtained and was in the hands of Lotzi's brother in the village of Rozsaly-Ungaria. But freshly-fallen snow made it impossible for me to set out immediately. During the first week in February spring began, earlier than for a hundred years. The snow melted, snowdrops and violets flowered and the fields were drying out; but then Lotzi the guide fell ill. He had caught a chill on his kidneys while dragging himself on all fours over the frozen frontier in December and was now suffering from hæmorrhages.

March 1957 . . .

The radio bulletins informed us that trains were circulating nearly normally in Hungary; only an occasional shot was heard now; the daily exodus of refugees to Austria was reduced from two thousand to about a dozen. Otherwise, the news did not give much cause for optimism; the Soviet Army had extended its control over the entire territory of Hungary; the frontiers were again rigidly patrolled.

On the 7th of March we heard that Lotzi was better and had sent for me to come to Satu Mare. The date of my departure was to be the moonless night of the 17th of March or else the following one. My last message for Montreux–Paris was sent the same evening, informing Alba of my imminent departure for Vienna.

# The Lost Footsteps

On the 14th of March the rising sun found us about seventy-five miles outside Bucharest heading northwards along the asphalt highway which leads to the Carpathian Mountains. I was travelling in a hospital car; the director of the hospital—Dr. Mircea Vulcanescu—was at the wheel; for over two years he had assured me that when the moment came he would see that I reached my friends in Cluj. Sandu accompanied me. I had left Bucharest without regret; the memories of the years I spent in prison had clouded its image. Only very occasionally did we pass another car or a lorry, but nobody took any notice of us.

By dark we came to the top of the Feleac hill; from this height (1,500 feet) I could see the fairylike sparkle of the lights in the city of Cluj. They were scattered widely in the broad, dark valley below. More than three hundred miles separated us from Bucharest, and there would be another hundred and fifty miles to cover before reaching Satu Mare, near the northern frontier of Roumania.

When we got to Cluj, the old hiding-place in Veronica's attic sheltered me for two days and two nights. My friend, Andrei Loghin, had suggested that I should break my journey here.

Our meeting, after an interval of seven years, moved us deeply. The professor, tall and wiry, his hair now white, was waiting for me impatiently. The surgery of Dr. Ion Borza seemed unchanged since the evening of our last meeting there in the summer of 1950.

"It's good to see you again! We meet in incredible circumstances. I don't even know where to begin," said Andrei.

The professor had made up his mind to escape with me to the West accompanied by his daughter and his son, a young doctor; he had lost his wife about a year before. He hoped that if I reached Vienna safely I would be able to raise the money for their journey. I promised to help him. My promise obliged me to blaze my trail to Vienna in such a way that it could also be used for *their* flight and this meant making certain alterations to the original plan.

It was his intention when he arrived in Vienna to publish his thesis on Intervention and to bring it to the attention of U.N.O. His theory had changed to some extent; he no longer believed in armed intervention by an international army; this, he thought, would have been a tactical mistake in the case of Hungary. But the Hungarian experiment had confirmed him in his view that the principle of national sovereignty, though valid, could no longer be regarded as absolute in the changed conditions of the world.

"This is what struck me during the Hungarian revolution," he told me. "The Western radio stations should have broadcast an invitation to the people of Budapest to await the arrival of a special delegation from U.N.O. The message should have been repeated hundreds of times. A 'white' aeroplane carrying the delegation should have landed at the central airport on the 10th of November, when the revolution was at its height. This gesture would have symbolised the desire of the peoples of the world for peace and, initiated by their Forum, it would, I believe, have been irresistible. I am convinced that hundreds of thousands of people would have flocked to the airport; and the Russians would never have dared to prevent the aeroplane from landing—still less to fire into the throng of people who had come to meet it."

I agreed with him that the U.N.O. delegates would have at once become the moral leaders of the people, and that a climate would have been created in which the nation could have found its way to freedom and peace. But for this, I argued, U.N.O. would have had to be a genuinely democratic Forum in which the interests of the smaller nations were not sacrificed to those of the major Powers.

In the two and a half years since my escape the Security Police had made numerous attempts to trap me and I was constantly on my guard to avoid making a false move. I could· describe my tactics at length but it might endanger the safety of many friends.

During these years of underground life I rarely left the comparative security of the homes which sheltered me. But now my journey to the frontier, which meant days on the road, would

expose me to far greater risks. However, my neat clothes gave me
the appearance of a doctor or an engineer. And, in case of an encounter with the Security Police, I pinned all my hopes on a set
of false identity papers. As well as these, Sandu, who was ac-
companying me, had got hold of a false document which certified
that we were both being sent by "Sovromoconstructia" to
supervise construction work near Satu Mare.

On the evening of Saturday, 16th of March, my friends took me
by car to within a short distance of Apahida, a junction about ten
miles east of Cluj. Here Sandu and I got a train for Satu Mare, the
last station on the line.

We arrived at four in the morning and we spent a day at Lotzi's
house, discussing our plans. Then Sandu returned to Bucharest.
He was to help Professor Loghin to arrange his journey to Vienna.

On Sunday evening—the 17th—Lotzi and I boarded a local
train which left at 7.30 for the little town of Halmeu which lies in
the north, towards the Russian frontier. This stretch of line was
only lightly guarded—for no one ever tried to flee to Russia! Forty
minutes later, and fifteen miles from Satu Mare, we got out at a
station just outside a village. A path by the railway line led us to
a level-crossing in the open country. A cold, heavy rain was soaking
the ground and making it slippery. A roof of clouds obscured the
sky; visibility was only about fifty yards. We struck across the
fields, keeping close to the thick lines of acacias. Even the most
experienced eye would have found it hard to distinguish us,
camouflaged as we were by those natural screens, dozens of
miles long, which protected the land and the crops from the
wind.

At 11 p.m. we caught sight of the church tower in Pelisor,
dimly silhouetted against the night sky; the distance separating us
from Hungary was now about a thousand yards. We had been
walking in a south-westerly direction in order to approach the
frontier in a roundabout way. The country was now completely
flat and bare, with only an occasional tree or clump of shrubs.
With every nerve taut, we advanced across the open ground. Every
twenty or thirty paces we dropped on all fours and stayed motion-

less for several minutes to avoid being seen by a patrolling sentry. Lotzi felt his way with a stout rubber stick over every yard we covered; I followed literally in his footsteps. At one moment the rubber stick was caught in the sharp iron teeth of a trap, like those set for wolves; the rubber deadened the click of the metal jaws and saved the guide's foot from certain fracture. Lotzi discovered thin wires hidden in the grass; twice he cut them, thus putting two luminous rockets out of action. Some time later the experience and prudence of the guide saved me from falling into a manhole; it was camouflaged by a net sprinkled with dry grass and had long, sharp iron spikes at the bottom.

It took us about an hour to cross this thousand yards which bordered on the demarcation line between Roumania and Hungary. Lotzi had caught sight of the frontier patrol, as they passed along, through his powerful field-glasses. A yellowish gleam in the darkness told us that the "strip of the lost footsteps" lay about fifty yards in front of us. The ground this side of it had been completely cleared of shrubs and trees; there was not even a hump behind which to hide.

The guide stepped calmly forward through the damp grass to the edge of the freshly-raked earth intended to receive and to retain the footprints of fugitives. With quick, precise movements he unrolled a piece of linoleum across the raked ground. Then, taking from his rucksack eight light squares of wood, he put one of them down on the linoleum and stepped on it, put down another and took another step, and so on until he had crossed the strip. I followed him. The crossing took us two minutes at the most. Now we pulled the linoleum carefully towards us, collected the pieces of wood and put everything back into the rucksack.

We set off towards the interior of Hungary. The rain poured down ceaselessly and we were soaked to the skin. By dawn the rain and the wind would have carried away our scent and wiped out any slight trace of our crossing. The physical effort and the nervous strain had exhausted us. We would have given almost anything to lie down for a few moments' rest, but we went on at a regular pace, for our further journey to Budapest depended on our meeting Lotzi's brother at the appointed place and time.

Half an hour later we found ourselves back at the "strip of the lost footsteps"; in the rain-filled darkness Lotzi had mistaken the direction. We turned and headed once again to the west, walking even faster to make up for lost time. At four a.m. we approached the village of Rozsaly, about six miles from the frontier. Here Denes, Lotzi's brother, was waiting for us on the outskirts, hidden in a pile of hay which had been lying on a threshing-floor ever since the harvest. The two brothers had agreed on this place when they met in December and the date of our arrival had been given in a postcard...

As I expected, the chaos following on the revolution in Hungary had made it easier to obtain a faked identity card, complete with photograph; a militia officer, originally from Rozsaly, had been tempted by my watches (their value had risen to astronomical figures) and had made himself responsible for the document, using the file of a schoolmaster as a basis.

We had covered fifteen miles in the pouring rain that night, lashed in the back by an icy wind. We had to press on to the station, for trains were running on time. It was beginning to get light when Denes bought our tickets. We slipped unnoticed into a second-class carriage; the platform was deserted at that hour and the station was outside the village. After we had been travelling for about two hours, the swaying of the train and the warmth of the carriage got the better of us and we fell asleep. Lotzi's brother had told us that only the trains running towards the towns near the Austrian frontier were guarded by special squads of Security Police. In fact, our documents were not once examined on the journey. We arrived in Budapest in the late afternoon. I was paralysed by exhaustion and could not rejoice as I would have wished at our wonderful success.

The capital astonished me. It had been a day of sunshine and the crowded streets seemed quickened by the fresh, warm air of spring. People walked about serenely, as though unaware of the walls cleft from top to bottom by bombs and gunfire. We also did our best to look calm and smiling in order to blend with the apparent mood of the city.

"Aunt Ethel" had died several years ago and old age, illness or the revolution had wiped out many of my other friends. However, the family of Andrassy, the engineer, and their little house in the suburbs had survived. It was quite dark by the time I knocked at their door. On Thursday evening, four days earlier, I had been the guest for an hour of Andrassy's sisters-in-law in Cluj and they had sent him a message to expect us. He threw the door open and welcomed us warmly. A Doxa watch with a central second hand, delighted the old mechanic and hospitality was showered on us.

After supper, assembled in the warm kitchen, we exchanged news. The events of September-October 1956—the outbreak of the revolution, the street fighting, the massacres, the collective hysteria—this was all told me by eye-witnesses. The Security raids still went on though they had been less frequent in the last three weeks, and units of militiamen armed with machine-guns patrolled the streets of the city day and night. And although on local trains only an identity card was asked for in a check-up, anyone travelling towards a frontier town was obliged, on pain of arrest, to have a special permit stamped by the Security Police.

# CHAPTER XIX

MY FIRST night's rest in the Andrassys' little house had a wonderful effect on me. I relaxed and my dream of escaping to the West, now half-way to becoming a reality, filled me with great happiness. Still, Vienna was a long way off, and I had been unable, so long as I was in Roumania, to make any preparations for the journey into Austria.

Two difficult problems confronted me: I needed a permit from the Security Police to get from Budapest to Szombathely, which lay inside the frontier-zone, and I needed a guide from there to the frontier, a distance of some sixteen miles. To whom could I appeal? Alexander Goldstein and Cornelius Markus, two old friends of Leon Pótócki, had vanished during the revolution. I decided to try and re-establish contact with my two Austrian guides, Stefan and Paul; but messages sent by post, now rigidly censored, would have meant months of waiting, and my safety depended to a great extent on reducing my stay in the capital to the minimum.

I got a glimpse of hope in the course of a conversation with Andrassy. Two of his grandsons had fled to Austria. "Who helped them?" I asked. "A neighbour—an engine-driver," he replied. The engine-driver had been his friend for nearly twenty years.

"Andrassy *Baci*, will you do me a favour?" I begged. "As you know, it is quite out of the question for me to get a permit to enter the frontier-zone. As things are, my only hope of getting there is by train. Could you have a word with your friend? Perhaps he'll think of a way to get me into Szombathely secretly."

"I'll try!" said the old man.

An hour later he came back accompanied by Josef, the engine-driver. The wrist-watches had once more proved their worth; they held a miraculous attraction for everyone in the Communist-dominated world. Josef promised his whole-hearted support. On

# The Lost Footsteps

Friday, March the 22nd, he would be on duty on the Budapest–Celldömölk–Szombathely line; after that he would be on other lines for a fortnight. He urged me not to delay as the situation in Hungary was so uncertain. I made up my mind at once to leave on the 22nd.

Lotzi, the guide, had by now set out for Roumania; Professor Loghin's flight to Budapest and his hiding-place there were now assured, so there was nothing to keep me in Budapest.

And now it was Friday, March the 22nd, 1957. Andrassy's son-in-law, Pytin, was with me in the carriage. I looked out at the travellers on the platform; there was not a great crowd. The sun was rising and the day promised to be fine. The train left for Szombathely—the terminus. There were only five coaches and we travelled comfortably and without a single incident as far as Celldömölk; here we entered the danger-zone.

The moment the train left the station, a squad of Security Police came into our coach. A subaltern and two sergeants, armed with sten guns, began their check-up at one end, while another squad of three started at the other. Their system of examining the documents was thorough, and there was not the slightest chance of flight.

Pytin paled when he was asked for his identity-card, but the inspection passed without incident. Now it was my turn; I held out my identity-card and my ticket as all the other passengers had done. The subaltern examined the entries and my photograph carefully, then asked: "Where are you travelling to?"

"To Sarvar."

"All right . . ."

He handed back my ticket and my card. He had checked that my ticket was for Sarvar. Sarvar lay outside the frontier-zone, and I did not need a permit to go there. My identity-card had proved its value. What I felt as I faced the Security agents is indescribable.

At the next station the police squad left our coach and went into the one behind us. Ours was a motor-wagon with a driver's cabin at either end, so they had to get out before they could pass along the train.

## The Lost Footsteps

We drew into the station at Sarvar. The coach disgorged its
passengers; we should have gone with them but, lingering behind
until we were alone, we moved quickly towards the driver's cabin
and squeezed into a small compartment where spare tins of oil and
petrol were kept. Josef had told us its whereabouts before leaving
Budapest, and in Celldömölk he had slipped us the key.

The train started off again to cover the last fifteen miles to
Szombathely. The head of the Security squad had ordered the
ticket-collector to see to it that passengers got out at the stations
marked on their tickets; any request to buy a supplementary ticket
towards the frontier was to be reported at once. We were still not
out of danger, as very often a further examination was made at the
terminus. At last, after another half-hour, the slackening speed and
grinding of brakes announced our arrival. The strain was growing
more acute each minute. The train stopped. After a few moments
Josef knocked softly on the door of our hiding-place.

"Come! Get out quickly! Hurry and mingle with the other
passengers . . . The police have just arrested two suspects; they are
taking them to the station police-point to hand them over. Good
luck and may God bless you . . .!"

The station square in Szombathely looked unchanged in seven
years. Two rickety old yellow trams stood waiting for passengers.
It was about lunch-time. From our outward appearance we could
have been taken for local people. A smile of pure happiness lit up
my face; the Free World was now only a distance of twelve miles
as the crow flies west of the town. Admittedly, these last miles
were the most difficult of all.

We called at three houses: at the first we were told that Arpad was
out for the day; at the second, we heard the tragic news of Demeter's
death in a shooting affray on the frontier; at the third we were
lucky. Gabor the carter recognised me at once, though he showed
the same incredulous surprise as all the others whom I had met
again after an interval of so many years. He shook our hands
warmly and asked us to come in.

"Well, Gabor! You've grown greyer since we last met!" I said.

"So have you. You look as if you've had plenty of trouble!"

"Did you imagine that our paths would cross again?"

"I certainly didn't . . . My nephew, Endre, told me in the autumn of '50 that you never got back to Austria. I suppose the revolution made it easier for you to come?"

"That's just what happened. But now, tell me, do you know how much the frontier control has been tightened up? How can I quickly get across into Austria, or at least as far as Endre's and Janos *Baci's* village?"

"Life is strange!" said Gabor shaking his head with astonishment. "We made friends that night when you came to our door and I can't think why, but we have often spoken of you in the years since. I don't know who you are, sir, and I don't even want you to tell me, but my heart tells me to help you . . ."

The old carter did know what was going on at the frontier: Soviet Infantry Units and Hungarian frontier guards were in joint control; the former barrage of barbed wire and mine-fields had been dismantled a year after Stalin's death. His successors had ordered this symbol of the Iron Curtain to be wiped out in the hope that their proposals for peaceful co-existence would be more readily accepted by the Western countries; the exodus of Hungarian refugees to Austria after the outbreak of the revolution in October 1956 had thus been greatly facilitated. But since about a month earlier a new barrage had begun to be put up under the supervision of experts from Russia. This was gigantic in size and the work on it had started from both ends of the Austrian frontier as well as in the middle. The first line of defences consisted, as before, of two parallel fences of barbed wire, more than seven feet high; behind this the ground was closely sown with mines to a breadth of fifteen yards; after this came a strip of narrow grass, and beyond that again a ploughed and raked "strip of lost footsteps." Altogether, the new defence system would have a width of approximately twenty-four yards, so that it would not be possible to cross it by any such contraption as the wooden bridge we had used before. Only an expert with mine-detectors could carve a way through the mined area, and the journey across, including the cutting of the wires attached to the mines, would take too long for the ordinary fugitive.

While the work on the barrage was being done by Russians, the Hungarian frontier guards were withdrawn, so that they should not learn how the mines were being hidden in the earth, and the whole operation was being carried out in the utmost secrecy.

Gabor advised me to give up my idea of asking the help of Janos *Baci* and Endre. The premiums paid by the Security Police for every refugee who was denounced had gone up and the network of informers in the villages along the border had been tightened. The situation was full of almost unavoidable possibilities of disaster. But neither could I remain long in the carter's house in Szombathely—certainly not later than that evening, for some of the neighbours had seen Pytin and me arrive there, and strangers in a house on the outskirts of a town near the frontier were bound to arouse suspicions.

Clearly, my only chance was to cross the frontier at a point where the work on the new defences had not yet begun. The old man himself offered to take me to such a place. It lay only five hundred yards from his native village of Bèrk, and only ten days ago his brother, who still lived there, had visited him, so that he had the latest information about that part of the zone. But as at any moment a team of Russian experts might be sent to that particular portion of the frontier, it was imperative not to lose a minute. We set out that very night, while Pytin, who had promised to look after Professor Loghin as far as Szombathely, returned to Budapest.

Darkness fell. For about an hour, I walked with Gabor over wide, freshly ploughed fields. His son was waiting for us in an acacia-grove with three saddled horses. He had set out with his cart before sunset for his plot of land, about a mile and a half from the northern boundary of the town, and had hidden the harness under sacks of hay.

We mounted and set off in haste; the horses' hooves made little sound in the grass and the newly-turned furrows. Stars shone in the clear night sky but there was no moon. The old man found his way instinctively for, as a carter, he knew every inch of the district. We headed due north—parallel with the frontier but about eight or nine miles inside the frontier-zone. For several miles we rode along the bed of an irrigation-canal where the mud swallowed the tell-tale hoof marks.

About ten o'clock, the lights of the village of Tömörd told us that we had already covered ten miles. Riding round to the west of the village, we dismounted. Leonard, the old man's son, led the horses into a thicket, gave them their oats and stayed to guard them. From that point we changed our direction to the West and continued on foot, making straight for the frontier.

For about five miles we splashed through muddy puddles in the blackness of a wood, following a path used for carting logs. At midnight we came out on the slope of a high hill.

"You see those lights over there on the right?" whispered my guide. "That's Frankenau, it's about half a mile inside Austria."

The lights of the little town made a distant glow against the night sky. Down below us in the valley lay the Hungarian village where seven years ago, when I came from Austria, I had spent the night in the byre of Janos *Baci* and Endre.

Old Gabor led me through the vineyards which surrounded the village and up another hill. His own village, Bèrk, lay about a mile away. I knew the topography of the whole of this region. This was the third time I was crossing it. The black upturned earth of a ploughed field absorbed us into its darkness as we threaded our way on the edge of another wood. Now the demarcation line was about three hundred yards in front of us, down below in the wide valley.

Silence shrouded the whole neighbourhood. The wood was above us, the ploughed field sloped down on our right. With great caution we left the shelter of the trees and crawled along the furrows. Part of the field belonged to Gabor's brother and when he had last seen him traps had not been laid in it; all the same Gabor felt his way with outstretched hands.

At the edge of the grassy valley a sentry usually patrolled in the shelter of some trees where he could watch the level ground for a considerable distance. This was our greatest danger.

The clear, star-lit sky ensured a visibility of between fifty and seventy yards. Crawling along the furrows made only an almost imperceptible rustle. We stopped to take our bearings.

The frontier to the Free World was about a hundred yards away. We could clearly hear the murmur of the stream on the other side. But we had come to the most risky part of our journey. We did not dare to crawl another yard until we had seen the sentry. The minutes dragged. It was as if the earth had halted on its axis. At the end of half an hour there was still no sign of the patrol.

Gabor whispered to me to lie flat and motionless till he came back. He crawled towards the black patch of the trees. It seemed an eternity until I sensed rather than heard his return. With his lips close to my ear, the old man whispered: "When I was on the edge of the ploughed land, I heard a groan coming from the thicket . . ." He had crawled there, to find the sentry stabbed with a knife; he had died as he was taking his pulse. Probably someone else was making his way to the frontier that night, and, determined to overcome all difficulties, had murdered the sentry. Gabor had brought back with him the dead man's rifle and the pistol. "Take the rifle!" he whispered; "it may be useful to you . . . I'll keep the pistol."

We did not know at what time the sentries were changed and at any moment a replacement might arrive and raise the alarm. Somewhere, far away on our right, a faint light appeared. Gabor reassured me by saying that it was probably an Austrian guard from Frankenau going on his bicycle along the road parallel with the demarcation-line. But as we watched the light, we saw that it was moving too slowly and irregularly for that, and when it came to within half a mile of us, we tumbled to the meaning of what was happening. A guard on this side of the frontier was searching the ploughed strip by the light of his electric torch for signs of any fresh footprints. Soon he was bound to come across the tracks of the fugitive who had killed the sentry. The old man whispered to me: "We mustn't lose a minute. I'm going back as we agreed:

otherwise, it might be much more risky for me. You must either come back with me to Szombathely or go on across the frontier at once."

There was no danger for me once I crossed the strip, for since the Austrian Peace Treaty had been signed, the Soviet occupation troops had been withdrawn and Austria was neutral ground.

"I'll go on!" I said. "Get safely home, Gabor!"

We shook hands. Gabor set off up the hill and disappeared, crawling on all fours towards its brow. He was making as fast as he could for a marshy stretch in the next valley where his footsteps would leave no trace. It would take him about three hours without a halt to get to the place where his son would be waiting with the horses, and he knew what would be happening behind him once the alarm had been given and police dogs had got on to our tracks on the ploughed land.

I covered about fifty yards on all fours, then stopped. I was now on a flat stretch of dry grass and I could see the clay-coloured "strip of lost footsteps" fairly clearly. The beam of the electric torch was nosing its way slowly from the right . . . Without a sound I ran the last fifty yards, and heedlessly, deliberately, registered my footsteps in the freshly ploughed strip of earth. Then, with extreme caution, I threaded my way for a hundred yards or so over the grass in a westerly direction until I came to the stream Gabor and I had heard. Its murmur guided me over the last stretch, straight to a steep bank, about four yards deep. I clambered quickly down into the bed of the stream, where the water came to about my knees, then, holding on to roots and tufts of grass, I pulled myself up with difficulty on to the opposite bank. I was now on Austrian territory, though not yet out of reach of gun-fire from a patrol on the other side.

I went on through the wood, opening a path through the dense undergrowth with my outstretched hands. I could not see more than a few yards in front of me. I was trying to press on westwards while at the same time veering a few degrees to my right in order to reach open country, as Gabor had advised me. But the thick shrub under the trees obliged me to keep changing my direction.

I had not been able to get a compass and I risked turning in a circle and arriving back at the frontier.

After about an hour of pushing through the branches, with my face and hands scratched and bleeding, my sense of direction was becoming more and more unsure. My only guide now was the star-lit sky but I only saw it in patches and, as the earth's rotation changed the position of the stars, I became increasingly confused. Suddenly I could see more light between the trunks of the trees, and a hundred yards further on I found myself outside the wood. According to Gabor, the walk through the forest should not have taken more than a quarter of an hour.

Open country stretched before me but the lights of Frankenau were nowhere to be seen. Without this landmark I could not be certain that I was heading westwards.

I heard a train; the sound grew louder, roaring and clanking, apparently in my direction, then dying away. A moment later another train passed going in the opposite direction. The railway line must be somewhere on my right. I knew that there was an Austrian line from Mannersdorf (a mile from the frontier) running towards Oberpullendorf. Everything seemed quite clear now. In order to get further into Austria I must keep on going to the right, I told myself.

Fairly confidently, I set off along a cart-track which followed the edge of the forest to the right. Twenty minutes later it turned to the left at right angles. With hardly any hesitation, I struck off through open country clothed with straggling trees and shrubs, convinced that I was heading westwards, until my path came to an abrupt end. In front of me, the ground dropped steeply to a patch of swampy water fifteen feet below.

Somewhere on my right a wild duck called loudly three times; I supposed it had been startled by my presence. Another wild duck answered it on my left, but much further away. It seemed strange that it too called three times.

Neither the ground along the bank nor the marsh below gave me any confidence. I turned back, meaning to rejoin the cart track. The duck called again, this time much closer to me. It was again

answered by a triple call from the distance. I had a sudden feeling
of imminent danger.

"Halt! Hands up!"

Instinctively I spun round. From among the bushes where I
had first heard the duck calling, a Hungarian frontier-guard was
hurrying along the bank. Covering me with his rifle, he ordered
tensely: "Drop your gun."

The murdered sentry's automatic rifle hung over my shoulder.
Urged by Gabor, I had kept it, though several times I had been
on the point of throwing it away, tired by its weight. Consciously
I had thought of it as little more than a souvenir of the frontier-
zone; its Soviet make was unfamiliar to me and I had made no
effort to understand its mechanism. Now I took it and held it at the
ready, determined not to give myself up alive.

"Throw it away at once!" shouted the guard angrily. That he
meant to capture me alive was obvious, or he would have fired.
Instead, he repeated: "Throw it away or I'll fire."

For a moment we faced each other across the few yards of scrub.
If I had known how to work the gun I would have fired. I took
three quick paces towards the guard. Surprised, he stepped back
to the edge of the bank. There he stopped and pressed the
trigger, but nothing happened except the dry clicking of the
firing-pin. The moment's respite while he looked down at his gun,
confused, concentrating on the mechanism, saved me.

I aimed my blow at his head; he ducked but the steel barrel of
my rifle caught him on the temple. At that moment his automatic
began to work and fired a long burst, but the bullets went wide.
A second blow, aimed with all my strength, caught him off balance;
he staggered, then the clayey soil on the edge of the bank gave
way under him and he tumbled over into the swampy ground
below.

The whole encounter had taken perhaps three minutes. I ran
back over the grass towards the cart-track. From the direction of
the marsh but now quite near came the triple call of the wild duck.
The help which the guard had summoned as soon as he had seen
me on the bank had evidently now arrived. Only my decision to

turn back and retrace my steps had forced him to go after me without waiting for the other sentry.

My best chance, both of cover and of at last finding my way was to follow the edge of the wood. I ran through the grass, ready to vanish among the trees at the first sign of danger. With my last ounce of strength I hurried as fast as I could in what I hoped was a westerly direction. But at the end of about half an hour I felt that I was again going astray. Exhausted and desperate, I decided to wait in the wood until dawn.

In the course of my journey from Bucharest I had distributed all my wrist-watches, so I had only an approximate idea of the time. I sat with my back against a tree-trunk and tried to keep awake and to think. How had I confused the landmarks which Gabor had described to me? "If you find your way when you come out of the wood you'll be all right," he had said. "Try to keep away from the stream if you think you are lost—it's dangerous near the stream." The stream crossed the whole of the district from north to south; I thought that I had heard its tinkle as I walked along the path which ended on the edge of the swamp; but there were places where the frontier line ran west of it.

What had really put me off the track was the sound of the trains. The sound waves had, indeed, started from the flat Austrian side of the border, but the line of Hungarian hills, which ran parallel to the frontier and a couple of hundred yards inside it, had echoed and amplified them.

The cold night air made me huddle closer to the tree-trunk. My head kept falling on to my chest. When at last I dropped off to sleep I had a nightmare of monsters and a stormy ocean.

## CHAPTER XX

I was awakened by the song of a bird; high above me a lark was trilling. I had no idea how long I had slept, but as dawn was only just breaking I thought it could not have been for more than half an hour. The first rays of the sun told me where the East lay; over there was Hungary; the road to the West lay in the opposite direction. My shirt, soaked by perspiration, felt like a corset of ice. Between the trees and the undergrowth I saw fields, some ploughed, some sown, stretching out into the distance.

The edge of the wood served me as a screen as I cautiously made my way towards the interior of Austria. After about a quarter of an hour, I crossed a highroad; here a signpost pointed to Frankenau. At the sight of this first proof that I was on friendly soil, all my fear and tenseness disappeared and I was filled with happiness.

The hills, the valleys and the villages, which daylight gradually revealed, were all familiar to me and the tall, slender, white tower of the church in Kleinmutschen—the village from which I had set out seven years before—seemed to welcome me. I offered a prayer of thanks to God. The glorious sun, the grass, the flowers, the wide world, happiness—all these had been restored to me.

My journey to Eastern Europe and my return to the West had taken exactly seven years—March 1950 until March 1957.

The first man belonging to the Free World I saw was coming down from the brow of a hill; with calm, wide-flung gestures, he was sowing seed into newly turned furrows. I watched him for a long time in silence; his work seemed to me symbolical; he was giving life to the earth; he was a man of peace and creation. I took from it a few grains, hoping that one day I could plant them and they would remind me of the joy of this morning.

# The Lost Footsteps

The gardens of the village of Kleinmutschen welcomed me as an old friend. But when Teta Franza saw me at her door, she drew back frightened; my torn and muddy clothes and my hands and face covered with scratches gave me, all too convincingly, the look of an escaped convict. Very soon, however, her fear vanished and she was fussing over me as though I were a son who had been missing for seven years in a war and had at last returned. The cuckoo-clock hanging on the kitchen wall struck nine. A distance of twenty-two miles now separated me from Szombathely in Hungary . . .!

At two o'clock that afternoon I set off for Vienna; the kind peasant woman had lent me a hundred-*schilling* note to pay my fare. From the luxurious 'bus I gazed avidly on the countryside, on the well-kept village houses, on the agricultural machinery and the tractors in the fields—everything enchanted me. When we had been travelling for an hour, we began to meet hundreds of cars speeding along the highway. The Viennese, tired after their week's work, were going for the week-end to the Rax Alpe—Schneegebirge, a mountain resort of great beauty.

My arrival in Vienna aroused in me a mass of contradictory emotions. The familiar boulevards, the shop windows, the throng of pedestrians, the general prosperity and splendour of the city, filled me with delight. But I was uneasy, for to a man in my position, without a passport, many doors were closed, and I wondered whether I would be able to find any of my old friends after so many years' absence.

Karl Böhm was sitting with his feet in a bath of hot water; so was his wife. All day long they had been on their feet selling fruit and vegetables in their little shop in the Sechshauserstrasse. In March 1950 I had put them in touch with my guides and asked them to make the arrangements for my return to Austria. Now they were at first stunned by seeing a man whom they believed to be dead, but when they had recovered from the shock, they immediately offered me hospitality. Their life had gone on calmly and peacefully, their main concern was their business on which their livelihood depended, and the heaps of vegetables and the crates of fruit left them with little time for thinking about other things.

Stefan, the blacksmith, had emigrated to Canada to join his brother, but Paul, the butcher, my second guide, was still living in Vienna, and I visited him that evening. Ghitti, his little six-year-old daughter, opened the door. A familiar voice called out: "Who is it?"

"Daddy, a man wants to see you."

When Paul caught sight of me he rushed forward to greet me, exclaiming: "Why, just today I was thinking of you! That's telepathy! I always expected you to turn up; I never believed you were dead. But you look as if you've been through terrible things. Come in and tell me . . ."

Even in Vienna I was not exempt from the possibility of arrest. Karl Böhm warned me that during the last few weeks the Austrian police had been arresting refugees from Eastern Europe and locking them up pending an inquiry. Obviously such an unpleasant event might befall me and delay or even prevent me from getting in touch with my friends in the West. On the evening of my arrival I booked a telephone call to Alba.

During the night I ran a temperature, probably caused by my exhaustion. Lying wide awake, I gazed into the darkness and tried to imagine my conversation with Paris; the call was to come through next day, Sunday, at noon. The morning seemed endless; then at last it was midday.

"Hallo, Paris? Hallo, Alba! Is that Alba?"

"Yes. Alba speaking!"

For a moment I could not go on.

"Did you get the notice of my call?" I asked. "I sent it last night."

"No." The short reply in a rather detached voice disconcerted me. "I came back late last night; the Exchange may have tried to get in touch with me while I was out . . . But who is speaking?"

"Silviu . . ."

"Silviu? Impossible! My Silviu? It's not possible! I can't believe it!"

"Yes. It's true."

"Oh God. Oh God! How I have longed for this moment . . ."

We were overwhelmed by happiness: after seven years and five months, we were able at least to speak to each other, though mountains, valleys, fields and rivers, as well as several frontiers, still separated us.

During the next four weeks we wrote to each other every day. It was impossible for her to get leave before the Easter holidays.

On Friday the 19th April, 1957—the day of our reunion—the rain, which had begun during the night, continued until lunchtime. The warm damp air was filled with the pungent smell of rotten wood and the dank odour of wet earth. The trees had put out young, anæmic, apple-green shoots. At 12 noon precisely, the blue Air France coach arrived with the passengers who had landed at the Vienna airport. Through the steamed windows I recognised the auburn curls of Alba. We smiled at each other.

We were the last to leave the waiting-room at the air station. We looked at each other. We talked. I felt embarrassed in my ragged coat and my ill-fitting old suit. Our separation had lasted so long, I had so looked forward to our meeting and now, here we were, standing stiffly side by side, hardly knowing what to say. It was only towards evening, in a little Espresso café, that we relaxed and felt the joy of being together again. We recalled the enchantment of our days together in Paris.

It appeared that my case had caused some agitation west of the Iron Curtain as well as east of it, and now Alba skimmed through the pages of a voluminous report and mentioned events and incidents which were unknown to me.

Communist spies had created havoc in certain circles of Roumanian émigrés, especially in Paris. Their activity had now been stopped but they had managed to avoid being identified. As a result an atmosphere laden with suspicion had arisen among the exiles. A parachute captain who had gained the confidence of some members of the section of the French Intelligence Service dealing with south-eastern Europe, as well as of Roumanians in Austria and France, had set off to Roumania to engage in so-called resistance activity; what happened on his arrival was a mystery, but the fact remained that a short time afterwards news came from Bucharest of the arrest of more than a hundred people. A young woman from Paris and a professor from Constantinople had vanished mysteriously in East Berlin; an Orthodox priest had disappeared in Vienna; all three were Roumanian subjects. Several months later the priest was seen walking freely through the streets of Bucharest . . . All kinds of theories were inevitably invented to explain the fate of these people; some of them were fantastic, others near to the truth. No one, however, succeeded in establishing the exact facts. Groups of parachutists who had been dropped during those years over Roumanian territory had been captured with bewildering rapidity by the Security Police. They had been inadequately prepared for what they had to meet; they did not know the extent to which the situation in Roumania had changed; these deficiencies, to which must be added certain grave indiscretions committed in the West, led to the destruction of nearly all of them. "So," I said to myself, "these no doubt were the sources from which the Interrogating Commission got its information about me, and from this it made its deductions about my purpose in returning to Roumania . . ." The intense pressure put upon me and the significance of the different phases of the interrogation were now at least partially understandable.

The solitary confinement in which I was held had prevented any leakage to the outside world regarding my fate. By the autumn of 1950 my friends in the West had given me up for lost. It was only in the summer of 1955 that they received the first news of my escape. By that time, however, it had become difficult and extremely risky to attempt to verify such news in a Communist country. When the Roumanian National Committee and other Western circles interested in the continuance of the Resistance Movement in Roumania were told of my reappearance, they tried to explain my five years' silence in two ways:

Either circumstances had obliged me to seek refuge with some partisan group in the mountains or to lie hidden in some town, or

I had fallen into the hands of the Security Police and been transformed into a Communist spy.

For a few months they wavered between these two hypotheses. Among them all, Basil Ratiu (former Military Attaché in Ankara and military adviser to the Roumanian National Committee) was the only one who had no doubt about me; in 1949 we had prepared together the plan of action for which I had returned to Roumania. He was the only one who insisted at Alba's request that money should be sent to me for my journey or that some other means of rescuing me should be found without another moment's delay. My first message that "Petre, by means of autotherapy, had cured himself of tuberculosis and would be grateful if his brother Gabriel (Basil Ratiu) would send him a tonic," perplexed them deeply and became the cause of heated discussions. The few lines I had sent in my own handwriting had been analysed by experts and had failed to satisfy them. Only after three months of argument and doubt did they decide to send me the small sum of 500 dollars; they agreed: "Let him try to find his way to the West and when we see what steps he intends to take, perhaps we'll be able to solve the mystery . . ."

So the money they had sent me had only been a means of testing me.

Basil Ratiu and Alba continued to struggle for me, but in vain, and in the summer of 1956 it was decided not to give me any further help.

Alba then appealed to Ion Ratiu, who was living in London. He could not believe that I had been abandoned to my fate. In order to convince him Alba asked him to come to Paris and talk it over with two representatives of the Roumanian National Committee. The meeting convinced him that I was not going to get any help from that quarter. Ratiu then generously offered to send me a sum equivalent to twenty thousand *lei* without delay.

A day or two after Alba's arrival in Vienna, Ratiu joined us. As he got out of the 'bus at the air terminal we looked at each other curiously. How strange it was! And what a coincidence! Ratiu was none other than my erstwhile colleague at the Law Faculty of the

Cluj University. We had not seen each other since our student days in 1938. And here we were, in fact, together; ourselves . . .! Yet the passage of those nineteen years and our experiences of life had altered us out of all recognition. Ratiu, tall and sturdy, now had grey hair and an air of maturity, full of self-confidence. The picture of him as he used to look in our student days passed through my mind, as though I were seeing a double image of him; but his youthful, springing gait was unchanged, and so was his cheerful smile . . .

We had long conversations, which lasted practically during the whole of his stay in Vienna. He told me the reasons which made him come to my aid at such a difficult time:

"Alba came to me in despair! She spoke to me of your disappearance in Roumania, where you had been sent years before by the Roumanian National Committee to carry out a political action. When you reappeared they abandoned you. Alba declared that as it was a question of life and death she was forced by circumstances to turn to me, invoking the old friendship that existed between us and appealing to my feelings as a patriot, of which she had had proof on other occasions. I helped you—knowing nothing of your identity at the time—simply because those who persuaded you to undertake that mission and who were solely responsible, refused to do anything to save you after shilly-shallying for more than a year. My own gesture sprang from a desire to help a Roumanian in danger who had been thrown into the battle against the Communists. From many points of view my action was imbued with a profound political significance, and I would have done it for any other Roumanian in your situation. After talking with the two representatives of the Roumanian National Committee in Paris about your case and hearing from them directly that they held nothing against you, I decided to help you without a moment's further hesitation."

The days spent together with Alba and Ion Ratiu passed like lightning. Then he left for London and she for Paris. From that moment began a phase of indescribable spiritual loneliness.

## The Lost Footsteps

People reaching the Free World from behind the Iron Curtain are often unhappy and frustrated during the first months after their arrival. Probably they have taken untold risks to reach the West and while doing so have been sustained by the belief that the moment they cross the frontier they will be able to relax in a state of security.

When this proves not to be the case, they suffer considerable psychological strain. They arrive penniless, often knowing no one who can establish their identity and political reliability; they have no papers and of course no labour permit. As a result they can neither travel nor work. In the eyes of the authorities they are illegal immigrants who may as easily be spies as members of the Resistance or simply individuals with a longing for liberty. Moreover, since the frontier is very close, they realise that they are still in danger of being kidnapped by Communist agents. Another fear is that, however good their anti-Communist record may be, there is only their word to prove it and so they may find themselves shut up for a long period while inquiries are being made.

I was lucky enough to know that I had plenty of people in the West, though not in Austria, who could vouch for me. But until I was able to contact them, I too lived in a state of continuous tension.

My anxiety was fanned by stories told me by other refugees, stories of kidnapping by Communists, of arrest and kidnapping by the Intelligence Services of certain interested Powers, of confinements in remote castles, of the use of lie detectors which registered emotion—an emotion which could well be produced by references to names of people and places associated with painful things, and produce a graph as characteristic of lying as of distress.

These refugees tried to persuade me that to obtain a false passport was a great deal easier than to establish one's identity. I paid no attention to their proposals, for indeed one of the aspects of life in the West for which I most longed was again to be able to be myself; the idea of acquiring one more false identity positively horrified me. Events proved that in my case at any rate their fears were groundless.

I applied to the Austrian State for political asylum; this, I thought, would give me at least a minimum of protection. The authorities were sympathetic and at once gave me a passport.

I was morally bound to remain in Vienna until I had arranged for Andrei Loghin's escape to the West, although the hope of finding the money necessary for his journey seemed infinitesimal. But even had I not been kept in Austria by my efforts on his behalf, I could not have left, for I had no visa for any other Western country. I was told by various consulates that the formalities would take months, and that visas for refugees were only granted to certain categories, to none of which I belonged. The period of spectacular aid to Hungarian refugees was over, so I had no chance of benefiting from that situation. Circumstances had made me into a "displaced person," devoid of possessions, rights and liberties, and I was only one of millions. If Western humanitarianism had been large-hearted enough to grant citizenship to all refugees, the psychological and moral levels of these millions of "pariahs" would have been radically transformed. Equality of rights and liberty would have been a sound basis on which to build a new life.

Soon I was without money. When we said good-bye Andrei Loghin had slipped ten gold coins into my hand. "They are my last," he said. "I give them to you with all my heart. Take them; they may be useful on the journey!" The Austrian money for which I had exchanged them in Vienna had covered my expenses for a month. Now I was supported by Karl Böhm; and he was barely able to make ends meet for his own family of five, yet he continued to allow me to sleep on my shake-down in their house and to share their meals.

As I could not raise the money for Andrei's journey I could not tell him to start, although it was imperative to cross the frontier soon. Paul, who was ready to set out for Szombathely to meet him, told me that the construction of the new barrage was going ahead rapidly, and that the gap along the frontier between Frankenau and Kosseg might be closed within two months. The chances of my benefactor's escape grew less daily. The appeal I sent to the Roumanian National Committee remained unanswered and my attempt to get hold of even a modest sum failed.

By June my own situation was very bad. Karl Böhm could no longer keep me, and I was beginning to spit blood again; my heart showed signs of damage while the lesions left by the thrashings on my legs and back reappeared and needed immediate attention. Meanwhile I had no money even for tram-fares, for I saved every penny for stamps.

I was obsessed by pressing everyday needs, but to whom could I appeal? One day I knocked at the door of the World Council of Churches, for Alba, who was ill in a hospital in Paris, had written suggesting that I should ask this charitable institution for help. The warm welcome and kind help they gave me at this time of bitterness and depression was a tonic which restored my hope and optimism. They got me into a clinic where I had the best medical care and where my treatment lasted for several months. On many occasions during my stay in Austria, this Christian welfare organisation came to my rescue at difficult moments.

After I left the clinic I lived incognito in a semi-clandestine manner in the hope of avoiding Communist agents. No one knew my address; I had no contact with anyone and my daily correspondence with Alba, who was now out of hospital, was my only link with the outside world. After seven years of almost uninterrupted confinement either in prison or in hiding, I longed more than anything to be out in the sun; the park of the Hofburg was my favourite haunt; sitting on a seat by a pool I used to spend whole days in that paradise. Mauve petunias leaned over the stone rim; fallen heads of lilac, white and red water-lilies rising from their flat, round collars of leaves, floated on the surface; pigeons, chaffinches and tits came to quench their thirst, and the sky with its floating wisps of cloud mirrored its infinite space in the water.

On other occasions I visited the art galleries or the museums or the old palaces of the Austrian capital.

Although I was moving about among bustling crowds, I lived

in complete isolation, communing only with myself, in an effort to solve certain problems.

The circumstances in which the Communists provoked the crisis of this century are known to everyone . . .! I asked myself repeatedly: "What constituted the superiority of my adversaries on the occasions when they got the better of me?"

As I was spiritually the product of a culture with its roots far back in time, bound up with the creations and fundamental values of the West, I had voluntarily thrown myself—in so far as my modest contribution lay—into the struggle along with millions of others to defend the modern way of life. But, although the aim of that struggle was the defence of very high moral values, the majority of those who fought for the cause in the Communist-dominated world were overcome. Why did this happen?

After analysing and meditating on this problem for years in my cell in the secret prison, I had succeeded in finding a reply to these questions.

In the course of the centuries, the founders of some of the great religions, together with certain philosophers of genius—inspired by the apparent harmony in the Universe—had created a real cult of this harmony which soon became the essence of a fundamental ethical principle. The partisans of harmony considered revolutions, war, strife in general, as accidental evils and sought solutions to avoid them or to lessen their effects.

We, the victims of Communism—believers in the ethics of harmony—followed the ideas of peaceful co-existence, respecting men who held different conceptions and interests and to this end we were using non-violent methods. We had studied the laws of the struggle of the opposites only superficially: at the decisive moment when social struggle was imposed on us and become inevitable, we did not know how to apply them.

On the other hand, our adversaries had eliminated the notion of harmony from their dictionary as if it had been created from pure fantasy. They proclaimed the struggle of opposites as the fundamental law of the Universe. They studied the rules with diabolical insistence and applied them mercilessly. In this respect they were superior to us, and destroyed us without compunction. . . .

It was my terrible clash with the Security Police which enabled me to discover my errors and gave me, at the same time, a strong impulse to analyse their ideology, their tactics and methods they used in order to find out the cause of their successes.

When I set out for Roumania in the spring of 1950, military war seemed to be the ultimate means of resolving the complex problems which had divided the world into two opposing camps. But in 1957 on my return to the Free World, the situation seemed to have changed radically. The fact that modern armaments imperilled the very existence of mankind, excluded the possibility of a military war or at least postponed it indefinitely.

The conflict between the two camps, instead of being less bitter, seemed to have grown more acute—with deeper roots. The struggle between them continued—behind the camouflage of a screen of pacifism—by every possible means short of military war (although the stock of arms was now gigantic and their potential exceeded human imagination).

Naturally, cosmic rockets and hydrogen bombs weigh heavily in the balance of forces! But it seemed that mankind had entered a new era in which it was becoming increasingly obvious that warfare would be carried out in the spiritual field: pure reason; ideas; science; philosophy . . . being now the decisive arms. But the Communists could be conquered or prevented from extending their domination only if—in this new era—they could be outflanked in the art of "the struggle of opposites" (the struggle between opposing forces). I now felt convinced that the free world had every chance of success with the condition of winning indisputable superiority in this field.

I asked myself very logically, whether—as a result of my experiences in the Communist world—I could still make even the smallest contribution to this gigantic struggle or whether perhaps the moment had come for me to withdraw from such a complicated situation. Would it not be wiser to give up the fight and retire to the narrow existence of everyday life, free from further conflicts and clashes?

I tried to come to a decision; to find a new orientation for my existence in the Free World. I strove to find a solution to this last quandary. The struggle with my adversaries had been a source of great challenge which had spurred me on for years. I longed desperately for some new incentive, some fresh aim to fill the coming years. But where should I look for it? During the years spent in my cell and those spent in hiding in Roumania, I had conceived a new system of action against the Communists. Now, in the peace of the Viennese park I glimpsed a perspective which attracted me more than anything else. My inner calm and self-confidence returned. I longed to dedicate myself to pure reason, to science, to philosophy, so as to be able to continue the struggle against my adversaries under new conditions, in the spiritual field. No amount of effort; no obstacle; no sacrifice would discourage me. Now I had before me an aim into which I could throw myself whole-heartedly. . . .

About this time a friend living in South America sent me a small sum of money, enough to keep body and soul together for about a year. Next Alba sent me two letters from a member of the Roumanian National Committee in New York. They brought me words of comfort which I never expected:

"I am so glad to hear that my friend Silviu is free. It is nothing short of a miracle. His great courage, power of resistance to tortures and his ingenuity deserve our respect. But I am glad above all that in spite of the trials he has undergone, he is determined to continue to fight and I am sure that his future activities will be of great help in the cause for which we are working. Please assure him of my love and friendship.

". . . I know you are impatiently awaiting my reply to your letter. I assure you that I, like you, have at heart the fate of our friend, who has so unselfishly risked his life for the sake of our country. I am sorry to hear that ill-luck continues to dog him even now, and still more sorry that all our efforts to support him have so far failed. This confession will explain my delay in answering:

I have been waiting to see what the result would be of our various attempts to send Silviu something more 'concrete' than fine words! Unhappily, I am not yet in a position to announce any success—all I can send are promises and hopes."

Later this friend wrote directly to me:

"I wanted to go to Vienna and shake hands and discuss all the things which might only be misunderstood in correspondence. Up to now, however, I have not been able to remove the obstacle which prevents me: lack of money. The same thing paralyses our friends in Paris and other places. All of them want to see you. It is hard to explain in a few words how we have got into such a state, but the international situation will help you to understand. No doubt you have seen that, since you left for Roumania, many things in the West have changed—and for the worse, unfortunately! As a result, the struggle of the various National Committees has become increasingly difficult and their activities have been curbed. No one is interested in political parties. But perhaps the little dog barking menacingly in the Soviet Sputnik may awaken the West and spur it on to firm and co-ordinated political action. In that case the aim and significance of our struggle will be better appreciated. But in any case, even if things take a turn for the worse, we must stay at our posts. However irritating our 'voices crying in the wilderness' may be—and we know that they are often a nuisance to those whose house is in danger but who prefer to sleep—we must never remain silent. At present, however, we are in a painful situation: we feel we must carry on with the task we have undertaken, but we know that, under the circumstances, it is impossible to fulfil it; this inevitably causes many disappointments and recriminations. In addition, we are not in a position to air our troubles and our sense of frustration for fear of harming the cause we serve.

"One thing I want to make quite clear, however: I rejoice wholeheartedly that God has rescued you from the dangers which you went to meet so courageously for the sake of our nation. And I am glad that after so much suffering, your health is almost restored and will soon allow you to begin a new chapter in your

struggle on behalf of Roumania. All those in the National Committee and in our political party who knew you, share my feelings
—all of them are full of gratitude and admiration. As to the future
. . . there will be further difficulties, but I beg you not to be discouraged, for however much adversity you may still meet, you will
win in the end!"

Now I understood clearly that my friends in the Roumanian
National Committee *had* wished to help me, but that their financial
position and the discouraging attitude of the Atlantic Powers, who
hold the fate of the nations behind the Iron Curtain in their hands,
had prevented them from taking decisive action to extricate me.
Unhappily, all of us Eastern Europeans have fallen between two
completely opposing worlds which, like gigantic mill-wheels, are
in danger of grinding us to dust. Under the circumstances, the fate
of Andrei Loghin may be considered as sealed; failing the generosity of the free world and the necessary financial help for his
journey, escape is impossible.

In August (1957) Alba came to Austria. Our meeting in the
Westbahnhof in Vienna was quite different from the one in spring.
Our daily correspondence had bound us closer together in a way
which is hard to express in words. We were both convinced that
nothing could ever separate us again.

Our intention was to try to emigrate to South America, there
to begin a new life. I hoped that after about ten years I would have
saved enough money to enable me to devote myself to the task
nearest to my heart. But the efforts made by the World Council of
Churches to facilitate our emigration failed. South America, sur-
feited with European refugees, had closed its frontiers for an
indefinite period.

In the autumn of 1957, however, Ion Ratiu told us that a
British publisher was interested in the story of my experiences in
far-away Eastern Europe. Here at last was something concrete.

Our departure for England seemed to me symbolical; I was
filled with new hope. Standing on the deck of the white ship
which brought us from Ostend to Dover, gazing at the thin line
of horizon where sea and sky met, I felt a sudden happiness, a hope

that perhaps the country I was now approaching would grant me asylum, security and the chance to have my say, as it has done to so many other lovers of liberty. Eastern Europe seemed a long way off and all that I had experienced began to fade into the past. And yet it was the past and its experiences which had nourished my spirit and given it new life.

This fragment from Tolstoy's *War and Peace* has always held great significance for me:

> "Dinner was nearly over and Pierre, who at the beginning had refused to speak of his captivity, gradually began to talk about it.
>
> " 'It's true, isn't it, that you were on the point of murdering Napoleon?' asked Natasha with a faint smile.
>
> "Pierre acknowledged that this was so, and setting off from that question, plunged into an account of his adventure. To begin with, he spoke in the slightly bantering tone which he was now wont to use in the presence of others and especially when speaking of himself; later on, however, when he came to describe the sufferings which it had been his lot to witness and to experience, he was carried away, without realising it, and began to relate them, controlling his emotion, as a man who was re-living, in memory, the powerful impressions of the past.
>
> "The servants, with gloomy, reproachful faces, kept coming in to change the candles in the candlesticks, but no one paid the slightest attention to them. Natasha continued to gaze at Pierre with lively, shining eyes, as if she wanted to understand even the things of which he did not speak. Princess Maria was silent. No one seemed to notice that it was already three in the morning and that bedtime was long past.
>
> " 'Some talk of misfortune; suffering,' said Pierre. 'But if someone were to ask me at this very moment: "Would you like to be once more the man you were before your captivity or would you prefer to go through it again?" I confess before

God that I would choose to be imprisoned again and to eat horse-flesh. We imagine that all is lost the moment we are forced to leave our narrow groove, whereas, in reality, it is only then that life begins to be novel and beautiful. As long as life lasts, there will also be happiness! So much of it, believe me!' "

Enquiries and gifts for the Underground Church may be sent to
JESUS TO THE COMMUNIST WORLD, INC.
P.O. Box 2947, Torrance, CA 90509